"Addi?"

Addison's heart twisted. She knew that voice, and only one man had ever called her by that nickname. Drew Bryant, her long-dead fiancé.

She shook her head. Clearly she'd let the stress and worry get to her. Drew wasn't here, wasn't even alive.

The screen door hinges squealed and the handle of the main door turned. A dream, she thought, it had to be a dream. As the door eased open, Addison leveled the shotgun at the man casting shadows across the weak moonlight spilling through the door.

"Addi, it's me, Drew. I'm here to help."

Addison fired.

The loud report deafened her to the splintering wood as the buckshot pelted the front door. The man rushed forward, taking the gun before she could fire again.

"It's *me*," he said, his voice lost in the ringing in her ears.

The single lightbulb came on and she covered her mouth, barely smothering the scream lodged in her

TO HONOUR AND TO PROTECT

BY
DEBRA WEBB & REGAN BLACK

Published in Great Britain 2015
by Mills & Boon, an imprint of Harlequin (UK) Limited,
Eton House, 18-24 Paradise Road, Richmond, Surrey, TW9 1SR

© 2015 Debra Webb

ISBN: 978-0-263-25307-8

46-0615

Harlequin (UK) Limited's policy is to use papers that are natural, renewable and recyclable products and made from wood grown in sustainable forests. The logging and manufacturing processes conform to the legal environmental regulations of the country of origin.

Printed and bound in Spain
by CPI, Barcelona

Debra Webb, born in Alabama, wrote her first story at age nine and her first romance at thirteen. It wasn't until she spent three years working for the military behind the Iron Curtain—and a five-year stint with NASA—that she realized her true calling. Since then the *USA TODAY* bestselling author has penned more than one hundred novels, including her internationally bestselling Colby Agency series.

Regan Black, a *USA TODAY* bestselling author, writes award-winning, action-packed novels featuring kick-butt heroines and the sexy heroes who fall in love with them. Raised in the Midwest and California, she and her family, along with their adopted greyhound, two arrogant cats and a quirky finch, reside in the South Carolina Lowcountry, where the rich blend of legend, romance and history fuels her imagination.

For Robert, if you never read past this page,
know that you're my treasure, full of the integrity,
insight and kindness that make real-life
heroes so special.

Chapter One

Addison Collins checked the fuel gauge, quickly calculating how many more miles she could put between her and the inevitable pursuit before they had to stop. Her brand-new BMW could've done that for her, but not this ancient, new-to-her Land Rover. That was what math was for, wasn't it? This was the perfect example she would keep in the back of her mind for the day her son complained about his math homework.

"Mom, how much longer?"

She recognized that tone. He was about to complain but not about math. Using the rearview mirror, she aimed a confident smile at her son. His bright hair gleamed in the sunlight coming through the window, but the glare on his face bordered on mutinous.

She couldn't blame him. They'd been on the road for two days straight and had another day left. Possibly more. "About another half hour and we'll stop again."

"I have to pee now."

"You'll have to hold it for a few minutes."

"A half hour is *thirty* minutes. A few is more like three."

Instead of maternal pride, Addison couldn't help

wondering why she'd ever been inclined to teach him the difference. "And how many threes are in thirty?"

"Ten." He turned his face to the window. "I still have to pee."

"All right. I'll find a place to stop."

"This car stinks," he said a minute later.

"The car is clean. It's just new-car smell." With a persistent undertone of mildew, but she kept that thought to herself.

"But it's an *old* car."

"True." *Patience will pay off.* "The car dealers spray a strong deodorizer to make it feel new." They had periodically rolled down the windows, but the heavy-duty deodorizer scent lingered, punctuating the mildew rather than overpowering it. This vehicle might be a major step down in value from her BMW, but the dealer in Arizona had been willing to meet her trade and cash terms without any questions, and that had been priceless.

"Why?"

"So they can sell it faster."

"Will our car stink like this when we go back home?"

"I don't know." It was the only safe answer because she hadn't yet found the courage to tell her son they weren't going back. She hadn't lied to him and she wouldn't start now, but she wasn't ready to discuss it. The words he needed to hear to understand the gravity of their new situation just weren't coming to her, and she wasn't ready to cope with the fallout when he realized he wouldn't see his friends again.

Her own grief was too fresh, her fear of the unknown too big. When she had a handle on her feelings, she would be better able to help him with his. *Coward*, an annoying little voice in her head muttered.

"It's yucky in here," he said, making a gagging noise.

He had a point, though she wasn't about to admit it. "I feel sick."

Addison's patience was fraying, but it wasn't Andy's fault they were in this mess. No, this was all her doing. She'd been the one to screw up their picture-perfect life by getting conned by a not-nearly perfect man. He'd looked like Mr. Right, and until a few days ago, she'd been sure he was the right man for both her and Andy. The only silver lining—and she was clinging to it—was that she'd learned the truth before the wedding.

"Roll down the window," she said. "Some fresh air should help."

His face brightened momentarily, then clouded over again. "Where's the button?"

She rolled her eyes. "Use that little handle thingy."

"Huh?"

She stretched but couldn't reach it from the driver's seat. The Land Rover was built so much wider than her sedan, and the only power was under the hood. How ridiculous that an old-school vehicle could stump them both. "The window isn't electric like you're used to. Just wind it down, remember?"

She had a few minutes of peace while the manual crank amused her seven-year-old son. In a few months, he'd be eight. Although less than a week ago she'd been kicking around ideas for his birthday party, now all bets were off. She didn't know where they'd be living by his birthday, only that she intended to be sure they were both alive to celebrate it—even if it was just the two of them.

She immediately pushed that train of thought off the tracks. Right now all Andy needed to know was that they were on a summer adventure. Providing for him, taking care of his education—those questions would be answered later.

"Are we there yet?"

Not even close. "Almost."

"Mom, I can't hold it much longer."

"Hang on." With her eyes on the road, she caught the squirming in the backseat. "There's a place at this next exit."

"How long?"

"Two minutes," she replied, her voice leaving no room for argument. "You can time me."

His small, straight nose wrinkled as he fiddled with the big Captain America watch on his wrist. He flipped up the red, white and blue shield cover and busied himself with the stopwatch feature. Her little man had begged for the watch for Christmas and had worn it from the moment he'd ripped open the package. Only his fear of ruining it made him take it off for bath time.

She happily nurtured his love of comic book heroes, and reading through various adventures with him was part of their bedtime routine. Even in the horrible, desperate rush to get away, she'd grabbed his entire collection. More than once she'd wondered if some part of his attraction to comics was genetic. Andy's father had been a soldier, a good man and a lifelong fan of the Marvel universe. Oh, what she wouldn't give to have him here with her now.

"One minute," Andy announced.

"My personal town crier," she mumbled, taking the exit.

"What's a town crier?"

Nothing wrong with her boy's hearing. "Lots and lots of years ago, people didn't have smartphones or clocks or watches, so someone would walk the town streets and call out the time. 'Three o'clock and all's well!' Like that."

"Huh."

"We're here." She pulled into the parking space closest

to the front door of the gas station, knowing that thoughtful "huh" sound meant more questions were dancing at the front of his brain. "You can unbuckle now."

"You made it with ten seconds to spare."

"Guess I should've been a race car driver."

"Did town criers drive this old kind of car?" he asked when she came around to open his door.

"No. Town criers were way before cars."

"Then how did they get around town?"

She held out her hand, her heart giving a happy bump when he placed his in hers without argument. "People walked or used horses and carts."

"That's weird. Horses poop a lot."

She laughed. "Everything has a by-product." Inside, she glanced around for the restroom sign, leading her son back by way of the motor oil aisle rather than the candy aisle. "I know at school you've seen pictures of cities before cars."

"And the museum field trips." He shrugged, his gaze roving across the labels at his eye level, his feet slowing as he tried to read the words and logos on each one. Grateful for the distraction, she wasn't surprised it didn't last. When she pushed open the ladies' room door, he stopped short in the narrow hallway.

"I'm a boy," he whispered as if she might've forgotten.

"Road rules, remember? We stick together."

"Mom." He scowled at her and folded his arms across his chest. "I'm too old to go in there."

She bent close to his ear. "I understand. I even almost agree."

"Almost?" He tilted his head, wary.

She nodded, smothering the smile for the sake of his pride. "But today it's a safety issue. We stay together."

"It's been nothin' but safety since we left home."

"I know. And it has to be safety for a little longer." She

silently vowed to make it up to him. Somehow. "Soon you'll have all kinds of new places and things to discover on our adventure."

"Promise?"

"Yes."

He looked back at her with the big, soft brown eyes that reminded her more and more of his father. His small hand patted her cheek. "If it makes you feel better, I'll stay with you."

"Thank you."

"But I want to make a new deal for when I turn eight."

"That's certainly up for discussion." Right now she had to be sure they lived that long.

With bladders relieved and hands washed thoroughly to the tune of the alphabet song, they cut through the store to get back on the road.

"Can I have a Coke?"

"It's 'may I,'" she corrected automatically. "And no. We have water in the car."

"Can I have a peanut butter cup?"

So much for her efforts to avoid the candy and junk food. "When we stop for dinner tonight, you can have a Coke and a peanut butter cup."

"Both?" His eyes went wide with hope.

She nodded.

"How long to dinner?"

She laughed and checked her watch. "A few hours." She wanted more distance between her and the man who had the resources to chase her off the edge of the world. Addison refused to think of him as her fiancé anymore. Although she'd done her best to blur any trail, to escape somewhere he didn't even know to search, she couldn't be sure it would work.

The idea of being so completely duped by Craig Everett

infuriated her. Worse, her relationship with him was now an embarrassment in both the professional and personal context. When she thought of how much she'd shared with that worthless excuse for a man, she wanted to shoot something. Preferably Craig. They'd shared lovely romantic evenings, family-type outings with Andy and lazy sleep-late weekend mornings. All of it made her feel dirty now.

Assuming she could evade Craig until she got word the authorities had him locked down, assuming she could eventually return to her life in San Francisco, she wasn't quite sure how she'd find the courage to look her friends or her boss in the eye again.

It was hopeless to think his arrest and illegal dealings wouldn't make news up and down the West Coast. More likely, it would be national news for a short time. Which meant she and Andy would be dragged into Craig's horrendous mess by association. Their lives would be picked apart and exposed for everyone in the world to judge. It was possible even her secluded destination in the uncharted depths of a Louisiana swamp wouldn't be shelter enough.

Because she'd been the idiot who nearly married an American traitor.

She buckled Andy into the booster seat and closed the door, stifling the violent words that wanted to pour out of her whenever she thought about what Craig had done. Telling herself she'd broken up his system and stopped him didn't help as much as it should. Maybe that would change with time. So many things did.

The facts crawled like a line of ants between her shoulder blades. The sensation grew worse when she considered the likelihood that Craig's slimy dealings had cost other women—other families—the grief she'd felt when

Andy's father had been killed in action on the other side of the world.

If Drew Bryant, her favorite soldier, were alive he'd…

Biting her lip, she pulled herself together. If Drew were alive, all of this would be irrelevant. Unnecessary. She, Drew and Andy would be a family, settled in some happy suburb or on farmland far from California. A road trip like this really would be a grand summer adventure. Complete with two drivers and possibly a brother or sister in the backseat with Andy. Even when she and Drew were children themselves, they'd dreamed of having a big family.

If Drew were alive, she wouldn't have been with Craig at all. It would've been up to someone else to catch that traitorous, double-talking jerk trading secrets and sensitive military information with who knew how many unsavory people.

If, if, if. Exasperated with herself, Addison slid into the driver's seat and moved the car to the gas pump. Might as well top it off while she was here. Hopefully it would save her a stop later.

No matter how she coached herself, she wasn't sure catching Craig qualified as a blessing in disguise, not when she knew it could cost her everything she held dear. But turning over the information she'd found had been automatic, a reflex she couldn't suppress any more than breathing. No one should profit from the pain and suffering of others.

Craig had made a fortune for himself and others through legal means. Discovering the fortune he'd amassed through illegal negotiations had shocked her. She couldn't fathom how he'd made that leap into predatory dealings. She'd only scraped the tip of the iceberg, but she knew without any doubt what would happen if Craig or his nasty colleagues caught up with her and Andy before the authorities took action.

She smiled at her son through the window as she pumped gas. Being the whistle-blower was difficult for anyone, but a single mom? Although she couldn't abide letting Craig go unpunished, she kept wondering if there'd been a better way to take him down. She'd completely altered two lives when she'd sent the files as an anonymous tip to the local FBI office. All she could do now was hide and pray for the best.

A few more miles down the road Andy piped up again. "Are we going to SeaWorld?"

She'd noticed the billboard, too, and the question wasn't unreasonable, but she found herself wishing for nightfall. "Not this trip, honey." Thinking of the crowds and security cameras raised goose bumps along her arms. An attraction like that could prove more risk than entertainment.

"Will Craig have part of our summer adventure with us?"

Only in my nightmares, she thought. "Not this trip," she repeated, glancing at the elaborate engagement ring that remained on her hand. Taking it off would have Andy asking still more questions she wasn't ready to answer. Once they reached the bayou she'd throw the damn thing to the nearest alligator. Imagining Craig's outrage over that move made her smile.

The diamond caught the waning sunlight and she wondered—again—which part of Craig's income had paid for it. Knowing wouldn't change how she felt about wearing it, but the aching, wounded part of her heart wanted the answer. She shut that down. There was no sense in being sentimental over a man who'd not only played her for a fool, but also traded lives for money with dangerous people. People who'd want to punish her for blowing up their system. People who were probably searching for her right now. Maybe it would be smart to sell the gaudy thing. She could invest the proceeds for Andy's college fund. That seemed like a fair enough solution.

"I miss him already," Andy murmured from the backseat.

"I know." Craig was the closest thing Andy had had to a father figure because his father had died before he was born. It made her cringe now, in light of his treacherous side business, but it would be another point of grief for her son when he learned that relationship was over. Forever.

Of all the challenges ahead of her, she dreaded navigating that particular tightrope. How could she ever adequately explain her choices to a seven-year-old who'd been so eager for a dad? In Andy's eyes, Craig had reached near-hero status. Now, thanks to her, in Craig's eyes she and her son were no more than risks to eliminate. That was more truth than Andy needed weighing on his young shoulders.

"Will the whole adventure be in this old car?"

"No." She'd hesitated to tell him where they were going, fearful that someone would overhear his chatter during a stop. "Do you think you'd like SeaWorld?"

"Yes! They have whales and dolphins and sharks and turtles and you can swim with them."

"That does sound like fun."

"Please can we go, Mom?"

"I can't make promises, but if it's possible, yes, we'll go to SeaWorld." Eventually.

"Cool! Jeff and Caleb will be jealous. We'll take lots of pictures, right?"

"Of course." As long as those pictures wouldn't jeopardize their secrets.

"I want to pet a shark."

You've already been too close, she thought, checking her rearview mirror. *We just didn't see his teeth.* Yet.

"We'll see."

"That means no."

"Not in our house," she said with more bite than she'd intended. "We've talked about that. I need to concentrate right now, okay?"

"Okay."

"We'll stop for dinner in two hours." She smiled, determined to regain her composure. "Can you set an alarm, please?"

"Sure!"

"Thank you." She checked her mirrors and stared at the long ribbon of highway cluttered with traffic. Once she saw Andy was focused on his handheld game, she turned on the radio, hoping to catch some announcement of Craig's situation. She wouldn't feel safe until he was in custody, and she wouldn't come out of hiding until she was sure his connections had been found. But she heard no updates.

Hours later, when Addison and Andy stopped for dinner, she ducked into a post office for one last precaution. An insurance policy of sorts, in case Craig found a loophole. Letting Andy push the buttons on the automated kiosk machine in the lobby, she breathed a little better when he sent the envelope into the chute.

Whatever happened next, now she could be sure someone else knew the truth about Craig and his involvement in her life.

"Are you mad?" Andy asked, taking her hand as they returned to the car.

"Not with you." She was definitely mad, but more than the anger, she felt a consuming, unfamiliar terror. All her life she'd known what to do and when to do it. There had been nerves and mistakes, sadness and joy along the way, but overall, she'd had a dream, created a plan and worked tirelessly to make it all a reality for her and her son.

"Then who're you mad at?"

She considered her answer as he boosted himself back up into the car. "Myself," she replied honestly. "I made a big mistake."

"Is that why we're on this summer adventure?"

Occasionally her son was too perceptive for her comfort. "Partly," she said with a smile. "But summer is the perfect time for a big adventure."

"We won't be in the car the whole time, will we?"

"Already asked and answered, young man," she said with a laugh. "I promise the real adventure will begin soon." She thought of the frogs and birds, the still, reflective black water and tall cypress trees where they were headed. He would love it all, so different from any camp or field trip he'd experienced. "You're going to have all kinds of fun."

"Promise?"

"Have I ever let you down?"

He actually gave it some thought before he replied, "No."

"Well, I don't plan to start now."

His grin, full of eagerness and love, was too reminiscent of his father. It had her heart aching for what might have been as they got back on the road. Since losing Drew before Andy's birth, she'd made a practice of focusing on the present. Of course she'd told her son bits and pieces about his real dad as he'd been able to understand them, but with no living relatives in the Bryant family, it seemed best for both of them not to dwell on what couldn't be changed.

Long after the dinner stop, as she crossed the state line into Louisiana, the news hit the radio. Federal authorities had arrested Craig at his posh home in San Francisco. Addison didn't breathe easy until the reporter finished the explanation with no mention of her name.

Understanding what he'd done, the scope of his crimes and that the FBI probably already knew she'd turned him in, she knew her anonymity wouldn't last long, but she intended to make the most of her temporary advantage.

Chapter Two

Andrew "Drew" Bryant remained in his seat, his back straight, palms relaxed on his thighs, gaze straight ahead. Maintaining a calm facade in all circumstances had been emphasized during his time with the Special Forces, but he'd mastered the skill as a prisoner of war. He'd memorized and evaluated every detail of his surroundings. The sleek, understated decor of the lobby, the expensive black leather seating and the polished chrome and glass accents might be found in any number of office buildings around the world, but the distinct lack of nameplates and office logos on the doors told him more than anyone behind those doors wanted him to know. At one time in his life he might've paced the marble-floored lobby impatiently, but not anymore. These days, he let the world come to him.

He was more than a little relieved the men in dark suits who'd picked him up twelve hours ago hadn't put a bag over his head. It could still happen, and if it did, it would test his fitful control. He took a deep breath. Calm was key. In every situation. No sense proving the army docs right about his uncertain mental state.

They'd left him alone and unrestrained, but he'd seen

the escort lock the elevator. If they wanted him to sit here, here was where he'd sit. He was in a high-rent office building, but the view from the window wasn't helpful, with no visible skyline beyond tall trees. The artwork on the walls and in the elevator was most likely original. In his assessment, that meant this place didn't get a lot of foot traffic.

Drew felt his heart rate tick up as another minute passed. He couldn't help recalling the last time he'd been snatched away from a normal day. Except that day hadn't been normal at all. It had been his wedding day.

On that occasion he'd been ordered to duty in the middle of the night and it had required half a pot of coffee to burn away the fuzzy aftertaste of his bachelor party. He'd left a note—unauthorized but nonnegotiable—for his bride. The woman who'd eventually given up on him. Not that he blamed her.

He kept his eyes forward, even as the sound of feminine high heels clicked across the marble floor on the other side of the door. Closer, closer, then fading away.

Had his bride chosen heels or flats? He recalled overhearing the debate with her maid of honor, but he'd never known the final decision.

The last time he'd been uprooted on the precipice of a major life event his commanding officer had insisted there'd been no time for even a cursory marriage ceremony. This time, someone with serious money and authority had pulled him away from a major basketball game between the top two teams in the Detroit recreational league. The score tied, less than five minutes left, he'd been forced away. Unable to stem the curiosity, Drew gave in and glanced at his watch. The game had ended hours ago and without his phone, he still didn't know who won.

It pissed him off. Bragging rights were riding on that

game, and these days that was all the stress he wanted, but life rarely cooperated with his wants.

Drew snorted as another minute clicked by on the wall clock. The kids he worked with in Detroit kept him from wallowing in self-pity after the army had shown him the door with an early retirement for medical reasons. Retired at thirty-six years old. Unbelievable. That hadn't been part of the plan. He rarely let it bother him, but today when something from his past was clearly interrupting his present, he couldn't shake off the irritation.

He knew this drill, knew someone from the alphabet soup of government agencies had pulled strings to drag him out of Detroit last night. But if it was so important it couldn't wait until the end of the game, why was he parked in limbo here?

The high heels approached once more and Drew shifted his face, his entire body into neutral. The heels stopped and the glass door opened with an understated *whoosh*.

"Mr. Bryant?"

"Yes." He stood, facing the woman who remained in the doorway. She was slender, her sleek navy blue dress making a professional and feminine statement. Noting the long legs and high heels, he pegged her as a dancer by training. Watching her approach, he knew she was an expert in martial arts, as well. If a woman like this was merely a receptionist in this place, he might be in more trouble than he could handle.

"Our apologies for the delay," she said with a polite smile. "I've been told you might appreciate this video while you wait. It shouldn't be much longer." She handed him a tablet and returned to her side of the glass doors.

He looked at the screen, baffled as he recognized the basketball court and uniforms of the players. It couldn't be… He sank back into his chair and, touching the icon, put the video into motion. "I'll be damned," he muttered, watching the last minutes of the basketball game.

Immersed in the video action, he forgot where he was, forgot to wonder why, and just enjoyed watching his team take the win in a nail-biting last-second shot. "Yes!" He pumped his fist and watched as one of the more headstrong kids from the neighborhood enjoyed a hero's celebration.

Drew took a deep breath, relieved and relaxed that his kids were making progress within the community. Something was finally going right. That neighborhood, those kids were coming together as a team and as a family of sorts. Knowing his small part in the overall puzzle made a difference was enough to keep him moving forward instead of stalling out.

A big accomplishment for a man who'd nearly lost his mind when the life he'd dreamed of slipped out of his grasp. *Stolen* was a more accurate term, but according to the army shrinks, that word held negative connotations. They wanted him to reframe, rephrase, re-everything when all he wanted was to rewind and make a different choice in the early hours of his wedding day.

"They're ready for you now, Mr. Bryant."

She was back and he hadn't even heard her approach. He knew better, knew he had to keep his mind off the past or it would swallow him up. Drew stood and smiled. "Thanks for this." He extended the tablet.

"You're welcome." She accepted the device with another courteous smile. "This way."

He followed the slender woman, the only sound the click of her heels, but even that went quiet when she turned down a carpeted hallway. They passed a bank of blacked-out windows of what was probably a conference room. When they passed another small reception area and one nearly closed office door, Drew's stomach dropped.

They were headed for the corner office, a destination that in his experience didn't ever add up to anything good. The woman stopped at the open door, announced him, then stepped back. Going forward was the only option. She closed the door behind him as he entered.

He felt underdressed in his gym clothes compared to the man in the dark suit and expensive tie. The man rose from his elegant chair and came around the desk quickly, hand extended. "I'm Director Thomas Casey." The grip was firm and brief as they shook hands. "Come have a seat, Mr. Bryant."

Drew couldn't hide his surprise. Thomas Casey was one of those names whispered in dark corners by people with the highest clearances. Among the microcommunity of black ops and special operations, the man who supposedly coordinated a crack team of "Specialists" was nearly urban legend. "I thought you were a myth," Drew admitted as Thomas returned to his big chair behind the desk.

"That's the way I like it." The smile was as firm and as brief as the handshake. "I appreciate your cooperation on such short notice."

"Didn't feel like there was much choice, sir."

"Call me Thomas."

Another surprise. "Sure."

"You saw the end of the game, I trust."

"Yes, thank you." He wondered if Thomas arranged for the game to be recorded, or if one of his Specialists had pulled it off YouTube.

"It came down to the wire."

Drew nodded. "Always better for both teams that way."

"Probably so." Thomas studied Drew another moment. "Solid effort and a close call incite more determination to win the next game. We understand that here," he said. "I've looked into your background as well as your present situation. What you're doing in Detroit is good work."

"I like it," Drew said, hiding his surprise at the compliment. "And I'd like to get back to it."

"I'm sure. Let's talk about that. It's not my practice to pull people away from good work, but I find myself in a tight spot. I believe your skills and knowledge would be helpful."

Drew waited in silence, curious. He no longer had the security clearance to even sit in this room. Thomas, having poked through his background, knew that. None of Drew's kids were into anything that would be of interest to the director. He couldn't think of a single way he could be helpful, but he'd listen. It would be rude not to after he'd been hauled out here.

"You aren't curious?" Thomas asked.

"I am." But he wasn't going to reveal anything to this master spook by asking questions.

"All right." Thomas gave a wry chuckle when Drew didn't elaborate. "Federal authorities made an arrest based on an almost anonymous tip."

Almost anonymous? Drew hadn't heard that phrase before.

"The person who shared the information requested that she be left out of it and we're doing our best to honor that from an investigative standpoint."

Drew wanted to stop Thomas right there, to point out that he wasn't in the market for a bodyguard gig, didn't have the head for it anymore, but he kept his mouth shut and his ears open.

"You've been through some hard times, Mr. Bryant."

"Drew is fine," he replied, wondering why the subject had changed. If this had something to do with the bastards who'd held him as a POW for six years in a cave in Afghanistan, he might opt in to whatever the director had in mind. A little revenge could go a long way toward healing. It was a dangerous line of thought, but Drew let it play out. Thinking about something and acting on it were two different animals. He'd learned that quickly as a prisoner and in the agonizing months of recovery that followed his escape and rescue.

"Do you feel you're fit for service?"

Drew met Thomas's assessing gaze. "Depends on the type of service, I suppose. The army found me to be more hindrance than help."

"Are you?"

"Didn't have the chance to find out," Drew blurted before thinking through a better reply.

"Tell me about your recovery."

Drew could see no way of avoiding the topic. Not in this room. Better to lay it out there than allow Thomas to continue to entertain his delusions. If the man managed to maintain myth status in a place like Washington, Drew could safely assume his personal secrets wouldn't leave the room.

Still, he played it close. "Long. Physically, I'd lost muscle mass to the malnutrition and poor conditions. That came back quick enough after a few weeks in the hospital with proper nutrition and a few months of physical therapy. They had to reset an arm and do a little work on my back."

He still felt guilty and selfish when he thought of those endless days with no contact beyond hospital staff and the occasional visit from a chaplain or army officials. He should have been full of gratitude, but instead he'd battled a terrible sense of loss and isolation no matter how they praised him for surviving.

"I heard your father died while you were a prisoner."

"Yes." His superiors had explained valid reasons for not publicizing his return to anyone, not even family. "They showed me the obituary, told me he was buried next to my mom."

"No one from your past knows you're alive. There's no reason to keep your survival a secret now."

"There's no reason to throw a parade, either," Drew countered. "A few people from my old neighborhood recognized me when I came back."

"I'm sure they were happy to see you."

"Pretty much." Almost a year later, he was okay with his neighbors, too. With his father dead, the only other person Drew had wanted to see was the bride he'd left waiting at the altar. She was the final piece of his recovery, and everyone who'd had a hand in it knew he needed to reach out to her. Too bad no one had warned him what he'd find.

Despite the years, having heard about his wedding plans from his father, the neighbors were eager to meet the woman they'd only seen in wedding announcement photos. When he'd felt strong enough, he'd gone looking for her and returned alone. After about six months his neighbors stopped asking about her.

"Took a while to get past all the sympathy," Drew said. It was all the explanation he felt Thomas needed on his personal life.

"That's reasonable."

It sure hadn't felt that way at the time, but it was done now and he had carved out a new place for himself. He might spend his nights alone, but based on the persistent nightmares, that was for the best.

The back of his neck prickling, Drew wanted to shift

the topic back to Thomas's invasion of his new life, but again he waited quietly for the director to make the move.

"Addison Collins." Thomas tossed out the name, like a bomb in the middle of his desk, and leaned back to watch Drew's reaction.

His body went cold at the sound of her name. Suddenly he wanted to talk about the POW camp. The injuries. The nightmares. The dirt cell and lousy food. Anything but *her*.

"Have you had any contact with your fiancée lately?"

"Former fiancée," Drew corrected. "And no." He didn't even let himself think of her. Not after he'd seen her playing freeze tag with another man and a little boy in San Francisco last fall. He'd been close enough to see the smile on her face, to hear her carefree, happy laughter. Close enough to see the ring on her finger sporting a diamond easily twice the size of the one he'd given her years ago. She'd been so obviously settled and content with her family that he'd walked away rather than ruin her day and twist up her life.

"Why do you ask?" He ignored the calculating gleam in Thomas's quick smile. Drew could no more hold back that question than stop the next sunrise. With a nearly audible snap, a piece clicked into place. "She's the tipster."

"Yes. And she's gone missing."

"So ask her husband." Drew's throat went dry and his palms went damp. Addi was fine. Had to be fine. He couldn't accept anything else where she was concerned.

"Well…" Thomas hesitated. "You haven't seen any of the news coverage on this?"

Drew shook his head. Knowing his emotional limits, he didn't do any more than scan the local headlines, and sometimes that was more bad news than he could handle.

"Craig Everett." Thomas opened a file and showed him

a picture of the man who'd been with Addi in the park. "He and Ms. Collins planned to marry at the end of the summer, but he's also gone missing."

Planned? "She's not married?" Had he missed an important chance to be with her? It was hard to think about that. He'd been so sure about what he'd seen. Maybe she'd been married and divorced before Everett came along.

"No marriage on record," Thomas confirmed. "What we do know is that she turned over damning evidence and abruptly left town. She hasn't been seen anywhere in just over two weeks."

It didn't make sense. Drew thought of the little boy, wondering if the kid belonged to Addison or Everett.

"The evidence Addison provided against Everett is excellent, but I think she knows more."

"If the evidence is so great, why do you need more?"

Thomas sighed. "Because I was informed last night that Everett escaped during a transfer between facilities."

Drew swore, unable to sit still any longer. He shifted in the chair, pushed a hand through his hair. "How'd you let that happen?"

"*I* didn't." The director's voice went cold. "Reviewing everything we have, I've concluded Everett's connections are too good. I believe Addison can confirm my suspicions and help me plug what must be a leak on the government side."

Better and better, Drew thought, but he couldn't get the image of Addison, scared and on the run, out of his mind. "What did Everett do?"

"Based on this initial evidence, he's used his contacts among import-export businesses to start a sideline brokering deals for controlled software and hard intel on human assets in sensitive areas. We're not yet sure if it started as his idea or—"

"She had nothing to do with that."

"You sound sure."

"I am." No matter how she'd moved on with her life, Addison wasn't a traitor. He could only imagine how angry she'd been to discover the secrets this Everett guy had been hiding.

"For the record, I agree with you."

No surprise. Thomas would've done all the background research on everyone involved in what must be a fiasco from the government side. It wouldn't take much legwork to look at Addison's background and find her first near-miss marriage. He clenched his fist. Her fiancé would've heard all about her past without the hassle of gathering intel. "Why am I here?"

"As I said, she's gone missing, and I think you're just the man to find her."

Would his past never stay buried? "I don't know anything about her anymore."

"Which is precisely the kind of advantage I'm looking for. No one on my team has found a trace of her since her BMW wound up in a used car lot in Arizona."

Just because she'd been south and east of San Francisco didn't mean she'd keep going that direction. "That leaves a lot of territory to cover. What about Everett?"

Thomas's expression clouded over. "Also off the radar right now. He could very well be searching for Ms. Collins, too, planning to buy her off or to silence her."

Drew understood which option was more likely. Addison had integrity in spades.

"My hope," Thomas continued, "is that you can find her first and bring her in. I can protect her."

Drew felt a hot lick of panic. This couldn't be happening. "What do you expect me to do? What do I tell her?" He'd seen the fallen hero obituary in the scrapbook his father had created. He'd read the few letters Addison had written to his dad in the months following their interrupted wedding and his capture. "She thinks I'm dead."

"I understand this is overwhelming," Thomas said. "We have resources here. Why don't you consider yourself a consultant? Give me a direction, some idea where she might be hiding, and help guide the team I send out to find her."

If Drew's gut instinct was right and Addison was heading to her home turf, Thomas's team wouldn't stand a chance. The woman he'd known, the woman he'd planned to marry, had always been ferociously independent and smart as a whip. If she was on the run and didn't want to be found, there was only one place she'd go. And if anyone cornered her there, she'd strike first and ask for identification later.

"No." Resigned, Drew accepted his fate. He couldn't leave this to anyone else. Whether or not he was thrilled by the idea of seeing her again, he figured he was the only one with a chance of convincing her to come out of hiding. "I'll find her."

"That's the best news I've had since they dumped this on my desk," Thomas admitted.

"I'll need gear."

"We have the best."

"I'll need cash for a car and cell phone in addition to the travel expenses."

Thomas pursed his lips. "Done."

"I'll find Addison, but I can't promise to bring her in." He cut off Thomas's automatic protest. "We both know she won't be safe until Everett and that leak are contained. She knows that, too. I'll monitor the news and do my best, but don't count on a quick resolution where she's concerned."

"Agreed." Thomas pressed a button on his phone. "My assistant will show you downstairs. Take whatever you need to get the job done."

"Yes, sir." If he thought about timelines and proximity, he'd lose it. Reminding himself life was a day-to-day effort, he focused on the first step: gearing up.

The T-shirt, warm-up pants and sneakers weren't going to hold up to what amounted to a manhunt through some difficult terrain.

Drew turned in his seat when the door opened and stood up as the receptionist returned. If he was right, if he still knew the woman at all, he'd soon be face-to-face with Addison. Surreal was a vast understatement. He couldn't decide if he should be terrified or ecstatic at the prospect. He supposed her reaction would help him decide.

Chapter Three

Thomas pushed his chair away from his desk and stood, restless and uncertain about what he'd just set in motion.

Not so long ago he'd been given a second chance and reunited with the only woman he'd ever loved. His personal success should give him hope for Drew and Addison, but he couldn't quite drum up that elusive emotion for this situation. Sending Drew to track down Addison could backfire. Not just for the two of them—three if he counted the little boy—but for the integrity of the operational mess he'd inherited.

It seemed more and more challenging lately to think of his Specialists as assets. They were all capable and strong people who, at the end of the day, were here as tools to be applied to specific purposes and operations. It was a particular trial when the people he assigned, like Drew, weren't even part of his elite program.

Time to hand over the reins. He stared through his big office window, blind to the stunning view. A knock sounded at his door. "Come in," he called without turning.

"I saw Bryant leave," Deputy Director Emmett Holt said. "Did he agree to help?"

Thomas loosened his tie as he returned to his desk chair. There was no need to stand on formality with Holt, who understood all too well what was riding on this operation.

"He agreed."

"But?" Holt sank into one of the visitors' chairs opposite Thomas. "You look like you've eaten bad fish."

"I feel a bit like that, to tell the truth. This could backfire. In a big way."

"Were there other options?"

Thomas drummed his fingers on the supple leather arm of his chair. "No." The whole reason they'd brought Drew into this was because Addison had disappeared. Completely. "But it's a lot to ask."

"He'll manage."

Thomas met Holt's sharp gaze. "I meant her. Addison's running for her life, for her son's life, and we're sending out a ghost to find her. She has no idea what happened— only that he never made it to their wedding."

"Then I stand corrected."

Thomas arched an eyebrow. "He won't manage?"

"No. *She* will manage."

It sounded like a magic-wand theory to Thomas's ears, and that was one theory everyone in his line of work always rejected. "He's not a trained Specialist."

"Oh, so that's the problem."

Thomas didn't like the half smile on Holt's face. "Explain."

"You feel guilty for sending an unqualified civilian after a high-value asset."

"That's not true." Where the hell was this coming from? He and Holt had different management styles, but this series of irritating questions wasn't typical. "Bryant might be a civilian now, but he could step in and train our recruits on anything at a moment's notice."

"So he's qualified."

"More than."

"Then I guess you're feeling guilty because we didn't have an equally qualified Specialist available?"

They both knew the roster and they both took great pride in the skills of the men and women on their team. "Why the hell are you being so difficult?"

"Because you need to ease up on yourself," Holt said, his expression somber. "The woman and her kid are missing, Everett escaped with some damned sophisticated help and you just sent out the best option for everyone involved."

"Thanks for the vote of confidence." Thomas wasn't sure how else to interpret that tidy speech.

"If that's what you need, you're welcome." Holt leaned forward. "We talked about it, looked at every asset before you brought Bryant in. He is the only choice for this mission."

Thomas knew that was correct. Even logical.

"Personally," Holt continued, "I believe he'll succeed, no matter how she reacts to seeing him again. He's resourceful. He'll bring her in or make sure we can."

"You're right," Thomas allowed, though he knew this decision would haunt him well into his retirement if it went wrong. He rubbed the palm of one hand with the opposite thumb. "I've never once forgotten that our Specialists are people. We demand more than we should—"

"But never more than we're willing to give ourselves," Holt finished for him. "That philosophy—*your* philosophy—is at the heart of our entire program. Don't ever doubt it."

"All right." Thomas raised his hands, palms out. There had been a time, not too long ago, when Thomas had doubted his philosophy and much more. He'd doubted Holt's loyalty to the Specialists and the nation at large.

Been certain he'd made the wrong call naming Holt as the next director.

No longer. Holt had proved himself in the field and protected the Mission Recovery office during a complicated attack from one of Thomas's old enemies. Not only that, he'd recently become family by marrying Thomas's sister. "Thanks for the pep talk," he said, the burden feeling a bit lighter. "It's the kid," he added, finally articulating the real issue. He and Jo wanted to start a family soon, and although his wife was as independent and resourceful as Addison, Thomas knew how far he'd go if someone took aim at his wife or their children.

"I figured," Holt said with a sympathetic nod.

"Cecelia is expecting you and Jo to join the family for July Fourth weekend."

"We're looking forward to it," Thomas said, more relieved than he should be about the change of topic. "Jo is making noise about getting a boat of our own when I retire."

"Want me to keep an eye out for you?"

"A casual eye." He recognized Holt's method of shifting the topic to something more normal. "But I don't want her to know I'm looking yet."

"Lucky for you, I can keep a secret," Holt said, heading for the doorway.

"I'm well aware." Thomas smiled as Holt walked out, the guilt of Addison and Drew's situation muted. For now.

He'd needed the reminder that Holt provided. If Drew had given the first sign that he'd cave under the pressure of the request, Thomas would've found another way to track down Addison.

As it was, he was back to hoping the reunion, although certain to be awkward and emotional, would result in capturing the traitorous Everett and the root of his network so Addison and her son could return to life without fear of retribution.

Chapter Four

Louisiana bayou
Saturday, July 5, 7:35 p.m.

In the fading light of another warm summer day, Addison came outside with two bowls of ice cream. Sitting next to Andy on the top step of the porch, she handed him one.

"We had ice cream last night."

"It's summer," Addison said with a smile. "And you've played hard all day. Besides, it won't keep forever." Her friend Nico, father of Bernadette, her best childhood friend, had given her permission to stay here in his mother's old place. He'd brought them out by boat and had delivered more supplies yesterday. Although she appreciated what the weather-worn shack provided, she didn't trust the ancient freezer on the back porch.

Andy didn't waste time arguing over the bonus treat and he dug in with enthusiasm.

As dark crept in from the edges of the swamp, the insects ramped up with an evening chorus that rose and fell with the soft breeze. In the tall marsh grass across the water, fireflies took flight. "Look." She pointed toward the soft twinkling.

"Can I catch some? Nico told me kids here use them as night-lights."

"Not tonight." She was tired and wary despite being as alone as a person could be out here. Other than Nico's, she hadn't even heard another boat in the area for days, yet she felt edgy as if they were being watched. They'd been here for two weeks, and according to the news, Craig continued to evade authorities as the story of his illegal dealings came out in dribs and drabs. "I did that a few times when I was your age," she said to her son. "Even once during a campout right here."

"Really?" His eyes were wide.

"Mmm-hmm. Mama Leonie, Nico's mom, lived out here more than in town. Nico's daughter was my best friend and we used to come here every chance we got. There was only one room then."

"No bedroom?"

Addison shook her head. "She didn't want one."

"Where did she sleep?"

"Outside on the back porch." Addison looked around once more, picturing it as it had been. "I always thought it was the best tree house."

"But it's not *in* the tree. I think we should call it a swamp fort." Andy twisted around and then leaned forward to peer through the slatted porch to the water below. "I like this part hanging over the water."

"It keeps the rooms cooler."

"Huh."

Addison smiled to herself. The conversation relaxed her. Feeling watched was simply paranoia, which wasn't unexpected. Nico had assured her no one came out this way much since Leonie's death a few years back. He promised that she and Andy would be safe in the old Voodoo Queen's place. Few people knew this place was still habitable. More important, only two people knew that Addison knew about it.

"This is a real adventure, Mom." Andy scooped up another big bite of ice cream. "I saw a frog out there." He pointed with his spoon toward the edge of the water. "And an alligator down that way." The spoon moved down the shore, away from the house.

"Are you sure?"

He nodded, his mouth full and a sticky stain of chocolate bracketing its corners. "Nico showed me how to spot 'em."

"Did he?"

"Uh-huh."

"He's the expert." Nico knew these swamps inside and out and stayed busy as a tour guide. When she'd knocked on his door in the middle of the night two weeks ago, he hadn't batted an eye at her request for help. Stomping into his boots, he'd taken her keys and driven her out to the edge of the swamp without asking any uncomfortable questions. After promising he wouldn't mention her arrival to anyone, he'd loaded two boats, tied them together and guided her out here. Once they'd unloaded and he was satisfied she had key supplies, he'd left her one boat and returned to his dock with the other.

She supposed other people might've felt obligated to help because she'd sent money back to help with Mama Leonie's health care and final expenses. But Nico lived by a different philosophy. You took care of your own, no matter how much time or silence passed between visits. That had shown through when he'd returned with a boat-load of supplies at midday, and he'd clearly spent some important time with Andy while she'd put things away in the house.

Now they had a stock of wood and charcoal, a generator and fuel to keep the small luxuries like the freezer, the ancient water heater and the two lightbulbs inside the shack going. They couldn't stay here indefinitely, but they could certainly stay through the summer and longer if she hadn't figured out the next step by then.

"Mom, the swamp is kinda creepy at night."

She felt herself smiling. "In a good way?"

"Yeah!"

"Nico told me his mom knew everything about the swamp."

"She sure did. And she loved to teach anyone who'd listen. She treated me like a granddaughter. I learned her secret recipe for pancakes when I turned ten."

Andy looked up at her. "Would she have been my grandma, too?"

"You better believe it. The two of you would've been best friends." She rubbed her hand across his small shoulders. "Leonie was very special. I loved coming out here to see her."

"This was your adventure place?"

Addison nodded. "Yes. And it's good to be back." More than she'd expected, really. It felt like home, even though she wasn't anywhere near the farm where she'd grown up in Mississippi.

"I think it's better than SeaWorld!"

"Just don't try and pet a gator." They shared a quiet laugh. "Tomorrow we can start exploring. I can show you what's—"

"Safe," Andy interrupted with a put-upon sigh. "You said we wouldn't have to be together the whole time on this adventure."

"I said we wouldn't have to be in the car the whole time. And you've been playing on your own, right?"

"Right."

"I just want to be sure you know what to do or where to go if you come across something dangerous." Or someone.

Craig wouldn't have the first idea of how to find this place, shouldn't even know about it, but she wanted to be sure Andy knew how to find Nico in case they were somehow injured or separated.

"That doesn't sound like an adventure."

"Oh, it will be."

Water splashed nearby. Andy turned to her with wide eyes. "Was that a gator?"

"Probably not. Gators slide into the water and most of the time they hardly make a sound or even a ripple." A small exaggeration, but worth the resulting expression of wonder on his face. "A sound like that's usually a fish or frog." Not a person, she reminded herself. People who slipped or splashed made even more noise.

"Nico taught you that, didn't he?"

"Mmm-hmm." She held out her empty bowl, let him stack his on top. "Take those inside to the sink, please."

"Do I have to wash 'em?"

"No, sweetie. I'll do it after bedtime."

She listened to his small footsteps, waited for the inevitable noise as the bowls and spoons landed with a clatter in the old porcelain sink. He rushed back out to join her a moment later, the screen door slapping shut behind him.

"About bedtime…"

She smiled into his serious face. "Yes?"

"It's summer, so there isn't such thing as a school night."

"I noticed."

"And we're on an adventure."

"We are." She knew where he was headed, but she waited for him to say what was on his mind.

"Could I not have a bedtime?"

She waited. This was the way they did things. He had to ask nicely even when he delivered sound reasons.

"Please," he added quickly with a winning smile.

"You still have a lot of growing to do," she pointed out. "Sleep is important for growing." Just after Christmas she'd bought him new tennis shoes, only to have him grow out of them within a few days. "Enough sleep," she amended, anticipating his next argument.

His face fell but only for a moment. "There were nights last summer that didn't have bedtime and we were at home."

"True." She drilled her finger at his belly, making him squeal and jump back. "There will be nights like that on our adventure, too."

"It's not even all the way dark yet."

"That doesn't mean it isn't late." And her son rose early, ready and eager for every day. She was more than a little grateful when she realized how well Nico had updated the place through the years. She wouldn't have to settle for instant coffee.

She patted the top step. "Come sit with me and we'll count the first stars."

Andy dropped down beside her, just a little sulky with his elbows on his knees and his chin propped on his fists.

"You can't see the stars if you're looking at the water."

He dutifully looked up, his lower lip poking out like a shelf. "Wow. There's lots up there already." Interested now, he forgot to pout.

They counted more than twenty as the sky transformed into an inky purple above the tall cypress trees. When she heard him yawn, she nudged him back inside the "swamp fort." Leaning against the doorway, she kept her weary little man on task as he chattered through the bedtime rituals.

The little things like pajamas and brushing teeth felt so normal even in Mama Leonie's rambling little shack.

"Which one will it be tonight?" She hefted the backpack full of comics onto the narrow bed near his feet.

His eyebrows drew together as he considered. "Will you tell me more about Mama Leonie?"

Surprised, she agreed. "Where do you want me to start?"

"Why did she live out here all alone?"

Addison gathered her thoughts, drew hard on her memory to recall the tales. She didn't want to scare Andy with voodoo stories, but she didn't want to paint Leonie as anything other than the wonderful woman she'd been.

"Nico's mama didn't live out here alone all the time. She raised Nico and his brothers and sisters closer to town."

Andy stared at the little room. "Because the swamp fort was too small?"

"Partly."

"Why not just make it bigger?"

"They already had a bigger house. Maybe I'll take you by it one day." Addison settled on the edge of the bed while Andy squished himself and his pillow into a comfortable position. Going through the familiar motions soothed her. "But she always had this place for herself."

"So it was her adventure place."

"In a manner of speaking, I suppose you're right. Mama Leonie came out here to meet with people who needed things. She practiced a religion called voodoo."

"She turned people into zombies?" Andy's eyes went wide as saucers but with more excitement than fear. Addison hoped it would always be that way, the opportunity for discovery outweighing potential distress.

"Of course not. She was smart and kind and full of compassion for people. She was more like a doctor or therapist."

"But voodoo has zombies."

"Comic books have voodoo zombies." Addison wondered if she needed to rein him in a bit. "In real life, voodoo isn't nearly so creepy." She walked her fingers over his foot and up his leg and tickled him behind the knee. He giggled and squirmed out of reach. "It's complicated but interesting, and the people around her counted on Leonie like they would a doctor or therapist." She stood and managed to kiss his forehead before he could protest. "Now get some sleep."

"Like a zombie?"

"If it helps you grow," she said with a laugh.

"Where are you sleeping?"

"I'll put my sleeping bag in here with you. After I take care of the dishes."

"And your quiet time."

That habit was one definite success in her parenting career. As soon as Andy had been old enough to understand, she'd taught him to appreciate the quiet time she needed in the evenings. "That's right. Now quit stalling and go to sleep."

"Did Mama Leonie ever do voodoo on you?" Andy asked before she could get out the door.

"Maybe I'll tell you that story tomorrow night."

"Ah, come on."

"Stalling. Love you, bear."

"Love you, too," he muttered, clearly resigned to losing the battle for more of a story.

She left the door cracked, the same way she did at home. It was a small compromise for him, but an added measure of security for her under these new circumstances.

At home during quiet time she would've heated water for tea and pulled out some reading for work or pleasure.

Here, hot tea meant lighting the wood-burning stove or the grill outside. On such a sultry evening, it didn't feel like a good idea to fill the kitchen with more heat. And she hesitated to start a fire in the grill at this hour.

Among the supplies Nico had delivered was a jug of homemade wine. She poured some into one of the mason jars that served as drink ware and carefully sipped. The sweet, light taste was a pleasant surprise and she bravely sipped a second time.

She washed and dried the dishes, stacking them back with the others on the open corner shelves near the small table. As a youngster she'd often been entrusted with this chore and had used a chair instead of a stepstool to get the job done.

The memories flooded through her, warm and comfortable, and for a fleeting moment she could almost hear the lilting voices filling the room with chatter and laughter. There had been good times here, each of them precious to her.

The creative "architecture" in the bayous was the polar opposite of the sleek designer spaces she'd left behind, and Addison found her fondness for this little shack and rugged natural surroundings hadn't changed. She'd learned early, from her own humble beginnings, that the value wasn't in the furnishings of a place, but the people who filled it.

Mama Leonie and her family by blood and choice had filled this place with love, encouragement and hope. *Still filled it,* Addison thought as a breeze ruffled the curtains at the window over the sink. For the first time since leaving the West Coast, she felt a sliver of doubt about running here. She didn't want to ruin the healthy vibe or cause any trouble for Nico and his family. The locals still revered this place because of all the good Leonie had done for them, but Craig wouldn't care about any of that. If he found her, he'd have no respect for the history and simply level whatever stood between him and her.

Too bad he'd never understand the biggest gap was full of intangibles, not physical obstacles.

"Mama Leonie, if you can hear me," Addison whispered, "I don't want to bring you trouble. There was nowhere else to go." Truly. Nowhere else Craig didn't know about. She looked down, twisting the engagement ring on her finger. What a fool she'd been to share so much of her life, of herself, with a man capable of such crimes. Why hadn't she seen through him? "I'm sorry if trouble follows me," she murmured into the silence. "Any help you can send would be appreciated."

She took off the ring and stuffed it in her pocket, scowling at the pale indentation left behind on her finger. The mark would fade and, with the bright days of summer, the pale line would soon fill in with healthy color. She'd taken a stand, done the right thing, and she had to trust the authorities to deal with Craig the right way. Soon.

Though her specialty was corporate law, she understood Craig and his legal defense team would make the most of every loophole available. Knowing the system too well to trust it blindly, she'd taken that final precaution and had mailed extra information on to a neutral party.

Addison paused at the cracked door, hearing Andy's steady breathing. They were out of harm's way. *Safe.* She repeated the word as she carried her glass of wine to the hammock on the back porch, screened in thanks to Nico's hard work.

Letting the hammock swing her gently, she reviewed every detail of her discovery, her report and her escape, looking for missteps, for anything Craig might twist to his advantage.

He could drag her into it by association, but she'd never had anything to do with his dealings. Although her firm hadn't balked at her request for six weeks off, she knew it was only a matter of time before she was unemployed. Her firm wouldn't tolerate the bad publicity of having her name dragged through the mud because she'd been idiot enough to nearly marry a traitor. Smart women weren't supposed to fall for the wolf in sheep's clothing. Her only saving grace was she'd found out before exchanging vows, but that wouldn't be enough to save her job.

She tipped back more of the wine, draining the glass, considering another glass. To pour or not to pour? became the most pertinent question. She used a toe to push off and send the hammock rocking again while she made up her mind.

It was so peaceful out here, the darkness so deep and quiet. She'd loved the West Coast city life, loved the challenges and perks of a high-powered, well-paying job. Being a single parent of an active, intelligent son had ups and downs, but at the end of every day, there was unconditional love. Everything about that life, except her son, was over. Where did that leave her? Where did she *want* to go next?

Money wasn't a big, immediate problem. Having been raised on next to nothing, she'd invested well and saved more through the years. Only Bernadette, as the executor of Addison's will and potential guardian for Andy, had access to those accounts.

She rubbed at the space between her eyebrows, wishing once more that there had been a way to warn Bernadette of the oncoming storm. But that kind of move would've been dangerous. During her relationship with Craig, she'd mentioned a few of their young and stupid antics in New

Orleans, and he'd taken care of Andy six months ago when she and Bernadette had spent a girls' weekend in Tahoe.

Did fools come any bigger than she'd been with Craig?

Rolling to her feet, Addison headed back inside with her mason jar. She'd done all she could, taken every precaution, including running here, the safest place she knew. There was nothing left to do but wait it out. She had nearly six weeks left before school started. Out here, with only Nico as a contact, surely that would be enough time for her to know how much farther she'd have to run to provide Andy with as normal a life as possible.

Walking inside, she closed the door and checked the load on the shotgun. It had felt odd in her hands at first, but after a few hours of practice, shooting at stationary targets and then moving ones, her hands and body remembered the routine.

Carrying the shotgun with her, she unrolled her sleeping bag on the kitchen side of the narrow bedroom doorway. Settling on top of the thick layers of fabric for the remainder of the night, Addison listened to the soft hum of the refrigerator. It seemed to underscore the gentle, content sounds of her son sleeping on the cot in the corner on the other side of the door.

Bugs continued whirring and chirping outside, and she heard the occasional splash from fish, frog or turtle beneath the stilted house. They were safe. Craig couldn't find them here. If he searched anywhere, he was more likely to start with the small plot of land in Mississippi that still held her name on the title. It was on public record, which she couldn't change now. Although he knew she'd loved visiting New Orleans, she'd never told him anything about her dirt-stained summers out here in the bayou.

Nico had promised to keep her presence here a secret as well as keep her informed of any suspicious strangers who might appear and ask questions. She had the radio, and maybe in a week or two she'd risk a trip into town to scour the internet for any warning signs and check in with Professor Hastings.

Addison discarded the idea immediately. Any contact with her friend and mentor earlier than planned would put her "insurance policy" in jeopardy. No one could know she'd sent him backup files of Craig's treacherous dealings as well as more incriminating evidence. She thought of all the names she didn't know on his contact lists, the lists she'd downloaded from his phone and computer before sending them anonymously to the FBI.

With any luck, they would keep that as an ace up their sleeve, the secret weapon he wouldn't be prepared to explain away in court. Combined with what she'd sent to Professor Hastings, Craig would never be free long enough to cause trouble for her or Andy. As long as they caught him.

As she drifted off to sleep, one hand on the stock of the shotgun, she almost believed it.

Minutes or hours later, Addison woke with a start. It was tricky, listening past the blood thudding in her ears, to figure out what had startled her. The refrigerator was quiet and she heard the creak of wind in the trees.

Not the wind, she realized, as the curtains over the sink were still. She strained for another clue, telling herself it was just another overreaction to new surroundings.

This time the quiet splash of water under the house was followed immediately by the soft rasp of a boat being pulled onto the grasses that lined the shore. Damn it all to hell. Someone had found her.

Immediate worry for Nico flashed through her. Guilt pricked her conscience. Had they hurt him to get a lead on her direction? Since Leonie's death, there had been no reason to head into this part of the swamp. Many of the locals believed she haunted the place, and they preferred to avoid even benevolent ghosts.

Addison gripped the shotgun and sat up without making a sound. It might very well be someone familiar with the shack and in need of shelter. If they'd noticed the generator was going, it made sense to stop and ask for help, but Addison prepared to shoot first and ask questions later.

For several long moments nothing more than typical night swamp sounds reached her. Maybe whoever had been in the boat just needed to sleep off a wrong turn. It happened, and hospitality was part of the odd society out here. If they stayed down there with the boat, they wouldn't have any trouble from her.

She'd just relaxed her hold on the gun when she caught the unmistakable creaking tread of the third step in the string leading to the porch. Addison tried to breathe, telling herself Craig wouldn't come by night and sure as hell wouldn't come to a place so rural without vocalizing his discomfort in the process.

But that had been the Craig she'd known—thought she'd known—not the greedy bastard who'd brokered terrible deals that ended with dead US citizens.

She listened, her palms going damp as whoever was outside climbed closer to the porch. Part of her wanted to run, to grab Andy and bolt through the back, but she'd only heard one person. She could take one person.

"Addison?"

The inquiry, delivered in a low whisper, only revealed that the speaker was male. Nico would've announced himself already, knowing she was armed and prepared to defend herself.

So who else out here could possibly know her name?

The intruder made no secret of his approach now. He leaned close to the window. "Addison? Are you in there?"

Without a porch light, the intruder's identity was impossible to make out, but he was nearly at the door.

"Hello?" The voice, a little stronger, sounded familiar. "Addi?"

Addison's heart clutched. She knew that voice, and only one man had ever called her by that nickname. Drew Bryant, her long-dead fiancé.

She shook her head. Clearly she'd let the stress and worry get to her. Drew wasn't here, wasn't even alive. This was probably just a vivid dream induced by Andy's talk of zombies. She took a deep breath and let it out slowly, urging her brain to wake up.

The screen-door hinges squealed and the handle of the main door turned. *A dream,* she thought, *it has to be a dream.* No one but Nico knew she was here. As the door eased open, Addison leveled the shotgun at the man casting shadows across the weak moonlight spilling through the door.

"Addi, it's me, Drew. I'm here to help."

Wake up!

Addison fired. The loud report deafened her to the splintering wood as the buckshot pelted the front door. The reactions of the stranger in front of her were like a bad mime, first ducking behind the door, then rushing forward and taking the gun before she could fire again.

"It's *me*," he said, his voice lost in the ringing in her ears.

The single lightbulb came on and she covered her mouth, barely smothering the scream lodged in her chest. "No. *No.*" This wasn't possible. It was a cruel twist of her overwrought imagination. She pushed to her feet, away from the man with Drew's face. Any second now she'd wake up from this horrible nightmare.

"Mommy?" It was her son's tiny voice that ripped through her confusion and brought her back to her senses. She had to protect Andy at all costs.

"I'm here, Andy." She couldn't decide. Comfort her son or confront the man in front of her.

"Take care of him." The man carefully leaned the gun against the wall closest to her. "Then I'll explain and you can shoot me if you want to."

It was such a Drew thing to say that she followed her instincts and tended to Andy.

"Why did the gun go off? Are we in trouble?"

"Someone startled me, that's all." She ushered her boy back into bed and pulled the covers up tight. "It's late. Go back to sleep."

"Who is that?" He rubbed his eyes.

"An unexpected friend." It was a simpler answer than explaining her possible hallucinations. "He doesn't want to hurt us." Apparitions and hallucinations didn't have enough substance to hurt anyone. She hoped. Whoever—whatever—was out there, he'd taken the gun from her all too easily. "He startled me and I fired the gun, that's all."

"I'm scared."

"That's understandable," she said with more calm than she felt with her heart pounding. "But I won't let anything bad happen. In the morning I'll tell you the whole story." Assuming she'd know the story by then. At least it gave her a bit of time to think of something logical.

They both gave the doorway a look when they heard the scrape of a chair across the wood floor.

"Promise?"

She pressed a kiss to his brow and wrapped him in a big hug. "I promise." Holding her son in her arms and smelling the sweet scent of his hair, she knew this wasn't a bizarre, unbelievable nightmare. The man in the kitchen might really be Drew. She tensed. If so, he owed her a detailed explanation.

"You'll tell me if I need to find Nico, right?" he whispered into her ear.

Her heart slammed against her ribs. She couldn't imagine sending her little boy into the swamp, even if they had talked about that very scenario as a safety precaution. "That's not necessary this time, especially not in the dark," she said. "For now I need you to stay right here in this bed." She leaned back, held his shoulders as she looked him in the eye. "Promise me."

Andy promised, gave her another fierce hug and released her to deal with the man in the kitchen.

Chapter Five

Drew heard the low voices in the other room and felt like an ass for his clumsy entrance. His hands shook and not from dodging the shotgun blast. He trembled for her. If there'd ever been any doubt, he knew for sure that he'd lost everything in that POW camp. Years of his life, sure, but so much more.

Addison seemed to grow more beautiful every time he saw her. Remembering her radiance the day before their wedding had carried him through those dark days in unthinkable conditions. Seeing her playing with her new family in the park had filled him with jealousy and later—much later—with a weird sense of peace. She'd found her place, the happy life she'd dreamed of, even if it was without him. And just now, despite the messy hair, her face pale with shock, the shorts and oversize T-shirt concealing the sweet curves of her body, he looked at her and saw the prettiest woman on the planet.

Not that he could tell her, even if he hadn't mishandled this completely. She wasn't his. He'd let her go, let her keep believing he was dead. He should've stayed in the boat under the house and waited until morning to talk to her. But he'd needed to see her.

He told himself the confirmation was required for the job. Waiting until morning and protecting people who might not need it was a waste of time and resources. He pulled a chair away from the kitchen table, sat down and tried to believe the lie.

No sale. Director Casey might've pulled him out of Detroit, but the official case had nothing to do with why he'd come out here in the dark. He hadn't come here for Casey. He'd climbed those steps and disrupted Addison's night simply to satisfy his curiosity.

Behind him the door opened and he felt her staring at him.

She crossed the room, keeping as much distance as the small space allowed. "This is impossible. You're real." She cleared her throat. "Alive, I mean."

"I am."

"Part of me expected you to vaporize while I talked with…" She tilted her head back toward the door. "With my son."

So the boy he'd seen in the park was hers, not Everett's. He wasn't sure why that made him feel worse about all this. "Leaving you on our wedding day wasn't my idea."

"And still you weren't there." She held up her hands as if she could wave away the accusation. "Forget it. We can't change whatever took you away. I was grateful you left the note."

He'd broken protocol with that, but he'd had to do something. It was their wedding day, for crying out loud. The note wouldn't have been nearly enough to earn her understanding, but it had been the only option.

"Come on, Drew. Start explaining."

Start where? Words failed him. His life had been a thousand times easier staying away from her. Lonely as hell, but easier. She'd moved on, had a kid, and the best way to honor her independence was to move on with his. He focused on his purpose here: to get her into Casey's protection.

"Speaking of vaporizing," he began, pointing at her. He realized the error of the phrase when her eyes narrowed dangerously. "Some important people are worried about you and your son." Casey couldn't have warned him about that detail? Where was the kid's father? "They asked me if I could track you down."

"What kind of important people?"

"People who want to keep you safe."

She pursed those full, rosy lips, then shook her head. "Congratulations. You of all people should know I came here because I didn't want to be found. Tell them you were wrong. Tell them you couldn't find me."

"Not a chance. I can't go back empty-handed."

"Of course you can. You *will*, since I'm not going any-where with you."

"Be reasonable, Addison."

"You first," she snapped, carefully pitching her voice so she wouldn't wake her son. "Tell me who sent you."

"You need help. You're in over your head."

"Give me a name, Drew."

He hesitated. "You've got the authorities running in circles looking for you all over the country," he hedged. Based on her mutinous expression, she wouldn't budge on this. The only name he could give wouldn't mean any-thing to her anyway. He weighed the mission goal with the usual security requirements. "Thomas Casey sent me."

"Alone?"

Drew nodded, wondering why she was so insistent about this.

"Who is he to you?"

"No one." He jerked a shoulder. "A man who gets what he wants. He sent an escort to pick me up in Detroit—"

"Detroit, *Michigan*?"

Inside his head, Drew swore. Was there anything he could do right here? "Yes."

"You've been living in the States?"

"Yes."

"You're not dead. You're living back in your hometown."

"Yes," he whispered, feeling miserable for causing the pain in her soft icy-blue eyes.

"For how long?"

He might as well lay out all the cards. "I've been in Detroit almost a year."

She turned her back on him. "Get out."

"I can't do that." How could he make her understand? Without her trust, he wasn't sure he could get her to cooperate, and he didn't want to resort to brute force.

She whirled around, her blue gaze full of fury and fire. "Sure you can. You've been in Detroit, letting me believe you were dead. You seem to have mastered staying out of my life. Feel free to continue."

His temper bubbled up to match hers. "It wasn't my idea to change the status quo." Irrational or not, she had a son. Not a baby or even a toddler—the kid was in grade school. "You didn't wait too damn long to get on with your life after the wedding," he said, pointing toward the closed door.

She reeled back as if he'd hit her and her voice turned brittle. "You can't stay here."

"I have to." He struggled for any remnant of sanity. His world, barely held together since his release, was breaking apart now that he was in the same room with her. "You need me."

"No, I don't," she countered. "I'm doing just fine on my own."

"Really? Craig Everett escaped federal custody."

"Shh." Panic flashed across her face as she glanced at the door. "He doesn't know anything yet."

"So Everett is the kid's father?"

Her gaze turned hard as she glared at him again. "I know he escaped and I guarantee if he'd walked in that door—" she stabbed a finger in that direction "—if it had been anyone else but you, my aim would've been right on target."

He believed her. He'd seen her in action on a shooting range. Years ago. "So you missed because it was me?"

"Yes."

He accepted the admission as a small positive sign. "We can go our separate ways after I get you safely out of Ev—his reach."

"How? Witness protection?"

"Possibly." He didn't know the details, but he trusted Casey with the task.

"No deal."

"Addi, be reasonable."

"I am being reasonable. As well as responsible. You don't have any idea just how connected Craig is. Witness protection won't be enough and it isn't fair to my son."

"Thomas Casey can keep you both safe."

"He's in some branch of government?"

"He is."

"No deal."

Drew bit back another string of foul words. "You're infuriating."

"Same goes for you." She crossed the room to the refrigerator, opened the door and bent to look inside. He tried to ignore the view as the soft fabric of her shorts hugged her backside.

"I think this is our first real fight," he said.

"Hardly," she muttered, handing him a bottle of water. "But it can be our last. Take this for the road."

"I'm not leaving." He twisted off the plastic cap and leaned back in his chair. "We never fought before...our wedding day." He forced the last two words out and then took a long drink of water.

"We fought plenty in the days and months after. You just weren't there."

"I'm sorry, Addi. If I could change it..."

"It was our *wedding* day," she whispered. "Why did they need *you*?"

His heart seized at the pain in her voice. Raw and fresh, she sounded exactly the way he felt every day. When he'd agreed to help Director Casey, he'd known her reaction would be volatile at best. He hadn't been prepared to deal with how much his appearance would hurt her. As she'd moved on with her life, he hadn't expected her to feel anything but initial shock at seeing him again.

But she didn't look like a woman who'd moved on, despite the evidence he'd seen for himself. Top of her field, gorgeous home in the right neighborhood and a son. That was the piece that slid like a knife between his ribs, straight to his heart. During his time as a prisoner, he'd fantasized about making love with Addi, about the family they would build in years to come.

She'd done that. With some other man.

"Why, Drew?"

He'd often asked the same thing and never found a decent answer. "I had the misfortune of knowing the key players in the area. Command said they needed me."

Her eyes went wide. "That's not what I call an explanation."

"It's the best I can offer."

With a derisive snort, she paced the small room, pausing near the front door. She pushed her hands into her hair. "You're supposed to be dead."

He wanted to take her in his arms and show her how alive he felt. How alive she made him feel now that he could hear her voice, smell the light citrus of her shampoo. He wrapped one palm around the other fist, massaging the tension in his hands. "For a time that's what I wanted, too."

"I didn't say I wanted you to be dead." She pushed loose strands of her golden hair behind her ears. "I heard the news from your dad. His face…" She gazed up at the slanted tin-roof ceiling. "He's the one who told me you'd died."

"You saw my dad?" He swallowed the swell of grief that came with every thought of his father.

"Sure." She nodded. "We spoke frequently after the interrupted wedding. He apologized to me that it didn't go as scheduled." She leaned back against the big sink and propped one foot on the other.

The pose transported him back to the days when she'd stand just that way, waiting for the first cup of coffee to kick her into gear in the morning. He'd counted on a lifetime of moments like this one, but fate had dealt him a different hand.

"And I saw him again about two months after that," she added.

Two months. It still bothered him the way the army had handled his capture. "They didn't waste any time pronouncing me dead."

"They being the army, I assume?"

He nodded.

"Are you surprised?"

"Not really." What surprised him was how much he struggled not to touch her. He wanted a rewind button, a way to go back and say no to that cursed assignment, no matter the consequences. "That kind of risk, the emergency operation, went with the job."

Her eyebrows shot up. "Past tense?"

"Yes." He looked away from the softer sympathy in her eyes.

"But they still tapped you to come find me."

"Not in a military capacity. The army decided I wasn't fit for duty anymore."

"What the hell?" Her eyes raked him from head to toe. "Who made that decision?"

"Addi, the details aren't relevant right now."

"Of course they are," she insisted. "If you're not fit for service, why would this Casey person call you?"

"My kind of luck. The sooner I get you to him, the sooner we can get back to our lives." Separate lives, if that was what she wanted.

"You seem eager," she said. She came over and took the chair across from his at the table. "What kind of life do you have to get back to?"

Not the kind he wanted, that was for damn sure. In the weak light he caught another glimpse of the thin gold chain she wore, but whatever charms were on it were hidden by the T-shirt. Early in their relationship, he'd given her a heart charm inscribed with their initials and the date they'd met. He was a sap for hoping she still wore it.

"Drew?"

He didn't want to talk about himself. His life was vacant, nothing but loss and heartache. Hers mattered more. "What kind of life did you leave?"

Her lip curled. "I left an illusion," she said. "And I won't let myself fall into the same trap again."

What the hell did that mean? "You can't stay out here forever."

"I could," she argued. "But I don't need forever. And

I sure don't need the certain failure of federal protection if they can't keep a traitor behind bars."

"All right. What's the plan?"

"That's none of your concern."

"I'm making it my concern."

She laughed, a bitter edge in the soft sound, as she propped her foot on the seat of the chair. He watched her run her fingertips over a small scar near her kneecap.

The blast of worry over an obvious sign of surgery was just one more irrational reaction added to the rest, but he couldn't stop himself from asking her what had happened.

"Nothing major. I tweaked it on a ski trip in Tahoe."

"When?"

"A couple years ago."

He should've been there. For everything. "I didn't know you liked to ski."

"Neither did I. It was a girls' weekend kind of thing."

Why did that flood him with so much relief? "I was in the middle of a rec league basketball game when Casey picked me up."

"Oh?"

"Since I, um, got back, I got involved a bit with the old neighborhood."

"Following in your dad's footsteps?"

Drew shrugged. "It was a starting point."

She bit her lip and pressed the back of her hand to the corner of her eye. "He was a good man, Drew." She cleared her throat. "The news of your death just tore him up."

"It tore me up when I heard about his heart attack," he confessed. "Long after the fact."

She shifted in her chair once more, her hand reaching across the small table, but she caught herself before making contact.

Smart, he thought. And he was grateful one of them had been. He couldn't be sure how he'd react to her touch. "You need to get some rest before we set out tomorrow," he said, standing.

"I'm not going anywhere with you."

"Staying here is certain suicide."

"How do you figure that? Unless you were followed, I'll be fine."

She had him there. Why couldn't he come up with a logical, convincing argument? Oh, yeah. He was distracted and overwhelmed by everything from her voice to her fierce determination. Watching her that day in the park had been bad, but this…this was a thousand times worse.

"I wasn't followed." His skills weren't that rusty. That strange sensation of being in two places at once, the phenomenon he'd first encountered in that damned prison cell, crept up on him now. It was something the shrinks discovered and referred to as a critical risk. Losing it here and now wasn't an option. He couldn't let his weakness put her and the kid in jeopardy.

With a deep, slow breath, he met her gaze once more. "I wasn't followed," he repeated when she continued to stare at him. "But I'd rather not deal with the swamp again tonight. I'll sleep down by the boat and we can discuss this in the morning."

ADDISON COULDN'T STOP staring at him, cataloging the differences between then and now. He'd always been fit, but now he looked as though he could afford to pack a few more pounds on that wide-shouldered frame. Plenty of definition in his arms and rippling under the snug dark T-shirt, but it wasn't quite *him*. She found the biggest changes in his face. Deep lines framed his eyes and mouth, and the tension in his jaw made her think he never quit clenching his teeth. What had he been through that had turned a strong, confident man into someone so haunted, hard and grim? She wasn't sure she wanted to know.

Dreamlike didn't begin to cover this. Her heart was stuck on "how" and "why" with frequent trips over questions about his new personal life. None of that mattered in the middle of the night in the bayou. She couldn't afford to let it matter come morning, either, but she could only win one battle at a time. It took all her willpower to push the right words past her lips. "You can't stay here."

"I can't leave."

She crossed her arms, fingernails digging into her biceps so she wouldn't reach for him again. Too tempting and far too risky. She suspected any physical contact would have her craving more, exactly as it had been between them from the moment they'd met. "You have to." If he stayed, she would lean on him. Worse, she would collapse or cling. Neither option was acceptable.

"Addi, sweetheart. You don't have to do this alone."

Again her heart tripped over the nickname, the sensation compounded by the familiar endearment and the sincerity shining in his brown eyes. "You have to go, Drew."

"Not in the dark."

"You made it here in the dark," she said ungraciously.

"Bad timing," he admitted. "And I did it for you. The same reason applies now. I'm not leaving until we reach an understanding."

She closed her eyes and counted to ten, remembering his mile-wide stubborn streak. Not unlike his son, when the man dug in, he wouldn't be budged.

Another worrisome thought chased the others through her mind. He didn't seem to know much about her and her son. Their son. Was it an act to throw her off? The obligations—personal and legal—niggled at her. Drew had a right to know Andy was his. "Fine. Take the hammock outside. We'll figure this out in the morning."

"The hammock," he repeated.

She cocked an eyebrow and stared him down in the same way she managed Andy when he was in a belligerent mood. "Screened porch. You found me. I trust you can find it."

"You won't try and sneak away?"

"Not unless you've suddenly become a sound sleeper." When they'd been together, it seemed he'd always slept with one eye open and his body ready to leap into action. She suppressed a needy shiver. Any kind of action.

"I wish," he muttered.

"So go on. We'll be here when you wake up."

With obvious reluctance, he walked out of the tiny cabin. She waited, listening to his soft footfalls as he walked across the rough planking to the other side of the cabin. When she heard the squeak of the hammock ropes, she turned out the lights.

Then she picked up the shotgun and moved her sleeping bag to Andy's side of the bedroom door. It was an immense relief to hear her son's soft, even breaths, confirming he hadn't been listening at the door the whole time.

Drew was alive. Her heart soared while her mind raced. What the hell was she supposed to do now? Drew was set on helping her, but she didn't see how his presence changed anything.

It infuriated her that her first instinct was to trust him. It was practically second nature to trust him, yet he'd been stateside all this time and had never reached out to her. That was the piece that cut so deeply and made her wary.

She knew the kind of friends Craig had on his side,

knew he'd be scouring the country for any sign of her. If Craig's contacts—the ones who'd surely helped him escape—had any link to this Thomas Casey, she was screwed.

She heard a noise and held her breath, praying fervently it wasn't more trouble. Tonight had given her one surprise too many. Whatever she'd heard didn't repeat itself, but she listened closely just in case.

Drew was *alive*. Her heart rejoiced even as she resented him for staying away.

She couldn't tell illusion from reality, didn't trust her intuition when it came to men anymore. Had the love and affection she remembered so fondly with Drew been real? She pulled the necklace from under her shirt and ran the two charms along the fine gold chain. Why would a man who loved her the way he'd once claimed stay away?

On top of that, a woman didn't get more wrong about a man than she'd been about Craig. The floor creaked as she shifted, trying to get comfortable.

"Mama?"

"I'm here," she answered her son's sleepy voice. "You're safe."

"'Kay."

As she stared in the direction of the ceiling, she vowed—again—to keep him safe. Physically and emotionally.

From the near-miss nasty stepfather and the unexpected arrival of his real dad, Addison knew keeping that vow would be a serious challenge.

Chapter Six

A few hours later, Drew came fully awake in an instant when he heard voices and movement inside the small shack. Calm voices, no sounds of struggle or distress. Sitting up, he scrubbed at his face. The hammock wasn't to blame for his bleary eyes and lousy mood. He'd survived far worse in years past. No, his current frustration, physically and with the mission, had everything to do with the woman on the other side of a very thin wall.

He wanted to kick down that wall along with all the others she'd built against him over the years. How could he have been thinking only of her while she'd forgotten about him? The killed-in-action report had an impact on her choices, he knew, and it was irrational to hold that against her. But being right here with her... Was it so much to ask that she want him, too?

Hinges creaked on the screen door and he listened to her soft steps come around the corner. Not wanting to advertise his past, he grabbed his T-shirt and covered the scars from his POW days.

She stayed on the other side of the torn screen wall, her arms folded across her chest. "You're still here."

"Told you I would be." He should never have agreed to this. Should've taken the offer to consult Casey's search. In a figure-hugging tank and cutoff denim shorts, her body was shown to perfection today. He'd always loved her generous curves, but it was clear she'd been putting in hours to keep herself strong and fit. He wanted to look away but couldn't stop staring. "Are you ready to get going?"

She shook her head. "Do you have to start in on that again?"

"Yes."

"No," she said, rubbing her finger where her engagement ring should've been. "Can't this wait? Coffee is brewing and breakfast will be ready shortly."

"Breakfast?" he echoed.

"Most important meal of the day, right? We can hash this out after we eat." She tilted her head. "I've got everything ready for Andy's favorite, pancakes and scrambled eggs."

The statement gave him a chill. Add a side of bacon and it would've been his favorite breakfast, too. How could she stand there as if it were a normal, everyday thing to have pancakes and eggs in the middle of the swamp when an escaped traitor was hunting her? "I need…" He coughed, clearing away the swell of emotions clogging his throat. "I need to check the perimeter."

There, that was much better than blurting out the needs his body urged him to share. What he'd noticed about her last night became more obvious in the clear morning light: her classic, Southern beauty hadn't faded a bit. It hadn't been artificially enhanced by his infatuation and unfulfilled longing or the poor lighting last night.

"You think someone followed you?" Her eyes went wide.

He cursed himself for worrying her. "No." The attraction, the damned pull of her, the need to protect, rode him as hard as ever. Annoyed, he stomped into his boots with more force than necessary, and the planked floorboards rattled. "But it's my job to keep you safe, and I'm going to do my job the right way. You've been here long enough for people to start talking."

"No one's talking about me. No one knows me out here anymore."

"Addi," he warned.

She held up her hands. "Fine."

He recognized the loaded delivery behind that single word. "If no one's onto you, it won't take me long to check."

"Are you okay?"

"Yeah." He scrubbed his hands over his face, remembering a few lazy mornings when they'd shared coffee and the paper in bed. Maybe they'd moved too fast back then and would already have burned each other out. He didn't believe it, but thanks to the damned assignment, he'd never know. "Hold a pancake for me."

"Andy's out of the bathroom if you want to grab a shower before the, um, perimeter thing."

"There's a bathroom?"

She laughed, the delighted sound washing over him, soothing him. "Nico made a few improvements despite his mother's simple wishes. The pump keeps a decent water pressure."

"Swamp guide and engineer."

"All Cajun," she said with a shrug.

"Yeah." He remembered the stories she'd shared with him. "I'll grab a shower when I'm back." He wasn't about to get stuck with his pants down—literally—until he knew they were safe. "Do you have a bug-out bag ready?"

"A what?"

"An emergency kit," he explained. "In case you have to run?"

She rubbed one bare foot up and down her shin. "We didn't bring that much along to begin with."

"I'll take care of it," he said. "If I'm not back in twenty minutes, I want the two of you to leave."

"And go where?"

"Deeper into the swamp. You'll figure out something."

"Drew—"

With his hand on the screen door between them, he hesitated, waiting for her to move. He needed even this small shield between them or he couldn't be responsible for the fallout. He wanted to hold her nearly as much as he wanted to keep breathing. "I'll be back in twenty."

"All right." She turned around, heading back into the cabin.

He couldn't take his eyes off the soft swing of her hips as she strolled away. He couldn't pull his mind back from the days when she'd welcomed his touch, when they'd held hands and talked about their hopes for the future.

"Hey," he called out.

She paused, glancing back over her shoulder.

"You didn't go the legal aid route. To the JAG office," he added at her blank look.

"They have no jurisdiction over Craig's dealings."

"No. Back then."

"Oh. A lot of things changed after…" She reached for her necklace.

The unspoken words were rattling through his mind. He knew she blamed him. He shouldered that old responsibility along with the new ones heaped on him by Director Casey. Trudging down the rickety steps while Addison ducked inside, he put his mind into guard-and-protect mode. No sense dwelling on what he couldn't have.

When he'd gone out to San Francisco and seen her with the man and boy, he'd known the fantasy that had carried him through his days as a prisoner was just that—fantasy. He didn't regret those fantasies; he'd just struggled to find his purpose without the army's guidance or Addison's support.

The youth center in his old neighborhood was up and running now, the renovation time shortened by his absolute lack of distraction. Absolute lack of a personal life. Drew checked the boat, pleased to find his gear still tied in place. Above him, he heard the muted voices of mother and son, and another flare of jealousy scorched his already raw heart.

"Focus," he muttered. He might be the only man on Earth able to find Addi, and that made him the only man who could keep her alive. He could radio his position to Casey's team or switch on one of the transmitters, but it would be one more thing on her list of unforgivables. Drew didn't want that. For either of them.

Coming in at dusk, watching and waiting until full dark to make his presence known, he hadn't been able to set much beyond the cursory alerts around the area. A calculated risk, but he'd been extremely cautious as he'd made a circuitous way through the bayou to Mama Leonie's famous shack.

Walking quietly along the water's edge, he kept an eye out for alligators or the more vicious human predators. He scanned the trees, keeping a careful mental record of where and when the shack was in view. He had a few dreamworthy gadgets from Casey's department, but he wasn't willing to blow them all at once. He wanted to give her protection without leaving a road map for Everett's connections. Anyone who could successfully stage an escape and avoid recapture for this long was undeniably dangerous.

Addison might think she was okay out here, she might

believe Everett wouldn't bother beyond a cursory search of her hometown in Mississippi, but Casey felt differently. Making a home in the bayou, off the radar, wouldn't be enough for someone determined to silence her. One day someone or something would slip and then all hell would break loose.

From what he understood, turning Everett in messed with the money and plans of several high-level bad guys. Although he admired her integrity and courage, she'd put a nice bright target on her head that wouldn't fade anytime soon.

Looking around, Drew had to side with Casey on this one. Although there was no connection between Addison and Mama Leonie's swamp home, it wasn't impossible to find this place. It might lack any evidence of civilization at first glance, but it wasn't far enough from the marked trails the professional guides used. Drew thought she was underestimating Everett as well as the local fascination with this place. He bent down, noting the size and shape of footprints that indicated children had been playing out here lately. That immediately vetoed his more lethal perimeter security options, but Drew's bigger concern remained: how long until her son encountered one or more of these kids and their seclusion was blown?

On top of all that, he knew Addison. She couldn't hide in the middle of nowhere forever. Her son needed an education, friends, community and support beyond the basics she could give him. She wasn't the sort to skimp on her values or priorities.

A breeze wafted through the treetops, sending them swaying. He checked his watch and swiftly reset a few "tells" so he'd know if anyone came this way.

When he'd completed the circuit, he grabbed the gear bag out of his boat and headed up the stairs to the shack once more. Reprieve over, it was time for round three. Maybe the third conversation would be the charm that convinced Addison to cooperate.

He walked in and set down his bag just inside the door. The kitchen, which a moment before had been full of happy conversation, went silent.

Addison forced a smile onto her face. "Right on time."

He nodded. "Perimeter is clear," he said.

"What's a perimeter?"

"We'll discuss it later," Addi replied, making a face that told Drew to shut up. "We held breakfast for you." She stood and crossed to the stove.

"You didn't have to." He wasn't sure what to do or where to go. He didn't want to sit down with the kid at the table, and there wasn't much room to help Addison with breakfast.

"We wanted to." She turned her attention to the griddle sizzling on the woodstove. "Drew, meet Andy. Andy, say hello to my friend Drew."

"Hello."

"Hi," Drew replied.

The kid looked at him, eyes narrow as he assessed Drew, then twisted around in his seat to look at Addison. "You said Nico was the only friend we had out here. You said everyone else was strangers."

"I didn't expect Drew to visit us out here."

What an understatement, he thought. "I didn't expect it, either," he added, bringing the kid's attention back to him. That day in the park, he hadn't gotten close enough, but now... "Where's your dad?"

"In heaven," Andy said.

Drew heard Addison drop something, but he kept his gaze on Andy.

"Mom says he watches over us."

"That's good. You know, I thought Craig Everett was your daddy."

"He was gonna be, but Mom said our plans got changed." Andy knew how to spit out the party line, but he obviously wasn't pleased about it. "I wanted a dad."

"Drew, would you like two eggs or three?" Addi asked, her tone overly bright as she changed the subject.

"Three," he replied, feeling happier than he should that this conversation made her uncomfortable.

"I timed you." Andy twisted his arm around to give Drew a good look at the watch. "Mom said to time you because I wanted to eat."

"That's a great watch." Drew admired the Captain America watch. "How long did you have to wait?"

"Nineteen minutes."

Drew gave an approving hum. "Thanks for being patient."

Addison put a platter of fresh pancakes on the table along with a small pitcher of syrup. "Take it easy," she said to Andy. "Everyone will want some."

"Okay." He looked at Drew again. "My mom makes the best syrup."

"That's a good skill to have."

He watched, mesmerized by the kid as he carefully smeared melting butter over his short stack of pancakes. Then, sitting up on his knees, Andy grabbed the syrup pitcher and drizzled the warm, maple-scented liquid as if he were performing for a commercial.

"Easy," Addi reminded him. "Eggs are nearly done."

Andy put the pitcher back on the table and grabbed his fork to dig in.

"Impressive spread, considering the limitations."

"Mom is resourceful," Andy said, expressing the big word slowly around his mouthful of pancakes.

"Chew first," Addi reminded him without looking away from the stove. "And swallow."

Drew got up and propped open the door, letting some of the heat out of the small room. "Smells so good, you're likely to draw in some company."

"I've told you no one knows we're here."

"Nico does," Andy piped up. "Drew does."

"No one *else*," she clarified. "Mama Leonie didn't have neighbors out here."

"I don't know. People might follow their noses to this amazing breakfast," Drew said, taking the bowl piled high with seasoned scrambled eggs. "Is this dill?" He inhaled deeply when she nodded. "Can't wait." What did it mean that she'd made his favorite eggs?

"Me, neither." Immediately, Andy looked contrite. "May I have some, too, please?"

"Sure, squirt. There's enough here for everyone."

"I'm not a squirt."

"No offense meant." Drew sat down once more, the small table barely big enough for Addi to join them. "Do you have a nickname you like?"

The boy slid a glance at his mother, thoughtfully considering the question. Recognition slammed into Drew like a cold fist. He'd seen that particular furrow between the eyebrows on his father's face, caught the same expression on his own face more than once. The boy might've wanted to be called Godzilla for all Drew knew. The shock had created a sudden, loud buzzing in his ears, momentarily blocking out everything else.

The resemblance through the eyes was uncanny. This kid had the Bryant family eyes. Drew's gut tied into a thousand knots. He couldn't believe it had taken him this long to see it.

The boy's father was in heaven. Or was supposed to be.

Everett would've been a stepdad. Drew's mouth went dry, but he forced out the obvious question. "How old are you?"

"Almost eight."

As the math clicked, the savory bite of eggs in Drew's mouth turned to mushy cardboard. The fresh air and warm scents of the hearty breakfast soured in his stomach as the truth hit him like a body blow. He was looking at his son.

Good Lord, he had a *son*.

They had a son she'd never bothered to mention when she tried to give him the boot last night.

"Addison, can I speak with you?"

"May I," Andy corrected with a syrup-coated smile.

"May I," Drew said through gritted teeth.

"Right after breakfast." She didn't meet his gaze as she sat down and served herself.

"I don't think this should wait."

"I disagree. Go on and eat while it's still hot."

He set down the fork, unable to tolerate another bite.

"What's wrong?" Andy took a big gulp of milk and then dragged another bite of pancake through the river of syrup on his plate.

"Nothing." Drew tried to smile. "Just full up."

"Mom's a good cook."

"I've always thought so," Drew agreed. It wasn't the kid's fault his mother had lied to him his whole life. Technically, it wasn't her fault, either, though that line was blurred by the way she'd tried to get rid of him so quickly. Maybe, when this news had a chance to sink in, he'd stop blaming her for the emotions tearing through him.

Eight years. She'd been pregnant on their wedding day. When the hell had she planned on telling him? He wanted to believe he would've found a way to tell the army no if he'd known that detail, but in those days he'd boasted a bigger-than-life confidence. He probably would've taken the assignment anyway, knowing it had been a quick-strike plan.

Nothing quick about eight years, he thought. She'd gone through all of it alone. Pregnancy, childbirth, Andy's first steps, first word, first day of school. Her parents gone, her fiancé—the father of her child—presumed dead. She'd done it all without any family support. No wonder she thought she could manage this situation with Everett on her own.

His hands clenched. He wanted to put his fist through the face of the man who'd overseen his torture. He'd missed too much of their lives, but if he had his way, he wouldn't miss anything from this point forward.

He studied Addi, but she was focused on her food. "You talked to my dad before. When?" With so many questions in his head, he couldn't seem to get the words out in the right order to satisfy his curiosity.

"I'll explain everything after breakfast."

He didn't believe her. Even knowing it was irrational, he wanted to blame her for this overwhelming sense of loss. "I'm done eating," he snapped, pushing back from the table. Andy's eyes went wide and Drew felt the shame of scaring him. "Pardon me." He sat down again. "It's been a long few days."

"It's okay." Andy nodded with a wisdom beyond his years. "Did you have to drive forever in an old car, too?"

Drew looked to Addi for an interpretation.

She finally met his gaze. "I traded my car for something older for our summer adventure. Andy soon discovered how much we rely on modern conveniences like power windows."

"I'm done," Andy announced. "May I be excused, please?"

"Yes. Leave your dishes and go brush your teeth. We'll go exploring in a little bit."

He slid out of the chair, then walked over to Drew and motioned him to lean down. "She lets you leave the table when you ask nice."

The advice, delivered in a serious whisper, had Drew grinning right along with his son. "Thanks for the tip."

ADDISON HELD HER BREATH, her heart thudding in her chest. The ornery grins on both faces were nearly identical. It made her ache for all the moments they'd never get back. She knew he was furious with her, the army, whoever else might have wrecked his mission. And after urging him to leave last night, she knew he had to be thinking she'd never planned to tell him the truth.

"Everett isn't his father."

"I've already said that." And by some miracle, she'd discovered Craig's true nature before he ever could be. "Andy liked him. Loved him like a dad," she admitted through the hurt and embarrassment. "He isn't happy with my change of plans."

"What did you tell him?"

She rubbed at the place where Craig's engagement ring had been. "You have to know this now?"

"I think I've waited long enough."

"Oh, please. That's bu— baloney," she corrected, glancing toward the bathroom. Appetite gone, she gathered dishes into a stack in front of her. "You walked back into my world less than twelve hours ago. Hardly a display of patience worthy of praise."

"You weren't going to tell me." His brown eyes were full of hurt and betrayal, but she refused to accept it as her sole responsibility.

"I told you plenty of times. You just weren't around to hear it."

"What the hell does that mean?"

"Watch your language." She glared at him. "And lower your voice. He doesn't need to hear us fighting."

"We wouldn't be fighting if you'd been honest with me."

"Like you've been so honest living in Detroit without so much as a note when you came home? I've never lied to you. I've never had the chance."

"What about last night?"

She shook her head. "I didn't lie."

"You sure didn't volunteer the information."

"I was in shock," she said in her defense. "The primary reason I let you stay last night was so we could talk about this today."

"Right." His glare would've sliced through steel, but she found herself equally infuriated with him. "When did you know?"

She knew what he was asking, but she made him clarify, just to buy herself a little time. "Know what?"

He stood up and in two strides he was towering over her. Pinned between his solid chest and the sturdy sink, she didn't feel the least bit threatened. No, her heart thrilled at his proximity and she inhaled his masculine scent. The woodstove had nothing on Drew when it came to creating heat.

"When did you know you were carrying my child?"

"Our wedding day." The memories came rushing back. With all the excitement of getting married, she'd barely had a moment to think about when and how she'd tell him. At the reception? Over strawberries and a single sip of champagne in the honeymoon suite? She remembered wanting to tell him before the morning sickness gave it away. "I did the test that morning."

Drew studied her, but she didn't know what she hoped to find. There was no reason for her to lie.

"I'm ready!" Andy came running in, shoes in one hand, ball cap in the other. "Can we show Drew the gator slide? Do you think the turtles will be out?"

Drew stepped back, his scowl vanishing as he knelt down to look Andy in the eye. "Have you seen any of the swamp by boat yet?"

"Uh-uh." Her son's eyes lit with excitement. "Mom said she'd teach me the boat later. Are you gonna take me out?"

Drew nodded. "If your mom says yes, I'll take you both out."

She had to fight the tears that threatened. How many times had she wished for this very thing? For Drew to see his amazing son, to be a part of Andy's life. Then she remembered what had brought him to their hiding place, what had dragged him away from his new life in Detroit. "Drew and I have a few things to talk about. Then we'll see if the boat is still an option." He'd been home for more than a year and hadn't so much as called to check on her. She wasn't about to hop in his boat and pretend nothing had gone wrong.

Andy's happy expression bottomed out. "You really mean it's not an option."

"No. I mean there's more to consider than a simple yes or no. Drew might have other things to do."

"Uh-huh." Deflated, Andy plopped down to put on his shoes. "Can we at least go see the gator slide?"

"Yes," she said with more enthusiasm than she felt. She turned to Drew. "Do you want to clean up first?"

"I think a gator slide takes priority."

She appreciated his understanding of Andy's impatience. "Let's head out, then."

Andy led the way down the steps and pointed out everything he'd learned about the swamp. It seemed as though every sentence began with "Nico said" or "Mom told me." Thankfully, Drew seemed content to listen, giving Andy his full attention and giving her space to come to terms with this latest upheaval.

Walking through the quiet swamp beside Drew, the first and only man she'd loved with her whole self, was a miracle in itself. But how could she make him understand and bridge the gap between them, not knowing where his side began? And how would she ever explain to her son that his father had fallen back into their lives like an angel from heaven?

Andy gave a cheer when she agreed to let him climb a tree. Drew gave him a boost, then stepped back to watch.

"I'm not leaving you out here alone," he said for her ears only, his tone firm. "Everett won't stop searching. You're a liability to him."

"I took precautions."

"While that's great, it doesn't change anything. You need to trust me to bring you in safely."

If only it were that easy. "Stay and play bodyguard if you have to. I understand why you feel you should, especially now, but I'm not going anywhere close to a government agency while Everett's loose."

"Then I hope Nico brought you enough supplies for three."

In all her fantasies of a real family vacation, Mama Leonie's swamp shack had never entered the equation. This was outrageous, yet, as she watched Drew advise Andy, as he encouraged their son, something about it felt absolutely right. It scared her nearly as much as it pleased her.

She reminded herself to stay firm. She couldn't allow the echo of her past feelings for Drew to color the tough decisions now. Thanks to time and circumstances, they were different people now. Even if she trusted that what she felt in this moment was real, she couldn't give in to emotions he might never return.

Chapter Seven

"What's a perm-a-meter?" Andy asked as Drew's footsteps faded down the steps and away from the shack.

Addison stirred the pot of gumbo simmering on the top of the stove. They'd eat as soon as Drew returned. "Perimeter." She waited while Andy practiced the word, praising him when he said it correctly. "A perimeter is an outline of an object or area. If you drew a line around the table, that would be the table's perimeter."

"Huh."

She nodded, smiling to herself. The whole day had been one question after another as Andy absorbed everything Drew said and did.

There were definite similarities, beyond the eyes and the fascination with comic books. Both Drew and Andy enjoyed exploring. From climbing the tree to watching fish ripple under the water of the swamp to spotting the various birds, they couldn't seem to get enough of their surroundings. Or each other.

"Why does Drew have to check it?"

So far, she'd only told him Drew was a friend, but she knew that wasn't going to satisfy her curious son for long. Or Drew. She dreaded bedtime when she couldn't use Andy as an excuse to avoid the hard conversation Drew was determined to have.

Why couldn't it be enough for him to know Andy was his? She didn't want to share her son. Anyone could look at Andy and know she'd been doing quite well as a single mom. Swiping the back of her hand across her forehead, she hated how childish that sounded.

Her emotions were twisted in agonizing clumps and she had no idea how to loosen them. There had to be a way through this mess so things could become smooth and familiar again. She took a deep breath. They were adults. Two reasonable people stuck in awkward circumstances. No one's fault, though a small, petty part of her wanted to blame him. If not him, then definitely the army, but that was a useless exercise that would only make her bitter.

Even as her wedding day fell apart, she'd understood why Drew had accepted the unexpected assignment. It made her feel like a horrible person to stand here wishing he'd stayed in Detroit. Not forgotten, but definitely part of her past.

Until this debacle with Craig, she'd done pretty damn well. As a mom and as a corporate attorney. She didn't need Drew and his sense of duty and honor throwing another wrench in her life plan.

"Will Drew stay with us for the whole summer adventure?"

Addison feared that was exactly what would happen. "He'll be with us for a while. I'm not sure how long." It would be impossible to outrun him, but she hadn't yet given up on finding a way to make him leave.

"I like Drew."

"I'm glad. He's a good person," she added. It made her ache to hear how much her son wanted a father. She'd done her best to instill a sense of his father in Andy, to let him know his dad loved him, but she was discovering a memory—even a heroic one—was a poor substitute for the real thing.

"He watches you."

Addison's pulse skipped. "What do you mean?"

"When you aren't looking he stares at you."

"Well." She didn't know what to say. "He keeps an eye on you, too. As our friend, he wants to be sure neither of us gets hurt."

"By alligators."

She nodded, laughed a little. "That's right." But she needed to prepare him for the worst-case scenario.

"I'm too big to be alligator food." Andy puffed out his chest. "Drew said so."

How had she missed that conversation? Addison ruffled Andy's hair, seeing the baby he'd been despite how much he'd already grown up. She knew she'd never recover if anything happened to him. She braced for an irritable reaction. "While I agree with Drew, that's no reason to forget safety."

"Safety's why I won't be alligator food."

"Oh, that is good news."

"Can we eat?"

"Just as soon as Drew gets back." She checked her watch, thinking of the twenty-minute time limit. The bag was by the door, a black-duffel reminder that trouble could fall on their heads at any minute.

"We didn't wait for Craig to eat with us."

"Sure we did." At restaurants.

"Did not."

She aimed a raised eyebrow at Andy. "I know you're hungry, but—"

"Hungry isn't a reason to be rude," he finished, plopping his head on his hands. "I worked up an appetite."

That conversation she remembered. "We had quite an adventure today. What was your favorite part?"

"Climbing the tree. Next time I'll go higher."

Not if she had anything to say about it. "What did you see?"

"More trees, just like Drew said I would. But you and him looked really small from up there."

She smiled, giving the gumbo another stir. "I guess that's fair. You look pretty small from over here," she teased.

"Hey!" Andy said when the joke sank in. "I'm getting bigger every day. I'm almost eight."

"All right, big guy, get down three plates and set the table."

It all seemed so normal to set a table for the three of them. She checked her watch, hoping they wouldn't have to run before they had dinner. Her pulse rushed for a split second at the first sound of boots on the steps.

"It's me," Drew called before the second footfall.

Andy raced to the door and held it open. "Hurry up. I'm hungry."

"Andy," she scolded.

"It's true."

"You held dinner?" Drew walked in and gave the table a long look.

She nodded, tried to smile.

"Let me wash up."

She stepped back from the sink. The small shack had felt roomy enough when it was just her and Andy. With Drew, it felt cramped and she was too aware of him. Maybe they should eat out on the porch. It would be cooler than in here with the woodstove, but before she could suggest it, Drew and Andy were settled at the table.

"How's the perimeter?" Andy asked, taking his time with the new word.

Drew glanced up at her as she served the gumbo.

"A learning opportunity," she said.

"The perimeter is fine," Drew replied. "This smells great."

Addison didn't miss the immediate change of topic.

"Craig doesn't like gumbo, but you have to eat what you're served," Andy said.

"His loss," Drew said. "Your mom's gumbo is one of my favorite things."

"Really?" Andy's eyes went wide.

Drew nodded, filling his mouth with a big spoonful. When he'd swallowed, he set his spoon down and applauded. "Just like I remember. How'd you manage this out here?"

"Nico was determined to give his mother all the amenities, even if they're decades out of date and rough around the edges."

"She didn't have a summer house, did she?"

Addison peered at Drew, tamping down the swell of doubt. If he thought they were in immediate danger, they'd be on the move with that black duffel bag by the door.

"This is her summer place."

Drew's gaze roamed across the room, as if he were taking a visual inventory. "Should I save room for dessert?"

"We have some ice cream in the freezer outside."

"We do?" Andy stared at her. "You said we ate it all."

"I said we finished the chocolate. Nico brought more and I wanted to surprise you."

"Sneaky," Andy said with plenty of admiration.

It was the highest form of praise from her son these days. "Can we eat it outside?"

"We'll see," Drew replied.

Addison let it go. Though she felt he'd overstepped, she wasn't going to say anything with Andy watching them so closely.

"What does that mean?"

Drew paused, a bite of gumbo halfway to his mouth. "I meant it would depend on how things go."

"Huh. Okay. With most moms it means no."

"Are you an expert on moms?"

"Pretty much. Me and my friends talk."

Drew's eyebrows arched as he struggled to keep a straight face.

"When my mom says it, it means she wants time to think so she won't have to change her mind later."

Drew's brown gaze locked with hers. "Good to know."

Addison managed to eat most of her portion of the gumbo while her son and his real father chattered about guy stuff. The reality slammed home, leaving her reeling. Given a choice, she would have all her nights just like this: a family dinner, aimless chatter, happy faces.

"Are you full? Mom?"

"Hmm?"

"You stopped eating," Drew said gently.

"Oh. I'm fine, thanks." She pushed her chair back from the table. "Who wants dessert?"

"I think I'd like to wait. Who's up for a boat ride?" Drew suggested.

"Tonight?"

"It could be fun."

She shook her head. "It's too close to dark."

Drew made a show of looking out the grimy front window. His big frame, so close, tempted her to touch. Years ago, it would've been her pleasure—and his—to reach out and kiss him, to take his hand, to share an embrace.

Not now. She crossed back to the table, telling herself it was more safety precaution than retreat.

"We could do s'mores."

"In the boat?" Andy bounced on his seat.

"Not in the boat. Fire and boats aren't a good combination. But maybe we could find a spot and build a fire."

Now she knew he was up to something, or more accurately, she assumed he'd found something on the perimeter check. "Andy, go brush your teeth and get your things together."

"I'll brush after s'mores. Before bed..." His voice trailed off at her stern look. "Yes, ma'am."

Addison snatched the dishes off the table and carried them to the sink. "What did you find?"

"Trouble," he said. "Could be locals, or not."

"Then they followed *you*," she snapped. "Lead them away and we'll be fine." It was a lousy argument and they both knew it, but she wasn't going to just follow anyone blindly anymore. Not even Drew.

"You promised to let me do my bodyguard thing."

"Fine." She rolled her eyes as she took out her frustration and scrubbed the dishes. "You're sure we have to move?"

"As soon as possible."

"Where?"

"I'll find us something."

"Uh-huh. Put out the fire in the stove and let me call Nico."

"That's not smart."

She planted her hands on her hips. "Not smart is wandering through the swamp at night without a destination. I'm making the call and we'll leave as soon as we clean up everything here."

"Addi, we need to go now."

"If there was time to eat, there's time to put this place to rights."

Together they had things almost done when Andy came out of the bedroom. "The toothpaste will ruin the s'mores," he complained, sticking out his tongue.

With a sigh, she stepped outside to radio Nico for suggestions on where they could go for the night.

DREW LOOKED AT his son, feeling a little less awkward with each conversation, but it was still strange knowing he'd missed everything up to this point.

"That toothpaste taste will fade by the time we find the perfect place to build a campfire," Drew said.

"How do you know what's the perfect place?"

"I'll tell you on the way."

"Why do we have to leave? I like it here."

"Me, too." Drew made a show of looking around. "It's pretty cool."

"It's a swamp fort. On stilts," Andy said.

"Should we make a bet on whether our next stop is on stilts, too?"

Andy frowned thoughtfully. "You can't put a campfire on stilts."

"Why not?"

"It wouldn't be camping."

"Ah." Drew dragged out the sound. "Good point," he noted. "What would it be?"

"Silly. If the campfire's on stilts, you can't reach it to roast marshmallows for s'mores."

Drew laughed. "You sure know a lot of stuff."

"Yes, I do."

Drew heard the porch creaking as Addi approached. "Did you get all your things out of the bedroom?" she asked her son.

"Most of it," Andy replied.

"Well, let's take it all, just in case."

"In case of what?"

"In case someone else needs to have an adventure here. It's not very big. They'll need room for their stuff."

"Okay," he grumbled.

They might as well take it all, Drew thought. Since she didn't seem to be in any hurry to cooperate with his advice. He gathered up the few items Addison had unpacked and put them in the small suitcase while Andy picked up the last of his possessions and stowed them in his backpack.

"Hey, what's that?" Drew asked, catching a glimpse of a familiar color scheme.

"My new Captain America comic book." Andy held it out. "Wanna see it?"

"Sure."

Drew sat on the bed, the mattress sagging, so Andy could watch him flip through the pages. "This is the new one."

"Uh-huh. I saved my allowance and Mom took me to get it. We read it every night."

"Is Captain America your favorite?"

Andy nodded. "Unless I'm mad."

"What do you read when you're mad?"

"Incredible Hulk!" He hopped off the bed and made a growling sound as he imitated the famous green monster pose. "Hulk, smash!"

"Wow. Remind me not to make you mad. You're scary."

Andy burst into a fit of giggles.

"Let's roll out," Drew suggested.

"Hey, that's from *Transformers*," Andy said.

"Sure is." Drew wanted to scoop up Andy and tell him

the truth, but Addi insisted on waiting. It was all he could do to hold in the news until she was ready.

They returned to the kitchen, and Addison's pale face worried him. "Did Nico have any ideas?"

She set the radio on the small table. "Yes."

"And?"

"I'll tell you on the way."

He knew that face, knew it was all he'd get until she was ready to share. "We have everything from back there."

"Great. Thanks." She pulled a cooler out of the corner and packed a few supplies from the fridge.

"Come on, Andy." He held out his hand. "Let's you and me get the boat loaded and ready."

"Wait."

He turned, saw the debate play out across her features. Her pale blue eyes were clouded with worry. "Andy can help me with the cooler."

"That's a girl job," Andy protested.

"Since when is food a girl job?"

Drew came to his rescue. "I think Andy means we're in Transformer mode. I'll send him back up to help you with the cooler the second we're done with this load."

She shot him an assessing look so long that he nearly begged for her to give him an inch of trust.

"Drew?" Andy piped up. "It takes me longer than a second to get up the stairs. I timed it."

"Go on," Addi relented. "If you're Transformers, I can find my super strength."

"You're sure?" Drew hefted the bug-out bag onto his shoulder.

"The sooner we get going, the sooner we all get s'mores."

That was all Andy needed to hear as he yanked Drew toward the door.

Andy got a tremendous amount of glee out of the rubber boat Drew had used to reach the shack. But he surprised Drew when he asked about taking the boat his mom had brought along.

"What boat?" Drew had assumed, with no evidence to the contrary, that Addi's friend Nico had brought them out here and left with the only boat.

"Over here."

Andy trotted up the bank and pulled back a screen of leaves, revealing an old flat-bottomed boat with a fairly clean motor and a full canister of gas.

"Nice." He'd looked around in the daylight and walked right by it. When had Addi learned to do that? Maybe he was as useless as the army claimed. "We can take both."

"I'm riding with you."

Drew was flattered but refused to leave Addi out of that equation. "If your mother agrees."

The little shoulders rolled back, determined. "I'll ask nice."

"That's the best policy," Addi said with a little huff as she joined them on the wobbly dock. "What's the question?"

"If we take two boats, may I please ride with Drew?"

Drew held his breath while he waited for her answer, surprised at how much he wanted her to say yes.

"I suppose."

She didn't sound thrilled about it, but Andy's enthusiasm made up for any lack on his mother's part. Drew wondered if it meant she was trusting him, or if it was simply more expedient to agree. Of course, she had yet to reveal their next stop.

He knelt in front of Andy. "You'll have to sit still."

The boy's head bobbed up and down. "I will."

"And we'll need to be very quiet when we're on the water. Can you do that?"

Andy mimed locking his lips and throwing away the key.

Getting to his feet, Drew looked to Addi. "Lead the way."

They pushed the boats into the water and paddled quietly away from the bank. The motors weren't worth risking the unwanted attention.

Though she was only a few yards ahead of him, he could barely see Addi's boat and he followed her more by sound than sight. Weak moonlight shifted through the treetops and splashed across the black water. The mirror-like surface shifted with ripples each time Addi's paddle dipped under, rose and dipped again.

Her years of city living and corporate success hadn't dimmed any of the skills she'd mastered in her youth. She was as at home out here as he remembered.

Moving through the night-covered swamp, with the subtle sounds of Addi's paddle ahead of him and Andy's soft breath behind him, his mind wandered back to the day he'd met her.

He'd come down to New Orleans with a few army buddies to celebrate Mardi Gras. Ready to party, he hadn't been ready to fall for the gorgeous blonde with the wide smile and pale blue eyes. Back then he didn't have a thought to spare for luck or destiny when his group of friends met up with hers in a blues bar in the French Quarter.

Over strong drinks and the sexy, low pulse of music, the soldier and the law student found some common ground despite their differences. Smart as a whip, only her soft Southern drawl gave away her Mississippi farm-girl roots.

He could still remember calling the next day, sweating as he wondered if she'd given him a bogus number and grinning like a fool when she'd eagerly accepted his invitation to lunch. From that moment, they'd been inseparable, holding hands, exchanging hot, breath-stealing kisses and longing for more of each other. By the end of the week, they were all but engaged, overlooking the tough romantic geography of her law school and his career keeping them apart.

That day, that first sweet memory and all the memories that followed had kept him going through every dark moment as a prisoner. His captors hadn't broken him because he'd had her in that sacred part of his mind, heart and soul. And while he'd had her, she'd had their son.

"You okay back there?" he asked, pitching his voice low.

"Yes," Andy whispered. "Is Mom okay?"

"She's doing great."

"How much longer?"

"No idea, but we'll have s'mores when we get there."

"Promise?" Andy asked around a yawn.

"I guarantee it." Drew balanced the paddle across his knees, listening. "Quiet for the rest of the way."

"'Kay," Andy whispered.

The swamp opened up and the sky above sparkled with starlight between the thick line of trees marching along the banks. It seemed the world held its breath, watching Addi guide her little boat around islands of cypress trees weeping with Spanish moss. He followed closely, keeping his boat on the same line as hers, unwilling to risk areas that might be too shallow.

They made it to the far side without any trouble and into another narrow waterway. At the slow pace, the only strain was on his patience, but he wanted to get far enough from the shack so he could determine the risk to her and Andy.

At last, she paddled for the shore, using a low-hanging limb to pull the boat in snugly. Her feet landed in the soft mud of the bank with a quiet smack and she had the boat out of the water before he could help. He had no idea what landmark she was using, but he was grateful to see the shadow of a smile on her face when they were all ashore, along with their gear.

"You really want to camp?" He had two tarps in the duffel.

"No. Our accommodations are just a short hike in."

He looked past her but couldn't make out anything but tall grass. Tipping his head toward Andy, he asked, "How short?"

"Five minutes," she answered. "You can time us," she said to Andy.

At just over four minutes per Andy's watch, Drew stared into what looked more like an abandoned survivalists' meeting place instead of a secluded spot to hide.

"This way," Addi said, adjusting her grip on the cooler. She turned into the trees and led them across a narrow strip of firmer ground into a clearing. With her flashlight, she spotlighted the modest, solitary square shack with cypress trees as footers.

"That's a tree house," Andy said.

"Another of Nico's engineering marvels." She climbed the stairs and nudged open the door.

She turned on the light and illuminated a one-room cabin with a half-size refrigerator, a two-burner stove and a pot for coffee on the miserly counter. At the other end of the room, two bare twin-size mattresses were balanced on plywood and cinder blocks. He couldn't decide immediately which shack he preferred.

"It's the best option," she explained. "No one's used the camp for years."

"If you're sure." Drew didn't like being so far from the boats. As soon as they were settled he would go back and hide them. "I'll build that fire for s'mores." Uneasy, he renewed his commitment to convince her to cooperate with Casey.

Andy dropped his backpack on one of the beds and spun around, clearly the recipient of a second wind. "Can I help?"

"Sure. C'mon."

Once they'd settled in for the night and Andy was asleep, Drew knew she'd ask him what he'd found that prompted the move. He also knew she wouldn't like the answer. Although the hard evidence was circumstantial, his gut instinct said Craig Everett or his associates were steady on her trail.

Chapter Eight

Washington, DC, 8:10 p.m.

Director Casey's phone vibrated in his pocket. He hesitated to interrupt dinner with his wife, but with so much on the line he had to check.

"I know what I got myself into," Jo said. With her warm and wry smile she waved him off to take the call. "Go on and do your thing."

Standing, Thomas rounded the table, bent down and brushed his lips across her soft cheek. "These days are numbered, I promise," he whispered against her ear.

She only grinned at him as he made his way out of the dining room.

The display on his phone showed a missed call from Deputy Holt but no message. That likely meant they had problems on an operation.

Thomas returned the call, cautiously hopeful the news wouldn't be awful.

"I know you're at dinner," Emmett began, "but this couldn't wait."

"Fill me in," Thomas ordered, braced for the worst after hearing the gravity in his deputy's voice.

"Craig Everett was spotted near the University of Mississippi, but we couldn't drop a net over him in time."

"He's not even trying to hide his identity?"

"Not a bit."

In a case like this, a fugitive behaving as though he were untouchable increased the odds of serious complications. "We expected him to search for Addison. He must be hoping she reached out to someone there. We thought the same thing at first."

"Yes."

There was a "but" coming and Emmett's reluctance meant Thomas wouldn't like it.

"Our tech team recently discovered alterations in Addison's personal history," Emmett said.

Damn it. "Financial?"

"To start."

"Crap. He's working to discredit her if she ever testifies against him."

"She must know more than she's already shared."

That would be good for the case, but it meant Everett would do anything to silence her. Thomas couldn't help thinking about the latest school picture of Addison's son in the file. Drew had to get to her first.

"He's afraid," Thomas said, thinking out loud. "He must believe she's capable of eluding him."

"Agreed." A world of concern weighed down the single word.

"How far did our team get before they lost Bryant?"

Emmett laughed. "They lost him just outside DC. Picked up the GPS in the car we provided again near Oxford, Mississippi, but lost him on the highway south. We assumed he was aiming for New Orleans. That man hasn't lost a step, no matter what the army thinks."

Addison had a few childhood connections in the New Orleans area, though no one who'd heard from her recently. "Then he's still our best chance at saving Addison and her son, so we can use what she knows to take down Everett and whoever he's working with." Thomas prayed the fast and loose plan wouldn't blow up in their faces.

"Whoever the leak is on the inside," Emmett said, "he's covered his tracks with a damned cloaking device."

"That will make it all the more satisfying when we expose him," Thomas pointed out.

"True."

He appreciated Emmett's determination to see justice served to a traitor. "Drew will find her. He'll bring her in." Thomas had to say it, if only as an affirmation.

"I took another hard look into Addison's life," Emmett said.

"What did we overlook?" If he'd dragged Bryant into this unnecessarily…

"Nothing, really. But she struck me as the sort to cover all contingencies."

"All right," Thomas agreed, curious now. Picking over the facts hadn't led them any closer to where she might be hiding. "That led you where?"

"Ole Miss law school is a pretty tight community. One of her classmates works for the FBI now."

Thomas didn't need the file in front of him to recall those details. "You think that friend lied in the interview to protect Addison? She said she hadn't heard from her."

"It might be a matter of not hearing from Addison *yet*. This woman is a hard-core overachiever. She doesn't leave anything to chance. It's one thing to send out the information authorities needed to make the arrest. But she's not stupid. She didn't blow the whistle on Everett without understanding all the implications."

"Keep going." They'd talked through this before he'd brought in Drew. What was Emmett leading up to?

"She has to recognize if not who, at least how Everett

was connected to his so-called investors. She sells her car and drops off the radar, but the big what-if is playing through her head the whole time."

"What if Everett wriggles off the hook," Thomas supplied.

"Right. The man knows her weakness is the little boy. Addison's a tiger, she's got something in place to make sure her son is safe and provided for if the worst happens."

"With Drew out of the picture, who would she trust with that kind of insurance?"

"I've reached out to a buddy at the FBI. He can check with Addison's friend. But I don't believe Everett would bother with the law school unless Addison mentioned someone there."

"She's got the family farm in Mississippi she inherited."

"Still no action there. Not even Bryant went through, as far as we can tell. I want to keep eyes on this law professor at Ole Miss. The file said he was supposed to give her away at the wedding."

"Another 'yet factor'?"

"If we're careful, I think we can ask again without tipping off Everett's connection."

"Don't put Addison's friends in jeopardy," Thomas warned. "We know that connection has significant access."

"Okay, I'll wait on that. One more thing," Emmett said. "About New Orleans."

Hope sparked in Thomas's chest. "Tell me it's good news."

"We lost Addison heading east from Arizona. Everett has been nosing around in Mississippi. Drew was last seen on the road to New Orleans. What if we set a trap Everett and his insider informant can't refuse?"

"Dicey." But he knew if it worked, Drew would be off the hook and Addison and her son would be safe. "We don't even know where she's hiding."

"No one does. That's exactly why it has potential. It gives us a chance to corner Everett with some discreetly placed bread crumbs."

Resigned, Thomas listened to the deputy director's idea, considered his available Specialists and gave his deputy the green light.

As he walked back into the dining room, Thomas felt the full weight of taking this chance. *Dicey* was an understatement, especially with the gross lack of real leads on Everett's government insider or even which department he served. But Emmett's daring plan, taking note of who responded and how, might be just what they needed to start peeling back the layers of the convoluted situation.

Chapter Nine

Louisiana bayou

From the elevated porch of Nico's sparse hunting cabin, Addison watched her son and his father build a small campfire. Small enough to avoid notice, she realized, wondering again what he'd found near Mama Leonie's shack. Drew showed Andy how to put the stones in a circle and the best way to stack kindling and wood so it would burn well.

Andy could've learned those same skills from her. She had in fact taken him camping in Northern California, but she recognized the differences. She could give her son the world, meet all his needs, but it wouldn't replace the father-son bond. Other men might step into the void occasionally as role models, but until now, she hadn't realized she'd given up on finding someone as good as Drew.

She put graham crackers and marshmallows on a paper plate and then broke a chocolate bar into pieces, hoping they wouldn't melt before she got them out there. The small tasks helped keep her mind off why she'd come back to the bayou in the first place. Whatever Drew had found, it had to be a coincidence. She respected his precautions, but Craig couldn't possibly have discovered ties that weren't on paper, ties she'd never shared with him.

Her past wasn't something they'd ever talked about. Looking back, she couldn't tell if she'd withheld the details because it felt as if she was betraying Drew's memory or if she just didn't think Craig would find it interesting. What did that say about their relationship? That it hadn't been real, even in the beginning?

She carried the plate piled high with s'mores ingredients out to Drew and Andy, watching her son grin as Drew gave an overblown, in-depth lecture on the importance of finding just the right stick for roasting marshmallows.

Being a mom, she could see things would get messy in a hurry. She set the plate on the next to last step and went back inside for bottles of water and paper towels. It was hard to believe Nico managed to keep this place a secret, but she was grateful. Drew claimed he could protect them, but she wasn't ready to rely solely on him. Craig had fooled her once. She wouldn't let anyone fool her again.

"We found chairs and we got a roasting stick for you, too!" Andy rushed forward. "Drew made it sharp."

"Thanks for the warning," she said to her son, avoiding eye contact with Drew.

They took places around the fire in folding metal lawn chairs that had seen better days. She wasn't sure she wanted to ask where they'd been stashed. Andy settled beside her, Drew across from them. She kept the supplies near her, just to make sure Andy didn't overindulge this close to bedtime. A few marshmallows went up in flames, but Drew shared his technique and Andy practiced until he could make them almost as well.

"This is a great summer," Andy said, his mouth full of his first successful s'more.

She couldn't argue. Indulging in the sweet, melting marshmallow, the gooey chocolate and the crisp graham cracker made her feel almost normal. The sensation was a welcome respite.

"Do you play any sports?" Drew asked her son.

"Soccer." Andy swiped a hand across his forehead, smearing it with dirt. "Mom says I can't play football yet, but I have friends who play already." He slid her a look.

She reached over and wiped his forehead before he could protest and squirm out of reach. "It's the coaching style that troubles me," she explained. Her son was tender-hearted and when she'd overheard the deep voices and tough words at practices, it raised her concerns. "They're in an eight-and-under league. It should be more fun than work."

Drew shrugged. "Moms worry a lot," he said in a stage whisper, making Andy giggle.

"What about baseball?"

Andy sighed, gazing longingly at the plate of marsh-mallows. "I want to try."

"And you will." She hadn't forgotten Drew's stories of playing for his high school team in Detroit. More correctly, of his being a star on the high school team. Her plan to surprise Andy with a week at a baseball camp this summer had been ruined when she'd discovered Craig's horrible dealings.

"There's a community league that plays year-round. I thought I'd enroll him just after school resumes."

"Really?" Andy jumped up and threw his arms around her neck. "That would be awesome."

"I played baseball," Drew said.

Andy's arms slid away, his enthusiasm and a barrage of questions carrying him over to sit by Drew.

She listened, balancing a mix of awe and irritation as Drew and her son—*their* son—talked about baseball. She knew Andy watched ESPN, and in San Francisco there was always plenty of sports news, but she didn't realize he'd absorbed so much. It wasn't as if they made a family habit of catching the local games on television.

While they talked, she wondered if she'd really been as overprotective as Drew implied. He'd been nice about it and it had felt as though he was backing her up more than criticizing, but still.

She watched her enamored son hanging on every word Drew spoke. If they'd had a ball and a couple of gloves, she could see this conversation playing out over a game of catch on a sunny afternoon. The image made her breath catch and she reached for a bite of chocolate, letting it melt on her tongue while she tried to relax. Drew wasn't intruding. Whether Andy knew it or not, this was his dad. Drew wasn't the type of man to force himself where he wasn't wanted. At least, he hadn't been.

Whatever had happened to him after the army thought he'd been killed clearly had changed him. She was only sure of one thing right now. She wouldn't risk Andy's heart before she knew Drew's intentions.

"When the summer adventure is over, I'll take you to a ball game. A professional game."

"That would be the best!" Andy turned to her. "Can I go?" He spun back to Drew. "Can Mom come with us?"

"Possibly," she replied with a calm she didn't feel. She didn't need Andy siding with Drew, though the hero worship had obviously set in. "Right now you need to go to bed. It's been a long day."

Andy's shoulders slumped, but he rallied quickly, knowing that sulking wouldn't help his case. "Okay. We're going exploring tomorrow, right?"

"Count on it," Drew said. "And you'll need a good night's sleep if you want to keep up with me."

Andy looked up at her, his eyes brimming with excitement that wasn't entirely fueled by sugar. "Can I—I mean, may I?"

"Of course you may sleep," she said, deliberately misunderstanding. Grinning, she added, "And yes. You may go exploring with Drew tomorrow."

Giving in was worth it for the sheer delight shining in Andy's eyes. They walked back into the cabin and she listened as he chattered on and on about riding in the boat with Drew.

"I like him, Mom."

"Mmm-hmm. I can tell."

"Do you like him?"

She couldn't lie to his earnest face. "Yes. He's a good friend."

"Will you come along when we go to the baseball game?"

Would she? Her heart and mind leaped to opposite conclusions. Of course she'd go, she thought, as would any protective mother with an ounce of sense. But her heart imagined how it would be, her son and his dad coming home and telling her all about their guy adventure.

"Mom?"

"We'll see how things go." It could be weeks or even months before she felt it was safe for Andy to be out in public. "First this adventure, then the next one."

"Okay. But I really want to go to a ball game with Drew." Andy wriggled into his sleeping bag on top of the bed. "He knows everything."

"He's had lots of experiences."

"Like this adventure is our experience?"

"Pretty much. You need to get some rest now. Which comic should we read?"

"Can Drew read it?"

The innocent request prickled along her skin like a

poison ivy rash. She didn't want to share this precious time. She had, in fact, long since given up on the idea of sharing her son. Marriage to Craig would've been a partnership, but they'd had an understanding that she'd have the final say about issues involving Andy. Craig hadn't protested. Drew would make his opinions known even when she didn't want to hear them. "Maybe Drew can read tomorrow night."

"Okay."

Addison ignored the heavy dose of disappointment and picked up another issue of Captain America.

"I could read it," Andy said.

"Sure." She nudged him over to the other side of the bed, her back propped against the wall and her son tucked against her side.

"I meant by myself."

She checked her first reaction and forced herself to smile. "How about you read it to me? Then I'll be here to turn out the light when you're done."

Andy considered, his small fingers tracing the vibrant design on the cover. "Okay."

She listened and turned pages as needed until Andy's eyelids drooped and his voice faded. Satisfied he'd sleep through until morning, she walked back out to the fire to confront Drew.

He was leaning back in one of the ratty chairs they'd found, his long legs stretched out toward the fire and his fingers laced behind his head. For a moment with the firelight flickering across his features, the years fell away and she was walking toward the man of her dreams. But life hadn't been so kind. To either of them.

"You have to stop that," she said, halting before she got too close to him.

His eyebrows snapped together as if he'd forgotten where he was, who she was. "Stop what?"

"Stop promising my son things you can't deliver."

"*Our* son."

She *knew* it. Knew it would come down to that. It didn't matter that his claim was valid. "It's not my fault you haven't been involved," she said. He'd left her once in the name of duty, and when he'd had a chance to set things right he'd left her again.

"Cut me some slack," Drew said, pushing a hand through his hair. "Leaving that day wasn't my choice, Addi. Mad or not, you have to concede that much."

She didn't feel inclined to concede anything at all. "Let's keep the focus on the here and now, Drew. You can't get his hopes up."

"Why not?" He spread his hands wide. "It's clear he wants a dad. Good news all around. I *am* his dad. I want to make his every hope come true."

"And how will you explain where you've been all his life?"

He sat up and shook his head. "We will find a way. Both of us. Together we can tell him so he understands."

"And so he accepts you." Why did that scare her so much?

"Is that such a bad thing? I intend to be a part of his life."

She hated the way her heart skipped at the image that popped into her mind. She could see it so easily, the three of them gathered around a dinner table or chowing down on hot dogs at a baseball game.

"From Detroit? You'll just pop in whenever it's convenient?"

"You know me better than that."

"I know the old you."

"I'm the same man." He sighed. "You could move closer to me. We could…"

She waited, but he didn't finish. "Are you in a good school district?"

"Probably not, but this swamp is hardly the pinnacle of academic power."

"This isn't a permanent relocation," she insisted. "Once Craig is back in custody, I'll find the right place to raise our son."

"If what little I've heard is any indication, you'll need protection. I can give you that."

She wanted to demand what he'd heard, what he thought he knew about Craig, but the day's events, the entire situation had caught up with her. Pasting a smile on her face, she searched for kind words. "Thank you for letting us stay out here." Weary, she sat down on the other side of the fading fire. It wasn't far enough away. "I know you want to take us in, that you think Casey can help, but I'm not ready to risk speaking with anyone connected to the government right now."

"What didn't you tell them?"

She shook her head, thinking of the package she'd sent to Professor Hastings. "It's better if you don't know."

"I'm not so sure about that."

"You'll have to trust me, then."

He snorted. "That's a bit easier if you trust me, too."

"I did trust you." Then and now, it seemed, but she had no intention of admitting as much. In her opinion, trust didn't have to mean giving up control of the situation. She wasn't sure Drew shared that opinion.

He came around to sit in the chair beside her. As he leaned close, his scent and heat crowded her. "Is that so?"

She nodded, unable to speak as her gaze drifted to his mouth. She remembered his taste, the way his lips had felt on hers. It was his taste, his expert touch that haunted her dreams and the recurring nightmare that she'd never find anyone else who could spark her passion. Had he changed, had his kiss changed? Or would it be a reprise of the way it had been: an explosion of heat and desire at first contact?

She wasn't sure which outcome scared her more, but she didn't get the chance to find out. Drew leaned back abruptly and tipped his face to the night sky.

"Do you remember the wedding rehearsal?" As soon as the question was out, she wanted to snatch it back, but it was too late. The lid was blown off the proverbial box where she'd locked away her memories of that precious time.

"Of course I do," he replied, still watching the sky.

"We practiced the kiss." She couldn't believe how much she wanted to practice it again. Had she lost her mind on some belated sugar overdose?

"The minister looked surprised when I dipped you back."

"Your dad was worried we'd make it a Hollywood production." She saw his lips tip in a faint impression of a smile.

"He knew better. He loved you."

And she'd loved him. Even through her grief-stricken anger that his heart had given up before he'd met his grandson. She remembered feeling as though the army had snatched Drew away and stolen his father as collateral damage.

She and Andy hadn't been enough to carry Mr. Bryant through the oppressive grief and loss. It wasn't fair to even think it—then or now. She'd known better even then, but it had required many expensive hours of therapy purging those destructive feelings so she could be a better mom. Based on the grim emotions churning inside her now, she might have to book some more time on a psychiatrist's couch when this was over.

"I kissed you on our wedding day," Drew said.

"What?"

"And every day since."

"Are you hallucinating?"

He met her gaze once more. "Did you know the stars are brighter on the other side of the world?" He picked up her hand, ran his thumb unerringly over the place where her wedding band should have been.

He'd lost it. Something inside him had snapped. What was she supposed to do with a little boy and a mentally broken bodyguard?

"Every night, whether I could see the stars or not, I imagined kissing you at the front of that church."

She yanked her hand away. It was too painful to hear, to think about. Her emotions were a jumble in her belly. She feared what his words might mean, feared this desperate need to give in to her body's persistent desire for him.

She—they—had a son to consider. Andy's physical and emotional safety came first; it had to. "I'm going inside."

"You're running away."

"Don't you dare judge me for doing what I must to survive."

"Are we talking about the present or the past?"

"Push me, Drew! Go ahead and push me further and I'll prove how well I can hide. Even from you."

It was a struggle, but she held her ground when he came to his feet in a move as graceful and quiet as a predatory cat. "Push you? Addi, I know a little something about being pushed. I understand limits and the dark places beyond them more than any other man you know."

She'd only ever known him. Had never wanted to know another man. "We should've been married." Again, the words that came out were different than the words she'd meant to say. What was wrong with her? She needed space, time. And a different bodyguard. This was too much to tolerate.

"You have to tell Andy about me."

Oh, but she had. Without any facts, she'd told Andy about Drew as a hero, a patriot, a strong, vibrant man who loved him no matter how much time or distance separated them. When she'd learned Drew had been killed in action, her connection with their baby buoyed her through the darkest days of her grief. She'd named their son after his father. Wasn't that enough for him?

"I won't let him down. Trust me, Addi. Give me a chance and I won't let either of you down again."

She wanted to believe him. Her heart already did. His earnest expression cracked the wall she'd built up as protection from loss and pain. From the first moment they'd met, Drew had been able to breach those barriers, but she'd built them up again—thicker and stronger—when she'd lost her husband before she'd said her vows.

Mired in that grim place, she'd been so jealous of people who had family. Simple survival meant she'd had to build some sort of defense against the world or wallow in self-pity for being denied the priceless gift other people took for granted. Her parents both dead before she'd finished her bachelor's degree, she had no living relatives on either side of her family tree. No heritage beyond stories to pass to her son.

"I plotted ways to get even with you for leaving me at the altar. They were funny and silly at first. Romantic challenges, you might say. They turned darker as the anger set in when weeks passed and I didn't hear anything more from you." Why was she telling him this? It wouldn't change anything. "I kept the note you sent."

"Thank you."

"I named Andy after you, hoping the killed-in-action reports were wrong and you'd be happy when you finally came back." She reached for her necklace, slid the two charms across the chain. "But you didn't."

Standing face-to-face with him, she knew there would never be a wall or any defense measure capable of keeping him out of her heart and soul. She dropped the necklace back under her shirt and pushed her hands into her pockets. With Craig on the loose, she couldn't bear the thought of putting Drew in any more danger. Bad enough Craig knew her weak spot was Andy. If he thought for a moment she cared for Drew, he'd be a target, too. She suspected Drew would blow off her concerns, but that didn't lessen them. "It's too late for us," she whispered. "We'll tell Andy the truth about you. We'll figure out a custody arrangement."

"It can't be too late for us, Addi." He paused, clearing his throat. "What we have is—"

"Was." She cut him off. "Past tense. What we had is over. Our wedding and every day leading up to it are no more than lovely, idyllic memories for both of us." She turned for the cabin before the tears filling her eyes spilled down her cheeks. "Too much has changed."

"Not for me."

She didn't reply. Couldn't. Oh, she heard the words. They landed softly on her heart, following her to the cabin and into restless, impossible dreams.

Chapter Ten

The next afternoon, under a hot summer sun, Drew glanced across the picnic blanket, watching Andy help his mother unload their lunch. He was a good kid, and Drew couldn't fault how Addi had raised him. They needed to tell him the truth, let him adjust to the idea of having a real dad. It wouldn't be easy—for any of them—but that wasn't Drew's biggest problem.

No, Drew understood the biggest struggle of his life was with Addi. Whoever said love at first sight didn't exist didn't know squat about it. Seeing her, he'd felt something inside him opening like a key in a lock. Curious, he hadn't fought it, just followed, and soon he'd experienced a love beyond measure. A love that hadn't shriveled under the long-distance pressure of her law school or his busy military career.

He felt awkward admitting it, even knowing she wasn't romantically attached to anyone, but he loved her still. Desperately. It made him vulnerable personally and in his role as her protector. Temporary protector, if she had her way. He was afraid to ask if she might have any emotions left for him. The answer was obvious enough—she'd been engaged to another man. She might not be able to deny the old physical spark, but he wanted more than her body. He wanted her heart once more. He just couldn't be with her and not be *with* her. The physical chemistry was a good start, but it went so much deeper. For him anyway.

But this wasn't the time to navigate that particular minefield. They had more immediate problems, and any mistake could be their last. If he didn't get her into Casey's protection soon, if he messed up and something happened to her or Andy, this op would accomplish the one thing the POW experience hadn't: it would break him.

The time between their introduction and their wedding had been the best of his life. Before Addi, he'd had family, good friends and the best support a career soldier could want. But she'd brightened up all of that. Loving her, being loved by her, had brought all those pieces together. Loving her made him stronger, gave him something even more significant, more personal to fight for. It sounded clichéd even in his head, but it was true. Loving her, believing she still loved him, had saved his life in that hellhole.

He looked at Andy, then at her. Loving her, he'd been willing to let her keep her new family and all the happiness he'd witnessed that day in the park. Now, knowing her son and their family of two was really his, he wanted it all, but he didn't know if he could give her what she needed in return.

Edgy and tense, she had reason to distrust the world, and if he admitted he'd tracked her down only to walk away, he'd give her a valid reason to distrust him.

"Aren't you hungry?"

He looked up as her shadow fell over him. "Famished." He didn't mean the food. Between their son and the imminent danger, he couldn't indulge his basic need to take and taste, to remind them both, on the most basic level, of what they'd once shared. She might not believe it was there, but he did. Instead, he decided right then and there to focus on what he could do. He could be the man he'd intended to be—her husband and a father—and he could keep them both safe until she trusted him enough to take her in to talk with Director Casey.

"Come on over and make a plate."

"I can't believe how well your friend stocked this place."

She smiled. "Based on that stash, I think he was planning an extended getaway. I feel a little guilty for taking advantage. I'll have to find a way to make it up to him."

"I like Nico's tree house," Andy said.

"Me, too," Drew agreed. Especially the wide porch that saved him from having to share the tight quarters with Addi through the night. "Has your mom taken you fishing yet?"

"Not ever," Andy said around a bite of ham sandwich.

"Chew first," Addi reminded him.

"I saw some fishing poles in that cubby under the cabin this morning. It would be a good way to spend some time this afternoon." Anything to create more breathing room. He couldn't decide if the temptation of being close to her was worse than the surge of grief whenever he thought of the time they'd lost. "If we can find some bait, we'll be set."

"What kind of stuff makes bait?"

He smiled at the boy. Drew wondered when it would stop feeling like a punch to the gut to look at his son. "The best bait is something that makes the fish curious enough to bite and get hooked. It could be a worm or a smaller fish. Some fishermen use fake bugs."

"Cool!"

"It all depends on what kind of fish you're trying to catch."

"Will you come, too?" Andy asked his mom.

Drew knew it was more than a good idea. Sticking together was necessary under the circumstances. At least if they were outside fishing, they couldn't keep arguing, and with Andy nearby, Drew would have a distraction from his perpetual need for Addi.

The three of them discussed the various fish living in the swamp and the different baits each fish preferred. Addi had looked perfectly content in the city with her fiancé and son, but out here she seemed equally at ease with her surroundings.

"You know, the best time to fish is early in the morning," she said. "Before the sun is up."

Andy's face sank with disappointment and his shoulders slumped. "Can't we practice today?"

"Definitely," she said. "But if you hope to catch anything, you should choose a cool and shady place."

The boy beamed once more. "Can it be just me and Drew?"

"Not this time," Drew answered before Addi had to be the bad guy. "But there will be other days when we can go out just the two of us." He met the hard look Addi aimed at him head-on. This wasn't a matter of overpromising. Come hell or high water, he would be a part of Andy's life from this point forward.

As they cleaned up the picnic and returned to the cabin for fishing poles and a bucket for bait, he kept an eye out for any sign of trouble. So far today, the only trouble was the prickly mother of his son. It was impossible to miss how they both used Andy as a shield, more than happy to talk to him but not each other.

He couldn't blame her, couldn't even imagine how difficult it must've been raising Andy alone. While they dug for worms he experienced a jolt of anger, like heat lightning, realizing how close he'd come to never knowing he had a son. Sure, he'd walked away in San Francisco, but she'd nearly pushed him away two nights ago.

It was a relief to head back toward the water, letting Andy's unending string of questions blur out the various levels of his worry and frustration. He taught his son how to cast a line, how to extricate the line from leaves and debris and then the more important lesson of sitting quietly while the bait did its work.

That last part proved the biggest challenge for the boy. Insects buzzed quietly out over the water and once in a while a fish would strike but not at their lines. Drew lay back on the grass, but Andy fidgeted.

"Who taught you to fish?" Andy twisted and knotted a bit of tall marsh grass.

"When I was growing up, my dad took me fishing on a lake that felt as big as an ocean," he answered quietly. "You couldn't see across to the other side."

"Where was that?"

"Michigan."

"We can almost see the Pacific Ocean from our house in San Francisco," Andy said. "But no one fishes there."

"What about on Fisherman's Wharf?"

Andy laughed, his small shoulders rounding as he tried to stay quiet. "No one fishes with poles and stuff out there. They get on boats and go way out from shore."

"Oh," Drew said. "That makes sense."

"How do you know about Fisherman's Wharf?"

"Stories and pictures. I've only been to San Francisco once." On the trip when he'd tracked down Addi and found her looking so perfect and happy with another man and this little boy. "California has a lot going for it. You must like it there."

"I live there," Andy said, as if that explained it all.

"I learned the whole San Francisco history from school field trips."

"Impressive."

"And books."

"You like to read?"

"Yeah." Andy leaned out and checked his line. "Did that move?"

"Not the way we want it to."

"Oh." He slumped back, then shifted, flopping down to mirror Drew's position, propping himself on his hands. "Mom and I read every night."

"History books?" He slid a glance at Addi, but she didn't seem to be listening. "Those would sure put me to sleep."

"No." Andy giggled. "Comic books. They're better for bedtime."

"Which is your favorite?"

"Captain America!" Andy bounced to his knees, then remembering they were supposed to be quiet, whispered the answer once more.

"He's pretty tough," Drew agreed. At Andy's age, he'd been into comics, as well, and Captain America had topped the list.

He chanced another sideways look at Addi while the little guy chattered on and on about the story and art in the latest edition. At this rate they wouldn't catch anything, but Drew didn't care. The kid's enthusiasm was contagious. It had been nearly twenty years since he'd given any real thought to the complex universes and alternate realities of comic books.

He let his imagination drift, wondering what it would be like to have been a part of Andy's life from the beginning. He couldn't fathom a responsibility more rewarding than raising a family. A wife, a few kids, a dog…

"Do you have any pets?" he asked when Andy stopped long enough to catch a breath.

"Not right now. My hamster died."

"No dog?"

"Mom said maybe after the wedding." Andy sighed. "But now we're not getting married."

Drew managed not to wince at the reminder that Addi had nearly tied the knot with Craig Everett. The perfectly styled Everett didn't seem like the dog type, but Drew hadn't stuck around for a full evaluation. Maybe if he had done more digging, he could've saved Addi from her current predicament. Maybe.

He and Addi had talked about adopting a big hound dog, but that had been when their plan was to live on a small acreage. Instead, she lived in a city-locked urban high-rise. He stared out over the still water, wishing he could go back and do things differently. It seemed like a lot more than eight years ago when he and Addi had dreamed of life with lazy summer days tucked between demanding careers and raising three or four children.

He battled back the more familiar swell of angry regret over what he'd lost in that damned POW camp. The world didn't owe him a thing, but there were moments, like this one, when it was tempting to think so. He hadn't indulged in self-pity under the horrible conditions of his imprisonment, and this wasn't the time to start.

"Andy, if you had a dog, what would you name it?"

ADDISON COULDN'T HELP smiling as she listened to Drew and Andy. Only pieces of the conversation floated back to where she sat in a patch of sunshine, trying to forget her circumstances. But the few words and phrases were enough to let her know they were getting along well.

She'd been invited to cast a line with them and to enjoy

the shade while they waited for something worthwhile to take the bait. But she was trying to show Drew she trusted him and meant to keep her word about making him a part of Andy's life.

Blame eight years of maternal logistics but she couldn't help wondering how they would make it work. She lived in San Francisco and Drew apparently had a life he enjoyed in Detroit. Just because they'd managed a long-distance romance ages ago didn't mean a long-distance family was doable.

Andy needed more than an occasional father figure. Now that it was possible, she wanted to give her son plenty of quality time with his real father. She suspected the relationship would benefit Drew as much as it would Andy. Not certain how it would affect her, she left herself out of the equation.

She rubbed a fist over her heart where it clattered against her ribs. In the early days after their postponed wedding, she'd had vivid dreams of Drew with the child she carried. Over the years, for the sake of her sanity, she'd let that fantasy go. Now, on this sultry summer afternoon, watching father and son, she felt it was a bit like being in the sweet bliss of those dreams again.

She shook it off, telling herself to stay practical. She'd raised Andy to know his dad loved him and had died on a mission, but she didn't know how to begin to explain this sudden shift of their reality. Andy was smart enough to know grown-ups made mistakes, but this qualified as a more serious error. Alongside her bad judgment in nearly marrying Craig and making that bastard Andy's stepfather, it would be a miracle if her son ever accepted her word on anything again.

How could one woman make so many wrong turns on such a carefully outlined path? No, she hadn't expected to be pregnant on her wedding day, but Drew would've been as thrilled as she had been. Losing him had changed everything, but she'd reworked the plan. She'd fled the Mississippi Delta and the haunting shadows of the memories they'd made for the West Coast and an urban life.

It had been the best option for her as a new lawyer, following the excellent money and perks that supported her as an unexpectedly single mother. She'd provided the best for Andy from his first nanny right up through his private schooling. She'd made a name for herself, rising swiftly to the top of her profession while staying involved as a parent and volunteer in Andy's activities. Sure, something had been missing—for both of them—but she'd done everything possible to compensate.

Andy popped up from the grass to check his line again, and this time Drew followed him. As she watched them deal with whatever had snagged the line, she understood there would be no compensating for the bond forming between them.

Andy idolized Drew already. Other than her fear of him promising things he couldn't deliver, she couldn't fault a single thing about how Drew interacted with their son. But she felt obligated to proceed with caution. It was up to her to protect Andy from the potential pain of losing his father again.

Drew might be her only ally right now, but there was no guarantee he'd stick around in the backwater of the bayous until the threats against her were completely neutralized. She'd blown the whistle on Craig, and he'd escaped custody once, confirming her worst fear. She didn't think he'd ever find her if she stayed off the grid out here, but she had to think of Andy's future.

"Mom, come look!" Her son raced up the bank, skidding to a stop beside her rickety chair. Grabbing her hand, he started to tug her to her feet. "Come on. We got a bite!"

"Way to go," she said. "You'd better help reel him in."

Andy stopped midstride, giving her a puzzled expression. "How do you know it's a boy fish?"

"Just an expression, honey," she said, waving him back down to the water's edge. If Drew wanted to step into dad shoes, she'd be happy to let him start with this topic. "Go check with Drew."

"Is it a boy fish?" Andy asked as Drew showed him the catch.

"This one is too young to tell," Drew said. He showed Andy how to remove the hook without hurting the fish. "I'm not sure fish care much about being boys or girls," he added, placing the fish in Andy's eager hands. "Be gentle," he instructed. "Toss him—it—back in."

"But fish have babies."

"Uh-huh," Drew replied warily.

Addison smiled, wondering how he liked parenting now.

"There has to be a boy and a girl to make babies," Andy declared, looking at each of them in turn. "We learned it in science." He held the squirming fish, looking it over from gills to tail. "Everything that makes babies has a boy and a girl."

"Well, this one is too small either way," Drew said. "Maybe we'll catch him—or her—again when he—or she—is older and we can tell for sure. But not if you don't put it back in the water."

Andy crouched, pushing his hands under and releasing the fish to streak away. "It's fast!"

"Being fast is the only way it'll survive to be a big fish," Drew said.

"Yeah," Andy agreed. He watched the water, his

sandals squishing into the soft ground of the bank. "Can we swim?"

"Only if you're done fishing," Drew replied.

"Will we catch anything real big?"

"Not if we go swimming."

"Huh."

Addison took advantage of her son's need to process the options. "I'm going back to check on the sun tea I started." It was the best excuse to make a graceful exit. "If you catch something for dinner, let me know."

"Hey, Addi?" Drew's voice followed her up the bank. "Can you cook gator tail?"

"Please. If you catch it, I'll cook it," she tossed back over her shoulder before she could stop herself. What was she doing flirting with him? They'd had a similar exchange during their first long weekend together after they'd met. It seemed Andy wasn't the only one all too ready to include Drew in their lives.

Determined to keep her distance and a firm hold on logic, she hurried back to the cabin, hoping he'd forgotten what she hadn't. As expected, the sun tea didn't need any attention. The water was turning a deep golden color as it brewed in the sunshine. When she spoke with Nico next time, she'd ask for some fresh lemons for lemonade. Andy would enjoy everything about that, including helping her make it.

She pushed her hands through her hair, lifting the heavy mass off her neck, letting the air cool her skin. With Andy well out of earshot, she found the radio and dialed in a news station, hoping to hear that Craig had been found and was back in federal custody. Would she feel safe enough to go back to civilization then? The answer wasn't clear. She suspected Craig had been dragged into this terrible operation by someone else, but she didn't have solid evidence to support the theory.

She changed the station, listened to a few reports on other situations, but hearing nothing helpful, she turned it off. What the hell had she been thinking? For the moment it was a grand summer adventure to wander the bayous, but that glow would fade soon enough. Andy would want to return to his friends and school. He'd want to play soccer and make sure she made good on her promise to let him try baseball.

Turning in Craig had been the only option, but she'd sure screwed up every aspect of her life in the process. Not to mention Andy's. The plan she'd been so sure about seemed increasingly rash with the hindsight of each new day. Hiding in a swamp didn't provide Andy with the social life and academic challenges he needed. How could she hope to manage indefinitely with nothing more than the barest essentials? He was growing up. He needed the structure and opportunities she'd originally put in place for him.

Maybe Drew was right. Maybe she should let him take her to this Casey person and ask for official protection. If she had someone to watch Andy... Taking a deep breath, she forced herself away from that fatalistic thinking. She was getting ahead of herself. There were weeks left of summer. Plenty of time for the authorities to unravel the material she'd provided about Craig's activities and make the world safe for her and her son again.

She'd created one hell of a mess and instead of resisting and resenting the one man who'd shown up to help her, she should show some gratitude. Assuming there wouldn't be fish, or gator, she opened the stocked cabinet and considered how to turn the supplies on hand into a dinner that would satisfy two big appetites.

Chapter Eleven

It didn't seem possible, but the mixed feelings followed Drew through the rest of the afternoon and into the evening. Getting to know his son, even if Andy didn't understand the real relationship yet, had been astounding. The kid wanted to know everything about everything. With every question, Drew fell a little more in love with Andy.

He thought the opposite might also be true, but he didn't dare ask Addi to confirm it. While he was trying to be respectful of her concerns and boundaries, he was eager for Andy to know the truth. Hell, he was an adult and he still ached knowing his dad was gone. From his perspective, it could only be a good thing for all of them if Andy knew he had a real father.

As she started nudging Andy through the bedtime routine, Drew offered to take care of the reading time.

She scowled. "Don't you have to check the perimeter or something?"

"I can read first," he pointed out.

She didn't look impressed by his suggestion, but Andy begged, adding big puppy-dog eyes to the drawn-out "please." Drew wasn't sure which of them was happier when she gave in.

"Just the comics," she said, shooting Andy a don't-mess-with-mom look where he waited on the bed.

It was impossible to mistake her meaning, and Drew fought the urge to argue. "Just the comics," he agreed. "Tonight."

He couldn't figure out why Addi was avoiding such an important conversation. Sure, Andy would have questions, but he'd also have two parents at his disposal to provide answers. She'd lost her own parents during college, a year or so before they'd met. She had firsthand experience with the gaping emptiness of losing a parent. Why couldn't she see her way clear to give her son a dad?

But she had almost done just that by nearly marrying Everett. She'd turned the bastard in, but Drew wondered how much she'd loved him.

"Turn the page," Andy prompted.

"Oh, right."

"I can wait if you're still looking at the pictures."

Drew had no idea what had happened to the story line. He quickly skimmed the panels. "No, I'm done."

"Okay." Andy didn't sound very convinced, but he turned the page and kept reading. "Do the sound effects," he said. "Please."

Drew complied, embracing the role with the same gusto his dad had used when Drew was a kid. He nearly burst with pride when Andy gave him a big thumbs-up when they finished. "Take it out to Mom, please? She'll want to know how it ends."

"You got it." Drew tucked Andy into his sleeping bag on top of the mattress. "We'll be just outside if you need us."

"'Kay," Andy said, yawning.

Drew turned out the light and eased the door closed as he stepped out onto the porch. He'd expected to see Addi, but the space was empty in both directions. For a moment, Drew panicked that she had been found and kidnapped.

"I'm over here." Her voice drifted up from the stairway.

He walked over, settled on the other end of the wide step and peered up at the sky. "Not the best place for star-gazing." The view was blocked by the tall trees on this side of the cabin. He waited, but she didn't seem inclined to converse. In fact, she'd been a little too quiet all night long. "Dinner was excellent. Thank you."

"So you said. Again, you're welcome."

He searched for another neutral topic, but the only thing he wanted to discuss was being honest with Andy or getting more details about her situation with Everett. "Was Andy born in Mississippi or California?"

She turned her head, giving him an expression he couldn't decipher. "Does it matter?"

"Not really. Did you, um, think about using my name on the birth certificate?"

Shaking her hair back from her face, she looked up at the treetops. "It should be a pretty moon tonight."

"Addi, come on. I have a right to know."

"I'm not ready for this, Drew. Not tonight."

"When?"

She blew out a sigh, clearly annoyed with him. "Just not tonight."

"You said—"

"You'll get your answers," she muttered. "Can we just enjoy the quiet for a while?"

In the past he'd had no problem sharing silences with her. Now, though, he could hear the clock ticking. Chalk it up to all his unexpected and unpleasant experiences, but he no longer counted on having time beyond the present moment. If she didn't want to talk, that was fine. But she could sure as hell listen.

"It was a three-quarter moon on our wedding day,"

he began. "I told myself I'd be back in the States making love to you by the full moon."

She didn't make a sound.

"No one ever explained to me how the mission was compromised," he said. "Could've been anything from intel to weather. Sometimes the people who claim to know guess wrong about who is working for which side over there."

"Over where?"

"The mission was Afghanistan. The prison camp was more like the fifth dimension of hell."

In the faint light bleeding through the doorway, he saw her catch her lower lip between her teeth. He wanted to kiss her, to soothe that spot with his lips. Imagining a negative reaction, he pulled his gaze away, focusing on the trees on the other side of the fire ring. It was a much safer view. For both of them.

"We went in as a team," he said, picking it apart one more time. Every time he went through those hours, he hoped to find an explanation. Maybe this time, telling her, would finally give him the insight. "A simple, straight-forward grab-and-go kind of thing. We were ambushed on the way out. Our target got killed in the cross fire and two of us were hauled away to stand trial."

"By what authority?"

Of course the legal ramifications cut through her sto-icism. He couldn't help laughing a little. "You know, at the time, I heard you say that very same thing in my head."

"You don't have to do this."

She said it softly, in a way that indicated she thought it would be painful for him. He bumped her knee with his. "Maybe I need to."

Her gaze rested on the place where their knees touched, and he assumed her silence was consent. Slowly, he cracked the lock on the door where he stored those awful memories, letting them out one at a time.

"The trial was a joke, obviously. They recorded me standing there in chains, listening to a long list of things I didn't do, spoken in a language I could hardly follow. Then they handed down whatever sentence fit their mood on that day."

"The army told us you were killed in action."

He wondered when and what she'd been told. "I'm sure the real story was buried under security clearances. I learned later that they staged my execution and sent my dog tags and the videos back to the army. It gave them free rein to do whatever they wanted with me after that."

Her shoulders slumped and her fingers toyed with the charms on her necklace.

He told himself she needed to know, needed to be aware that he could crack under the wrong pressure. Sure, he'd convinced himself, and her, that he could be her bodyguard, but there were chinks in the armor. The army had seen it first, forcing him into retirement. As much as he wanted to get Addi into Casey's protection, he recognized now that she was safer out here in the murky places of her past. A man like Everett didn't understand the nature or culture in the bayous. If Drew cracked out here, Addi and their son might still survive. Same went for a leak in the government that even Casey might not see coming.

"Emotionally it couldn't have been much different than what you probably went through." Only the night insects answered him. "You know, like the five stages of grief."

"I know them," she bit out.

"Right. So I was in denial that the capture was serious," he admitted. "Sure, it was obvious I was in trouble, but

I didn't believe it would last. As a United States soldier I was sure someone would track me down and pull me out."

She slid those charms across the fine gold chain.

"Denial lasted me a good couple of weeks. I was trained to be patient, to look for the right opening. I knew they wouldn't leave me out there without good reason. So I did what I could to gather useful intel.

"My captors ignored me at first. They weren't what you'd call hospitable, but they didn't do anything obnoxious. I kept my mind on you. More denial, I suppose. In my head I was with you every day, imagining the perfect apology so you couldn't resist me."

"I'm sure I would've caved instantly, whatever you'd planned," she confessed.

Progress! Instead of a fist pump, he rubbed the scars on his knuckles. "They marched me across the mountains for a week, and while I was sure they'd taken another soldier that night, I never saw him. When we reached their camp, when I saw it was a prison, I went full-tilt pissed off. That held me for months, the anger during the day and dreaming about coming back to you at night. It even held me up when the torture started, but it wasn't long before I was bargaining."

Her face turned and the pale moonlight caressed her cheek. He wanted to touch, to feel the softness of her skin under his fingers, but he resisted. "I didn't bargain with them, just God, the army, the universe. We're trained for that crap, you know."

She shifted closer, by intent or reflex he didn't care. Their bodies brushed at shoulder and thigh and inside he rejoiced at her unspoken support.

"Movies and books tell you the reality is worse than the training. And everyone thinks they know how they'll deal with it. But until you're in it, you don't know there's something beyond the pain or the humiliation when your body gives in," he said. "The worst part is not knowing where the end of the line is."

She gave a little gasp but didn't interrupt him.

"It's impossible to underestimate the value of knowing there's a time limit for any given activity. June has thirty days and then July begins. If you hate June, you know there's an end, right?"

"Right," she whispered.

"There was none of that. It's all an untenable, unending hell. The food barely met the definition, and a body reacts before it adjusts." He laughed. "In the early days I complimented the food, saying it tasted like pork chops just to piss them off, to prove they couldn't break me."

"But they tried." She covered her mouth with her hand. "Sorry."

"Of course they tried," he agreed. "That was their job. Mine was to heal up and stay alive. They thought I had some valuable information about military installations, in their country or ours, I'm not sure. I heard them torturing other prisoners about the same stuff, but I didn't hear anyone give up anything you couldn't find on the internet."

"Impressive."

He snorted. "I suppose. I just don't think that crew understood the layers of protocol and firepower they'd face if they attacked." *Thank God,* he thought. "Every damn day that I could think clearly enough I bargained with the mud and air and the rats in my cell," he continued. "Just for it all to end. The shrinks say the depression gets mixed in, that the stages cycle through and repeat or something like that."

"Yeah, I heard the same thing."

Somehow, knowing she'd grieved, knowing she hadn't just left their wedding day relieved to be free of him made him feel better. Stupid, but true. "Acceptance," he said on a sigh. "I can't really pinpoint when that kicked in. Had to be after the first year. But accepting the situation gave me more days when I looked for a way out. In the cells we developed allies, identified the human rats planted to erode our flagging morale or to get information we wouldn't admit during the interrogations."

"Drew."

"That's existing as a POW." He knew she was fuming and it made him admit the rest. "Eventually you find a way out. It took me nearly six years before I finally managed to escape, but I was the only American that day. The only good news was, surviving the elements felt like a cakewalk after torture and interrogation."

"OH, DREW." ADDISON swallowed, grateful he hadn't gone into more detail about what he'd endured. The few scars she'd noticed on his hands and just under his collarbone were surely just a tiny preview. He was leaner than he'd been, and she suddenly wondered how long it had taken him to get back to this point. Six years of horrendous conditions compounded by nothing but pain and loss when he returned home. She couldn't imagine it. Admiration for his fortitude had her wishing she could ease just a small piece of his burden. "I'm so sorry." She covered his hands with hers, leaned in just a little more.

"You don't owe me an apology." He brushed his lips across her temple.

Countless times in his absence she'd missed that touch, that tender move that made her feel so cherished. She'd wished a thousand times that he'd walk back into her life, and now that he had done so, she'd made him feel unwelcome.

"How long have you been in the States?" She stroked

her thumb across the back of his hand. Feeling the hard ridges of scars, she nearly wept for how he must've earned them.

"Two years give or take. I've spent most of that time in hospitals and rehab facilities."

"They should have called me." She gazed into his eyes, but his expression was hard to read in the night shadows. "*You* should have called me."

"I couldn't," he said, his gaze drifting to her lips. "I—I was too broken. You wouldn't have wanted to see me like that."

"Impossible." She shook her head. If he'd called, if she'd known, she would've been by his bedside in an instant, been with him through every step of his recovery.

"Even now, Addi—"

She silenced him with a kiss. A gentle, sweet touch of her lips against his. Barely more than a whisper, but she felt desire sizzle through her bloodstream.

"Addi," he murmured, brushing his thumb along her jaw. "You need to know I could still break. Some sounds, certain contact throws me off. If something happens—"

"It won't. I trust you." She kissed him again, lingering this time, enjoying the way her body remembered him.

"Hang on." He took her face in his hands, held her just out of reach. "Let me say it."

"Okay."

"If they find you and I…falter, promise me you'll run."

She couldn't stand the idea of leaving him to fight for the sole purpose of buying her time to escape. Not now. Her fingers curled around his hands, slid down his wrists. "I promise," she lied. He wouldn't listen to reason right now, and logical arguments were the last thing on her mind.

With his taste on her lips once more, need for him roared through her like an unquenchable craving. A need for him she thought long dead. "Seal it with a kiss?"

He hesitated so long she wondered if he'd forgotten all the *x*'s and *o*'s under the red lipstick print she'd added to her signature with every letter she'd sent him. Then, finally, with agonizing deliberation, he covered her mouth with his. His warm, firm lips washed away the tension she'd been carrying and her body went pliant.

Angling, she parted her lips and the first tentative stroke of his tongue had her moaning. He tasted of strong coffee and spices from dinner and the delightful, edgy temptation she remembered. Her pulse drummed in her ears. Here was the kiss, the passion she thought she was incapable of ever feeling again. She couldn't get close enough to his heat, his heart.

His whiskers rasped under her fingertips as she rediscovered the shape of him. Leaner, yes, but still Drew, the man she loved. Had never stopped loving. She wanted to tell him, but she knew he wouldn't believe her. She'd rather show him how nothing had changed.

She grinned as he pulled her across his lap, his hands sliding up the back of her thin tank top. Pressed against him from breast to core, his thighs hot and strong under hers, she felt complete, powerful. The danger of her present circumstances forgotten for the moment.

She kissed him deeply, reveling in the warm, sensual haze that had always come over her when she was with him. Only him.

His erection nudged at her through the denim shorts and she gripped his shoulders as she rocked against him. She moaned, the friction of the fabric between them deliciously unbearable. He made that familiar rumble of pleasure in his throat as she rocked again, sucking lightly on his tongue.

Being a single mom hadn't left her much time for dating, and her few experiences had never compared to Drew. She'd thought motherhood had killed her passion. Now she knew better. The most intimate parts of her—body and soul—wouldn't settle for anyone but him.

She dipped her head, trailing kisses along his hard jaw, down his throat and across the scar under his collarbone. His pulse raced under her mouth.

His hands covered her breasts through her shirt, thumbs bringing her nipples to hard peaks through the thin layers of her bra and tank top. Her head dropped back as she arched into his touch. She was tugging at the hem of his T-shirt, desperate to get it out of the way, when an owl called from a tree nearby. She jerked back, remembering where they were and that their son was resting on the other side of a thin wall.

"We can't do this."

"What?" He stared up at her, his eyes glazed over, his breath quick.

She pushed against his shoulders, using every ounce of her willpower to scoot out of his reach. "This, Drew." She gulped in air. "This isn't the right time."

"Right time," he echoed, pushing a hand through his hair.

Suddenly she felt too exposed, as if the entirety of the swamp stood by, judging her. "We're outside." A lousy excuse and the wrong thing to say as his eyes locked with hers. Her cheeks flooded with heat when she realized they were both recalling a particularly erotic interlude during a weekend camping trip in a Mississippi state park.

"We'll go inside," he said, catching her hand.

"No." Only one of them was thinking clearly. She

pulled free. Inside was worse than outside with Andy asleep in one of the two beds. She'd never had cause to explain a man in her bed to her son, and she wasn't about to start now. Remembering how it had been between her and Drew, she vowed that when they made love again—if things went that far—their son wouldn't be within hearing distance. "This—" she waved a hand between them "—has to wait."

"Okay." Drew pushed to his feet and moved to the bottom of the steps. "I'll just do a perimeter check."

"Don't bother. We're safe," she said. "Everett doesn't know about my connections here."

But Drew left without another word. She watched him go, debating the wisdom of waiting outside for his return. Better, she decided, if she hurried in and pretended to be asleep when he got back.

Her legs were rubbery, her skin prickling with every sensation as she tried to settle down in bed. She needed the rest, but her body wanted the exciting promise of pleasure in Drew's arms. It shocked her, embarrassed her a little how much she'd wanted him. Needed him. One kiss and she'd blotted out all risk, all thought of his commitments as well as her own.

What did that mean for the future, assuming they survived Craig's inevitable efforts to find her? Her heart already had designs on reclaiming what they'd lost, but that wasn't practical.

Was it?

Exasperated with herself, she rolled to her side, putting her back to the door. She closed her eyes, but it was an exercise in futility until he came back.

Finally she heard him, deliberately clearing his throat and scraping the dirt from his boots on the top step. She placed her hand on the shotgun anyway until the door opened and she heard his voice.

"All clear," he murmured.

She didn't dare reply.

Chapter Twelve

Only when Drew heard Addi's breath even out did he let himself doze off. It didn't qualify as sleep, disturbed by the contrast of recalling her sweet body in his hands and the imminent danger he sensed closing in on them.

There'd been no sign near the markers he'd placed, but he felt the threat lurking in the shadows. Paranoia was a symptom of what he'd survived, and he struggled to keep his weaknesses at bay. Another move would cause more problems than it solved. Telling his body to stand down, he closed his eyes. With Addi a mere arm's length away, he couldn't stop wishing he'd done things differently.

If he'd escaped the prison sooner. If he'd just said no when the knock had sounded on his hotel room door. He thought of what she'd endured without any support and kicked himself for not grabbing the minister and insisting they exchange vows before the mission. She would've had access to his military benefits that way. He had known how to make the most of his available time and he'd squandered it.

In a twilight sleep he had that sweet dream of her walking down the aisle, but this time she wore a cotton tank top and denim shorts. It sounded just as miraculous when she said, "I do."

The floor squeaked, tearing him from the dream until he realized it was Addi rolling over.

What would it take to get her to open up about those years? He'd probably shared more with her than he should have, but in the moment he couldn't have stopped the tide of words. He finally understood what the shrinks meant about finding a confidant. Her reaction, those hot kisses, had been unexpected, filling the desolate places in his soul and smoothing out the raw edges.

He was dreaming of their first kiss as husband and wife. This time they were at the front of a small chapel with sunlight streaming through stained-glass windows. She wore a white gown worthy of a princess, and he'd just lifted her veil when he heard the slide and scrape of something near the cabin.

Awake once more, he held his breath, listening and counting the passing seconds. At the count of eleven, he heard the unmistakable sound of boots on the ground.

No time to waste wondering how they'd been found—it was time to go. With dead calm and absolute silence, he looked over to Addi. She was already sitting up, the shotgun across her knees. Good woman.

"I'll look," he whispered. They needed some idea of what they were up against. "Take the bag and wait with Andy."

She nodded, moving quietly to do as he said.

He headed for the door, leaving his pistol in the holster at his hip. Based on the sounds that had woken him, he assumed the boats had been spotted despite his efforts to conceal them. They'd have to push through the swamp and hope they found a safe place to hide. He intended to clear a path.

Wincing as the door hinges creaked, he dropped to one knee just outside the opening, braced for any reaction.

A silhouette rushed up the stairs, handgun raised. Clearly not a case of hunters or kids messing around. Adrenaline zipped along his nerves, bringing all his senses to high alert. Waiting for the perfect moment, he reached out and grabbed the black boot just before it hit the top step. Before the man could shout, Drew flipped him feet over head back down the steps.

In the commotion, he heard two more low voices check in by radio. A team of three. It made sense. Three men in a strike boat would be agile and mobile and feel confident about overpowering a scared mother and child. But were other teams searching other pockets and cabins in the swamp?

Only one way to find out.

Using the shadows, he eased back against the wall of the cabin, watching to see if the others showed themselves. A man passed under his position, heading for his pal at the bottom of the stairs. He heard the whispered comments and the call for reinforcements.

Damn.

Make a stand or run?

Run.

It was the best option. Out in the swamps they had the slight advantage of understanding the terrain. In the cabin, they were sitting ducks with limited ammunition. He crept back inside, hoping Addi didn't shoot him before he could get them out. He found her tucked between the beds, shotgun loaded and ready.

"Take the bag," he said. He scooped Andy into his arms. "Down the steps and bear right to the swamp. I'll follow you."

Eyes narrowed, she gave a short nod and opened the door. When they cleared the steps without incident, he felt a prickling at the back of his neck. It was too easy.

He paused behind the wide trunk of a live oak tree. "Stay behind me," he instructed.

Her eyes went wide and her lips parted on a protest, but he didn't have time to debate and discuss. He winced as his boots splashed into the shallow water, followed by hers.

Someone shouted, but they didn't heed the warning. A bullet whizzed by and he felt a moment's panic that the shooter had hit Addi. "Keep going," she said, putting a hand on his shoulder.

He did. Covering Andy's head with one hand, he moved as quietly and swiftly as he was able.

"Where we going?" Andy whispered sleepily.

"Some bad guys showed up."

"Really? Why?"

The excitement wasn't necessarily the best reaction, but it beat panic in Drew's opinion. "I'm not sure."

"Did you shoot 'em?"

"No."

"Are you gonna?"

"If I have to. I won't let them hurt you."

"I know that."

The little boy's certainty fueled Drew's determination and steadied him more than he would've thought possible.

"I can ride piggyback and you can shoot."

And the boy would be between them, better protected. "All right, but you have to stay awake and stay quiet."

"I promise," he whispered.

They paused long enough for Drew to get Andy situated on his back. "Anything?"

Addi shook her head. "I heard them at first but not now."

"So far they aren't in front of us," Drew said, slowing the pace a bit.

"When the trees break, we should follow the inlet."

"Why?" he asked.

"Better cover."

She would know. He led the way as they alternated running with pauses to listen for any pursuit. Drew checked his watch as the first hour went by.

He halted their march when he caught the low rumble of an outboard motor on the water nearby. They froze, sinking back into the cover of tree trunks and bushes away from the shore. At his back Andy wriggled away from the tickling fronds of a fern, but the boy didn't make a sound. Thankfully, he didn't snap the offending stalks, which would leave a clear mark for those trailing them.

Addi touched his arm. "Do you—"

She stopped short when the motor died. Drew strained to hear anything helpful, but a radio crackled and his stomach knotted with dread when he realized they were caught between their pursuers and another team.

Damn it. Someone on the other side of the swamp must have spotted them. Given a rifle, with or without night-vision goggles, Drew would've made a more aggressive choice. Still, he had to do something to buy them a bit more time.

"Wait here." He settled Andy next to his mom and handed her his gun. "For backup." He set the timer on Andy's watch. "Start moving when that goes off. I'll catch up."

Any protest she might've launched died when they heard another radio exchange. This time on the shore. Too close. With a nod for Andy to start his watch, Drew slipped into the darkness and went to reduce the odds against them.

The moonlight drifted across the water as he crept along the shore. The boat, a dark rubber tactical vessel, floated just out of light. One man searched the shoreline with binoculars, while another remained seated near the motor. A third man kept his assault rifle ready, muttering instructions into his headset periodically.

Drew found a rock and tossed it out into the water, away from Addi and Andy's hiding place. The response was controlled, much as it had been when he'd tossed the man down the steps. A well-trained team of at least six.

Checking back with the team on the boat, he listened for any movement from the team trailing them. He was nearly on one of them before he realized it. Drew recovered from the surprise first, applying a choke hold. When the man slumped unconscious against a cypress tree, Drew relieved him of his weapons and radio. He listened to the comms as he circled wide of the place where Addi and Andy waited.

They should break any second now; the watch alarm and movement would cause another reaction, giving Drew better targets. It was the hardest thirty seconds of his life, but when they started moving, he used the stolen weapon and picked off the shooter on the boat, causing that team to run for cover. Then, like a snake coiled to strike, he waited for the last two men of the first team to come by.

When he caught up with Addi and Andy, they were making decent progress toward the inlet. "Just me," he called out, his voice sounding too loud in the night swamp.

She stopped and turned toward him, putting Andy behind her and raising the shotgun. "You're alone?"

"Yes."

Even in the mottled shadows of the dark swamp he could see her shoulders relax. "Good."

"It's a small window," he added, coming closer. "We have to move quickly. There were two teams and I expect they have reinforcements."

ADDISON WATCHED AS he settled Andy on his back once more. She wanted to ask what he'd done, but she wouldn't do it in front of her son. Idolizing Captain America in the comics was one thing, but the finality of life and death in the real world was completely different.

"Did you get 'em all?" Andy whispered.

"No," Drew replied in kind. "Just the ones in my way."

"Huh."

"Quiet," she reminded her son. The night was far from over. "We'll stop soon." She hoped they made it to a place safe enough to give them time to develop a new plan.

Drew had offered to take her to safety, to tell her story to Casey, and she'd stubbornly refused. For good reason, she reminded herself as they progressed through the swamp. What she'd discovered about Craig made her skin crawl more than the idea of napping beside an alligator. As a corporate attorney, she had a basic understanding of international business law. As an intelligent person, she knew how to dive beneath headlines to see how world events would affect the interests of her clients.

"What day is it?" she asked, suddenly unable to remember.

Drew sidestepped a low-hanging branch, slid in some soft ground and caught his balance before he replied, "After midnight, so officially it's the eighth."

On the tenth, less than forty-eight hours away, if Professor Hastings didn't hear from her, he would go public with the additional information she'd compiled on Craig. The details included his bank records and his latest trips abroad. Surely someone, maybe the person who'd sent Drew to find her, could use that to see justice done.

As they followed the inlet deeper into the swamp, the muscles in her legs burned, her tennis shoes were soaked and squishy and the shotgun grew heavy in her arms. She wasn't ready to stop. Every splash of water, every call of an owl made her press on.

Another motor sounded, but this one was far distant and pitched differently than the attack boat.

"Not them," Drew confirmed, helping her over a fallen log. "Wrong sound."

She managed to get in another full breath. "Hiding in here gives us plenty of reaction time to any boats coming this way," she said, convincing herself.

"Down this inlet a boat's more likely to run aground," he agreed.

She jumped, belatedly recognizing the sound she'd heard as the soft scrabble and swish of an alligator sliding into the water.

"Let's stop here," Drew said.

"You should keep going," Addison said, gasping for air. "Andy's asleep on your shoulder. Keep heading that direction and you'll find someone to help you."

From one step to the next she'd hit the limit of her endurance, but she would not be the reason either Drew or her son died. Her arms and legs were scraped and scratched and she'd likely itch from a thousand insect bites by morning. All of which were trivial. "I've got enough shells to hold them off while you go."

"We'll camp here."

"Do we have a tent?" Andy asked, rubbing a fist across his eyes.

"Shh." She looked up at Drew, unable to make out his expression in the darkness. "Drew, you can keep going. I'll hold my own if they find me here. It's me Craig wants."

"I'm sure we've lost them," he replied in a tone that told her the discussion was over. She remembered that same tone when she'd pointed out the multiple pitfalls of a long-distance relationship.

She pulled together her fragmented attention, another sign of exhaustion. Any argument would more likely reveal their position than change his mind. As much as she wanted to keep going, she didn't have any energy left. Besides, if the roles were reversed, she wouldn't leave him behind, either.

Saving her strength as well as her breath, she conceded, slipping the bag off her shoulder and letting it fall to the ground. The zipper sounded too loud against the backdrop of nature's night creatures. Biting her lip, she prayed the people after them weren't as familiar with the sounds of the swampy environment.

Taking in their position and the potential dangers from nature and man, they chose a place to create a sheltered hideout. Drew talked her through the process of laying out a tarp and settled Andy on it as soon as she was done. The excitement and escape had taken a toll on him and before long, he was curled on his side, sleeping deeply.

Together she and Drew cast camouflage netting between the trees. The humidity and temperatures had dropped with the night, and a light breeze stirred the air as they settled into their hideout.

"Get some sleep," Drew said. "I'll keep watch."

She stretched out next to Andy, the shotgun between her and Drew, but she couldn't relax.

"I'm sorry," she murmured at his bulky shadow.

"What for?"

She trembled, grateful for the dark. His voice, pitched low so he wouldn't wake Andy or draw unwanted attention, lent a distracting intimacy to the moment. "Not going to see Casey when you first arrived."

He snorted. "How much does Everett know about your life out here?"

"Nothing." Just the mention of his name made her

tremble. "My past wasn't something I talked about." Sharing anything about her humble life up to law school would've bored Craig. Sharing anything after she'd met and fallen in love with Drew had been too sacred for anyone but her son and therapist. "Seems I didn't know him well, either." She'd realized he had serious connections with too much information access, but she'd never thought he would hire a team to hunt her down. "At worst, I figured I'd be dodging private investigators for a while. Not…" She didn't want to call them mercenaries or assassins, but that left her searching for the right word. "Not anything like this."

"Something brought him close."

"It wasn't me." The words came out with more heat and accusation than she intended. "I didn't mean it was you," she added quickly. "But you're right. Something led him to look in this direction."

"It has to have been someone in town who saw you pass through."

Unfortunately, that was a safe bet. "Everyone has a price and Craig certainly has the money to meet it."

"What about Nico?"

Nico wouldn't have turned on her for any amount of money. "He's the closest thing I have to family." She sat up, drawing her knees to her chest and wrapping her hands around them.

"We'll make it, I promise. You should rest."

"I can't," she admitted. "I'm too wired." Too afraid one of those men would kill Drew or Andy to get to her. "Thank you for your help."

"If you really want to thank me, let me take you to a team who can fully protect you."

"How?" She wanted to hear he had the perfect escape plan, even as part of her cringed at the idea of leaving the swamp. Populated areas meant witnesses, security cameras and all the things that made it easier for Craig to track her down.

"I'm not without abilities," he muttered.

"You've proven that. Repeatedly," she said, scooting closer to him. His firm, sculpted shoulder turned to stone when she rested her palm there. "Without you, I'd be at Craig's mercy right now."

"How? What did… Forget it."

She sighed, assuming the question he couldn't quite spit out. "What did I see in him? Right now, I feel like I must've been an idiot blinded by the polish and charm."

"You fell in love with polish and charm?"

"Hardly." She hadn't fallen in love at all, but how could she explain that without sounding heartless? "I'd known him a long time. Or thought I did," she amended. "Yes, the sophistication was one layer of the attraction."

Drew shifted away from her touch and she let her hand fall. It wasn't smart to get attached to Drew. She couldn't afford to entertain the idea of a future when she and her son might be on the run for a long time. *Our son,* she thought. Regardless of the short acquaintance, it was clear Drew was as invested in Andy as she was. Would he insist on serving as a bodyguard indefinitely?

Whatever had led Craig here, she knew she had to completely change things up if they were to escape. She had their passports and knew a few places abroad well enough to get started as an expat. The problem was Craig knew those places, too.

"What I need is a new identity. Know anyone who can create false IDs?"

"Of course." His tone was gruff. "But Everett won't let you anywhere near an international airport long enough to use them."

She knew he was right, though she wondered if it would make a difference if she and Andy were traveling as a family of three. With Drew. Craig wouldn't be looking for that. The thought brought with it a flood of sweet images. Things she'd dreamed of and forgotten through her pregnancy and during the day-to-day details of raising a child alone.

Warming to the idea, she did the math. The money she'd tucked away would see three of them through for a few months. That would be long enough to develop a better plan if Craig continued to evade the authorities. She was about to suggest the family escape when his voice rumbled through the night.

"You won't have to run forever, Addi," Drew said, iron underscoring his words. "It won't come to that. I won't let it."

Another delicious tremor shivered through her. This man had a power over her that she'd never be able to overcome. Her desire was her problem and while her heart and body told her to never let him go, she couldn't know what he wanted or needed. Other than Andy. Whatever she and Drew would be to each other in the future, she would have to consider the father-son bond and relationship, as well.

"I'm too edgy," she said suddenly. "Why don't you rest and I'll keep watch?"

"Why don't you watch the water and I'll watch the trees?"

It felt like a manageable truce as they rested back-to-back. He was so solid, so confident, she felt a flutter of hope that he could get them out of this. He might call himself broken, but he sure didn't sound, feel or behave that way to her.

"Have I said thank you?" She couldn't recall precisely,

but she didn't want him thinking she took any of his help for granted.

"Yes."

The swamp, unable to be truly silent, murmured around them for long minutes.

"Have I?"

She felt his words where their backs touched as much as she heard them. "Have you what?"

He reached back and, finding her hand, gave her a warm squeeze. "Said thank you?"

Chapter Thirteen

Her mouth dry, she could barely articulate a response. "For what?"

"For our son. He's—" Drew coughed "—he's amazing."

"He wants to be Captain America," she said, feeling her lips curve into a smile.

"There are easier careers than being a soldier."

"Life tosses crap at everyone, Drew."

"I know."

At her back she felt his shoulders rise and fall. He knew all the pitfalls and heartbreaks she'd faced before they'd met and fallen in love. The reverse was also true. She knew how his inherent need to serve and his sense of duty and honor had led to his army career. Those very qualities had drawn her to him like moth to flame and kept her heart tied up even when she hadn't realized it.

If Craig had his way, Addison might not have another chance to share Andy's early life with Drew. And if she ever convinced him to take Andy to safety, he needed to know so he could better connect with their son. Not that she had any doubts about his ability on that score, just so she'd feel no regret if the worst happened. She trembled at the thought.

"Are you cold?"

"No." How could she be with him at her back? "It's summer."

"Come here." He shifted around, moving almost silently, until his back rested against a tree. Holding her hand, he pulled her next to him.

"What about keeping watch?"

"You can still see the water, right?"

"Right." She felt the grin spread across her face. So little had changed about him.

"I'm so sorry I missed our wedding."

His statement hit her like a sucker punch. It was the last thing she wanted to talk about.

"Me, too." Last night, when she'd told him she knew the stages of grief, she hadn't been exaggerating. Like him, she'd gone through each stage multiple times. The first time it was a mild thing, irritation mostly that the army had called her groom away. But when Drew's dad appeared at her door, holding out those dog tags... It clawed at her still, that dreadful feeling of being scraped raw.

Then denial, clinging to the strange mythical "sense" women often claimed that warned them of some terrible fate befalling a spouse or child. "Talk about denial," she said. "I extended the reservation at the hotel for a week, sure that you'd be right back."

He lifted her hands to his lips, kissing her knuckles. "I was sure of that, too."

"I believe you." She could almost hear the mortar crumbling as the wall she'd built up around her heart weakened more under his gentle assault. "I finally went back to the apartment and wandered through the local job offers."

"Anything exciting?"

"For the two of us starting out, sure."

"But?"

"When your dad came to the door and gave me the news…" Her voice trailed off as tears filled her eyes. She blinked them away, determined to hold up her side of the watch-keeping. "I had to get away from the things we'd planned."

"Of course you did."

His easy acceptance and understanding made her feel guilty all over again. "I moved to San Francisco during the second trimester."

"What were you thinking? You're a Southern girl."

She heard the humor in his voice and she chuckled. "I was thinking about schools, hospitals and providing for our son."

"You did good, baby." He wrapped an arm around her shoulders, pulled her in closer still.

She laid her hand on his thigh, slipping so easily into their old, tender habits. "Being pregnant got me through those early days." And her first round of real grief. Or was that the second? Both? Either way, while he'd been fighting to stay alive, she'd had something to live for. Their baby had become the sole purpose of taking the next breath, the next step forward while she waited for the pain of losing him to fade. Still, she'd gone through those stupid five phases again, twisted up with the typical hormonal and emotional turmoil after Andy's birth.

"When did you find out it was a boy?"

"On my first doctor's visit in the new city. I cried so hard and started calling him Andy immediately."

"You know I'd do anything to go back and change what happened. To be there for you through all that."

"I know." Addison sighed and pushed at her hair. "I believed it back then, when I thought you'd come back.

And I believed you were an angel watching over us when they told me you'd died."

"And now?"

"I believe you want to be part of his life."

"Addi…"

She waited, but he didn't say anything more. "It's done, Drew," she said, hoping to bridge the gap at last. "Trust me, I never felt abandoned." God-awful lonely. Furious that life would demand so much. Often weary, shouldering the burden on her own, but never abandoned.

"How can you say that? I left you at the altar."

She felt her lips twitch. "You know very well I never actually got that far."

"Why didn't you use my last name for Andy? And you could've gone to the JAG office for support."

She'd thought about turning to the army's legal branch, especially for the benefits that could've been arranged for Drew's son. But after hearing Drew had died on a mission, she needed space from the military. She'd been fortunate enough at the time to find work that made that option possible. "He's Andrew Bryant Collins," she explained. "I wanted to honor you, for the sake of all three of us, but different last names as he went through school felt like more of a challenge than I wanted to tackle at the time."

"Fair enough." His chest rose and fell on a heavy sigh. "I look at him and think about all the things I've missed." He toyed with her hand. "Just when I get mad about being cheated, I feel guilty that you've had to do it all alone. I don't want you to be a single parent anymore."

Was he saying he wanted to be part of their future? Andy was nearly eight, but there were plenty of milestones left. At thirty-five, she still had time to expand their family with a brother or sister for Andy. It was all too easy to picture a quick, quiet wedding followed by the rest of their lives together. As a family.

The world didn't toss out second chances like this all the time. A silly, sweet proposal was dancing on the tip of her tongue, an echo of how he'd once proposed to her. The timing would be terrible or perfect, depending on his view of their circumstances. She just had to muster up the courage to ask him.

"Good Lord, Addi. Will you ever forgive me?"

She already had. "You couldn't prevent what happened that day and it seems like you're determined to make up for lost time now." She realized she was well on her way to forgiving him for hiding since his return, as well. "Following me through the bayous is above and beyond the call of duty for a former groom."

"Stop saying things like that," he grumbled. "It was supposed to be a few days. Two weeks, tops. Not the better part of eight years."

"And you should stop those kinds of comments." Six years of torture, deprivation and abuse while she'd had six years of first-world comforts, decent therapists and the company of their delightful son. Nothing could ever make that even out. "We both need to let go."

"Yeah." He rolled his shoulders as if he could shrug away the burdens she knew they were both carrying. "Do you have any pictures? From the wedding day," he added.

"Only a few of the setup, getting dressed, that kind of thing." Those snapshots were in the safe-deposit box, where she'd stowed them the following year, unable to look at them anymore. "Why?"

"I'd like to know if I was right."

"About what?"

"Thinking of you in your wedding dress walking down the aisle toward me kept me going. When I dreamed, it was of you. Any star in the sky got hit with my wish to see you again."

She swallowed and blinked away the sudden surge of tears.

"There were a few variations, but one dress was the default, I guess you'd call it," he said on a weary chuckle. "I said my vows countless times a day, determined to live long enough to say them to you."

He'd told her he'd imagined their day, but to this level of detail? It shouldn't be shocking because she'd felt much the same, but it was. Or maybe that was the chemistry zipping through her bloodstream making her feel so attuned to him. "What kind of dress did you imagine?"

"Strapless," he rumbled in a sexy growl. "White and strapless. You wore pearls."

She nodded. They'd discussed that once. She wanted to wear her mother's pearls when she married him. It had never occurred to her to wear those pearls to marry Craig.

"There was lace at the top," he continued. "Snug at the waist. I could feel the lace under my hands when I pulled you close for our first kiss as husband and wife."

Goodness. She wasn't sure she could remember how to breathe.

"The bottom skirt swept out and away in a short train, I guess you call it."

He had been pretty close to what she'd chosen. If she ever had a chance to marry this man, she promised herself that was the dress he would see.

"Am I close?"

"It sounds lovely."

"But am I close?"

"There was lace," she admitted. She was torn between affirming his fantasy and maintaining the element of surprise. Just in case. "When I get back to the city I'll show you the pictures."

"Okay."

He didn't sound too happy about the idea and she wondered which part turned him off. As she understood it, when he'd come home he'd basically hidden himself away. Maybe the old memories and obvious mutual attraction weren't enough to start over with. He wanted to be part of Andy's life, but maybe she'd changed too much. Maybe she couldn't live up to his memory of his Southern girl.

"I heard you tell Andy you'd been to San Francisco once."

She felt the tension ripple through him. "Uh-huh."

"After, um, you got back."

"Yeah."

Would she have to pull out the story word by word? "When?"

"About ten months ago."

That would've been shortly after she'd accepted Craig's proposal. "Did you do any sightseeing?" she prompted when he didn't volunteer anything more.

"Like Fisherman's Wharf?" He fidgeted beside her. "No. I saw you with another man and a little boy. You were playing in a park near your condo. I watched for a little while."

Why hadn't she noticed him? She thought back, unable to pinpoint any day that stood out. Trips to the park happened too frequently. "Why didn't you say anything?" she demanded, anger spiking even though it was far too late.

"I couldn't." His voice cracked. "It was obvious you had a family, that you'd moved on. You were happy." He squeezed her hand. "I went back to the airport and waited for the next flight to Detroit."

Had she been happy? Happy enough, she supposed,

with her healthy son, an excellent job and a considerate man who wanted to be her husband.

If Drew had walked up to them that day, what would she have done?

"I had to leave," he said. "No other choice."

"I disagree."

"You're allowed to do so."

She didn't appreciate the cold finality of that statement. "I had every right to know you were back. Alive."

"Did you? What would that have gained?"

"It would've gained you a son!"

"I didn't know that," he shot back.

Biting her lip, she held back the torrent of useless accusations and predictions. He'd come out, seen her happy and left. She tried to see it from his point of view, but she was too wrapped up in the pain as she imagined him walking away.

"You were *happy*," he repeated. "I couldn't mess that up. Sure, I'd wanted you to be happy with me, but I refused to be responsible for causing you trouble or making you miserable."

The pain in his voice was unbearable. "But walking away caused you pain."

"Not as much as you think."

"What?"

He sighed in the dark. "Seeing you happy and knowing one of us had found a good life helped me heal. It gave me hope and courage to make a life for myself."

"Oh." She had to wait for her heart to catch up with his words. "I wish you'd said something." When she thought of what he and Andy had missed—what she had missed— her heart broke all over again. For days lost and time wasted. If she'd gone to the JAG office with news of her pregnancy, would they have told her when he'd returned?

She could wish and hope they might have at least told him he had a son.

"I understand, truly I do." Though she didn't believe she had enough courage and integrity to have done the same if the roles had been reversed. Guilt and tenderness and more love than she could hold rolled through her in waves. She turned away from the water, trying to make out his features in the weak moonlight. For too short a time this remarkable, heroic man had been hers. Always thinking of others first. Honorable. Strong. It was no wonder she'd never let another man close to her heart. Who could've measured up? She'd put him on a pedestal—for herself and Andy—but she'd known even from day one that he wasn't perfect.

Just perfect for her.

She rose onto her knees and gifted him with a kiss. It was a poor reward for his remarkable courage, yet she put all her heart into it.

The moment spun out, the sweet contact quickly transforming into something hotter and deeper, stripping away the world until it was only the two of them. God, she'd missed this mesmerizing pull that made her feel weak and strong at the same time. Memories of this kind of passion had haunted her since she'd walked away from the church, alone and pregnant.

Reluctantly, she pulled back, her breath coming in small, shallow sips as she fought for control. Beside them, by some miracle, her son slept on.

"Take him, Drew," she whispered, sitting back on her heels.

He didn't answer and she worried she hadn't actually said the words aloud.

"Please," she begged. "It's the best solution. You can get Andy to safety. I'll deal with Craig and come find you."

DREW SHOOK HIS HEAD. "I'm not leaving you out here alone." He admired her courage, understood where it was coming from, but he refused to budge from her side. She'd never be alone again if he had any choice in the matter.

"You could keep him safe in Detroit," she pleaded. "Craig doesn't know anything about you."

"No, Addi. We'll get through this together." He turned her so her back rested against his chest while he used the tree for support. Her legs were pale, bracketed by his, and their hands linked lightly across her waist. In the quiet, he thought she might sleep, but soon she was toying with the charms on her necklace, a sure sign her brain was still working overtime.

"What's that?" He couldn't quite squelch the jealousy, wondering who'd given her something she valued so much.

She tensed. "You heard something?"

"Relax. I was asking about the necklace. You didn't wear anything like that—"

"When we were together," she finished for him.

"Exactly." It felt so natural to hear her do that again. They'd often finished each other's sentences or train of thought. He'd been curious about the necklace since he'd noticed it that first night at Mama Leonie's shack, but he wasn't sure he could cope if the answer involved Everett.

Now, after hearing everything she'd never shared with Everett, he suspected she'd never loved the man. Which gave him hope that the bastard had nothing to do with the necklace. She wasn't wearing an engagement ring, either. Not even the one he'd given her.

He waited while she fidgeted, watching her rub one toe up and down her opposite calf. Bug bites or nerves? Likely a bit of both. He knew she wouldn't lie to him, but somehow it made him feel better that she didn't just offer up a quick answer.

"You remember that necklace you gave me for our three-month anniversary?"

He'd never forgotten the little heart-shaped charm inscribed with their initials and the date they'd met. "You rarely wore it."

"That's not true." She made a little noise of impatience. "I just bought a longer chain and you know it."

"Maybe," he teased. He remembered that she didn't like anything right up close to her throat. Except his lips. The thought, the memories of having her in his arms, under him, sighing his name made him hard. Not the time or place, but he promised himself he wouldn't leave her, and he definitely wouldn't let her resume her old life before they had a chance to rediscover the explosive chemistry between them.

"Between the necklace and the engagement ring you gave me, I felt loved and safe. Weird, but true."

It didn't sound weird at all to him. "In my cell, I used to think about holding hands with you, remembering how your ring felt between my fingers."

"Drew."

The way she sighed his name had his whole body aching to claim hers.

"That charm felt like my anchor. A talisman. I nearly panicked when that little diamond came loose one day."

"Did you find it?"

"Yes, through a fit of tears," she said. "A jeweler reset it for me, but I worried about it anyway." She took a breath and held it. "When your dad told me the awful news, he gave me your dog tags."

"What?" A chill raised the hair at the back of his

neck. He couldn't quite picture his father doing something like that.

"For the baby," she explained. "He stood at my door and told me the chaplain had delivered the news. He couldn't bring himself to do a formal memorial service, but he wanted me to have something to show our child.

"When he left, I slipped them over my head and wore them alongside the necklace through the rest of my pregnancy," she whispered in a raw voice. "And the delivery, too, so it felt like you were there with us."

He stroked her shoulders. Speaking was impossible.

"I'd had to take off the engagement ring during my last trimester. I slid it onto the same chain with your tags. On the day that would've been our first wedding anniversary, I decided to set the tags aside for Andy, but I had the jeweler make these charms first." She held them up, even though it was too dark for him to see. "One is a miniature of your dog tag and the other is the heart charm, but I had the date changed to Andy's birthday."

Same initials, only a slightly different meaning. Was it any wonder he loved her? "What about the engagement ring?"

"It's in a safe-deposit box waiting for the day when Andy wants to propose. I thought you'd appreciate giving him that option."

"You were right." Her thoughtfulness, her care for preserving the best of what they'd had only proved how right they'd been for each other. He'd been so lucky to find her. Would he be lucky enough to keep her?

"When Andy was four, I showed him your dog tags and really started explaining who you were. Andy has them still." She twisted around, frowning. "Unless they were left behind at Nico's cabin."

He hoped not, for Andy's sake. He kissed her right on

that crease between her eyebrows. "We'll go back and look if he doesn't have them." Drew had been motivated to protect Addi and wrap up this mess before, but he was doubly motivated now.

In the bag he'd packed two transmitters that would call in Casey's reinforcements. It was tempting to activate one right now and get the hell out of here, but it would potentially give Everett room to escape again. If Everett thought he'd lost all hope of stopping Addi, he would surely disappear.

When they left this swamp, Drew wanted to be sure they wouldn't be looking over their shoulders for danger the rest of their lives. Besides, Addi wouldn't rest until justice had been served to Everett.

So close. The moment that was accomplished, sooner if it proved necessary, Drew would hit his knees and beg for her to take him back. He could practically smell what life would be like with her. Waking up each morning next to the woman he loved as their son slept in his bedroom down the hall. He could hear the patter of small feet as they filled a house with children. He wanted to see her pregnant, experience every minute of that with her, if she was willing.

He stroked his hands up and down her arms, just needing the contact. She'd worn his dog tags in one way or another since he'd disappeared. Surely a shrink would agree that it symbolized a commitment of some sort. He wanted to believe, like him, she'd never given up on the dreams they'd shared.

He cringed as she went back to watching the water. They were out here partly because of him, and she deserved his best to overcome it. If by some cruel twist of fate Everett got the better of them, he knew a shrink wouldn't be enough for him to recover. He just couldn't lose her again. "Addi?"

"Hmm?"

"If I'd come forward that day in the park, would you have taken me back?"

"The minute I'd been revived from fainting."

That scenario was laughable. "I don't think so. You didn't faint when I found you in the swamp."

"I was in mama-bear mode and not about to let anything near my son. *Our* son."

Her correction was sobering. "I'm sorry I didn't come forward. You might not be in this mess if I had."

His skin sizzled when she rubbed a hand along his thigh. "I'll grant this isn't ideal, but I choose to believe we're right where we should be. The lost time is unfortunate, but I hate to think how long Everett would've gotten away with his illegal deals if I hadn't recognized something was off."

"There is that," he agreed.

They seemed to be out of words again and a companionable silence fell over them as they kept watch. He thought she might've dozed as her head rested on his chest, but it didn't matter. He was alert enough for both of them.

Once more he considered activating a transmitter, and then rejected the idea yet again. He'd use both of them, but not until he could put one of them on Everett.

"Drew?"

"Yeah."

"In the morning I want us to tell Andy the truth."

"About me?" The silk of her hair brushed his arm as she nodded. He swallowed. "Okay." He had no idea how she'd start that conversation, but he'd happily back her up.

"Then I want you to take us to Casey."

"If you're sure."

"I'm sure we've wasted enough time and energy with this game of cat and mouse. I'd rather get back on the offensive."

He was all for that. "What changed your mind?"

"Having you as an ally."

As an answer, he felt that was a good start. "Then that's what we'll do." He pressed a kiss to the top of her head and tried not to think about what she would do when the threat was eliminated and she had the world at her feet again.

Whatever happened, he wanted her to know one option was to reunite as a family.

Chapter Fourteen

Having never drifted into a sound sleep, Addison came fully awake at the sound of a boat running aground downstream. The black water of the swamps disguised all kinds of debris that frequently tangled up motor blades and dented or cracked hulls. Sunken logs, inexplicably changing depths, root systems and animal habitats all combined to make the swamps an ever-changing environment. Navigating the area was less about maps and direction and more about knowing what to watch for along the way. It had all seemed to come back to her, like riding a bike, since she'd arrived.

The sudden outburst of angry voices and resulting commotion made it a safe bet the frustrated boaters were likely part of the team hunting her. Why couldn't they shake them? The rising sun put a glow behind the trees to the east, but there were shadows still working in their favor. They needed to decide on the fastest route to rendezvous with Drew's friend Casey.

With her hand on her shotgun, she looked to Andy. Drew was already there, waking him gently and urging him to be quiet.

"Mom," he whispered, tugging on her free hand. His eyes were wide and a little desperate. At first she thought it was the situation, but then she realized he had to pee.

The very normal need made her smile. In as calm a voice as she could muster, she let him know where to relieve himself.

She exchanged a look with Drew and knew telling their son he had two parents would have to wait, not just for nature's call, but until they could speak without fear of capture. When Andy was ready, she looked to Drew. "Which way?"

"We're pinned between two teams."

Panic threatened, but she kept her gaze on him. "What do you mean?"

Drew raised his chin in the direction of the trees. "A team went by about two hours ago and again half an hour ago in the other direction."

"Are they lost?" she asked hopefully.

"I don't think we're that lucky."

Damn. She calculated the choices. It would be so easy to trudge up the swamp and let Everett's men haul her in. The move sounded foolish, but she felt it would give her back some control, especially if Drew used the time to get away with Andy.

The words were on her lips, but Drew was already shaking his head. "Don't you even think about it. We'll do this together."

"Fine." The odds were stacking up against them anyway, and working together was better than struggling alone, she had to admit.

Although hiding deep along the inlet had given them better protection through the night, now they were stuck. Drew boosted Andy onto his back again while she slipped the bag across her body and checked the load on the shotgun. They didn't risk the noise or movement of tearing down their shelter. "Your call," she said. "I'll follow you."

His brown eyes held hers for a long moment as he silently confirmed her full meaning.

She wished he'd hurry up and start moving. At this point the direction didn't matter; she just wanted to get on with it. Standing here waiting to be discovered was making her antsy. She didn't know exactly what he had planned, only that she trusted him to make the right call. For all of them.

"We'll circle back to Nico's cabin."

She nodded. If the radio was still there, if the boats were intact, they had better options.

They set out at a brisk pace and soon crossed the broken twigs and stomped undergrowth from where the other team had been wandering through the night. It wasn't the ideal family hike and she gave a start when Andy asked about fishing.

She held a finger to her lips.

"But it's early. The fish will be biting."

"Another time, I promise," Drew said, cutting short the protest.

"I can walk," Andy started again a few minutes later.

"I'll let you prove it later," Drew answered.

"Promise?"

"Yes."

"'Kay."

Addison shook her head at the two of them as she fell into step behind Drew. His long legs made quick work as he marched along in the fresh tracks left by the others. No point asking why; she was sure he had good reason for taking this route. It was certainly easier walking in areas already torn up by people who didn't care about leaving a trail.

The voices from the boat faded, but the occasional attempts to restart the motor cut through the natural morning sounds of the swamp, jarring her every time. A shout from behind had her turning and she caught movement from the direction of their inlet camp.

"We've been spotted."

Drew shifted gears, his long legs creating distance. She jogged behind him, hitting the dirt when a gunshot sent a flock of birds into the air.

"Run!" Drew put Andy down, placed their son's hand in hers and sent them on, turning back to deal with the attack.

She ran as fast as Andy could go, sliding into the only cover as soon as she spotted a knot of bushes. Sinking to her knees in mud, she propped Andy on her hip. "Tell me if someone comes up behind me."

She waited, willing Drew to join them. She wouldn't let him change the definition of *together* now. He jogged into view moments later and offered her a hand out of the muck.

"They're trying to flush us out," he said as another bullet bit into a tree well above their heads. "Either they've never used those guns, or they want you alive."

It wasn't much relief and she had no confidence that Everett's orders would leave Andy and Drew alive, too.

"Too bad. I don't want them at all."

His smile was edgy and dangerous. "Then we'd best hurry."

THEY REACHED THE tree line near Nico's cabin and skidded to a stop. Drew was surprised it was still standing. He'd expected them to have burned it to the ground, eliminating Addi's options. He didn't see any activity and the place appeared deserted, but the fire pit had been used recently. Probably this morning, he thought, catching the faint scent of wood smoke in the air.

Only a short hike between them and the boats they'd left. Everett's men would be on them any minute, and if they didn't move now, it would be open season on Addi. "We'll go for the boats." And deal with it later if they were no good.

They made it across the clearing and through the marsh grass and trees to the far shore. Spotting the boats they'd pulled onto the shore, he stopped, assessing the area for any threat. It was the perfect spot for an ambush. If he only knew how many they were up against.

"That's Nico's boat." Andy pointed.

"Right." But Drew's boat, the faster of the two they'd brought, was missing. Drew knew Addi trusted the old man, but if Everett had turned him, it explained how they'd been found.

"Craig doesn't know anything about Nico or his mother."

"You're sure?"

"Yes," she said through clenched teeth. "The water is our best hope to escape."

Knowing she was right didn't make it any easier to race across the open space, into what could easily be a trap. He was surprised when no one rushed from the shore or the water to intercept them.

Beyond a quick prayer of gratitude, Drew didn't waste any thought on their good fortune. At first glance, both Addi's and Nico's boats looked to be in good condition.

"Help your mom," Drew said to Andy while he took up a covering position. "Can you start either motor?"

"Sure."

Another three-round burst of gunfire chipped away at the knot of mangroves they'd used as a dock the other night.

Behind him Addi cried out and his blood turned to ice. "Are you hit?"

"No."

"Andy?"

"No." Her voice was choked with tears.

He turned. Addi had gathered Andy into a tight embrace, blocking the boy's view of the boats. "Oh, no." He saw the body of an older man with graying hair and a rangy build floating facedown in the water behind one of the boats. Produce, dry goods and a box of sodas were scattered around the body.

"It's Nico." She gulped, struggling for composure.

"Addi, I'm sorry."

"Nico?" Andy asked, straining for a look.

"You keep your eyes on the water," Drew instructed him. At seven—nearly eight—he didn't need to stare death in the face. "Let me know if you see anything moving out there."

"Okay."

He wanted to comfort them both, but escaping was the priority.

"Can you get the other boat in the water?"

She nodded as another shot splintered the stilt. Drew fired into the trees, hoping to pin back Everett's men for just another minute or so.

"Ready."

He heard the motor start. "Go on, then. Leave the bag."

"Not without you."

"I'll catch up." The boat wasn't that fast. "Stay near the bank."

He heard a splash, then the rumble as the motor revved.

Spotting movement at the tree line, he squeezed off a three-shot burst and the pained scream confirmed he'd hit flesh. He could hold off Everett's men, giving Addi and Andy time to get away. Someone on this swamp would help her. He just had to give them the chance. He'd been trained to hold the line and—

"Drew!"

It was Andy's screech that tugged him away from that sucking abyss that whispered he was only good enough as a sacrificial distraction. They'd warned him about moments like these when the past would cloud the present. Although he was more than willing to do whatever kept Addi and the boy safe, this wasn't the best place to make a stand.

How could he have forgotten about the other team on an attack boat? She needed him. Too much swamp remained between her and Casey's protection. Drew reached into the bag and pulled out both transmitters. He shoved one into his pocket and toggled the switch on the other, tucking it into the mud near the mangroves. Assuming it didn't get shot to pieces or carried away by an animal, it would give Casey's men a place to start searching and hopefully result in a decent burial for Nico.

As Addi urged the boat out into deeper water, Drew scrambled along the bank, trading fire with the men behind them. Anticipating the best place to join her, he hollered and pointed. She waved back, acknowledging. There was something to be said for knowing a person well.

"Mom, wait for him!" Andy's cry carried across the air, filling him with determination. He wouldn't miss, wouldn't renege on his promise to see her and Andy through this.

When Drew glanced their way, the boy was lying low in the boat, his head barely visible. Whatever Addi had said had calmed him down. They had a great kid, he thought, rounding the point and jumping into the water. He ignored the idea of any wildlife as he trudged through the waist-deep water to the waiting boat. He came up to the side, tossed in the drenched gear and wet gun first, then pulled himself in.

His boots were barely clear of the water before Addi gunned the motor. The bow reared up a little before the boat leveled to skim across the swamp.

Heedless of his soaked clothing, Andy crawled closer to give him a hug. "Seventy-three seconds."

Ah, so she'd distracted him by making him timekeeper again. "Is that good?"

Andy shook his head. "It was too long without you."

"But I made it." He gave his son's shoulder a squeeze.

Andy nodded. "I'm glad a gator didn't get you."

"I'm glad the bad guys didn't get you."

Another hug. Drew thought he could get used to this.

"Are you going to stay with us forever?"

He looked back at Addi, but she didn't seem to hear anything over the growl of the motor and her eyes were on the water ahead of them. "That's up to your mom." But he sure hoped it worked out that way.

"But she's gonna have a baby. You have to stay and be the dad for it." His face clouded with worry, that familiar Bryant frown creasing his brow.

"What?"

"You and her were kissing. I saw. Kissing makes babies."

Drew was not getting into *this* right now. "Andy, the three of us have a lot to talk about."

"I want you to be my dad."

"I'd be honored." It was the best he could do, considering the poor timing of this conversation. "The three of us will— Get down!" he shouted as another attack boat approached behind them. He pushed Andy to the little protection offered by the hull of their shallow flat-bottomed boat and reached for the shotgun. It was the only dry weapon.

Addi twisted around, then swerved across the swamp as she searched for cover behind an outcropping of trees. Their boat wasn't fast or agile and Everett's men had no intention of allowing them out of this swamp.

A warning shot fired from the shore just as she made the turn. Though Drew was prepared to shoot back, it wasn't worth the risk of Andy getting hit in the cross fire.

They'd been flanked by a team of professionals. The best they could do was surrender and hope the orders were to take them in alive. "Time to cooperate," he said, lowering the shotgun and raising his hands.

Her face went pale, but she nodded, cutting the motor and raising her hands, as well.

A voice boomed from shore, "Addison Collins!"

She faced the man shouting at her. "Yes?"

"Mr. Everett wants you to come with us. Put up a fight and we'll shoot you where you are."

"I promise you I'll find a better opportunity," Drew said under his breath. Or he'd die trying.

"*We* will find a better opportunity," she said, her mouth set in a grim line.

The attack boat came up alongside them, the leader clearly irritated by their resistance. "I'll come with you," Addi replied when they demanded it. "Just let my son go."

Drew was impressed by her courage, knew she had to ask, but he wanted to keep Andy with them.

"All of you or none of you," the leader said, raising an assault rifle.

"Be reasonable. He's a child."

"Would you rather I let him go right here in the swamp?"

Based on what Drew had seen, it wouldn't be much of a hardship for Andy, but he kept that opinion to himself.

"Well?" the leader demanded.

"All of us." Addi sent Drew an apologetic look as the men tossed them a line and tied their small boat to the attack boat.

He knew she'd weighed the decision and he murmured reassurances as he kept Andy tucked by his side. None of them, not even Andy, said a word as they were towed through the swamp to a dock and transferred to a big black SUV waiting there.

Chapter Fifteen

Drew reviewed the limited options as the SUV barreled down the road in the direction of New Orleans. The driver, weaving in and out of traffic, clearly wasn't worried about the authorities intervening.

Drew had the second transmitter in his pocket, but his hands were cuffed. The crew was well armed. Drew recognized the semiautomatic pistols in each holster and assumed the men were more than proficient. So far the five-man team had shown a disturbing level of efficiency and a cold calm that only cranked up Drew's adrenaline response. He was now certain that last night's seeming inept work by these guys had been about ensuring that Addi was captured alive.

He reminded himself that he'd survived hell once already. Nothing Everett dreamed up could be worse than what Drew had endured as a POW. Yes, there was more on the line beyond his own life, but he would not cave to the fear of failure.

He didn't know Craig Everett beyond the little insight Addi had shared, but the man had been given an excellent strike team. Casey would be very interested in this development.

The city came into view and Drew waited for his opening, knowing it would be a narrow window. With a clear path to a weapon, he could flip the whole scenario to their favor. Every fiber of his being was braced to save Addi and Andy from whatever Everett had planned.

He and Addi had been cuffed at the wrist with plastic zip ties, but Andy's hands were free and the boy was buckled into the seat between them. Drew wasn't naive enough to believe that minor concession was a positive thing. Everett was working for someone connected and ruthless.

The driver slowed down as the traffic got heavier. Drew leaned over Andy's head. "Whatever happens," he murmured to Addison, "whatever they do, don't tell them anything."

Her eyes welled with unshed tears, but she gave him a smidgen of a nod.

"We'll get through this. All three of us." He bumped his elbow against Andy's shoulder in a small show of assurance as the driver turned down a narrow alley between two warehouses.

Drew believed Casey and his team of Specialists had to be closing in. Thinking anything else would erode his confidence. He ran through a mental checklist of the details Addi's former fiancé didn't know about her. His men might've found them in the bayou, but not because of Everett's knowledge of her past.

Had to be that leaky contact. Had to be, Drew thought again. Everett wouldn't have wasted time searching for Addi around her college haunts if she'd told him her real origins or given him any indication how much she valued her family roots.

The car slammed into Park and the driver cut the engine. Drew decided not to dwell on the obvious concern that their captors weren't hiding location or faces. He'd cheated death plenty and intended to keep up his winning record now that he had two amazing reasons to stay alive. The men in the front seat climbed out and the back doors opened a moment later, flooding the vehicle with bright morning light.

Drew hopped down, hiding his trepidation behind a cocky squint. "Nice place."

"Shut up," the driver said, pushing him toward the nearest door.

New Orleans was a fine town, but this grimy industrial area wasn't the sort of area preferred by a man like Everett. This seedy environment was, however, just the sort of place Drew could navigate with expertise. Places like this lurked in the shadowy corners all over the globe, always controlled by the man with the most money and biggest weapons.

Gang graffiti decorated nearly every rusting surface. Drew wondered how much Everett's men had paid, in dollars or blood, to gain temporary control of this area. The ripe scents of trash, grease and stale fuel stained the thick, humid air. Drew hoped to turn his unfortunate affinity and experience with this kind of place into an advantage. Surely the powers that be would grant him that much, giving him a chance to create something good from the sorry remnants of his career.

"Where are we?"

Andy's small voice sliced right into Drew's heart.

"I'm not sure," Addi said, "but we're together."

Drew didn't turn, picturing mother and son holding hands as Everett's men pushed them into the dreary interior of the warehouse. Two cars were parked near a wide garage door. Three battered couches and an oversize flat-screen television made up a seating area in the far corner. The windows of what might have been a supervisor's office were covered with peeling black paint. An odd mix of industrial equipment was scattered around the space, but the stack of crates along one wall looked too new to be anything but valuable.

Drugs or guns. Drew hoped like hell this gang was the gunrunning sort. He could hardly beat the crap out of this crew with drugs. He needed a weapon.

The office door opened as they approached and out stepped Everett, looking preppy in a short-sleeved polo shirt, creased khaki slacks and loafers; Drew understood Addi's comment about polish and charm. It wasn't hard to picture them as an attractive power couple, able to give Andy every advantage. Drew wanted to bloody that smug face beyond all recognition.

"Addison, so good to see you again." Ignoring Drew, Everett reached for her hands, hesitating when he saw she was cuffed. "That's ridiculous. Take those off."

The driver shook his head. "Not recommended."

Drew smothered a grin, remembering how Addi had clocked the other man when he'd grabbed Andy with too much force.

"She won't hurt me," Everett insisted. To Addi, he said, "This can be over in minutes. A few answers and you and Andy can be on your way."

The driver made a snorting sound as he sliced through the zip ties binding Addi's hands. Whatever delusions Everett was under, Drew knew they weren't supposed to survive this meeting.

As soon as her hands were free, Addi slapped Everett across the face hard enough to knock him back a step. The red handprint bloomed instantly across his freshly shaved cheek. Drew wanted to crow with pride.

"Told you so," the driver muttered.

"Screw you," Everett said to the driver. "Keep these two under control." He shoved Addi toward the office. "I just need a few minutes."

Drew knew she wouldn't break, yet it took all his will-power not to make eye contact as Everett led her away. Neither Everett nor his men could know how invested he was, or they'd kill him where he stood.

ADDISON HEARD CRAIG close the door behind her and she rubbed her elbow where his hand had dug hard into her arm. In all the time she'd known him, he'd never shown a ruthless side. Oh, she'd known he was a formidable force in a financial negotiation or conference room, she'd known he kept fit, but he'd never demonstrated this dark edge. She supposed that was why the truth of his illegal dealings had been such a shock.

He shoved her into a cold metal folding chair and leaned back against an old metal desk, folding his arms across his chest. "Let's do this the easy way," he suggested. "Tell me what you think you know and who you've told about your theories."

"What theories?"

"This isn't a game or a courtroom, Addison. You ran away from home flinging accusations at me." His quiet, unflappable tone strained her composure. "It's been expensive tracking you down and I intend to make sure the investment was worth it." He reached out, running a fingertip across her sunburned cheek. "You forgot the sunblock."

She refused to flinch. If he was focused on her, Drew could get Andy out of harm's way. Getting that sunburn while her men had been fishing might be the last truly happy moment of her life. She wouldn't let Craig cheapen it. "How did you find me?"

He shook his head, his eyes hard as stone. "I'll ask the questions. You'll answer them."

"And then you'll let us go," she said, refusing to make

it a question. Though he nodded she wasn't buying it. She wanted to rail, to shout and scream that he wouldn't get away with any of this. Not after what he'd done and what she assumed he would do in the coming moments.

"Addison, who have you talked to?"

"No one." Technically it was true. Talking to Drew didn't count, as he was officially "deceased" and she hadn't shared any details of Craig's activities. She'd sent emails and one snail mail package as insurance. Her stomach clenched as she realized that insurance would be used if Craig had his way here.

He blew out a heavy sigh. "You're wasting my time. I wouldn't have been arrested unless you blew the whistle on me. You're the only one who had access."

She pulled on the composure that had served her so well through depositions and negotiations during her legal career. "I don't have any idea what you mean."

Craig leaned forward, his lips twisted in a menacing grin. "Why did you run from home?"

She nearly blurted out the "adventure" answer she'd given to Andy, but she didn't want to divert Craig's attention. "There was a death in the family. My presence was requested."

"Bull." Craig leaned back. "You don't have any family beyond your son."

"That isn't true." Mama Leonie was family. Nico was family. Bernadette and Professor Hastings were family. Maybe not by blood, but some bonds went deeper, some roots were stronger. She didn't expect a money-grubbing sellout like Craig to understand that.

"Answer me!" Craig shouted. "Who else have you told?"

She shook her head. "No one."

Craig grabbed her shoulders, shaking her hard enough to make her teeth clack together. "Addison, cooperate."

The chair rocked back when he released her with a violent shove. "Answer my questions now or I can't protect you."

A chill of fear skittered down her spine. She didn't fight it, embracing it instead and using it to hold her ground. "I have nothing to say to you, Craig."

He stared at her for another long moment, then moved around her chair and tapped twice on the door. In the interminable silence, she heard the squeak and scrape of footsteps in the warehouse coming closer to the office.

Two men hauled in Drew and tied him to a chair at the other end of the room. Addison felt a wave of dread. Her hope of him saving Andy fizzled and died. Her son was alone with these terrible men. She had to find a way out of this nightmare or her dream of a family would be crushed again.

"Who is this?" Craig demanded.

My heart. My love. "A friend," she said, hoping to protect Drew.

Craig snorted. "Here's how it will go, Addison," he began. "I'll ask you a question. You'll answer me, or your *friend* will suffer. Is that clear?"

"We don't know anything about your problems," she replied. Drew didn't want her to talk, so she wouldn't talk.

"We'll find out, won't we?"

She kept her gaze on Craig, not risking eye contact with Drew. If Craig discovered this was Andy's real father, if he discovered how much she loved him, Drew would pay. And he'd already been through more than any person should endure.

"Why did you run from San Francisco?"

"I came out here to help a family in need," she replied honestly. She and Andy were a family, and they'd definitely needed to get away from Craig.

Craig raised a finger and one of the men behind Drew came around and punched him in the belly.

She closed her eyes. "That was an honest answer."

Craig bent over, bracing his hands on his knees to look her in the eye. "They are going to rig a battery to your friend and electrocute him for every lie you tell me."

"Craig, this is insane. I can't help you."

He gave another signal and suddenly Drew's body jerked and seized. Addison's resolve faltered.

"Don't talk, Addi," Drew rasped as his body recovered.

"Addi?" Craig turned on his heel. "You told me you despised that nickname, that it was weak."

"Is there a question in there?"

Craig flung an arm toward Drew. "Who is he to you?"

"My best friend," she said as her heart raced on with more of the truth she would never share with Craig. *My heart. My should-be husband. My son's father. My soul mate.* She'd been delusional to believe she could be satisfied with bland contentment when she harbored all this passion for Drew. Alive or dead, no one else had meant the same to her. Or to Andy.

"I was your best friend. We were supposed to be on our honeymoon now."

"With blood money!" she shouted, furious.

"It all spends the same," Craig said with a slimy smirk. "You can't judge me, Addison. I know who your clients are and how you 'negotiate.'" He mocked her with air quotes.

"I never traded innocent lives for personal gain!"

"No?" Craig signaled and Drew's body started quaking again.

"Stop it!"

"Tell me who you've told."

"Don't talk!" Drew whispered between electricity-induced spasms.

Addison wouldn't dishonor Drew by giving in now, no matter how much it hurt her to watch him suffer. "We'll get out of this," she promised.

"You want out of this? Tell me the truth!"

Addison shook her head.

Craig scrubbed a hand over his mouth and closed his eyes. "Get the boy."

"No!" Drew and Addison shouted at the same time, but Craig's men were already moving, dragging Drew away.

Tears streaked down her face. "You can't do this," she cried out. "He trusts you."

"Your choice," Craig said as Andy was led into the office. "Whatever happens now is on you."

Andy's eyes were wide as they led him to another chair out of her reach. "Mama?"

She blinked away the tears, determined to be strong for her son. "Don't worry. We'll be out of here soon." As long as Drew was breathing, as long as her heart beat, they would see that Andy survived.

"Well?" Craig raised a finger, bringing those horrific battery cables too close to her son's small body.

The blood in her veins turned to ice. "If you so much as pluck a hair from his head, I'll kill you."

Craig laughed. "Start talking, Addison, or I'll prove just what an incompetent and incapable mother you are."

She swallowed, her jaw clenched as she tried to smile at her son. "Andy, get your stopwatch ready." Anything to distract him. "Press Start when I say go and Stop when I stop talking."

"'Kay." He chewed on his lower lip as he concentrated.

"Go." She met Craig's hard gaze. "About six weeks ago, while I was cooking dinner, your phone beeped with a text message and I checked it. One of the names was familiar. You remember the ambassador's assistant arrested for human trafficking?"

Craig scowled, gesturing for her to continue.

"Curious and a bit worried on your behalf, I started doing some digging into your financials. I didn't actually speak to anyone about you. I gave the authorities a place to start looking into a troubling association. I trusted that if you were innocent you'd cooperate. If you had been innocent they wouldn't have arrested you."

"But you left town."

Andy interrupted, announcing the time on his watch. She beamed at him. "Good job."

She looked up at Craig. "I left because I didn't want Andy getting dragged into your problems."

"Too late."

"Apparently," she agreed. "How did you find us?"

"It doesn't matter."

Oh, she was sure that it did. If Craig's contacts had compromised Drew's friend Casey, they were out of allies.

"Who else did you notify about your discovery?"

She shook her head.

"How many volts do you think his little body can take?"

"Shut up, Craig," she snapped, adrenaline pounding through her system. She might not have Drew's skills, but she had the benefit of being in full-blown mama-bear mode. "I've cooperated. Now let us go. I promise you'll never hear from us again."

"Not so fast. I know you too well. You always have a contingency plan."

"Not this time," she insisted. "There wasn't any time. Discovering what you've been doing spooked me. I did what I could, then did what I felt best protected Andy."

"I don't believe you."

She shrugged. "That isn't my problem. You did this to yourself," she started, unable to keep a leash on her temper. "Quit lashing out at us with your guilty conscience. I've answered your questions. Now let us go."

"Who else knows, Addison?"

"No one!" Professor Hastings wouldn't open the package unless she failed to make contact on the tenth.

"I'm satisfied," a voice declared. Addison hadn't noticed the cell phone on the desktop. Craig must have had it on speaker this entire time. "Clean up and come in."

"Yes, sir," Craig said, his face a mixture of relief and regret. He tucked the phone into his pocket and turned to the men flanking Andy. "You heard him. Let's clean up."

Addison cringed as they urged her son out of the chair. He raced across the room and took her hand. "It'll be okay," she said, determined those words wouldn't become a lie. "You did a great job."

"I know," he said, his smile wobbling. "Drew told me the secret of how to be brave."

"Good." Probably some quote from one of their favorite comic books. Whatever it was, she was grateful for the positive influence. Andy's hand felt so small in her grasp. She vowed to find a way out of this. Her son would grow into a man and she and Drew would be there to watch and support him along the way. She had to seize the first opportunity, she thought, praying she'd recognize it. "You'll have to tell me that secret sometime," she said as they were shoved roughly into the back of one of the cars parked inside the warehouse.

"But he said you taught the secret to him."

"Is that so?"

"Did you forget it?"

"Of course not," she said, though she had no idea what

secret Drew had credited to her. Whatever it was made Andy feel better and that was the important factor.

"I love you," Andy said, scooting across the backseat of the car to sit close to her side. "Where are we going now?"

"I'm not sure," she admitted, battling back fear. *Where had they taken Drew?*

The driver twisted around to face them. "You like to swim, kid?"

"Yes," Andy replied warily.

"Well, I'm supposed to find the perfect swamp swimming hole for you," he said with a nasty smile.

Addison didn't need a translator to get the hidden meaning. Craig—or whoever was calling the shots here—planned to silence them permanently. "I don't have my swimsuit, Mom."

"It'll be okay," she assured him.

"Or dry clothes. Or a place to put my watch," he added. A worried frown clouded his face.

She wanted to tear Craig apart for this. "We'll figure it out," she said. "I don't want you to worry about anything."

"We can't leave without Drew!"

She glanced around, seeing no sign of him. "He'll find us," she said. Or they would find him. She wasn't giving him up without a fight, whether or not he wanted to stay in their lives after this.

"Oh, you'll see him soon, kid. It'll be a regular family picnic."

With that cryptic comment the driver started the car. The big overhead bay door rose with a groan and scrape of neglected metal and a rattle of chains across a squeaky pulley.

As bright sunlight flooded the space, Addison shielded her eyes against the glare. This man planned to kill her and her son out in the swamp, where nature would be more than happy to clean up the mess. Odd as it sounded, even in her thoughts, she felt a surge of gratitude that Craig knew so little about her.

Chapter Sixteen

From the backseat of the black SUV, Drew watched the white sedan pull out of the warehouse and take the lead. He had three men with him, two in the front seats and one back here with him. That left only one or two with Addi and Andy, which gave her a fighting chance.

He'd heard the orders to dump their bodies in the swamp and had been overwhelmed with relief when he'd seen her and their son walking to the car rather than being carried. No big surprise that Everett was too squeamish to do the dirty work.

When Everett had taken Addi into the office, Drew had used the distraction to turn on the transmitter. With Andy's help, he'd managed to drop the device into the couch where they'd been ordered to wait. He hoped Casey could mobilize a team quickly enough to snare Everett.

Now if only his body would just get over the inconvenient and unexpected electric shock. It felt as though his blood would never stop sizzling. His thoughts were clear, which was a plus, and any pain was repressed by his determination to rescue his wife and son.

Wife. The word was as soothing, as easy in his mind as swinging gently in a hammock on a shady porch. He wasn't sure when his brain had finally accepted the status his heart had never relinquished. He wasn't sure it mattered. Whether he had to wait an hour or another ten years for her to love him again, Addi was his wife in every way that mattered. No one would tear them apart again and no one would cheat him of another precious minute as a family.

"Can I have some water?" He tipped his head toward the bottle of water in the cup holder in the console.

"No," said the man seated next to him.

Drew snorted. "Are you planning to give me a last meal?"

"Hell no." This denial came from the driver. "You don't have long to suffer."

Through the windshield, Drew saw the sedan with Addi and Andy two car lengths ahead. No other guards were in her car and both drivers were being very cautious on the return trip to the bayou.

"A little compassion could make a big difference," Drew said.

"Compassion? For who?" The guard in the passenger seat snorted. "I'll shoot you right here if you don't shut your trap."

"You shut up," the driver balked. "Unless you want to detail his brains out of the upholstery."

"Why work that hard? We can dump the car near the projects and it's someone else's problem."

Drew nearly laughed as the men argued with each other, confident their captive was no threat. Keep believing that, he thought, fueling the delusion by slumping in his seat and leaning against the door.

They left the paved roads a few minutes later, following the sedan into the shady wilds of the bayou. This part of the world had always intrigued him with how quickly the terrain shifted from polished civilization to raw and unforgiving. Of course, the dangers shifted, too, from man to nature. At least nature didn't pick sides; it went after any threatening intrusion with equal fervor.

"Better head deeper," Drew muttered. "You dump us here and our bodies will pop up too soon."

"What do you know about it?"

"More than you do if you're thinking of stopping here."

"Ignore him," the guard in the front passenger seat said. "We do it the way the boss wants."

"Does your boss even understand the bayous?"

The guard in the backseat plowed a big fist into Drew's jaw. "You're wasting your last words."

Drew shrugged but kept silent. Wherever they stopped, he knew which man in this car to attack first. He only hoped Addi had figured out the same weak link in her car.

He hated that she and Andy were scared, but he also knew she had a well of strength and courage to draw from. Any woman who'd raised a child dealt with any number of false alarms and real scares on her own. Andy was a good kid, but that didn't mean he hadn't stirred up his fair share of trouble along the way. Addi's courage wouldn't falter, despite the overwhelming odds. The soul-deep fighter in her hadn't changed.

When he lined that up with her insider knowledge of the swamps and bayous out here, he felt a ray of hope flickering like sunlight through the cypress branches high above. Everett might have hired quality muscle to do his dirty work, but Drew and Addi held the real advantage.

Smart men would take them way back into the bayou, shoot them and sink their bodies in the deepest water. He didn't think this crew would be that patient. A few minutes later the team proved him right as they followed a dusty service track into a protected wildlife area.

"Triple homicide on federal land." He shook his head. "That won't end well for you."

The guard in the backseat pulled his gun and aimed it at Drew's temple. "You were saying?"

Drew stared him down, willing his body to hold still. The best time to strike was yet to come. He let them pull him from the car and managed to maintain an outward air of defeat as the driver of the sedan hauled Addi and Andy to the bank of the swamp.

It was as if time slowed, each second standing well apart from the previous and the next. Every beat of his heart might have been as long as a minute as his mind cataloged each detail. His senses were primed, his body ready to react. Drew felt the brush of the air on his skin, heard the rustling of leaves above and the absolute silence of the mirrorlike water.

Only one other time had he felt this timeless, out-of-body sensation. He looked around as they prodded him to stand next to his son. No surprise how Everett's men planned to proceed. The guard with the gun would raise his arm and it would be a simple double-tap to the back of each skull. In moments, the only two people he loved in this world would be dead before their bodies fell into the water, a feast for the scavengers.

Andy, his hands free, reached up to hold Drew's cuffed hands. "Mom says it'll be okay."

Drew looked down into those wide brown eyes, so like his, and saw more awareness than any nearly eight-year-old kid should know. "She's right." One way or another they would all be okay. He scanned the water and what he could see of the banks. Whatever the next moments held, he would ensure the two of them made it out alive.

Over their son's head he met Addi's gaze. Her eyes were bright, lit with the dangerous fire of a protective mother ready to do battle. "Trust me?" He slid his gaze to the water and back to her.

She smiled at him. "Always."

Behind them the men were debating who should shoot Andy. Drew shifted his weight, bracing his feet wide. His hands gripping Andy's, he twisted around. "Let the kid go."

"Hell no," the man who'd driven the sedan said.

"He's a kid." Drew was trying to push anything that might resemble a sympathy button in one of these four bastards. "A little kid."

"Who shouldn't spend the rest of his life missing his mommy." The sedan driver circled his finger. "We're doing him a favor," he sneered. "Now cooperate and we'll make it quick. For them," he added with a laugh.

Drew shook his head. "I'm sorry, son." He squeezed Andy's wrists. Turning back to the water, he tossed Andy out into the shallow water of the swamp.

Reacting instantly, Addi lunged for the nearest of Everett's men, taking him down with a shoulder tackle a professional football player would envy.

It amazed Drew that he could fall any deeper in love with the woman, especially amid a fight for their lives, but it happened.

Guns fired in a rapid burst of violent noise, but Drew didn't care. Andy would find shelter, Addi was holding her own with one guard and the three remaining men were no real challenge. He rushed forward to safeguard his family, feeling a smile bloom across his face as he swung his restrained hands out, batting away the executioner's gun, then plowing an elbow into the man's jaw. When he dropped to all fours, Drew kicked him hard enough to crack ribs and leave him breathless. "Stay down," he growled, picking up the man's gun.

A blow to Drew's kidneys caused more irritation than pain and he countered with a sharp, swinging kick to the second man's head. He put a bullet through his knee to keep him down and tucked that pistol into his waistband. Three down, one to go.

"Andy?" he called out.

"He's safe," Addi replied.

Drew glanced back and saw Addi holding the guard she'd tackled at gunpoint. "Shoot the tires," Drew shouted as the weak link from the SUV raced for the vehicles.

She put a bullet into one tire on each car, even as the jerk turned and shot recklessly in their direction. Drew's vision turned red at the edges and he fired back, calling out to confirm Addi hadn't been hit.

The man dropped his gun and begged for mercy, scooting backward as Drew advanced. "I'll cooperate, give a statement, whatever you want," he stammered.

"How thoughtful." Drew backhanded him. "You missed your chance for any mercy from me."

"Drew," Addi said from behind him. "We're okay."

"We'll put them in the sedan and push it into the swamp," he said.

"You can't do that," the man with cracked ribs protested. "Th-the gators!"

Drew stood tall, keeping the gun on the pleading man. "You're right. We could get fined for animal abuse."

"I'm willing to risk it if you are," Addi said, coming up beside him.

He just stared at her, amazed and grateful. "Where's Andy?"

"Safe," she assured him. "He scrambled up the bank and into a tree."

Drew followed her gaze. Andy's clothes were wet, but

he was tucked in tight in the strong bracket of a tree. "Good job."

"My watch still works!" He pumped his small fist. "Can I come down and help push the car?"

Drew thought it sounded like a fine idea. "Sure."

He stepped back, swaying a bit. His vision blurred, making it difficult to get his bearings. "Addi?"

"Right here."

He didn't believe her; her voice sounded too far away. The adrenaline had carried him this far, but on the downward slope of the rush, he felt the wounds where a bullet, maybe two, had tagged him. "No big deal, Addi. Take Andy…get safe…" He couldn't catch his breath, felt his heart thundering in his chest. He shook his head to clear his vision, but it didn't help.

"I'm not leaving you. Let me take a look."

Stupid to shoot out the car tires, he thought, sliding hard to the ground as his knees gave. He should've had her shoot the bastard. He tried to slow his thoughts, reassess his injuries. Damn it, this wasn't about blood loss or injury. They were only flesh wounds. He was having a panic attack.

"I'll be fine," he said through clenched teeth. He shook his wrists. "Get these off of me."

He told himself he'd done well and had held it together when it mattered. Still, they weren't off the hook yet. Everett's men were down for now, but the survival instinct would have them attacking Addi again if they had an opportunity.

Drew tried to stand, but Addi held him down with a firm hand on his shoulder. "Stay put a minute."

He stared up at the sky, hoping the clear blue day would calm him down. No such luck. He closed his eyes tight, fighting against the useless anxiety. She still needed him.

He needed his body to get back on task. He heard her snapping out orders and felt his hands finally drop free. A small weight landed on his chest and he opened his eyes as Andy wrapped his skinny arms around Drew in a fierce hug.

"What's wrong with you?" Andy asked.

What wasn't wrong with him? How could he explain post-traumatic stress and a full-blown panic attack in terms Andy would understand? "I'll be okay in a minute."

"You got shot."

Drew glanced at his biceps where blood stained the torn sleeve of his gray T-shirt. "Looks like it."

"Does it hurt?"

"Not much." Not nearly as much as fighting the fear that he'd be locked up again, away from his son and the woman who should be his wife.

"Then why don't you breathe right?"

"Andy, hush," Addi scolded.

"He's fine," Drew said on a weak laugh, waving off her concern. His breath shuddered in and out and his lungs resumed normal function. To his surprise, answering the questions helped give him a focal point, something the shrinks suggested early in his treatment when the memories and nightmares had overwhelmed him.

"Did you see which one of them shot me?"

"That one." Andy pointed to one of the men on the ground near the edge of the swamp. "You kick really high."

"Thanks." He ruffled his son's hair. "The army taught me."

"Like Captain America?"

"I think the shield would've been helpful."

"You could've knocked them all out with one throw. Before…"

Drew saw the moment Andy remembered Nico. He pulled Andy in for a hard hug. "The bad guys will pay for everything they did. Your mom and I will see to that."

"If Nico could've kicked like you…"

It wouldn't have made any difference, but Drew understood the real problem. "Want me to teach you that kick?"

Andy nodded. "Will you throw me again? It was fun."

"Maybe later." Into the clear water of a pool. Between guns and alligators, he'd known this particular corner of the bayou was the lesser danger.

Andy looked from Drew to his mom. "What'll we do with all of 'em now?"

"I'm still for putting them in the swamp," Drew said.

"Me, too," Andy crowed, bouncing to his feet. "Let's go."

"Drew," Addi chided. "What happened to caring about the wildlife?"

"If we use the sedan, someone will come haul it out sooner rather than later. It's a classic."

She rolled her eyes. "Fine."

The man protested as he and the others were loaded at gunpoint into the car. None of them seemed to realize what Addi had known from the start: the swamp wasn't terribly deep here. The men would be uncomfortable and, because of their ignorance, they'd be too frightened to move. Hopefully that fear would give law enforcement time to get out here and arrest the four of them.

ADDISON WATCHED, TRYING not to laugh, when the bargaining started. The four men had no idea they were safer in the swamp than on dry land with her. She was more than a little disconcerted knowing how easy it would've been, how good it would've felt to kill the men so willing to murder her family.

Family. It was a beautiful word and it felt more real now than it had since her ruined wedding day.

She kept sneaking looks at Drew as he and Andy pushed the car into the water. If anything nibbled at those four men in the car, she wouldn't be the least bit sorry for it. She'd had her chance, known as she held the gun that a self-defense plea would've assured her acquittal, but she'd managed to do the right thing. In no small part because her son was watching, but she'd taken her cues from Drew, as well.

She'd been awestruck watching him fight, heedless of the personal danger as he overpowered the other armed guards. Her mind zipped back to the moment before the fight, when nothing more than a look had fully explained his intentions.

How was it they still had that connection? Without words, she'd known he would get Andy out of harm's way. She hadn't expected him to throw Andy into the swamp, but knowing the threat in the water was minimal so close to the service road, it made perfect sense.

The men shouted, screamed, really, as the car partially filled with water. She had zero sympathy, smiling as Drew and Andy swaggered back to join her near the SUV. "There's a spare tire."

Drew grinned and her pulse fluttered. "That will get us back to town."

"Then what?"

"I suggest we find a landline and make a phone call so Everett doesn't slip away."

"I'd like to wring his neck."

"Because he fooled you?" Andy asked.

How much had Andy heard the other night? Or today, for that matter?

"That's one reason." Addi wondered how best to

answer the question. Only a few weeks ago he'd looked up to Craig as a father figure. "He did some bad things," she began carefully, searching for the right words. "When we met him, when we let him be part of our lives, I think he was more of a good guy."

"He changed?"

"Yes." Drew knelt down, looking Andy right in the eye. "Craig Everett was good to you once, right?"

"Yes." Andy's eyes gleamed with tears. "I don't want him to marry us anymore."

"Not a chance," Addison said, smoothing his hair back from his face. "You never have to see him again."

"He won't ever be my dad?"

"Absolutely not," Addison replied, looking at Drew. They really needed to tell their son the truth. But it felt like a big risk when she didn't know what kind of life Drew wanted.

Bodyguard duty was one thing. Rekindling their friendship and rediscovering their long-buried passion was understandable. But what did Drew want from her after this crisis was over?

He'd made the choice once before—to leave her alone with her new life. She understood his reasoning but couldn't help wondering what choice he'd make now.

"Let's get that tire changed and get moving," Drew said, interrupting her thoughts. "I don't want to risk them getting brave enough to bolt."

"They can't be brave," Andy said as she boosted him into the backseat.

"What do you mean?" she asked.

"The secret to bravery," he replied, clearly exasperated to be stating the obvious.

Except it wasn't obvious to her.

"They don't have someone to love," Andy said. "Or

someone who loves them back to make them brave. Did I get it right, Drew?"

"You sure did."

Addison stared at Drew for a moment before realizing that he needed her help changing the flat tire. He called out for Andy to time them. They finished in record time. She rounded the car and climbed into the driver's seat.

"Maybe I should stay," he muttered, his gaze on the partially submerged sedan as if he were suddenly uncertain where they went from here. "I can make sure they don't get away."

"No." She wasn't letting him out of her sight. Not until they had things well and truly settled. "We stick together."

Chapter Seventeen

The drive back into the city went by in a blur and Addison's thoughts were a jumble of questions she couldn't answer. Questions for Drew, but she wouldn't ask until she had a few answers for herself. What did she want next? Returning to San Francisco felt wrong, even if she took the rest of the summer to help Nico's family recover from the devastating loss.

What if she moved back home? Was this a better place to raise her son?

"Don't worry, Addi," Drew said. "Everett won't escape."

"It's not that."

"No?" He sounded surprised "Then what?"

"Just about everything else," she admitted. "But it can wait until we know Craig is in custody and we get you patched up."

Drew nodded, his lips pressed into a thin line.

"Are you hurting?"

He shook his head. "Let's drive by the warehouse."

"Okay." She knew he wouldn't put them in danger, and this time they had the advantage of loaded guns. "I still think we should've used one of the phones."

"We can't risk tipping off Everett's contact and giving whoever the hell it is another head start."

"It's hard to fathom any one person having this kind of reach."

"You took extreme measures when you fled."

"I did." And Drew had found her anyway. She glanced into the backseat, pleased to see Andy gazing out the window. Bless his heart. She didn't want all this to haunt his dreams. He was just a little boy.

Sirens blared in the oncoming lanes, and law enforcement vehicles sped their way before veering toward the warehouse Craig had been hiding in.

"I hope they're on our side," she said, goose bumps raising the hair on her arms. If Craig managed to escape again, she might never be free.

"Let's stop here," Drew said.

Addison pulled to a halt behind the perimeter created by men in various law enforcement uniforms.

"Open your door slowly," he instructed Addison. "Andy, stay right where you are."

"Yes, sir," her little brave boy affirmed.

"Oh!" She pointed through the windshield. "There's Craig." Her breath caught in her chest. "In handcuffs." She hoped it wasn't just for show.

"Consider him locked down for good," Drew said. A satisfied smile tilted his lips.

"How can you be sure?"

"Because the man next to him is Thomas Casey. The guy who recruited me to find you."

She wanted to believe, to share Drew's confidence. "You sound sure of him."

"There's only one other person I trust as much." His eyes darted to the rearview mirror. "Well, two."

Addison looked at him, but Andy asked the question she couldn't find her voice to pose. "You mean you trust him like you trust us?"

He nodded, holding Addison's gaze. "I do."

This wasn't the time for tears, but she'd pined all of Andy's young life to hear those two words from Drew.

He reached across the seat and brushed away the tear that rolled down her cheek. "Don't worry," he said softly, somehow understanding her fears. "We'll figure everything out."

She nodded, her throat clogged with her heart and all her churning emotions. Hope and love were easy to identify, but they were shadowed by uncertainty. She knew what she wanted, but would Drew want that, too?

The man Drew pointed out turned their way, striding through the chaos to meet them. "Come on," Drew said. "I'll introduce you and then you'll understand why I'm so confident this is the last you'll see of Everett."

"All right," she managed, wanting to believe him. As Drew made introductions, Addison studied Director Casey. There was a hard edge under the business-casual polish, but his sincerity as he addressed her son won her over.

"Do you have enough information now?" she asked abruptly, unable to tolerate any more small talk.

"I might have a few more questions, but thanks to both of you, the trap my deputy set worked perfectly. We have Everett as well as his contact inside the Department of State."

Addison sucked in a breath and looked at Drew, thinking of the implications. "That is a long reach." Department of State personnel were typically informed of military operations around the globe. An insider leak like that might even have led to Drew's capture.

"Well, it's cut short now. I anticipate closure on several questionable situations as we investigate."

She shivered, thinking of how terrible it would've been

if she'd exchanged vows with Craig. "He wasn't like that when we met." Her gaze drifted toward the warehouse, confirming that Craig remained in cuffs and was surrounded by hard men in black tactical gear. "I don't know when or what made him change."

"Thank you for doing the right thing," Casey said. Turning to Drew, he added, "We have a team searching the bayous for you." He reached for the radio clipped to his belt. "I need to call them back."

"Actually," Drew said, "they should probably pick up Everett's team."

"They were gonna feed us to the gators." Andy's voice held more pride than fear. "But Drew stopped them and then we sank their car."

Addison bit her lip, letting the conversation play out. Her son had earned a few bragging rights after everything they'd survived.

"You look a little wet. Did you fall in?"

"Drew threw me into the swamp so I wasn't in danger."

"I see." Casey arched an eyebrow at Drew. "I'm glad they didn't hurt any of you."

Addison's mind flashed to Drew being tortured with a battery, beaten and shot. She opened her mouth, but Drew put his arm around her. "We all came through."

"We did," Andy agreed. "Mom and Dad—I mean Drew—attacked the bad guys just like Captain America." He tipped his face to Drew. "Without the shield. I watched it all from a tree. But then I helped sink the car."

Addison lost the rest of the conversation. Andy had called Drew Dad. In her heart the moment felt as big as when he'd taken his first steps or the first time he'd called her Mama. She slid a look at Drew, but his impassive expression gave her no hint to his feelings. He must've heard it. Would it change anything?

"I might just need a statement from you, young man," Casey was saying.

Andy's eyes went wide. "From me?"

"You think you can describe the people you saw?"

"Yes, sir!"

"If it's okay with your mom, we'll step over here and you can tell me everything."

Andy looked up at her hopefully.

"Go on," she said. Apparently Casey's instincts were accurate and he'd noticed she and Drew needed a moment to themselves.

"You were hurt," she began. "Shot and—" she had to swallow "—tortured again. Because of me." The tremor started in her hands as her calm facade cracked apart.

Drew caught her hands and pressed them between his. "You didn't cause any of this. Everett did and he'll pay the penalty."

She leaned close, dropping her forehead to his shoulder, breathing in his warm scent. She could be strong and still be allowed her weak moments. It had always been that way with him. "Thank you."

"For what?"

"For all of it." She forced herself to look up, to meet his warm brown gaze. "I couldn't have saved Andy without you."

"You'd have found a way." His big hands smoothed across her shoulders and down her spine, as if he might simply erase the tension built up there. How could a touch calm and soothe in one moment and ignite a whole new kind of delicious energy in the next? It was just one more of Drew's many talents.

"How long before you head back to San Francisco?"

"I have a few calls to make." First to Professor Hastings and then to her boss to resign. After that, it would be reaching out to Bernadette and Nico's family. Taking a step back, afraid of being hurt by Drew's reaction, she took a big breath and blurted out her decision. "I'm not going back to California. I've decided to stay out here. Andy and I need…" *You*, she thought, but she wouldn't put that kind of pressure on him. "We need a change of pace. I have enough cushion built up until I find work that suits me in this area."

He reached out, winding a curl of her hair around his finger. He'd done that the night they'd met. "You're moving back to the family farm?"

She nodded. "I think Andy will like it out there and any adventures we have will be a thousand times safer."

"It must be pretty run-down."

"No." His face fell and she wished she'd kept the truth to herself, if only so he'd be enticed to help her make a few repairs. "There's a realty service that's kept it up for me."

"Surprised Everett didn't know about it."

She'd never told Craig much about her past. It hadn't felt relevant then, but now she understood it had been a way of keeping Drew's memory safe and treasured. He'd been the gold standard no other man could measure up to.

She was being an idiot here. They both were. "You could come with us. Give yourself a chance to heal up before you head back to whatever is waiting for you in Detroit."

"Is that what you want?"

"Which part?" She wanted the dream that had been snatched from her so many years ago. She wanted family dinners, picnics and baseball games. She wanted movie nights, stargazing and all the joys that came with sharing life's ups and downs with her soul mate. If he wanted that, too.

The words tangled in her throat, so much to say that

she didn't know where to start. She pressed up on her toes, her hands clutching his shoulders for balance as she kissed him, letting him feel everything she wanted.

"I want you to be happy, Drew," she said, breaking the kiss. "This time your happiness has to come first."

HIS HANDS RESTED lightly at her trim waist. Happy? Did he dare take what he thought she was offering? "The day I met you I understood what being happy felt like. It sounds cheesy, but it's true."

She pressed her lips together, her pale blue eyes bright. After everything he thought he knew about her, with all the desperate hope crashing through him, he didn't trust himself to read her reactions correctly. Nothing for it but to barrel on. If he held back now, he'd never shake free of the regret. "I never stopped loving you, Addi. Loving you got me through the darkest days of my life. Give me another chance. Give *us* another chance to have what we once dreamed of. Please."

Her gaze drifted over to where Casey and Andy were talking. "He called you Dad."

"I heard." It wasn't the response to his revelations he'd anticipated, but he wasn't above using Andy as a way in. He wanted to get to know his son and he believed with a little time he could win Addi back, too.

"He's a smart kid." A tear slipped down her cheek and she swiped it away impatiently. "You're the only man I ever wanted him to address that way."

"Does that mean…"

"I never stopped loving what we had, Drew." Her words were tender, but she stepped back again. "I don't think my heart is capable of loving another man like I loved you."

Past tense. Damn it. Sensing the worst, he shoved his hands into his pockets to keep from grabbing her. Every muscle in his body was ready to hold and cling, but he worried that if he made a move before she was ready, he'd scare her away.

"You should know what you're getting into," she said, her eyes on their son.

"Tell me." Good or bad, nothing she could say would sway him from wanting to be part of their lives, however she'd have him. They had a son who wanted and needed his dad and his mom.

"The routine can be monotonous," she began. "School, homework, bedtime."

So far, no problem.

"Moods—"

"Yours or his?"

"Both," she admitted, her lips tilting. "There's soccer and laundry and meals."

"I like to eat," he said, warming to the topic. "I can even cook."

"This is serious."

"I know."

"A commitment."

"I'm ready." He caught the quick hitch of her breath, pressed his advantage. "Whether you can love me again or not, I love our son. Let me be there for him."

"But I want you to be there for *you*." She crossed her arms and glared. "What about your community work in Detroit?"

He shook his head. "Sweetheart, it was a place to hide. Those programs are in good hands, though I wouldn't mind checking in on the kids periodically. I was marking time, that's all, just to keep from interfering in the life you'd created without me."

"There hasn't been a day since we met that you weren't

in my life." She tapped her fingers against her heart. "I've been raising Drew 2.0."

"And doing a fine job." He couldn't stand it; he draped an arm around her shoulder. "Let's go the rest of the way together."

"You mean it?"

He nodded. "We have another shot, Addi. Either push me away or tell me you'll marry me so we can get to work on the other three kids we wanted to have."

"You remember that?" she asked on a shaky laugh.

He moved so they were facing each other again. He wouldn't leave room for any doubts. "I remember everything. We wanted four kids and the farmhouse for summer vacations, and by this time I was supposed to be looking for a unit that wouldn't send me away quite so often."

"We were good at the long-distance thing."

"We're better together." He kissed her until they were both breathless. "You were going to teach law once the kids were all in school. On our twenty-fifth anniversary I was going to re-create our honeymoon."

"You thought that far ahead?"

"From the moment you agreed to marry me."

"Where were we going on our honeymoon?"

He had her now, he knew it. "Eight years ago, it was Belize."

"Oh, that sounds nice."

"Now I'm thinking Disneyland."

"Disneyland?"

"It's a family-friendly kind of honeymoon. We'll get a suite," he added with a suggestive wink. "Plus, it puts a positive spin on these major changes in Andy's life and gives him a chance to say goodbye to his friends."

"Don't say that too loudly."

"Why not? Does he hate theme parks?"

"He loves them," she said, gazing up at him. Her mouth curved in her most beautiful smile, her beautiful eyes glowing with happiness. "You'll be an amazing dad."

"I'm crossing my fingers that I'll be half as good as you've been as a mom."

"What if I'm a lousy wife?"

"Not a chance."

"You sound pretty certain. I've been doing the solo act a long time. What if I'm too set in my ways?"

"Not a chance," he repeated. "From where I'm standing you've been making our dreams come true."

"But the most vital piece was missing," she murmured, lacing her fingers with his. "You."

"I'm yours for as long as you'll have me," he said. "I love you, Addison."

"I love you, too. I always will."

"So say you'll marry me and let's start making up for lost time."

"I'll marry you." She wrapped her arms around his neck and pressed her soft body to his. "On one condition."

"Name it."

"Promise me you won't answer any kind of phone or summons until we exchange vows and you kiss the bride."

He threw his head back and laughed. "It's a deal."

"I might not let you out of my sight between now and then."

"That works just fine for me."

"I can't wait to be your wife."

"We're getting married?" Andy raced over and threw himself into their hug. "You'll be my dad?"

Drew nodded. "I always have been, son."

"Yes!" Andy did a fist pump. "Wait." He stopped his victory dance and stared up at his mom. "Always?"

"It's true," she replied. "Your dad was lost for a long

time and no one knew he was even still alive. But he's back now and we're going to be a family."

Drew had never felt more certain about anything when she smiled at him that way. All those wishes on all those stars were finally coming true. "We'll tell you the whole story as soon as we're out of here."

After a brief exchange with Casey, they were cleared to leave, with a protective detail as a final precaution.

Nothing and no one could stop them now.

Epilogue

New Orleans, Louisiana
Saturday, August 2, 4:45 p.m.

Addison smoothed a hand over the soft, sleek skirt of her wedding gown, stunned by the absolute lack of butterflies in her stomach. Nerves were expected for any bride, and considering her rocky road to this day, she would've been entitled to plenty. But she knew Drew would be there this time and not just because he sent her a text message update every ten minutes.

She laughed when her phone chimed with another one, this time with a shot of Andy in his tuxedo, practicing serious ring bearer faces in the mirror. She was about to have the happy beginning she'd dreamed of and Andy was about to start a lifetime with his father.

She thought of the farmhouse they would turn into a home after their honeymoon. They would be a family at last. Complete and whole and stronger for the fire that had forged their relationship.

"You made the right choice. Then and now." Bernadette smiled as Addison checked her reflection one last time.

"I did." She'd gone back and forth about the dress. Drew hadn't seen the original, and during the whirlwind planning for today, he'd carefully avoided any reference to their first wedding attempt. She and Bernadette had shopped boutiques and she'd tried on gowns in various styles, but nothing else felt as right as the gown she'd chosen the first time.

With her mother's pearls glowing above the strapless sweetheart neckline and the lace that hugged her curves from bust to waist, she hoped to make Drew's jaw drop. But she hadn't done a complete carbon copy of the day he'd missed. That wouldn't honor what they'd been through. Instead of an updo with a veil, she left her hair down in loose waves, pulled back from her face with luminous pearl-studded combs.

"Take your bouquet and let's go or Drew will think you've left him this time."

She laughed. "Never!" As she waited out of sight for Andy and then Bernadette to enter the small chapel, she sighed happily.

"Ready?" Professor Hastings offered his arm.

"More than." She beamed. "Here's to the first moment of the best days of our lives."

"You look lovely," he whispered, making her smile as the music changed for her procession.

She felt lovely. She'd felt confident and beautiful in the dressing room, but when Drew's eyes locked with hers the awareness shifted to an all-new high. With him in his tuxedo, with their son by his side, her world felt complete at last. It was a priceless image she'd hold in her heart forever.

Her steps were sure, her smile unquenchable as she approached the altar. At last she and Drew could seize the dream that had been stolen from them eight years ago. The words and motions of the ceremony barely registered, her heart was so full of Drew and the sheer joy between them.

With the exchange of vows and rings, she heard the words that mattered most, the words she so recently thought would never be spoken for her—"I now pronounce you husband and wife. You may kiss the bride."

Drew's lips were warm and gentle and a loud cheer nearly blew the roof off the chapel when they turned to face everyone who'd come to celebrate their wedding.

Her arm linked with Drew's, she felt as if she were floating on a cloud down the aisle.

"Happy?" Drew asked as he helped her into the carriage that would take them to the reception.

"That's not a big enough word for everything I feel, but it's a good start." She looked at him, seeing the happiness and love in his eyes. "You can't be worried I'll have regrets."

"I'm not." He gave her hand a squeeze, rubbing his thumb over the gleaming gold of her wedding band. "It's hard to believe this day is real. It's a miracle."

"Yes, it is."

"But we're not the same people we were when we first attempted this," he said.

She patted his thigh, so grateful she'd have the rest of her life to share affection and passion in equal measure. "Allow me to disagree. We've both had some hard mileage in the years we were apart, but it made us stronger individuals. Nothing we've been through changed my soul-deep love for you."

"I love you, Mrs. Bryant."

Sweeter words were never spoken. His sexy grin made her pulse jump. She tipped her face up for a lingering, searing kiss this time. "I love you, too, Mr. Bryant. It will only ever be you for me."

"He'd make one hell of a Specialist," Emmett said quietly to Thomas as Drew and Addison mingled with their guests at the reception. "If not in the field, as an instructor."

"I offered," Thomas said as the happy couple moved

out in front of the band for their first dance as husband and wife. "He turned me down."

"Our loss."

"Yes, but I sure don't hold his priorities against him." Thomas slid a look across the table where his wife was chatting with his sister and Emmett's wife, Cecelia. How much longer before he and Jo could get started on their own family? "Drew and Addison have done more than enough for their country. They need some space to make up for lost time."

As if on cue, Andy rushed onto the dance floor and Drew scooped him up. The three of them swayed to the music and hope radiated like sunshine from the young family.

Emmett escorted Cecelia out when the music changed and Thomas walked over, extending a hand to Jo. The happiness was contagious, he thought. With his wife in his arms, and the romance swirling around them, he pushed away thoughts of work, enjoying the hard-earned peace of the present moment.

Tomorrow was soon enough to think about the next assignment.

* * * * *

The woman's lips tilted up at the corners briefly as she drove out onto the street. "Hank has resources most people don't. Not even the government."

Rip riffled through the contents of the packet, glancing at a passport with his picture on it, a name he wasn't familiar with on the document. "Chuck Gideon?"

"Better get used to it."

"Speaking of names...we've already kissed and you haven't told me who you are." Rip glanced her way briefly.

Her eyes narrowed and her lips firmed. "No, I haven't."

"Is it a secret, or are you going to tell me?"

"It's probably best if I don't tell you my real name."

"Why? Do you have a shady past, or are you related to someone important?"

"For this mission, I'm related to someone important." She twisted her lips and sent a crooked grin his way. "You. For the purpose of this operation, you can call me Phyllis. Phyllis Gideon. I'll be your wife."

NAVY SEAL
NEWLYWED

BY
ELLE JAMES

Published in Great Britain 2015
by Mills & Boon, an imprint of Harlequin (UK) Limited,
Eton House, 18-24 Paradise Road, Richmond, Surrey, TW9 1SR

© 2015 Mary Jernigan

ISBN: 978-0-263-25307-8

46-0615

Printed and bound in Spain
by CPI, Barcelona

Elle James, a *New York Times* bestselling author, started writing when her sister challenged her to write a romance novel. She has managed a full-time job and raised three wonderful children, and she and her husband even tried ranching exotic birds (ostriches, emus and rheas). Ask her, and she'll tell you what it's like to go toe-to-toe with an angry three-hundred-and-fifty-pound bird! Elle loves to hear from fans at ellejames@earthlink.net or www.ellejames.com.

This book is dedicated to all the families of military personnel who have kept the home fires burning and welcomed their loved ones home with open arms.

Chapter One

Hunkered low in the underbrush, Navy SEAL Chief Petty Officer "Rip" Cord Schafer gripped the M4A1 rifle with the SOPMOD upgrade and inched forward, carefully placing every step to avoid tripping, snapping branches or making any other loud noises. Loaded with sixty pounds of equipment specially selected for this mission, he was ready for anything.

Gunny took point, leading the team into the Honduran camp, keeping to the darkness of the jungle. Moonlight shimmered through the occasional break in the dense overhead canopy, barely making it down to the jungle floor.

Rip had his headset in one ear and listened for sounds of the camp with his other.

Montana eased up behind Gunny, followed by Sawyer, then the newest SEAL, Gosling, with Rip bringing up the rear.

Their mission: extract one undercover DEA agent from a terrorist training camp deep in the jungle of Honduras.

No matter where he looked, Rip could detect no sentries standing guard or patrolling the compound. Strange. The DEA agent had been adamant about being pulled out. He'd feared for his life and had been concerned the information he needed to pass on might be lost.

In his brief plea to be extracted, he'd given specific

GPS coordinates. When Gunny reached the position, he held up his fist.

The team stopped in place and hugged the earth, waiting.

He pointed to Montana and Sawyer and gave them the follow-me sign.

The three surrounded the door of the building. Gunny nudged it open and disappeared inside. Montana and Sawyer followed. Gosling and Rip remained outside, providing cover.

Seconds later, they hustled out a man wearing rumpled clothing, his shoulder-length hair straggly and unkempt. He ducked low and moved quickly between them, hurrying toward the path leading out of the camp.

Gunny motioned for Gosling and Rip to fall in with the team. They had their man, and it appeared as though they were going to make a clean getaway with none of the terrorists aware of the agent's departure.

The hair on the back of Rip's neck stood straight up. The entire mission had been too easy. If there was any real danger, wouldn't there have been sentries on alert, wielding machine guns and willing to cut down anyone who stepped into range?

They cleared the edge of the camp, heading back to the river and the waiting boat.

Gunny was in the lead again, followed by Sawyer. Montana was in front of their extracted DEA agent and Gosling behind him.

The agent stumbled for a moment.

Gosling didn't adjust his stride in time. He caught up with the man then gave him a hand to right himself.

The sharp report of gunfire ripped through the night, shattering the silence.

Gosling collapsed where he stood.

Another shot rang out and the DEA agent grunted and crumpled to the ground.

Instinct made the remaining members of the SEAL team drop to their bellies.

His heart slamming into his ribs, adrenaline racing through his veins, Rip low crawled to the two men who'd been hit. He shone his red penlight over Gosling. The man had taken the bullet in the throat. By the dark stain spreading in a wide blob on the ground around him, Rip suspected the bullet had cut a hole in the young SEAL's jugular vein. He lay sprawled on his side, his body completely still. Rip covered the wound with his hand, but nothing he did could slow the flow of blood.

"Roll call," Gunny spoke into Rip's headset. One by one the other team members reported in.

"Montana."

"Sawyer."

"Schafer," Rip said. His heart in his throat, he reported, "Gosling took a hit."

Sawyer spun around and low crawled with his weapon in front of him to where Gosling lay unmoving. He jerked Rip's hand off the wound. "Damn."

Gunny muttered a curse, "Status."

For a moment Rip closed his eyes, thinking of his last conversation with the young petty officer. Gosling's wife was expecting their first child. He'd been so proud, scared and excited all at once.

Sawyer answered, "Gosling's dead."

Though Rip knew it, hearing Sawyer's confirmation made it all the more real and heartbreaking. Overwhelmed with grief but knowing they still had to get the agent out, he moved toward the other downed man a yard away. The agent had been hit in the chest. Without the armor plate the SEALs wore in their vests, he hadn't been protected.

"*Our guest?*" Gunny demanded.

Rip felt for a pulse. As he pressed his fingers to the base of the man's throat, a hand snaked out and grabbed his wrist with surprising strength.

In the darkness of the night, Rip could see the whites of the man's eyes staring up at him.

"*Set up,*" *the agent said, his voice nothing more than a guttural whisper. He reached up to the medallion around his neck, yanked it free and pressed it into Rip's hand.* "*Find out who.*"

"*Who what?*" *Rip asked.*

"*Status on our extraction?*" *Gunny's voice sounded loud in Rip's ear.*

"*Conscious, but not good,*" *Rip replied, stuffing the medallion into his pocket.*

Shouts could be heard in the village behind them as the occupants raised the alarm. Lights blinked on and headlights lit the night. The tap, tap, tap of gunfire broke through the night's silence.

"*Let's get out of here.*" *Gunny raced back to where Sawyer and Rip were leaning over the wounded men.* "*I'll take the agent.*"

The agent gripped Rip's arm and refused to let go.

Rip straightened, bringing the man up and throwing him over his shoulder. "*I've got the agent. Get Gosling. He deserves a proper burial.*"

Cursing, Gunny hesitated only a moment before pitching Gosling over his shoulder, muttering, "*This wasn't the way this was supposed to go down, damn it.*"

Rip didn't wait. With the deadweight of the wounded agent bearing down on him, he took off at an awkward lope racing through the trees and vines toward the boat they'd left in the nearby river. Silence wasn't necessary. Speed was.

Montana ran ahead to get the boat engines started. Sawyer brought up the rear, covering their sixes as Rip and Gunny carried their burdens over the uneven floor of the jungle.

Shots rang out behind them. A vehicle full of angry terrorists raced toward them. Sawyer held them at bay, firing short bursts of rounds into the night. He ejected his clip and without missing a beat slammed another home while running backward to keep up with the other SEALs.

When Rip reached the boat, he jumped on board and laid his charge on the deck. He manned his position behind a grenade launcher, waiting for Sawyer to emerge from the tree line.

Gunny jumped on board, dropped Gosling on deck and took a position behind a machine gun.

As soon as Sawyer cleared the trees, Gunny opened fire on the oncoming sets of headlights.

Rip launched a grenade, aiming at the line of vehicles barreling through the underbrush.

As Sawyer leaped aboard, Montana hit the throttle, spun the craft around on the water and gunned it, sending it speeding downriver, bullets plinking off the hull and hitting the water around them.

Not until they were a good mile downstream did Rip glance down at Sawyer working over the body of the DEA agent.

Rip shook his head. The mission had gone like clockwork. They'd been out of the village, on their way back. What the hell had happened? Rip glanced at his teammate's lifeless body on the deck of the boat. Gosling was dead. Two shots were fired and then none until the terrorists had loaded up in their trucks and given chase.

Whoever had fired the first two shots could have taken out more, if not all, of the SEAL team. Why hadn't he?

When the boat reached the helicopter landing zone, Sawyer rocked back on his heels, his shoulders slumped.
Gunny shot a glance back at him. "Well?"
Sawyer shook his head. "He's dead."

"HEY, SWEETIE, WOULD you like a drink?"

Rip blinked up at the waitress standing beside him with a tray in her hands. For a full thirty seconds he couldn't remember where he was. He'd done it again. The shrinks he'd seen in the past had said part of post-traumatic stress disorder was flashbacks to events that had an indelible impact on him.

"Excuse me?" he said, buying time for his mind to reconnect with his surroundings.

"Would you like a drink?" the waitress repeated.

He shook his head. "No, thank you."

The woman moved away to the next customer in the casino.

Rip stared around at row after row of brightly lit slot machines, pinging, ringing or plinking in the darkness. For a long moment he wondered how the hell he'd gone from a hot, humid, bug- and snake-infested jungle to an upscale casino in Mississippi.

Then he remembered all the events that had led up to this meeting. All that had happened since getting back from Honduras.

He stared around the dimly lit room.

What's keeping him?

The past six weeks since their failed mission had been a blur. Rip had been back on duty with his team, while covertly researching the odd medallion the DEA agent had shoved into his hand.

The medallion had been a clever disguise for an electronic storage device on which were stored hundreds of photos of the terrorist training camp and crates of American-made weapons and ammunition disguised as World Health Organization donations.

And based on the botched mission in Honduras, someone higher up didn't want the agent or anyone else exposing who was providing the weapons from the States. How else could a sniper have known exactly when and where they would be unless someone had tipped them off?

Rip had pilfered a copy of the after-action report, developed the pictures and was in the process of piecing things together when an assassin started stalking him. He'd found out that details of their mission had been leaked. Not only after its failure, but before it had even been launched.

Someone, possibly in a high-ranking political position, wanted that agent dead and had sent the SEALs in to get him out of the village and into the open so a sniper could take him out. It was the only answer he could come up with given the limited information he had.

Rip was in hiding, officially missing and presumed dead. The Navy still thought he'd been swallowed by the Pearl River after being shot during a live-fire training mission with Navy SEALs Special Boat Team 22. If not for the help of former SEAL James "Cowboy" Monahan and Rip's old friend FBI Agent Melissa Bradley, Rip might not still be alive. The two had persevered, and searched the river until they found him holed up in a shack in the Mississippi bayou.

Lucky me. Rip snorted.

Now, after spending the past three weeks recovering from his gunshot wound, Rip was finally able to pursue his self-appointed mission.

He'd gotten his commander and the few members of his team who'd been involved in his rescue to keep his survival on the down low until he could find the persons responsible for the death of the undercover DEA agent.

He couldn't engage his team in this mission without disclosing to the world and to whoever was responsible for the assassination of the agent that the Navy's Chief Petty Officer Cord Schafer was alive and well. In order to keep from becoming a target again, it was best if he remained "dead" until he resolved the situation.

Only, he knew he couldn't do it on his own. He needed a partner, a cover and fake passports to get him down to Honduras without raising red flags to the terrorist organization or the traitorous Americans supplying them with weapons.

Sitting in a crowded casino in Biloxi, Mississippi, with a baseball cap pulled low over his brow, he waited for his contact, not knowing who he was or what he looked like, only that Cowboy's new boss, billionaire Hank Derringer, was sending one of his operatives from Covert Cowboys, Inc.

Rip glanced up every time a man slowed near the slot machine he was only halfheartedly playing. He looked for a man in a cowboy hat and boots, but most of the men in the place were hatless, gray-haired and wearing comfortable loafers.

Glancing at his watch once again, he started getting nervous. He hadn't been out in public since the mercenary had shot him. Feeling exposed, he sat at the designated position in the selected casino, at the exact time he was supposed to meet his contact.

Where the hell was his cowboy?

Shoving another token into the machine, he punched the spin button without caring what pictures he'd land on. He was surprised when three cherries lined up on the screen and tokens plinked into the tray below.

Soft, slender hands slid over his shoulders and down the

front of his chest, and a sultry voice whispered in his ear, "Getting lucky, sweetheart?"

Nerves stretched to the breaking point, Rip fought the urge to grab the arm, spin around and slam the person to the floor. Instead, he spun on the stool in such a way he had the woman sitting across his lap before she knew his intentions.

Her eyes widened briefly and then narrowed. "Wanna take your winnings and buy me a drink?" She had long dark brown hair, green eyes and a lean, athletic figure dressed in a red cotton sundress that screamed tourist.

Though he gave the appearance of being happy to see her, his hand on her wrist was tight. She wouldn't get away easily or without raising a ruckus. He smiled at her and, through his teeth, he demanded, "Who the hell are you?"

She smiled back at him, cupped his face with her other hand and patted his cheek, not so gently. "I'm your contact, so play nice and pretend you're happy to see me."

For a brief moment he frowned.

She laughed out loud. "If that's happy, you're a terrible actor. Make like we're a couple."

"Since I didn't get the memo, I'm a little slow on the uptake. Let me set the stage." Getting past the shock of his contact's gender, Rip had to admit she was a lot prettier than any cowboy he might have expected. He wrapped his arm around her waist, then slid his hand up into her dark brown hair and pressed the back of her neck, angling her face toward his.

"What are you doing?" she said, her eyes widening.

"I would think it was obvious. I'm showing you how happy I am to see you." Then he captured her mouth in a deep, lip-crushing kiss.

Apparently she was so shocked that her mouth opened. Rip slid his tongue in and caressed the length of hers.

At first her hands, trapped between them, pressed against his chest. But after a moment or two, her fingers curled into his shirt and she kissed him back.

When he finally came up for air, it took him a second or two to come back to his senses and remember where he was, yet again.

He stood so quickly, he had to steady her on her feet before he let go of her. "Let's get out of here."

"What about your winnings?" she said.

He scooped up enough tokens for two full cups, carried them over to a gray-haired senior citizen and dumped them into her slot machine tray. "Congratulations, you're a winner." He kissed the woman's cheek, grabbed his contact's hand and headed for the door.

The woman whose hand he held hurried to keep up with him in her bright red cowboy boots. "You were playing the dollar slots."

"So?" he countered.

"That was probably a couple hundred dollars."

"Then that woman will go home happy."

He tipped his baseball cap lower over his forehead, slid his arm around her waist and smiled down at her as he stepped out into the sauna-like Mississippi late afternoon sunshine. "Where's your car?"

"This way." She guided him to the parking lot and stopped beside a large black 4x4 truck with twenty-inch rims and tinted windows.

"Seriously?" Rip shook his head. "This is yours?"

"One of the perks of working for Hank Derringer. That and an arsenal of every weapon you could possibly need." When she hit the key fob, the engine started and the doors unlocked. She opened the driver's side door and nodded to the passenger seat. "Hop in."

"How do I know you really work for Hank?"

"You don't. But has anyone else shown up and told you he's your contact?"

"No."

"You have that." She raised her eyebrows, the saucy expression doing funny things to his insides. "So, do you trust me, or not?"

His lips curled upward on the ends. "I'll go with not."

"Oh, come on, sweetheart." She batted her pretty green eyes and gave him a sexy smile. "What's not to trust?"

His gaze scraped over her form. "I expected a cowboy, not a…"

"Cow*girl*?" Her smile sank and she slipped into the driver's seat. "I grew up on a ranch, I've worked with cattle and horses and I know the value of a hard day's work. I spent eight years with the FBI. I also know right from wrong and tend to be loyal to a fault, until the person or organization I believe in breaks my trust." Her lips firmed into a straight line. "Are you coming or not? If you're dead set on a cowboy, I'll contact Hank and tell him to send a male replacement. But then he'd have to come up with another plan."

Rip considered her words and then acknowledged he didn't have a lot of choices with only a couple of week's reprieve before he had to turn up alive or be buried by the government. He rounded the front of the truck and climbed into the passenger seat. "I'll go along for the ride and maybe you can convince me you're up for the challenge."

"Please. I don't normally have to justify my existence to the people I work with. I'm a trained operative. I don't need this assignment. However, from what Hank told me, you need all the help you can get."

"I'm interested in how you and Hank plan to provide that help. Frankly, I'd rather my SEAL team had my six."

"Yeah, but you're deceased. Using your SEAL team would only alert your assassin that you aren't as dead as the Navy claims you are. How long do you think you'll last once that bit of news leaks out?"

His lips pressed together. "I'd survive."

"By going undercover? Then you still won't have the backing of your team, and we're back to the original plan." She grinned. "Me."

Rip sighed. "Fine. I want to head back to Honduras and trace the weapons back to where they're coming from. What's Hank's plan?"

"For me to work with you." She pulled a large envelope from between her seat and the console and handed it across to him. "Everything we need is in that packet. Passports, cash, credit cards and new identities. We also have at our disposal Hank's jet, a Citation X, capable of cruising at Mach 0.9, almost the speed of sound. Say the word and we can be in the sky within twenty minutes. It's waiting at the airport."

Monahan had only good things to say about Hank and all he could do for the operation, otherwise Rip would have been more hesitant getting the billionaire involved. With a DEA agent and one of his SEAL teammates dead, and himself almost killed, he was determined to find the one responsible. But after losing one of his SEAL brothers, he was hesitant about getting anyone else caught in the crosshairs. "Hank sure pulled all of this together fast."

The woman's lips tilted up briefly as she drove out onto the street. "Hank has resources most people don't. Not even the government."

Rip riffled through the contents of the packet, glancing at a passport with his picture on it as well as a name he'd never seen. "Chuck Gideon?"

"Better get used to it."

"Speaking of names…we've already kissed and you haven't told me who you are." Rip glanced her way briefly.

Her eyes narrowed and her lips firmed. "No, I haven't."

"Is it a secret? Do you have a shady past or are you related to someone important."

"For this mission, I'm related to someone important." She twisted her lips and sent a crooked grin his way. "You. For the purpose of this operation, you can call me Phyllis. Phyllis Gideon. I'll be your wife."

Chapter Two

Tracie Kosart had recognized the man in the casino immediately from the photo Hank Derringer had given her and realized that could be a problem. Even with his shaggy long hair, the breadth of his shoulders, the stubborn set of his chin and the steely look in his gray-blue eyes set him apart from the other gamblers there hoping to score a big win.

Though he'd been slouching on the stool, he looked as if he could spring into action at a moment's notice. Now as he sat opposite her in the interior of her truck, he filled the space, his shoulders seeming to block her entire view.

"Phyllis, huh?" He stared at her, his eyes narrowing. "You don't look like a Phyllis."

"It doesn't matter." When he looked at her so intently, it made her body heat and her belly tighten.

"Missy?"

"What?"

"Jasmine, Lois, Penelope? I could list names all day." He pinned her with his stare, a sassy smirk on his face. "You might as well tell me."

"Penelope?" She shot a glance at him, her mouth twitching as she fought a smile. "You think I look like a Penelope?"

"Some parents have a sense of humor." He raised his brows. "Well?"

She sighed. "Tracie. My name's Tracie Kosart."

"That's better." He stuck out his hand. "Nice to meet you, Tracie. And by the way, the name fits you better than Phyllis."

She took one hand off the steering wheel to shake his, an electrical surge racing up her arm from their joined fingers. Tracie yanked her hand back and wrapped it tightly around the steering wheel, willing the surge of fiery heat to fade.

"You and Derringer seem to have this all worked out." Rip leaned back in his set. "Where to first?"

"We've looked over all the photos the dead agent left you, along with the after-action report from the extraction operation and we really don't have much to go on. Yes, they prove the terrorists are receiving American-made weapons in World Health Organization boxes. But we don't know for certain who is sending them or at what point they are packaged to ship via WHO." Tracie shifted the big truck into Drive and pulled out of the parking lot.

Rip nodded. "I'm betting the World Health Organization didn't send those boxes."

"What we need is one of those guns so that we can trace the serial number on it back to the manufacturer. Short of going to Honduras to get one, we should exhaust all other stateside options first."

"Okay, what options?" The SEAL beside her crossed his arms, which made his biceps appear bigger than they already did.

Tracie had to focus on the road to keep from openly drooling. The man had testosterone oozing from every pore. For a moment she forgot Rip's question—then it came back to her. "I was hoping you had some ideas. We think the DEA agent's boss had to have been receiving data from him. He might have other operatives inside the terrorist group or in nearby towns."

"And how do we find Dan Greer's boss?"

Tracie snorted softly. "Hank already has. He was able to tap into the DEA database and extract that information." Hank had the connections, the computer power and a technical guru who could tap into any system.

"I'm surprised Hank hasn't already contacted the agent's boss."

A muffled beep sounded in the console between them. Tracie lifted a cell phone out of a cup holder and glanced down at a text. Her lips formed a broad smile. "As a matter of fact, he has. We have a meeting with Morris Franks in Atlanta in three hours."

Rip gave her a doubtful smile. "Honey, it takes a lot longer than three hours to drive to Atlanta."

She turned onto a highway and jerked her head toward a green sign with an airplane depicted in white. "What did I say about having Hank's Citation X available?" Tracie softened. As a former FBI agent, she remembered how unbelievable Hank's assets were when she'd first been exposed to them. "Prepare to be impressed."

Instead of driving through the terminal area of the Biloxi airport, she drove on to the private businesses' hangars along the runway and parked outside one of them.

As they climbed out of the truck, the door to the structure opened and a man stepped out. "Right this way, Mr. & Mrs. Gideon. I'm Tom Callahan. We've topped off the fuel, your pilot has performed the preflight checklist and he's filed the flight plan. The jet is ready for takeoff whenever you two say the word." Tom smiled. "And congratulations on your recent marriage."

Tracie almost did a double take until she remembered that was their cover story. "Th-thank you."

A hand settled at the small of her back. "It all happened

so quickly, we're still getting used to it, aren't we, dear?" Rip guided her through the doorway into a reception area.

Tom led the way past a desk to another door that opened into the hangar where a shiny new Citation X airplane sat on the tarmac. The huge hangar door slid open, sunlight cutting a wide swath into the dim interior.

"Shall we?" Tracie asked.

Rip waved a hand. "Ladies first." Tracie climbed the short set of stairs into the cabin and took the first seat on the far side.

Ducking to keep from bumping his head, Rip entered the cabin and dropped into the seat beside her.

As soon as they were aboard, a flight attendant pulled the door closed, and the engines ignited.

Soon the small jet, with seating for twelve, taxied down the runway and lifted smoothly into the air.

"Okay, now I'm impressed," Rip whispered. "How long will it take to get to Atlanta?"

Tracie glanced at her watch. "We should be there in less than an hour. In the meantime, we should go over what data the DEA agent was able to pass off before he died and the after-action report, one more time to see if we missed anything."

RIP STARED ACROSS the narrow aisle at Tracie.

With her long, slender legs crossed at the knees and one of her red high heels bouncing with barely leashed energy, she still didn't look like a trained operative. He was less than thrilled at the idea of Hank sending a woman to help him. He'd rather have had a man to work with. Women tended to complicate things. His natural urge to protect women and children might get in the way of a success-ful operation. *This operation has been dangerous thus far and will only get worse. I'm not entirely sold on the idea of working with a woman.*

"If it makes you feel any better, I used to work for the FBI. I received my training at Quantico and I've been a field agent for more than five years. I worked undercover along the Mexican border to help stop several drug- and human-trafficking rings. I know how to handle a gun, and I'm not afraid to use one."

Rip nodded in deference to her risky and dangerous duty assignments. "Have you ever been in the jungles of Honduras?"

"No, but I've been held hostage in a cave in Mexico and survived. I know what hard work, prior planning and enemy engagement is all about. Don't let the dress fool you." She raised her hand, holding the cell phone up. "But, if you're still worried about working with a woman, I can contact Hank now and have him send another agent to replace me."

He liked her spunk and the fact she wasn't taking any crap from him. Rip sat back in his seat. "What I don't understand is why Hank sent you. I thought he was all about cowboys."

She shrugged, making that movement look entirely too sexy, her creamy white shoulders in stark contrast with the bright red dress. "As I already mentioned. I grew up on a ranch. Hank likes his cowboys—or girls—to have that ranch-life work ethic and sense of morals and values."

"I don't know Hank Derringer. All I have to go on is my buddy Jim Monahan's word."

Tracie's lips quirked upward and she stared out the window. "Hank and his team saved my life. I have nothing but respect for the work they do."

"Just what is it he does?" Rip asked.

"He champions the truth and justice when other organizations can't seem to get it right or have corruption in their ranks." As she spoke, her jaw hardened and her mouth pulled into a tight line.

"Why did you give up on the FBI?" Rip asked.

"You know that part about corruption in the ranks?" She snorted. "Well, let's just say, I wouldn't be alive if I had relied only on the organization I had sworn into."

"Surely not all of the FBI is rotten." Rip studied her.

Tracie glanced his way. "No, not all of the agents are. But Hank made me an offer I couldn't refuse. After two of the agents I worked with went bad, I was ready for a fresh start."

Rip turned away and stared out the window. He knew how she felt. As a member of the Navy SEALs, Rip had been trained to rely on his brothers in arms. When one went bad, as one had on the mission in Honduras, it shook his entire foundation of trust. Especially since the bad apple had been the leader of the mission, the now deceased Gunnery Sergeant Frank Petit. Rip's friend, James Monahan, a man he'd put his complete faith in, had helped to expose Gunny for the traitor he was.

What worried him even more was that they still had no idea who had paid Gunny to leak the information about their mission. He suspected it was someone higher up. Someone in Washington.

For a long moment, he sat in silence, reliving the past few weeks. He was only just recovered from the assassin's gunshot wound. If not for his best friend and a former SEAL teammate, he wouldn't have made it. That fact alone gave him hope for humanity. There were good people out there. His glance shifted to Tracie. She might be one of them. Only time would tell.

After what seemed like only a handful of minutes, the jet began its descent into Atlanta.

The plane's tires kissed the runway with barely a bounce

and, after rolling it into an open hangar, the pilot brought the aircraft to a complete stop.

The flight attendant lowered the stairs and stood to the side.

Rip stepped down first into the dim interior of the hangar and held out his hand to Tracie.

For a moment, she refused his proffered hand, her brow puckering. Then she laid her fingers in his.

The last time he and Tracie touched, he'd felt an electric jolt. This time was no different and the fire raced all the way through Rip's body. What was it about the woman that had his body on high sexual alert? To get his mind off her, he leaned close and asked, "If the DEA agent was terminated for what he knew, how has his boss managed to stay alive?"

Tracie nodded. "Perhaps he doesn't know anything."

Rip ground to a halt. "In that case, we're wasting our time."

"We won't know that until we meet with him." Without slowing, Tracie strode across the hangar lengthening the distance between them.

A man appeared at a doorway. "This way Mr. and Mrs. Gideon. Your car is waiting."

Rather than be left in the hangar, Rip ran to catch up, falling in step beside Tracie.

A sleek black limousine waited at the curb, the chauffeur holding the door. He didn't speak a word as he held the door open while Tracie and Rip slid inside.

Once the door was closed, Tracie turned to Rip. "Have you considered the fact that Morris Franks's willingness to talk to us might be an indication he knew more than he let on to others in his own department?"

Rip's eyes narrowed and he stared out the windshield

as if trying to see into the future. "Or, he could be looking for more information himself."

"I suppose we'll know soon enough. The hotel isn't far from the airport."

Tracie sat across the limo from Rip, not any single part of her body or limbs so much as touching him. Rip found himself wanting to reach across the short distance and pull her into his arms. The scent of her hair was doing strange things to him. Funny that even with her incredible legs and the classy way the red dress fit her body, the smell of her shampoo was what got to him most. It set every one of his nerves on edge and his groin tightened.

As a SEAL assigned to Special Boat Team 22—conducting missions and training their own team for missions as well as other SEAL teams—he hadn't had the time nor the inclination to pursue a lasting romantic relationship. Not that there were many women to go around when he was stuck in the backwater swamps of the Mississippi bayous at Stennis where SBT-22 was headquartered.

If he were to pursue a woman, Tracie wouldn't be the one. She was some kind of special agent for Hank Derringer. She didn't have any more time than he had to get involved. Not that they would even be compatible. She was too…

Rip struggled to find the right word.

The tightness of her jaw and the slightly narrowed, beautiful green eyes said it all. Intense.

He'd bet she was just as intense in bed. Again his groin strained against the denim of his jeans. Now was not the time to think about getting naked with a woman. He had a job to do.

As a dead man, he needed to resolve the case so that he could resurface alive before the Navy processed him out of a job.

"We're here," Tracie said as the limo slid up beside the curb in front of what appeared to be a three-star hotel only a few blocks from the airport. "The driver will remain nearby in case we need him on short notice."

Rip nodded and glanced at the hotel. "Once inside, who do we ask for?"

"We don't. We check in as newlyweds." Tracie glanced his way. "You'll need your driver's license and credit card. Our guy is in room 627. We'll make our way up to his room after we check in."

Rip pulled out the wallet Hank had provided and familiarized himself with the contents and his new name. *Chuck Gideon.* "Who came up with the name?"

"Does it matter?"

"No." Rip got out, rounded the vehicle and beat the chauffeur to opening Tracie's door. "Mrs. Gideon, shall we get a room?" He winked and smiled.

Tracie's eyes narrowed slightly and she placed her hand in his, allowing him to pull her to her feet on the pavement.

His fingers tingled where they touched hers, but Rip schooled his expression, determined to give no indication that Tracie had any effect on him.

As soon as she was on her feet, she let go of his hand.

Not to be deterred, and using their married status as an excuse, he rested his hand at the small of her back. A slight tremor shook her body. Inside the lobby of the hotel, Rip adopted his role. "We'd like a room for the night."

"Just a moment, sir." The hotel manager's fingers flew across the keyboard. "We have one suite left on the seventh floor."

"Perfect," Tracie smiled. "We'll take it."

Rip grinned at the manager. "She can't wait to get me alone." He held up her left hand, displaying the diamond ring and wedding band on her finger. Then he held up his left hand, displaying a matching wedding band. "Newlyweds."

The manager smiled and handed them two key cards. "Congratulations."

"Let's wait to get the luggage until we've seen the room," Tracie said, with a flirty bat of her eyelashes.

Though Rip knew it was all part of the act, it didn't stop his pulse from leaping and his blood from thrumming hot through his veins. They stepped into the elevator. Before the door closed, Rip pulled Tracie into his arms and kissed her soundly.

The elevator doors slid shut and Tracie pushed him away, straightening her dress unnecessarily, her hands shaking. "We don't want to look overeager."

"Don't you think newlyweds are anxious to get to their hotel room?"

Tracie shrugged. "I wouldn't know, never having been a newlywed." Her words were tight and it was as if a shutter descended over her green eyes.

"Well, I guess that answers one question."

"Oh, yeah? What's that?"

He smiled, liking that he'd shaken her with his kiss. "You've never been married. So you're not married now."

Turning her back to him, she said, "What does it matter?"

"I would think it would matter a little since we just kissed."

"All part of our cover. It didn't mean anything."

"If you were married, wouldn't you hope that your husband would be a little jealous of the man kissing his wife?"

"I would hope he'd understand it's part of the job. Not that I'm getting married anytime soon."

"Why not?"

"I'm not convinced marriage is all that great."

Having been a SEAL for seven years, Rip had much the same perspective, though he'd never voiced his opinion on the institution. Tracie made him reconsider his own stand on matrimony. "I think marriage is okay for some."

Tracie's lips twisted as she glanced up at him. "But not you?"

He countered with raised brows. "Or you?"

"Marriage is hard enough when the two parties involved live under the same roof all year long. My jobs in the FBI and now on Hank's team have kept me moving. I don't have the time or the inclination to set down roots."

The door opened on the seventh floor. Rip took the lead, turning toward the stairwell instead of the room the hotel manager had assigned them. Tracie was right behind him.

He hurried down the stairs checking for security cameras. He'd seen one in the hallway on the seventh floor, but not in the stairwell. One floor down, he opened the door.

Movement captured his attention. Two men were entering the stairwell at the opposite end of the long corridor. The last one through looked over his shoulder at Rip and Tracie before shoving the guy in front of him the rest of the way through the door and crowding in behind him.

"Damn." Tracie ducked past Rip and ran for room 627. The doorjamb was splintered and the door stood ajar. Tracie pulled a pistol from her purse and shouldered her way inside, gun pointed.

Rip dragged the HK .40 from the holster beneath his shirt and rushed in after Tracie.

"Franks is dead." Tracie turned toward him. "Whoever did it got away."

"The two in the stairwell." Rip ran back to the stairwell. He took the steps two at a time, jumping over the railing as the staircase made a turn. He landed and repeated the process until he hit the ground floor where he burst through the doorway. As dark sedan rushed by, one of its windows lowered and the barrel of a pistol jutted out.

Rip threw himself to the ground as the sharp report of gunfire blasted the air. He rolled beneath a truck and out the other side, jumping to his feet. Another shot shattered the truck's passenger window.

Hunkered low with the body of the truck between him and the fleeing vehicle, Rip sucked in a breath and dared to poke his head over the top of the hood, praying he'd have enough time to get a fix on the license plate of the sedan. Already, it was too far away and getting farther.

Rip ran across the grass, cut through a stand of trees and made it to the street as the getaway vehicle turned onto the main road.

He hammered his pistol's grip into the driver's side window, cracking the glass.

The driver cursed, and the vehicle slowed for a second. Tires squealing, it leaped across the crowded roadway, and three other vehicles crashed into each other as the drivers slammed on their brakes.

With the pileup blocking Rip, the killers got away.

Farther away from Tracie and the scene of the crime than he felt comfortable with, Rip jogged back to the hotel, and raced up the six flights of stairs.

Tracie was still in room 627 with the dead DEA supervisor.

Rip nudged the door open with his foot, breathing hard, his shirt torn and dirty.

"What happened?" Tracie asked.

"They got away." Rip kicked the door closed behind him, careful not to touch anything. "Have you called the police?"

She shook her head and held up gloved hands. "No. And I've been careful not to leave prints on anything. We can't blow our cover. There's still a lot of work to do."

"What about the surveillance video for this floor?"

"I'll get Hank to work on that. Right now, we need to find any information that Greer might have left for us." She slapped a pair of latex gloves in his hands.

Rip pulled on the gloves and glanced around the hotel room. Drawers littered the floor, a small suitcase lay upside down beside the drawers, clothes were strewn around the room as if someone had gone through them in a hurry. Pillows had been tossed off the bed and the mattress lay at an awkward angle, the sheets in a rumpled heap beside the dead man.

"The room's been tossed. If there was anything to be found, don't you think the killers would have gotten to it first?" Rip asked.

He glanced at the door. Not only had the killers splintered the frame, the chain lock had been ripped out of the door itself.

"The chain on the door was torn off. The agent knew someone might try to get to him." Tracie checked the closet, the empty room safe and behind the dresser. "Nothing."

Rip found a set of keys beneath the corner of the bed. "Think he might have left something in his vehicle?"

"We can check, but we better make it quick. It won't be long before someone sees the broken door and discovers the body. We don't want to be around when the police get here."

Rip nodded. They couldn't afford to be tied up answering questions for the police. Their fake documents would only hold up until authorities tracked down their real identities. "Did Hank have the access to erase our fingerprints from the FBI and military databases?"

"As far as I know, he removed us from all grids."

A sense of loss washed over Rip. His identity had been erased from the military system. He'd always been proud of his connection with the SEALs. Having been removed from the system made him feel even more disconnected than his fake death.

Rip squared his shoulders. He didn't have time to grieve his own death. Palming the car keys, he jerked his head toward the door. "Let's go."

Chapter Three

Leading the way, Rip took the staircase down to the ground level.

Tracie followed more slowly in her high heels, listening for others entering the stairwell or raising the alarm about a killing in the hotel.

So far, nothing had gone according to plan, which was right on par for the life of an FBI agent, or a Covert Cowboys, Inc. operative for that matter. Rarely did she have complete control over what happened, but she'd rather be in the position of giving the orders than taking them. She frowned at Rip's back.

The massive breadth of Rip's shoulders gave her a modicum of confidence. At least he was capable of defending himself and possibly her, if hand-to-hand combat became necessary.

Outside in the parking lot, Rip hit the unlock button on the key fob. A nondescript gray economy car's lights blinked and the vehicle let out a mechanical beep.

Thankfully, the car was parked at the side of the building, not in clear view of the lobby or the hotel manager, and hopefully out of range of security cameras.

Without wasting time, Rip dove into the car and thoroughly searched the interior before he gave up and popped the lock on the trunk. It was empty.

"Check under the mat where the spare tire and tools are located," Tracie suggested.

His hand already skimming over the edges of the trunk lining, Rip found the tab to pull it upward. Beneath the felt-covered liner was a large envelope tucked next to the spare.

A siren sounded in the distance. Tracie's pulse leaped. "Grab it and let's get out of here. We don't know if that siren is headed this way."

Rip grabbed the packet, dropped the car keys on the ground nearby and peeled off the gloves, tucking them into his pocket.

Rip put his arm around Tracie, tucking the package between them as they made their way toward the limousine the driver had parked in the far corner of the hotel parking lot.

With Rip so close, Tracie had a hard time concentrating and she stumbled.

Rip's hand on her arm steadied her. "You all right?"

"I'm fine," she said. "Which is more than I can say for Franks." Before Rip could reach for the back door, the driver hopped out and opened the door for Tracie. Rip helped her into her seat, leaning across to slide the package onto the seat beside her. In the process, he stole a kiss.

Startled by the feel of his lips on hers, Tracie froze, her mouth tingling, her hands pressed to her chest to still her furiously beating heart.

When Rip rounded to the other side of the vehicle and slid in beside her, his jaw tight.

"Was the kiss necessary?" she whispered.

"It was part of our cover," he said, his lips twitching in the corners.

"Well, warn me next time," Tracie muttered.

"Sorry, I thought you'd want me to act like the love-sick bridegroom."

He had a point. He also had her trembling, and that just wouldn't do.

He winked at her and glanced at the driver. "For now, just get us away from the hotel."

The driver nodded and shifted gears, setting the limo into motion.

Rip pressed a button and the privacy window between the driver and the passengers slid upward.

As soon as they were back on the main road and Tracie was certain they weren't being followed, she opened the packet and peered inside.

"What's in it?" Rip cast a quick glance her way.

"Photos and some printouts from the internet." Tracie thumbed through the contents.

"Photos of?" Rip queried.

"People. They appear to be Latino." She handed one to him. The image was at an odd angle, as if whoever had taken it hadn't been focusing on the subject. "This is marked as Juan Villarreal."

Rip's eyes narrowed and a muscle ticked in his jaw. "Villarreal was the leader of the terrorist camp we raided in order to free the DEA agent. He's the one in charge of the group using the US-supplied weapons. The photos are probably more of those taken by Greer while he was embedded. I'm surprised they made it all the way to his boss in the States. I had the feeling the flash drive he gave me before he died was all the evidence he managed to get out. Find anything else?"

"More photos and a hand-drawn map." Tracie pulled the map out of the packet and unfolded it in her lap.

Rip leaned over the map. "Looks like the layout of the camp before we raided. I don't think it will do much good now."

"Maybe not, but the photos might help." Tracie gathered

the information and slid it back into the packet. "We need to get this information to Hank and let him run it through his computers."

"And how will we do that?" Rip asked.

"Back at the airport. Everything we need is on the airplane."

Rip studied the controls on the armrest and hit the one marked mic. "Driver, take us back to the airport."

"Yes, Mr. Gideon," the chauffeur responded.

Tracie shot a brief text message to Hank telling him what had happened and to clear the hotel's video feeds of their images.

They arrived at the hangar within minutes and entered the big space where the airplane sat waiting for them.

An attendant hurried over to them, "We've topped off the fuel and checked all fluid levels. As soon as the chauffeur indicated you were on your way back to the airport, the pilot conducted all preflight inspections and is ready to file a flight plan."

As they approached the aircraft, the steps were lowered. Tracie climbed aboard first, followed by Rip. The flight attendant secured the door behind them. Tracie led the way to the middle of the plane where she flipped one of the tabletops open, revealing a computer screen. She tapped several keys, and in moments she had Hank's face up on the screen. "Hank, we're back on board the *Freedom Flight*."

"Glad you're safely aboard. Brandon wiped the security video of any images including you and Schafer."

"Good. I'm not certain how soon the body will be discovered. Your help with the security footage should give us some time to get out of Atlanta. We found some data in the DEA boss's vehicle. I'm scanning it now."

She raised another part of the table, revealing a computer scanner, and fed the documents they'd found in the DEA agent's vehicle into the machine.

Hank's attention shifted to something beside his monitor. "Got them. I'll have Brandon double check the identities of the men in the photos. But I can't move on nailing the suppliers of the weapons until we have some serial numbers."

Rip frowned and leaned close to Tracie so that he could see and be seen by Hank. "The only way to get serial numbers is to go back to Honduras and get them off the guns."

Hank nodded. "Afraid so."

Rip's gaze captured Tracie's and then returned to Hank. "She can't come with me. It's too dangerous."

Hank's brows rose. "Miss Kosart's a trained professional. She knows the risks."

"Look, frogman, I can speak for myself." Tracie shoved him aside. "I'm on board. So we're headed to Honduras as planned?"

Hank smiled. "You can opt out, if you feel it's too dangerous for your liking?"

"I've been in worse situations," she said, her lips thinning.

"Exactly. You might not want to go to that extreme again. The men in that terrorist camp are pure evil and have little regard for women."

"Hank's right," Rip confirmed. "It's not a good place for a woman."

"Or a man." Tracie crossed her arms. "If we don't go in for the additional information, how will we stop whoever it is selling American weapons to terrorists?"

Rip opened his mouth to say something, but the stubborn set of Tracie's chin made him realize he wouldn't get her to change her mind. Instead, he turned to Hank. "I won't be able to focus on the mission if I'm worried my partner can't keep up or will be captured and tortured."

"She's your partner. We can't activate your SEAL unit and send them in again. They've been in once and that got one of your men killed. Someone is dirty on the Fed side. Until we find that person, we can't count on the secrecy of the operation if we involve your unit or any other government agency."

"I trust my brothers."

"So did Gosling." Hank stared straight into Rip's eyes. "Tracie can handle it."

"Yeah," Tracie said, her ire up. "I don't need you or any other man telling me what is too dangerous for me. We go in together or, if you think it's too dangerous, I'll go alone."

Tracie stared at Rip, holding his gaze, daring him to try to override her decision.

Finally, Rip shrugged. "It's your funeral."

"That plan is not in my books." Tracie aimed for confident, when inside she wasn't quite as certain. The kidnapping in Mexico had shaken her more than she cared to admit.

"Then you're deluding yourself. You're headed right into trouble."

Her chin tilted upward. "That's my choice."

The flight attendant appeared. "If you would fasten your seat belts, we can get underway."

Rip frowned into the screen. "How do you propose the two of us sneak into the terrorist camp?"

"I've got that covered. You will be the guests of a friend of mine." Hank grinned. "You're honeymooners, I'm sure they have tourists wander off the beaten path on occasion. And Rip you will be especially prone to wandering off. Your cover is a wealthy entrepreneur looking for potential investment property."

"On my honeymoon?"

"My contact has the story spreading already. You're

notorious for your arrogance and disregard for anyone but yourself."

Rip snorted. "I'm an entrepreneur in a violent, nearly lawless country?"

Tracie's brows rose. "Are you afraid?"

He met her stare with his own, his lips firmly set into a straight line. "Not for me. If you recall, I've been there. I know what the terrorists are capable of."

"Then you'll be the best guide to get us back in there." Tracie nodded at Hank. "We're good to go."

Hank tipped his head. "Glad to see you two agreeing. Your flight plan has been filed. Brandon tells me you're number three in line to take off. My contact, Hector De-Vita, will greet you on his private landing strip. I'm sending two of my best bodyguards from CCI to provide some backup. They should arrive soon after you."

"Only two?" Rip's lips thinned. "Honduras is overrun with rebels, terrorists and guerillas, and you're sending only two of your best bodyguards for us?"

Hank smile. "DeVita will augment with several men of his own. He's in the security business, providing bodyguards and human shields to the wealthier members of Honduras's population. The plane you're on is fully equipped with an arsenal of weapons you might familiarize yourself with."

Tracie harrumphed. "Some honeymoon."

"Nothing but the best for my baby," Rip winked at her.

"Good luck, you two. Make use of the satellite phone if things get tough. I'll answer at any hour."

When the call ended, Rip stared across at Tracie. "I felt better going in under the cover of dark with my SEAL team."

"What? You're not up for a frontal assault in full daylight with only a girl as your sidekick?" She leaned back in her chair. "No guts, no glory."

The giant hangar door opened to let in the afternoon glare. The plane taxied out into the sunshine. Within minutes, they were in the air, winging their way to Honduras.

Tracie closed her eyes. "You might as well get some rest. Once we hit the ground in Honduras, we'll need all our faculties to pull off this information-gathering honeymoon."

Once they had serial numbers or even a manifest, they might have a chance of tracing the weapons back to those in the United States who had sold them. Nothing like barreling into a potentially hostile situation pretending to be a newlywed couple to get your adrenaline pumping.

Knowing they were headed into a hotbed of danger in the steamy Central American jungles of Honduras didn't stop a chill from slipping across Tracie's skin.

Whatever happened, she refused to be taken captive ever again. If the terrorists wanted her, they'd have to kill her before she'd surrender.

RIP REMAINED AWAKE, studying all the information they had on the case. He reviewed every photograph to glean as much insight as possible from the details in the images they'd obtained from Franks…everything from the faces to the crates of weapons.

After the botched retrieval of the DEA agent by SBT-22, the terrorist camp had probably moved to another location, taking advantage of the jungle's canopy for concealment from satellite photography. Finding them would be a challenge.

Beside him, Tracie had leaned back in the contoured seat with her eyes closed, the steady rise and fall of her chest letting Rip know she'd fallen asleep.

His attention shifted from the computer to the sleeping woman beside him.

Her long, soft brown hair fanned out around her shoulders, and her dark brown lashes made shadowy crescents against her cheeks. Apparently, she was caught in a not-so-pleasant dream. She shivered again and whimpered.

Her eyelids twitched, her eyes beneath them darting back and forth. Her fingers clenched the armrests and a tremor shook her body. Rip motioned to the flight attendant to bring a blanket. He took it from her and laid it across Tracie his hand finding hers.

She let go of the armrest, fingers curling around his, squeezing so tightly she nearly cut off his circulation.

"Tracie," Rip whispered. "Wake up."

Her head turned from side to side and she whimpered again.

"Tracie, wake up." Rip made his entreaty more forceful. He didn't like seeing her in such distress. What kind of dream was it to make her so upset?

When she still didn't wake, he leaned forward and captured her face between his palms. "Tracie, it's okay. You're just dreaming."

The CCI agent's eyes blinked open, the startling green of them piercing Rip through the heart with the anguish reflected in them. She stared around at the interior of the plane. "What...where?" She shook her head and her gaze locked with Rip's.

He stroked his thumbs across her cheek. "Remember me? I'm your husband." He winked and pressed a kiss to her forehead, liking the sound of the word on his lips. What would it be like to be Tracie's husband? "You were having a bad dream." He leaned back, letting go of her face.

Tracie touched her fingers to the place he'd kissed and

frowned. "Oh, it's you." Dragging in a shaky breath, she let it go slowly and sat up. "I'm sorry. For a moment I forgot where I was."

"I take it you weren't in such a good place in your dream." He tucked the blanket in around her sides.

Sitting up, Tracie adjusted her seat to an upright position and pulled the blanket up to her chin, her body trembling. "It was only a dream. How long have we been flying?"

"Two and a half hours."

"That long?" She pushed her hair back from her face and slipped an elastic band around the thick hank, securing it in a ponytail at her nape. "I must have needed the sleep. What about you? Did you rest?"

"I can rest when we solve this case, and I can return to the land of the living."

Tracie's lips twisted. "I know this must be difficult for you to play dead and alive at the same time. Hopefully, we'll get in, get out and the terrorists will be none the wiser."

Rip snorted. "That's what we planned when we went in to get Greer out." He glanced out the window into the clear blue sky. "That's not quite how it worked." Gosling's wife had been devastated when she'd gotten the news of his death. She'd almost lost the baby.

Tracie laid her hand on his arm. "We'll do the best we can. You should get some rest."

He leaned his head back and closed his eyes. "What were you dreaming about when I woke you?"

A long moment of silence stretched between them.

Rip opened one eye.

Tracie stared straight ahead, her face pale and drawn. Finally, she spoke. "I was dreaming about Mexico."

Closing his eye again, he allowed his lips to quirk upward in a wry grin. "I take it you weren't dreaming about a vacation to Cozumel?"

"Not hardly."

Rip opened his eyes.

Tracie had turned her head away and stared out the window. Her back stiff.

"Dreaming about being held hostage by members of a drug cartel?"

She nodded.

Rip slid his hand over hers and gently squeezed her fingers. "I'm sorry."

Tracie turned to stare at where their hands touched. "It happens."

"Yeah, but it's not something you get over that easy. I'd bet you have PTSD."

She shrugged. "What do you do? Give up?" She shook her head. "Not my style." Her hand slipped from beneath his.

Rip's grip tightened before she got away. "Sometimes it helps to talk about it."

"Thanks, but I did enough talking to the FBI shrink." She tugged again and he let go of her hand. "I want to get on with my life, not dwell in the past."

"I get it."

"Perhaps we should look at the weapons Hank sent for our use," Tracie suggested.

The flight attendant cleared her throat. "Mr. Derringer also provided additional clothing, if you'd like to change." She opened a small closet with an arrangement of clothing hung on hangers that included several nice dresses in light colors typical of warm climates, a man's light gray suit and a white linen suit next to it.

"Oh, please," Tracie said. "Wear the white one. It reeks of spoiled, rich playboy."

"I thought I was going for wealthy entrepreneur."

"True, but that white, with your dark hair, will make more of a first impression. Very sexy."

Rip's brows rose and his lips curved upward. "You noticed?"

Tracie shrugged. "I'm an agent. It's my job to notice things."

"Uh-huh."

"Fine." Tracie frowned. "Wear the gray one. I don't care." She disappeared around a curtain at the rear of the plane with one of the dresses.

Though he tried not to, he couldn't help watching Tracie's bare feet beneath the curtain. The red dress pooled on the floor and she stepped out of it, then light yellow filmy fabric puddled on the floor of the plane and Tracie's feet stepped into the middle of it.

Something about her bare feet had Rip's blood singing through his veins at Mach 5. He had the urge to yank the curtain back and feast his eyes on her naked body.

A slow chuckle built in his chest and he nearly laughed out loud at what he expected her reaction would be if he followed his urge. He rubbed his cheek where he guessed she'd slap it. But, damn, it would be worth it. The woman had his insides tied in knots.

Tracie emerged, wearing a beautiful dress that hugged her breasts, emphasizing the ripe, rounded fullness while drawing attention to the narrowness of her tiny waist. The skirt flared out and fell to midthigh. Long legs stretched from what seemed like her chin to her slender feet encased in nude, strappy stilettos. She was pulling her hair up into a sleek French twist, her arms raised, head tucked low.

For a moment, Rip could only stand and stare. When she finally glanced up, she caught him gawking.

Snapping his mouth shut, he took the white suit off the hanger and stepped behind the curtain, coming out when he had the white trousers on, a black button-up shirt, open halfway down his chest and the jacket hooked on his finger and slung over one shoulder.

Tracie stood beside the closet, arms crossed over her chest, a cocky look on her face. When she caught sight of him, her mouth opened as if to say something and closed again without uttering a word. She swallowed hard, the muscles in her throat working. "I—" Her voice came out in a tight squeak. After clearing her throat, she finally managed, "I was right. Damned sexy." Then she turned on her stilettos and marched back into the cabin.

Rip chuckled. If he wasn't mistaken, the woman had been tongue-tied by him in a white suit. Who'd have thought a man in a white suit would have that much of an effect on a woman. He'd have to ask Hank where he'd gotten this one. It would be worth it to invest in something that inspiring. Especially if Tracie thought it made him look sexy.

He returned to the cabin with a wide, satisfied grin on his face.

FOR THE NEXT thirty minutes, Rip and Tracie poured over the racks of rifles, grenade launchers, pistols and explosives with which Hank had seen fit to equip the small armory on the airplane.

Rip tucked a HK .40 caliber pistol in his boot, then he grabbed a nine-millimeter Glock in a shoulder holster and slung it over his shoulders.

The flight attendant stepped up behind him and offered to hold the white linen jacket that went with the tailored white trousers, while he slipped his arms into the sleeves.

Though the sleeves were long, the entire outfit was surprisingly comfortable and cool. Used to heavy battle-dress uniforms, bullet-proof vests and helmets, Rip felt somewhat naked and exposed in the suit.

"Smile. You're supposed to be on your honeymoon without a care in the world." Tracie adjusted the collar of his shirt beneath the jacket and patted his chest. "You look more like a kid in his itchy, Sunday best."

Rip fidgeted. "I'd rather go in with my M4 on automatic."

"Well, we can't. We're honeymooners and guests of Hector, so act like you're in love." Tracie's eyes widened and a smile curled her lips. "Unless you've never been in love." Her brows climbed up her forehead. "You haven't, have you?"

He shook his head. "Haven't had the time. I was a little preoccupied with SEAL training straight out of Navy basic and saving the world one bad guy at a time for the past seven years."

She smiled at him. "Let me guess…it's a tough job, but—"

"—someone has to do it." With one arm, he captured her around the waist and clamped her body against his, his other hand reaching up to cup her face in his palm. "Is this better, *mi amore*?" He bent to claim her lips with his. At first he did it to prove a point, but when her body pressed to his, it triggered a response he wasn't prepared for.

Her arms slid around his neck and her breasts pressed against his chest, he couldn't break the kiss to save his life.

Not until a discreet cough sounded nearby.

Her cheeks flushed, the flight attendant gave him a weak smile. "Sorry, but Hank's on the satellite phone. He wants to talk to you two before we land."

Tracie stepped away and wiped the back of her hand over her mouth. "Tell him we'll bring him up on the computer." She took a seat at the monitor and clicked the keyboard, bringing up a video feed of Hank.

"Tracie, Rip." Hank nodded. "We have a little information on the man called Carmelo Delgado we thought you should know. He's a coffee plantation owner. Though they don't have photos to back it up, the Feds think Delgado is a key player with the rebels. His plantation has never been targeted and he keeps a heavy contingent of gunmen employed to protect his interests. Locals say that he is well-known in Honduras for his ruthless disregard for the law and life and for the way he treats women. Or should I say beats women?"

"Sounds like a nice guy," Tracie said, her voice flat.

"Be careful around him," Hank said. "He's dangerous and he could be one of the rebel leaders."

"We'll keep that in mind. Did you find anything else?"

"I don't know if it means anything, but there is a photo of Senator Craine in San Pedro Sula this year. He's been in several of the Central American countries negotiating trade agreements between the different countries and the US."

"So?" Rip stared at the screen, studying Hank Derringer's face. He didn't look like a billionaire. He looked like a rancher with his weathered skin, shock of white hair and a blue chambray shirt he might wear out to the barn to muck stalls.

"Brandon found a photo of Craine and Delgado at a trade meeting, shaking hands."

"Flight attendant, prepare for landing," the captain said over the intercom.

"We're about to land," Tracie told Hank.

"We're still searching for more clues. If we find anything else, I'll call you on the satellite phone." Hank rang off.

Rip took his seat across the aisle and buckled his seat belt, his mind not on the information Hank had imparted but on the kiss that had left his head spinning and his pulse hammering. She was such a distraction, he was afraid he'd lose focus when he needed it most.

Turning his back on Tracie, Rip leaned toward the window, staring down at what appeared to be a jungle rushing up at them, when in fact they were plummeting toward the treetops.

The adrenaline coursing through his veins spiked at the speed of their descent. He peered closer as the Citation X circled, dropping toward the canopy, slowing as it approached the ground.

A wide slash opened up in the green carpet below, revealing an expansive field with a magnificent hacienda sprawled across a hilltop, its stucco walls painted a pale terracotta and accented with creamy white trim. The place had a dark terra-cotta tiled roof and richly dark wooden doors. A sparkling pool provided a splash of blue with palm trees lining the tiled deck.

To the north of the house stretched a long, level green field of grass with several wind socks along its length. It appeared to be more of a fancy playing field than a beautifully manicured and level landing field.

The Citation kissed the turf, the pilot reversing the thrust to come to a swift stop on the grass-covered landing strip. From all appearances they'd landed in a tropical paradise.

The peace and tranquility of the lush setting was short-lived. As they taxied to a halt, several topless Jeeps, with machine guns mounted on them, exploded out of the tree line headed straight for the Citation.

The pilot's voice sounded over the plane's intercom, "Relax, our host assures us the approaching vehicles are his men coming to greet us and ensure our safety."

Rip frowned, patting the Glock in his shoulder holster. "They don't look like the welcoming committee."

Tracie bit her bottom lip. "I hope they're on our side. I'd hate to take live fire from one of those guns." She peered out her window, her brows furrowed.

Even if they'd wanted to, they couldn't take off again and leave. Not with Hector's men surrounding their plane with weapons pointed at them. Now that they were in Honduras, they were Hector's guests, like it or not.

Perhaps a little danger was just what Rip needed to wipe away the aftereffects of that kiss. One thing was certain, it had left an indelible impression on his lips and his libido. Pretending to be a lusty, loving honeymooner wouldn't be such a burden to bear. Turning off the act at the end of this charade would be an entirely different story.

Chapter Four

Tracie's heartbeat rattled in her chest and the hum of blood banging against her eardrums seemed louder than the plane's engine. What bothered her most was that it had nothing to do with the fear of landing on a short runway in the jungle or the fact that they were surrounded by big, mean-looking men armed with weapons that could cut them down in seconds.

No, her elevated heart rate had more to do with the one man who'd dared to bend her to his will in a soul-defining kiss that she would not soon erase from her memory.

Holy hell.

With her back to him, she pressed her fingertips to her pulsing lips. More than anything, she wanted to ask the pilot to take her back to Texas where she could tell Hank that she wasn't the right person for the job. He could get someone else who would be more professional when playing the part of a happily married woman. Someone who could separate truth from fiction, keep them distanced and remain sane throughout the mission.

Oh, her body had the lusty, newlywed part down. The disconnect came when she reminded herself that this was all a ruse and that when this job was over, there would be nothing else between her and the SEAL. After their mission, the man, with his burly muscles and blue eyes she

could fall right into would go back about his business of
saving the masses from fates worse than death, and protecting the country's freedom.

She would return to Texas and her next assignment with
Covert Cowboys, Inc. Her and Rip's paths would never
cross again. What would be the point of a relationship with
such a man? Not that there was anything happening between them. They were both playing their parts, nothing
more.

Oy. Then why was her heart still pounding?

The flight attendant lowered the steps into place and
Rip headed for the doorway.

Tracie's gaze followed him as he made his way down
the steps, his swagger so sexy it made her belly tighten.

She left her seat and followed, sucking in a deep breath
before stepping into the doorway and smiling down at him,
slammed with the heat and humidity of the Honduran jungle. She could do this, she thought, reminding herself again
that it was just an act.

Rip stood at the bottom of the steps and held out his
hand, the white of his smile rivaling the brilliant sunshine.
"Come on, sweetheart. Our host is waiting. The sooner we
meet with him, the sooner we can start our honeymoon."
He winked. "You did bring that sexy teddy you got at the
bridal shower, didn't you?"

Her heart stopped in her chest as she stared down at
the elegantly handsome SEAL dressed in the white linen
suit. God, he looked like a million dollars and the man of
every woman's dreams with his darkly tanned skin and
megawatt grin.

Squaring her shoulders, she forced a broad smile and
took his hand, descending with deliberate slowness to give
the appearance of a woman tempting her new husband with
a sexy turn of her ankle, ready to enjoy every minute of

her honeymoon. "I did, darling. It's on top in my suitcase. As soon as we can get to our room, I'll give you a private viewing of me in it."

Before her stilettos touched the ground, he swept her into his arms and bent her over in a sexy and deeply satisfying kiss that stirred her in a thousand different ways all at once.

When he let her up, she batted at his chest. "Oh, baby, save it for the bedroom."

"Why save it, there's much more where that came from, and besides, I can't keep my hands off you." His fingers slid along her spine, down over her bottom and squeezed, pressing her pelvis to his thick thigh.

Tracie leaned up to nip his earlobe. "What are you doing?" She hissed through a broad, fake smile.

"Playing my part, sweetheart. Playing my part." He bent, captured her beneath the knees and swung her around, her filmy skirt floating out around them. "Where's Senor De-Vita?" he asked the nearest guard.

"You are to come with me." A scary man with heavy brows and a wicked-looking AK-47 Soviet-made rifle jerked his head toward a Jeep similar to those surrounding the plane. The leader didn't wait for Rip or Tracie—he strode to the vehicle and climbed into the front seat.

Rip carried Tracie across the grass and settled her into the backseat. A man stood between the front seat and backseat holding on to the machine gun, his gaze skimming across Tracie's shapely legs.

Tucking her dress around her, Tracie covered as much as she could, then slid the edges of the material beneath her to hold the dress down.

Rip climbed in on the other side of the Jeep. Before he was completely settled, the driver gunned the accelerator, sending the SUV into a tight one-eighty and headed back into the solid wall of jungle. A road appeared in front of them, winding through trees to an imposing gate and an even more imposing concrete fence topped with concertina wire.

A chill rippled along Tracie's spine. The fence and gate looked more like the kind you'd see at a prison compound than at a wealthy man's hacienda in the tropics.

Once they cleared the gate, the trees thinned and opened onto a wide knoll that must have been a good ten acres of manicured lawns. Gracefully designed landscape surrounded the sprawling hacienda with a tall concrete and stucco wall rising up to provide yet another imposing barrier around the owner's home. At least this one didn't sport concertina wire.

As they neared, huge, ornate, steel double doors opened. The Jeep entered the circular driveway and came to an abrupt halt in front of a wide set of elegant stairs, leading up to the glass and wrought-iron entrance.

A man stood at the top of the stairs, dressed similarly to Rip in a white linen suit, white leather shoes and a smoky gray shirt beneath the jacket. A thick gold chain shone through the V of his shirt's neckline, reflecting sunlight off the links.

His hair was full, dark and smoothed back from his forehead, falling to brush the tops of his shoulders. He wore a goatee and his eyes were shiny black. When he smiled, his white teeth shone in stark contrast against his bronze-toned skin.

The Jeep driver shifted into Park, jumped from his seat and circled around to Tracie's side. The man who'd greeted them at the plane climbed out of the Jeep and spoke to the man on the steps in swift Spanish to which the man replied sharply.

Rip took Tracie's arm in a firm grasp and helped her

from the Jeep and then addressed the man on the steps. "You must be Hector DeVita."

Their original welcoming committee and chauffeur backed away from their boss, settled in the vehicle and drove away, leaving Tracie and Rip alone to face their host.

Only they weren't alone. Tracie counted no fewer than four men bearing assault rifles—two positioned at the corners of the front of the hacienda, and two a couple steps behind Hector. All four men were dressed in black trousers and black T-shirts, and they wore sunglasses that hid their eyes.

"*Si*, I am Hector DeVita." The man in white spread his arms wide. "Senor and Senora Gideon, welcome, *por favor. Mi casa es su casa.*" He stepped sideways and waved them up the stairs and past him into the shadow of the entrance. "Hank has told me so much about you. I understand congratulations are in order."

Tracie adjusted inwardly to the use of their fake married name, while smiling politely at Hector. "That's nice since he's told us so little about you. I hope we can rectify that misfortune."

"Certainly," he said. "*Por favor*, step inside. The day is *muy caliente*, and I think a cool drink is much needed."

A servant dressed in a powder-blue guayabera shirt and dark pants opened and held the door.

Tracie stepped inside onto a gleaming white marbled foyer with impossibly high ceilings that created a sense of elegant spaciousness. A sweeping staircase with mahogany railing curved to the right to a second level.

"Your home is lovely," Tracie said.

Hector gave a slight bow. "*Gracias*, Senora Gideon."

"Please, call me Phyllis."

Hector took Tracie's hand and raised it to his lips, press-

ing a light kiss to her skin. "Phyllis, you are *muy bonita.*"
He clutched her fingers longer than she liked.

Rip held out his hand to Hector, forcing the man to acknowledge him and release his hold on Tracie. "Nice to
meet you, Senor DeVita. You can call me Chuck."

"Chuck." Hector shook Rip's hand and let go. He turned
to the interior of the luxurious hacienda and waved a hand
toward the staircase. "My servant will show you to your
room. Once you have had time for a short siesta, I would
be pleased if you would join me for dinner. We get so few
visitors here. At that time we can discuss your visit and security needs while you honeymoon in Honduras."

Chuck nodded. "I look forward to dinner." He hooked
an arm around Tracie's waist. "But for now, I'd like that
siesta. I haven't had two minutes alone with my new wife
since the wedding."

Hector's brows rose. "A beautiful woman is not someone to be ignored. If I had such a lovely wife, I would not
waste my honeymoon on business."

"Phyllis is not only gorgeous—she's an astute business-
woman and she's as eager as I am to begin our search for
additional investment property and businesses." He winked
at her.

Though she knew his playful look was all for show, the
sparkle in his blue eyes and the way he smiled at her made
Tracie's stomach flutter and heat rise up her neck to bloom
in her cheeks. "But of course. I love the challenge of finding a diamond in the rough and turning it into something
of value. It gives me a thrill every time."

"Were you my wife, I would find other ways to excite
you, *mi amore*," Hector said.

Rip's eyes narrowed and his smile slipped as his arm
tightened around Tracie. "Make no mistake, I know how
to please my wife in *every* way."

"Trust me, I didn't marry him just for his brain." Tracie laid a hand on his chest and stared up into his eyes, channeling every sexy move she'd seen in the movies. "He knows me," she whispered and leaned up on her toes to press a kiss to his cheek. "I am a bit tired from the flight." She looked around, ending the conversation that was becoming more uncomfortable by the minute.

"Of course." Hector snapped his fingers and a young woman in a powder-blue dress with a white Peter Pan collar hurried forward. She executed a little curtsy and said, *"Por favor, sigueme."* With a hand motion for them to follow her, she led the way up the stairs and down a long, wide hallway. Arched windows looked out over the glimmering pool surrounded by palm trees and bright splashes of blooming bougainvillea bushes.

If the entire compound were not surrounded by a high concrete fence, with security guards positioned at each corner and several in between, it could easily be mistaken for paradise. Knowing what lay beyond the walls and hidden in the jungles, or even roaming the streets of the cities, Rip knew Honduras was a country in desperate times. The government had little control over the rebels, the military often siding or collaborating with them in order to stay alive.

They walked in silence to the room Hector had assigned them. The servant opened the door and stepped inside, switching on lights. Calling the space a room was an understatement.

The bedroom alone had more square footage than Rip's entire apartment back in Mississippi. Through an arched doorway was a sitting room with a chaise longue, a desk and a leather executive chair.

The maid spoke in halting English, *"El banjo*—the bathroom is here." She led the way through another arched doorway into a bathroom in stark black and white, the counters solid slabs of white granite, specked with flashes of silver and black.

A huge walk-in shower could have fit six people and sported no fewer than four showerheads. The fixtures were polished, gleaming and sparkling clean. Fluffy white towels lay on the counter and near a tub big enough for two people. Lit candles flickered all around, adding to the sunlight shining through a glass brick wall.

"If you need anything, *por favor*, just ask." The maid backed out of the bathroom.

Rip and Tracie followed her to the door of the bedroom, closing it softly behind the maid.

"Wow," Rip said.

Tracie spun and placed a finger over his lips, then stood on her toes to kiss him, pulling his head down so that she could nibble his ear and whisper, "The entire room could be bugged or monitored by video." Louder, she added, "Kiss me."

Rip obliged, gathering her into his arms. While he kissed her, he closed his eyes halfway, glancing around the bedroom from beneath his eyelids. A trained SEAL, he was used to sneaking into villages, or towns, carrying a healthy array of weapons and explosives. Sometimes he searched for surveillance devices on the exteriors of buildings, but for the most part, finding them hidden in a room was a whole new skill to add to his arsenal.

He ran one hand down her back and cupped her bottom, his other hand pushing the hair off her neck, his mouth following his hand, tasting her skin up to her ear where he nipped her earlobe. "You're the expert. What do we look for?" he breathed into her ear.

She winked at him and then turned her back. "Unzip me, please." Tracie pulled her hair aside allowing him access to the zipper.

His heart leaped and he stared down at her. While he would love to get naked with the beautiful former FBI agent, what had made her come around to the idea so quickly? Especially considering the added probability of their movements being recorded.

She spun around, smiled and whispered between her teeth, "Just do it." Giving him her back again, she waited, holding her hair up.

While he obliged, his knuckles skimming across the silky, soft skin of her lower back, Rip tried to keep his mind off the scent of her shampoo, the curve of her shoulders and the flare of her hips.

Forcing his mind away from what he was finding inside Tracie's dress, he stared around the room, checking corners, wall sconces and the chandelier hanging at the center of the room. His breath hitched. At the same time he skimmed the soft, rounded curve of her bottom beneath her dress, he caught sight of a small black device attached to the wrought-iron chandelier.

"Got one," he said softly as he reached the end of the zipper.

Tracie turned and let the dress slide off her shoulders. "Where would you like to begin?" she said loud enough to pick up on any listening device in the room.

Rip's stomach flipped. Hell, he'd like to begin at her lips and taste every inch of body. Unfortunately, she was talking about the location of the camera he'd found.

The yellow dress fell to the floor, pooling around her feet. Wearing nothing but her bra and panties, she batted her eyes, lifted the filmy garment in her hand and paused. "Aren't you going to get undressed?"

"You don't have to ask me twice." He took the dress from her hands and tossed it in the air. The fabric caught on the wrought iron of the chandelier, effectively blocking the view from the miniature camera perched there.

Standing at the bedroom door, Rip switched the light off, to keep the dress from getting too hot on the lightbulbs and catching fire.

Moving quickly and efficiently, Tracie slipped into a silk robe that had been left on the bed. Then she made her way around the room checking behind the wall sconces, beneath the edges of the furniture, inside vases and behind the king-size bed's headboard. When she skimmed her fingers along the underside of the nightstand, she came across another device and pulled it from its mooring.

Rip followed suit, combing over the sitting room and the bathroom, discovering a camera and a listening device in each. Over the cameras, he tossed hand towels. The listening devices he pulled free from the furniture where they were mounted.

Collecting the one Tracie had found, he wrapped them tightly in one of the fluffy towels and stuffed them into the back of a drawer. If the listeners were concerned about the sound being muffled…too bad.

Rip didn't relax until they'd completed a thorough search of the room and Tracie stopped in front him. "I think we got most of them," she said quietly. "But don't let your guard down."

Nodding, Rip sighed. "I don't know about you, but I could use a shower and that siesta."

Tracie smiled. "I'm a bit tired after the flight and everything else. You can go first."

Speaking louder, Rip offered, "Sweetheart, it's our honeymoon, we can shower together." Then he cupped the back of her head and kissed her neck. "Just in case we missed some."

Tracie wrapped her hand around the back of his head. "I'm not showering with you."

His lips trailed across her jawline and back to her earlobe. "I promise not to look."

"Or touch?" she asked.

He raised three fingers. "Scouts honor."

Tracie's brows furrowed. "Why do I get the feeling you've never been a Boy Scout?"

"Probably because I never have." He turned her away and patted her silk-covered behind. "Now go get the water warmed up. I like my showers like I like my women, hot and wet."

Tracie's gasp and the frown she tossed over her shoulder at him made him chuckle. Her cheeks flushed a healthy pink and her eyes flared. He gave her a head start of thirty seconds and then joined her in the bathroom.

Tracie had the shower water running and her silk robe hung on a hook outside the tiled walls of the large walk-in shower.

Rip studied the mirror. Call him paranoid, but he couldn't be certain the mirror wasn't hiding another camera, given the amount of surveillance devices they'd taken from the room.

He told himself he was playing a part. Hank had said from the time they touched ground in Honduras until they left, they had to be completely convincing, even with his contact, Hector. He wasn't absolutely certain of his allegiance to Hank or his alliances with the rebels in Honduras. But he was the best provider of security in the area, with a reputation that had made him a very wealthy man.

For the sake of the mission, Rip shed his white suit and hung it on another hook before stepping into the huge, stone-tiled shower.

Tracie stood with her back to him, her long brown hair

covered in soap suds that slid down her slim athletic, naked body, big suds slipping off the rounded globes of her bottom.

As quickly as he stepped into the shower, he slipped behind her, and clamped one hand around her waist and the other over her mouth.

Chapter Five

When thickly muscled arms wrapped around her waist, Tracie slammed an elbow backward and stomped her bare heel into the instep of her attacker.

Rip bit down on his tongue to keep from yelling out loud, and let out a pained hiss. "Damn it, it's me."

Her body went rigid, the shower pelting her skin and Rip's face as he leaned close. "I wasn't sure if the mirror might be two-way or hiding a camera. So I got in the shower like we're a newlywed couple." He dropped his hand from her mouth, but didn't loosen the arm around her waist until he was certain she wouldn't attack him again.

Her hands crossed over her breasts and she hunched her shoulders. "Then why did you grab me?"

"I knew I'd startle you and didn't want you to scream."

Tracie snorted. "You got the first part right. Now let go of me and turn around. It's not like we have to take this charade all the way."

"I'll let go if you promise not to hit me again." He groaned. "I think you broke one of my ribs."

"I'm not making any promises or apologies," she said.

He let go anyway and stepped back, admiring her body, before he turned away with equal twinges of guilt and regret.

Switching one of the other showerheads on, he squirted

a handful of body wash into his palm from a dispenser on the wall and rubbed it into his hair and over his shoulders. It was too flowery for his liking, but he imagined it was some high-dollar brand used exclusively by the rich. He preferred a plain bar of soap.

Tracie cleared her throat behind him. "This is awkward."

Rip glanced over his shoulder and caught her looking over hers. He grinned and gave her his back again. "You obviously haven't been in the military. Modesty is the least of your worries." He spoke low enough his voice wouldn't carry outside the shower walls or over the sound of the running water.

"I suppose bullets rank higher on your scale of concerns."

"Yup."

"I guess you had a point. I just wish you'd warned me before we both got in the shower."

"I didn't think about the mirror."

"It's probably just that—a mirror."

"Better safe than sorry."

Tracie snorted.

"By the way," Rip hesitated. "You have a beautiful body." He smiled, knowing his words would get to her.

He wasn't disappointed by the gasp behind him. His smile broadened until he was hit in the head with a sopping washcloth.

"Hey." He turned and grabbed her around the waist as she pulled her arm and the cloth back for a second attack. "I just call it as I see it."

"You weren't supposed to see it." She struggled to free herself from his hold. "Let go."

"Not until you quit swinging at me." The more she wiggled, the more Rip became aware of her rounded, wet breasts pressing against his chest. Before he could will his natural reaction away, his body responded, his groin tightened and his member hardened, pressing into her tight belly.

Tracie froze. "Uh." She bit down on her lip. "Is that what I think it is?"

"Did I mention that I think you have a beautiful body?" He started to set her away from him, but her arms wrapped around his waist holding him against her.

"This is really awkward," she whispered, her voice breathy.

"I'll just leave the shower. You can have it to yourself." He didn't want to leave at all but was afraid that the longer he stayed, the more he'd want to do more than was strictly necessary to nail the role.

"Don't move. I'm naked." Her eyes were round and her cheeks bright pink. And damned if she wasn't biting her lip again.

It was bad enough her naked body was pressed flush against his, but biting that lip did all kinds of crazy to him. It wouldn't take much and he'd be beyond his ability to control himself. And for Tracie's sake, he needed to maintain his control.

Trying not to breathe too deeply and add more friction to the movement between their chests, Rip suggested, "How about I close my eyes and back away."

"Please don't move," she repeated, sounding as if she couldn't get enough air into her lungs.

He reached up and pushed a wet hank of hair out of her face, that little bit of movement making him even more aware of every inch of her skin touching his with the shower's spray heating the space between them. "If I don't move now…" Rip ground his teeth together, his fingers curling around her arms, preparing to push her away. To hell with the possibility of a camera behind the mirror. He couldn't take much more and not…

"What?" Her hands slid up his back.

"What, what?" he said, his mind a blank, all his blood rushing south to another extremity.

"What will happen if you don't move?" She sucked in a breath and let it out slowly, as if it gave her strength and permission to continue to hold him. "You feel it, don't you?" she asked, her words barely above a whisper.

He leaned his head back, letting the shower's spray pelt the back of his head, trying to beat sense into him, one drop at a time. "I feel, a whole lot of you, rubbing against me." He straightened, his grip tightening on her arms. "And it's making me crazy."

"Uh-huh." She nodded. "Same here."

That made him give her a double take. "So what are we going to do about it?"

She shrugged, her breasts rubbing up and down on him. *Sweet Jesus.* She was killing him.

"There's only one thing we can do."

"Yeah? Then tell me. I've never been good at guessing what goes on in a woman's mind. And will you make it quick? I'm about to come undone."

"This." She wrapped one hand around his neck and pulled his head down so that she could press her lips to his. "And this." Her other hand slid down his back to his buttocks, cupping him and pressing him closer. "You see, I figure there's a physical attraction here."

"You think?" He groaned, let go of her arms and skimmed his hands down the curve of her waist. He trailed his fingers over the swell of her hips and cupped the backs of her thighs. In one smooth motion, he lifted her, wrapping her legs around him, pressing her back against the tiles. "What was your first clue?"

"The kiss." She brushed her mouth across his. "Maybe

if we get the elephant in the room out of the way once and for all, we can concentrate on what's more important."

"I like the way you think." He positioned her over his swollen member, ready to drive the point home.

Tracie's hands on his shoulders pressed down and she hovered over him. "One thing…"

His heart hammering against his chest, adrenaline and lust raging through his veins, Rip could barely hear her through the blood pounding in his ears. "What thing?"

"Protection?" she said. "I don't suppose you have some?"

His body on fire, his brain disengaged, it took a moment for Rip to realize what she was saying. "Damn."

"Damn you have to stop to get it or damn you didn't bring any?"

"Damn to both." He buried his face in her neck and moaned. "I had some in my old wallet. Not in the new one."

"This bathroom has just about everything a guest could want…you don't suppose…"

Rip set Tracie on her feet and dove out of the shower, nearly slipping on the tiled floors. Trailing water everywhere he stepped, he riffled through the drawers one at a time.

One had extra washcloths, another had an array of bath salts. Still another had unopened tubes of toothpaste and individually wrapped toothbrushes. When he'd just about given up, Rip opened the bottom drawer in the farthest cabinet and found a supply of lubricants in every flavor imaginable and at least two-dozen foil packages.

He was back in the shower carrying his prize, his ardor no less urgent.

But Tracie had the washcloth draped over her front, barely covering the important parts.

Rip sighed. "Nothing like an important interruption to kill the mood, right?"

She shook her head. "No. I'm perfectly prepared to go through with this." Letting the washcloth fall to the floor, she stepped forward, holding out her hand. "Let me. I'm sure that as soon as we get this over with, we won't be nearly as distracted."

Rip held the packet out of her reach. "You make this sound like the cure to a disease."

"Well, in a way, it is. Once we…do it…it will take away the mystery and we won't be thinking about what it might be like. We can get on with our purpose for being here without unnecessary distraction."

He could see where her thoughts were headed, but her logic was faulty. Once they consummated their relationship, it would only be the beginning. He already knew he'd want more. By the look on Tracie's face, she thought this would be the end and they'd put their physical attraction for each other to bed, so to speak.

Tracie propped her hand on her hip, a worried frown denting her forehead. "Don't you want to have sex?"

Water ran over her shoulders and dripped off the tips of her dusky rose nipples.

Oh, yeah, he wanted it.

He had to clear his throat to answer. "Yes, I do." His member couldn't get any harder. "But, honey, this won't stop here."

"It has to. We are consenting adults with jobs that take us to the ends of the earth. Most likely we won't see each other again. Besides, I'm not interested in anything more than a one-night stand."

A spike of anger jolted through Rip. "Isn't that the man's line?"

"I've been there. Once the lust fades, all you have is regret, and both individuals looking for a way out without hurting the other."

Though he wanted her, Rip knew this was all wrong. "Baby, I don't know who hurt you in the past, but that's not how it works with me." He stepped back, turned and left the shower and her in it.

A sloppy, wet slap sounded behind him and he spun to find a wet washcloth on the floor near his feet. Grumbling echoed inside the shower.

Let her stew. He had some thinking of his own to do. And his thoughts were clearer away from her.

TRACIE STOOD IN the shower, steaming hotter than the water. What just happened? She'd given the SEAL permission to make love to her with no strings attached, demanding no promises for the future. Most men would grab at that opportunity and accept what she was offering, no hesitation.

Not Rip.

She wanted to rant and rave and throw a whopping temper tantrum like a five-year-old deprived of her favorite doll. Only she wasn't five, and she had been all lathered up and ready for some hot and heavy sex. Frustrated beyond anything she'd ever felt she turned the handle on the faucet. Cold water sluiced over her body. Her breath caught in her throat and she shivered, but remained standing in the cool water until the heat of her desire chilled and she could think beyond the sight of Rip's rippling muscles and stiff erection.

Damn. What was wrong with the man?

Or was it her? He didn't desire her enough to take her up on her offer? No, he'd been just as turned on by her as she was by him.

She shut off the water and peeked around the corner of the shower stall. The bathroom was empty of the man she couldn't get out of her thoughts.

Quickly drying off, she slipped her arms into the robe

and pulled it over her body, cinching the belt around her middle before gripping the door handle. Sucking in a deep breath, she squared her shoulders, determined not to show any of her disappointment over Rip's blatant rejection.

Pulling the door open, she stepped through, her chin tilted at a slight angle, determined not to show any emotion to the man.

Tense and slightly hesitant, she stepped out of the bathroom into the bedroom, her belly tight. Her breath caught and held.

The room was as empty as the bathroom. Rip had left.

All the air left her lungs, and a deep sense of disappointment washed over her. Good grief. Had she scared him so badly he'd tucked his tail and run from the room? Wow. Way to shoot a girl down.

Her ego completely deflated, Tracie flopped on the bed, wearing the silk robe and nothing else. Maybe if Rip came back soon, he'd rethink his refusal, part the edges of the robe and take her.

Her heartbeat kicked up a notch and her breathing quickened. Every time she heard a noise, she hoped it was coming from the hallway. At one point she heard footsteps on the tiles outside her door. They paused. She held her breath in eager anticipation, her groin tightening, her body tense.

Then the footsteps moved on.

Releasing the breath she'd been holding, Tracie rolled to her side, tucked her hand beneath her cheek and closed her eyes. If she wasn't going to get the sex she needed to slake her appetite for the man, the least she could do was rest up. She didn't know when they'd head out of the compound in search of the rebel fighters…er…investment property, but she wanted to be ready when they did. Rip had warned her that the guerilla fighters were dangerous and would prefer to shoot first and question later.

She lay with her eyes closed, willing herself to sleep, but the scene in the shower keep replaying against the backs of her eyelids. If she'd kept her mouth shut, she'd be in the middle of what she guessed might have been the best sex of her life.

Rip would be a superb lover. Rough but gentle, aware and insistent on satisfying her needs, the complete opposite of her former fiancé.

She'd met Bruce Masterson on the job when she'd been an FBI special agent. They'd worked a case together and Tracie had been infatuated with him. Still fairly new as an agent, she'd looked up to the man who had several more years experience than she did.

Unfortunately, she'd mistaken infatuation for love and had agreed to marry the bastard before she realized he was linked with one of the deadliest and most traitorous men smuggling drugs and trafficking women and children into the United States: their regional director.

She'd been so blind to their deception, trusting them because they were on her team—supposedly the good guys.

Sadly, Bruce had never loved her. Their engagement had only been a front to help hide his nefarious activities. His deception had cost Tracie her ability to trust men.

Hank Derringer was the exception. If not for him and Covert Cowboys, Inc., she'd be dead. Their relentless pursuit of her and her captors saved her life. But the knowledge that the people she'd worked so closely with in the FBI had been rotten to the core had shaken her to the foundation of her beliefs.

Aside from Hank and the agents he'd assembled in CCI, Tracie didn't know who to trust. That lack of faith in humanity had led to her decision to leave the FBI and go to work for Hank, seeking truth and justice when the police, FBI, military, CIA or other government agencies couldn't seem to get it right or had their hands tied by the powers that be.

She wanted to trust Rip. Admittedly, he was slowly winning her over. After Bruce's betrayal, she'd vowed never to trust another man with her heart. Perhaps that's why she'd spoken up when she did and told Rip that a one-night stand was all she wanted. She was teetering too close to the edge with Rip as it was.

Sleep was the farthest thing from her mind. Instead of lying in the bed, moping about failed relationships and her lack of trust in humanity, she should be up, celebrating a near miss. If she'd made love to the man, she might have broken her vow to herself.

Tracie flopped onto her back and stared up at the high, coffered ceiling with the ornate chandelier hanging at the center, her yellow dress draped across a hidden camera. Her heart beat strong and steady and her mind lurched forward to the task at hand. Since sleep wasn't coming, she might as well get up and get moving.

First thing on her list was to learn more about Hector DeVita and his fortified compound. If he was an ally, good. She'd know what he had available to her and Rip in their quest to find the rebel hideout. If he turned out to be shady, then she'd at least know what they were up against.

Chapter Six

When Rip left Tracie in the shower, he knew Tracie would think he'd run away. So be it. As a SEAL, he didn't have much time at home. Why waste it on people who didn't give a damn about him? When he was not out fighting battles, he wanted to feel emotionally safe and surrounded by people who cared for and meant something to him.

In the short time he'd known Tracie, he'd come to respect her and he couldn't deny his attraction to her. But one-night stands weren't his style.

His buddies might jump at the chance, claiming life was too short to pass up an opportunity to get lucky. But that was why Rip made every connection count. And he suspected a connection with Tracie would be worth the effort to make it real. Hopping in the sack to get sex out of the way wouldn't make him forget her, or forget what they might have between them.

In the bedroom, he found that, while they'd been in the bathroom, their suitcases had been offloaded from the plane, the clothing unpacked into the dressers or hung in the walk-in closet. He checked to see if the staff had found the wadded up towels stuffed in the back of the drawer. The towels were gone, along with the devices. Damn, they were efficient and, if Hector hadn't figured out before they'd removed the equipment, he'd know now.

Rip selected a pair of light gray trousers and a white button-up shirt—he left three buttons unbuttoned at the top. Still aroused by his naked encounter with Tracie, he didn't want to further tempt himself by being there when she emerged. Slipping into a pair of expensive loafers, he left the room, pulling the door closed.

Out in the spacious hallway, he looked back the way they'd come and turned his back, choosing to search the path yet untraveled. He wandered down the hallway and pushed through a door that led out onto a terrace overlooking a large, beautifully designed infinity pool with water running over the edges in a continuous, soothing flow.

"Join me, Senor Gideon," Hector called out from below.

For a moment, Rip didn't respond, not recognizing the use of his fake name. When he realized Hector was talking to him, Rip descended a set of wrought-iron stairs to the patio surrounding the pool.

The Honduran sat at a bistro table, an iced drink in his hand. "Can I offer you a drink?"

"Yes, thank you. Whatever you're having will be fine."

Hector waved a hand and a servant appeared. He gave the man instructions in Spanish and the servant hurried off. With a smile he faced Rip. "My staff informs me you found my surveillance equipment." He tipped his head. "Well done."

"I like my privacy, even when I'm enjoying the accommodations of my host."

Again, Hector smiled like a gracious host. "I understand perfectly. I hope you did not take offense."

"Not at all," Rip responded.

"Where is the lovely Senora Gideon?"

"She was tired after the flight and chose to sleep through the hottest part of the day."

"And you don't find her company...stimulating enough to lie down with her?"

The servant appeared at that moment with a drink on a tray. He set it down in front of Rip and walked away.

Rip raised the glass and drank, then set the glass on the table. The alcohol took the bite off his irritation with Hector's questions about Tracie. "Jack and Coke. Perfect."

Hector's lip lifted on one side, in recognition of Rip's attempt to steer him away from personal questions. Their host lifted his own drink and held it up. "To your beautiful bride."

Raising his glass Rip tapped it to Hector's. "To my wife. She's an amazing woman, and she's mine." He stared hard over his glass at the man across from him.

His host raised his other hand and chuckled. "How is it you say? Message received?"

Rip relaxed against the back of his chair. "Hank didn't tell us much about you, only that you were a shrewd businessman, the best in security in Central America and somewhat of a ladies' man."

Hector shrugged, the movement smooth and elegant. "I am a rich man. There are many women who would be happy to be with me. But it is rare to find one who isn't interested in only my money."

"And you think Phyllis isn't interested in my money?"

His head canted to the side as Hector considered Rip's question. "It is said that the eyes are the window into a woman's soul. Your wife loves you. She may not know yet how much she does, but it is clear."

If only. Rip bit down hard on the inside of his mouth to keep from blurting out that he didn't have her love and he wasn't in love, though the thought of loving Tracie appealed to him. Not many women would understand the life he led.

Having been assigned to different tasks all over as an

FBI agent, Tracie was aware of what it was like to be away from home for long periods of time. Some women wouldn't understand when he couldn't come home for months at a time. Tracie would. Hell, she might be out on assignments of her own.

But what was he thinking? When they had the information they needed and traced the weapons sales back to their source, this gig was up.

His belly tightened.

He'd go his way. Tracie would go hers.

Rip leaned forward. "Hank said he was sending two bodyguards to accompany us while we're out looking at potential properties."

Hector nodded. "He informed me of his plan. He also said you might need more protection and to provide for you only the best and to bill him. I've set aside four of my most trusted men to accompany you. If you like, I can go with you, as well."

Rip held up his hand. "I wouldn't want to take you away from your day-to-day operations."

"It is no problem. I grow bored sitting in my little oasis. So tell me. What is it you're looking for?"

Having done a little research, Rip leaned forward like an eager entrepreneur. "I'm interested in owning my own coffee plantation." Drawing on the satellite images Hank's tech guy had sent plus his own knowledge of the area in question, he proceeded. "My sources told me that there is a coffee plantation near the small town of Colinas Rocosa. From what I've read, they've been successful with rudimentary irrigation techniques. I want to see their operation and the land surrounding it for the potential to expand."

Hector's eyes narrowed. "I am familiar with that area. Carmelo Delgado is the owner that plantation, and it is surrounded by jungle and a river. I seriously doubt Senor

Delgado will sell. The plantation has been in his family for a very long time. It is also a very dangerous area. *Los Rebeldes del Diablo* are known to run the land. I can show you other coffee plantations not nearly so close to trouble."

Rip shook his head. "The other areas are far more expensive. If I can get this coffee plantation at the price I want, I can afford to expand operations."

"Can you afford to pay *Los Rebeldes del Diablo* to keep them from killing you or your workers?"

Pretending to consider Hector's words, Rip tipped his head to the side and touched his chin. "You run a security firm. I could hire your services to protect my interests."

Hector shook his head. "I provide bodyguards for wealthy business owners and their families. I install expensive surveillance equipment in warehouses, stores and homes. I am not equipped to guard entire plantations against *Los Rebeldes del Diablo*. They are an army unto themselves."

"If you won't do it. I'll take care of it myself."

"How?"

"I'll hire mercenaries to stand guard over the land." Rip narrowed his eyes. "Or I'll pay the tithe to *Los Rebeldes del Diablo*. In the meantime will you provide the bodyguards I need to protect me and my wife so that we can get to the plantation?"

"Surely, you are not considering taking your wife with you? It is suicide."

"My wife is quite aware of the dangers. She has a gun and knows how to use it."

"Then not only will she be in danger of attacks by *Los Rebeldes del Diablo*, but if she is caught by the authorities carrying a weapon, she will be thrown in jail." Hector held up a hand. "Honduran jails are no place for Senora Gideon."

"Did I hear my name?" Tracie stepped out of the house onto the tiled decking.

Rip noted she wore thin, harem pants in a pale cream and a silky watermelon-pink blouse that draped her breasts and tiny waist, emphasizing her curves rather than hiding them. Rip's pulse picked up and his fingers clenched into a fist to keep himself from reaching out to her.

Hector stood and pulled a chair out for her, pushing it in as she settled on the cushion. "You did. I was just enlightening your husband on the dangers of traveling in the countryside."

"Are the guerillas still active in this area?" Tracie asked.

Hector nodded. "You did take note of the fences and concertina wire you had to pass through to get here, did you not? These precautions are necessary to protect what is mine."

"We are prepared to take the risk." Tracie smiled at their host and leaned back in her chair, crossing one slender leg over the other. "Hank is sending two of his best bodyguards."

Hector's jaw hardened. "It won't be enough."

"Hank said that you would augment our protection with whatever else we would need. And we'll need transportation, too."

A muscle in Hector's jaw ticked. "I can provide the SUVs and four men to escort you. I advise you to travel in the daylight and not linger too long in one place. If you don't announce that you are coming, you have a better chance of getting in and out without being accosted." Hector waved his hand. "Unless, of course, *Los Rebeldes del Diablo* have checkpoints set up on the roads. In which case, you should turn around and get out of there as fast as you can."

Tracie inhaled and slowly released the breath… "Understood."

His lips thinning into a straight line, Hector snarled. "You may *think* you understand. These men are ruthless.

They cut down a woman and a six-year-old child while I watched helplessly from my office window in Tegucigalpa."

Tracie laid a hand over Hector's. "I'm so sorry."

Though Rip could appreciate her compassion, he didn't like the way Hector turned his hand upright and gripped Tracie's. But he held his tongue.

Hector continued, his head down, his gaze where his hand held Tracie's. "They are ruthless and have no regard for life, and no remorse. All they know is how to threaten and follow through with their threats by killing anyone who crosses their paths."

"Why don't the people rise up against them?"

"The guerillas are armed. The citizens of Honduras are not. And the citizens value the lives of their loved ones. If they try to fight against the guerillas, *Los Rebeldes del Diablo* steal their wives, husbands and children and kill them or hold them for ransom."

"That's terrible." Tracie's brows tugged together.

"So you see, if you want to look at a coffee plantation, I implore you—look somewhere else. Perhaps another country."

Rip leaned back, his arms crossing over his chest. "I know I can make this work. I'm not afraid of the *Diablos*."

"You should be." Hector shifted his gaze to Tracie. "If not for your own sake, then for your wife's."

Tracie smiled reassuringly. "Chuck will protect me. I'm sure we will be okay surveying the plantation. After all, we'll go during the daylight and return here before dark."

"*Los Rebeldes del Diablo* do not confine their terror to the shroud of darkness. They have been known to walk into a restaurant or café in the middle of the day and kill everyone in it."

"Then we will stay out of restaurants. Tomorrow Chuck and I want to see *le Plantación de Ángel* coffee plantation."

With a sigh, Hector stood. "I can see that you are not to be dissuaded. I will inform my men that they will ride with you or follow you to the plantation and remain there until you return."

"Thank you, Hector." Tracie glanced at the man. "I can only imagine the anguish you felt at witnessing the deaths of that mother and child. It's such a senseless act to kill innocents."

Hector slowed on his way back into the house and turned again to face them. "Honduras is my home, but sometimes I hate it so much I wish to leave. I will have my assistant make arrangements for your visit to the plantation. Hank's bodyguards are scheduled to fly in tonight. I will not be at dinner, but my staff will see to your meal. Dinner is served at seven." He didn't wait for a response, disappearing inside the house.

TRACIE STARED AFTER the owner of the hacienda, her heart tight in her chest. "He could be right. Perhaps it is too dangerous to go in broad daylight."

"I want to see how many eyes and ears are employed by the rebel leader and how far out they are stationed," Rip said. "We need to know where they get their groceries and supplies. In order to find out where those boxes full of weapons came from, we have to find members of the *Diablos* and follow them back to their camp."

"Yeah, but wouldn't it be better to sneak in under cover of nightfall and do the same?"

"They will have moved from their last location after our attempt to extract the DEA agent. We don't have their coordinates and, most likely, they've chosen a well-concealed spot in the jungle, beneath the canopy and out of view of our satellites."

"Couldn't you get satellite images that show heat signatures?" Tracie asked.

"I'm sure military intelligence is working on it, but there are miles and miles of jungle out there to scan. In the meantime, we could have already found the camp, located a name and traced it back to whoever is selling the weapons to them."

Tracie sighed. "Then we do it."

As they'd been talking, the sun had been steadily sliding toward the horizon, the shadows lengthening. Lights came on in the pool and a servant worked his way around the patio, lighting tiki torches. The atmosphere became more and more intimate as the sky darkened.

Alone with Rip, Tracie couldn't help but feel uncomfortable about her attempt to seduce him in the shower. Apparently he was not nearly as attracted to her as she was to him, or he would have taken her up on her offer, no questions asked.

With desire flaring up in the pit of her belly, Tracie leaned forward, prepared to run. "If you'll excuse me, I think I'll go change into something more formal for dinner."

As she started to rise, a hand halted her progress.

"Just to make things clear," Rip whispered. "I would have made love to you."

She tried to pull away, her cheeks heating with embarrassment. Had he read her mind? "I know a brush off when I hear it."

His grip tightened and he gave a quick yank, forcing her to fall forward to land in his lap.

"That's better." He nibbled at her ear, while whispering, "Now we look like a newlywed couple and you have proof that I find you extremely attractive."

The hard ridge beneath the placket of his trousers nudged

her bottom and a thrill shivered across her body. Oh, yes, he was attracted. "Then why walk away?"

His hand clamped on either side of her face, forcing her to look him in the eyes. "Because you're a smart, beautiful and wonderful woman, and you deserve more than a fleeting affair." He leaned closer, brushing his lips across hers. "And I mean to show you how much more you deserve than a one-night stand." His words were low, his breath warm against her lips and then he crushed her to his chest, his mouth claiming hers.

Unable to resist, Tracie wrapped her arms around his neck and gave in to the desire that had been building since she'd first met this incredible man.

His tongue slid along hers in an urgent caress, drawing a heartfelt moan from deep in her chest. Warm, strong hands slipped down her back and up her sides, his thumbs skimming the underside of her breasts.

So caught up was she in his seduction, Tracie didn't hear anything outside her own moans and the blood pounding against her eardrums.

Rip raised his head, reluctantly releasing her lips.

The man she'd first seen wearing the powder-blue servant uniform when she'd entered the hacienda stood ten feet away, his head downcast but peering up from beneath heavy black brows. When he was certain he had their attention, he spoke quietly, "Pardon, Senor, Senora. Dinner will be served in fifteen minutes."

"Thank you," Rip said without releasing his hold on Tracie's body.

After the servant left, Rip stared into Tracie's eyes. "That's just a taste of what you could have."

Her body on fire, Tracie wanted nothing more than to retreat to their room and make mad, passionate love to this man. But there was more than sexual desire emanating from his eyes. He held her gaze with an intensity she could imagine he used to attack any challenge, including taking on the enemy. "Just so you know, I'm not good at relationships. Bruce, my ex-fiancé is a perfect example of how lousy I am at it. I don't think he was really ever interested in me to begin with."

"Then your fiancé didn't deserve you." He dragged in a deep breath and let it out. "I guess I have more work to do on that front." His hands wrapped around her hips and lifted her off his lap to stand on her feet.

She wobbled for a moment, still affected by that kiss.

"Go, change into something more formal. I'll see you at dinner." He turned her and patted her bottom, propelling her forward.

Torn between being annoyed and flattered, she thought about slapping him for patting her fanny. Instead, she chose to scurry away before she threw herself into his arms and begged him to take her back to the room, not send her back on her own.

Tracie entered through the back patio door and turned down a wide, airy hallway, heading for the wing where their room was located.

Halfway down the hallway, Hector stood staring at a portrait.

Her feet making very little noise, Tracie was almost to Hector before he noticed her.

He stiffened and stepped back.

Tracie glanced at the portrait of a woman and a small boy and it hit her.

Hector had witnessed the murder of a woman and a small boy at the hands of the guerilla fighters.

A lead ball dropped to the pit of her stomach and her eyes burned with unshed tears. "These are the woman and child you were talking about, aren't they?"

He didn't respond at first, a muscle ticking in his jaw. Finally, he nodded. "I had known Marisol since we were both children. She had such a hard time getting pregnant. When Alejandro was born…" Hector broke off, scrubbing a hand through his dark hair. "I'd never seen her happier."

"You must miss them terribly."

Hector nodded. "I'd give anything to have them back."

"I imagine you would."

He closed his eyes and seemed to draw himself up before he turned to her. "Hank did not tell me why you and your husband really came to Honduras. It is not a honeymoon getaway for most people."

Having just witnessed Hector's raw emotions about the loss of his wife and son, Tracie was tempted to blurt out the real reason they were there. But she bit down hard on her tongue, remembering Hank's entreaty not to trust anyone, even his contact.

Tracie shrugged. "In case you haven't figured it out, Chuck and I love a challenge. We like adventure and working through difficult situations. It's what makes our relationship so exciting." *Among other things*, she added silently.

Hector held her gaze for a long moment before nodding. "Very well. If you have other goals in mind, please keep me informed. I might be able to help you."

"Thank you. I will." With a smile, Tracie edged past the man. "I need to change for dinner. Thank you for helping out with our security and for letting us stay in your beautiful home."

He gave her a slight bow. "It is my pleasure."

Tracie hurried away. Feeling as if she were still being watched as she rounded a corner, she glanced back and saw Hector standing exactly where she'd left him, his gaze following her.

A shiver of apprehension coursed down her spine. Hank wouldn't warn her to trust no one without reason. Still, she felt guilty for deceiving Hector, when he'd opened up to her about his loss.

Back in the bedroom, Tracie avoided looking at the king-size bed where she and Rip would sleep that night. After the kiss they'd shared, she wasn't sure she could lie beside him and not want more.

Oh, hell. She knew she wouldn't be satisfied to just sleep with Rip. She wanted all of him, but was she willing to open her heart to a man? Especially a man who had heartache written into every muscle in his body? He was a SEAL. They'd never see each other and he'd be all over the world, possibly with a different woman in every port.

No. She couldn't risk her heart. Not so soon after her former fiancé had proven he was traitorous to the country she loved and had lied to her during their entire time together.

A little voice in her head reminded her that not all men were the same. Still, she wasn't ready to trust her instincts again. Not yet. Maybe never.

Chapter Seven

Dinner was conducted in silence. Rip forced himself to eat, fueling his body for whatever was to come. Despite his resolve, the devil on his shoulder was pushing him to make love to Tracie before he had her full commitment to the possibility of a longer-term relationship.

He didn't know how long he could hold out and not take her to the next level, especially if they would be sleeping in the same room. For certain, he couldn't lie in the same bed and not touch her. It would be the floor for him. Hopefully, the discomfort would help to cool his desire.

As he sat at the long teak dining table that could have hosted a party of twenty, he stared across at Tracie.

She wore a simple black dress crisscrossed low in the front, exposing so much of her breasts, he couldn't look at her without his gaze drifting lower.

She'd twisted her silky brown hair up into some fancy knot at the back of her head, the long line of her throat tempting him nearly as much as the low-cut neckline of her dress. Several times he'd had to swallow hard to keep from groaning out loud.

When the meal was finally over, he nearly leaped to his feet. "I think I'll go for a walk."

Rising with more grace, Tracie raised her brows. "That sounds lovely. Do you mind if I join you?" Her lips quirked at the corners as if she knew he couldn't refuse her and knew he wanted to.

With the possibility that anyone could be watching, Rip nodded and held out his hand. "Please. I haven't had nearly as much time with my new bride as I'd like." He pulled her arm through his and guided her to the rear of the house and out through the patio door they'd gone through earlier.

The pool shone a soothing blue, the lights beneath the water tempting him. Later he'd come out on his own and swim a dozen laps to burn off some of the energy smoldering throughout his body. He wasn't used to taking things slow and he hadn't had an opportunity to work out since he'd met up with Tracie on this crazy mission Hank Derringer seemed to be in charge of.

Past the pool, several steps led down into a garden filled with every type of flower imaginable. Soft lights illuminated the path, pointing up to showcase one or another flowering bush or vine.

With Tracie so close, her bare arm touching his, Rip could almost imagine they really were on their honeymoon, enjoying a walk through a resort's grounds. When he reached a rose arbor, he stopped and turned her to face him, gathering her hands in his. "For the sake of our cover…"

Pulling her close, he circled her waist with one arm and cupped her chin with his free hand. Then he bent to kiss her.

Before his lips connected with hers, the rumble of an engine broke through the silence and darkness.

Tracie's body stiffened and they both turned their heads toward the sound.

It grew louder as an aircraft appeared, silhouetted against the moonlit sky.

"Think that might be our bodyguards?" Tracie asked, still standing in the circle of Rip's arm.

Rip returned his gaze to her face, her green eyes inky

dark and reflecting the light from the moon. "Right now, I really don't care. All I seem to be able to think about is kissing you."

Her gaze returned to his and she smiled. "Then what are you waiting for?"

"I haven't a clue." He captured the back of her head in his hand and kissed her, long and hard, his tongue pushing through to tangle with hers. When he finally came up for air, he leaned his forehead against hers. "What am I going to do with you?"

She brushed her thumb across his cheek and replied, "Make love—" Her words halted and she pressed her hand against his chest. "Never mind. Perhaps we should greet our bodyguards and fill them in on our plans."

"I wonder how much Hank told them?" Rip still wasn't sure about the Texas billionaire he had yet to meet.

"I suppose we'll find out." She led the way back to the house, walking a step ahead of Rip. He wanted to catch up to her and hold her arm like he had as they'd walked out to the garden, but he sensed she was putting distance between them on purpose.

As they entered the hacienda, Hector was descending the staircase. When he reached the bottom he met Rip and Tracie halfway across the wide foyer. "I believe Hank's men have arrived. My team are bringing them to the hacienda."

"Thank you." Rip moved up beside Tracie and slipped his arm around her waist. "I'd like to speak with them before we turn in for the night. Tomorrow will be a full and hopefully fruitful day."

"I've briefed my team on your needs. The man in charge speaks fluent English and will coordinate the details with your bodyguards once you decide on a plan. My men are prepared to ride out with you tomorrow as early as seven in the morning."

"Thank you, Hector." Rip held out his hand. "Your hospitality is exceptional."

Hector placed his hand in Rip's. "Say the word. I can do more."

"Thanks, but you've already done more than we could have hoped for."

With a nod to Rip and then Tracie, Hector backed toward the stairs. "If that is all you need of me, I will bid you *buenas noches.*"

"Good night," Tracie echoed.

Rip merely nodded, his attention shifting to the hum of engines outside the front of the house.

He cupped Tracie's elbow and steered her toward the grand entrance.

A servant rushed forward and opened the heavy wooden door before Rip could reach out to open it for himself. He just couldn't get used to someone else doing things for him.

As when he and Tracie arrived, two Jeeps pulled up in front of the house, each mounted with machine guns. One had four of Hector's men on it with one manning the gun. The other Jeep had three of Hector's men and two additional men in the backseat.

As they climbed out of the back of the Jeep, they spoke in Spanish to the men in front. Both men had dark hair and swarthy skin and wore blue jeans and faded heather-gray T-shirts with no identifying marks on the fabric. With their appearance and nondescript clothing, they could easily have been any tourist or local.

The first one out walked up to Rip. "You must be Mr. Gideon. I'm Carlos Rodriguez, and my partner is Julio Jimenez. Mr. Derringer sent us to provide for your security while you're in Honduras. We can also translate for you if the need arises."

Rip nodded. "Call me Chuck."

Carlos nodded and repeated, "Chuck." He turned to Tracie. "Mrs. Gideon, it is a pleasure to meet you."

Tracie took the man's hand and shook it. "Please, I'm Phyllis. And it's nice to meet you, as well."

The men who'd brought them from the airplane jumped into the Jeeps and kicked up gravel as they spun out of the driveway and away to their posts, leaving the four of them alone.

Gripping Tracie's arm, Rip nodded toward the two men and said, "Let's walk."

Carlos fell in step with Rip on the opposite side of Tracie. "Hank said you might run into trouble with the guerillas who have taken over this area of Honduras. I'm not certain how much help the two of us will be against an entire army of them."

"Our host, Hector DeVita, has promised us the use of four of his men. Phyllis and I want to explore opportunities around the town of Colinas Rocosa. There is a plantation near there we want to pay a visit to, and Phyllis is interested in the town itself. If I'm not mistaken, there is a fiesta scheduled for tomorrow. Once we've concluded our business with the plantation owner, we'll join the festivities."

When they were far enough away from the house, Carlos stopped. "For the record, we're here to help a brother," he said and lifted his shirt aiming his tight abs toward the moonlight.

For a moment all Rip could see were dark spots across his skin. But as his gaze focused in on them he made out a tattoo of tiny frog footprints.

Rip smiled and relaxed. "I'm glad you're on board." He held out his hand. Carlos gripped his forearm and nodded solemnly then jerked his head toward Julio who also lifted his shirt and displayed another set of frog prints. Rip extended his arm to him, as well, and they clapped hands on each other's shoulders.

These men were SEALs. Whether they were on active duty or had since separated from the service. But once a SEAL, always a SEAL, and they stood by each other.

Knowing they had his six made him feel better about the mission. When they had a chance to get away from Hector's compound, he'd go into more detail with them. Having established that the men Hank had sent were just what he needed, Rip circled around and headed back toward the house.

"Did Hank send anymore information about the investigation?"

Carlos shook his head. "No. But he has Brandon working hard to find anything that will be of use to us."

"Good. Hector's men want to meet with us this evening to go over the timing of our travels tomorrow." Rip turned to Tracie. "I can fill you in on the details later, if you'd like to call it a night?"

Tracie chewed on her lower lip for a moment before nodding. "I'll leave you men to it. I am tired."

They'd arrived at the front of the hacienda and the steps leading up to the massive wooden front doors.

Rip walked Tracie up to the door and leaned down to touch his lips to hers. "I'll be up as soon as I nail down the details of our expedition tomorrow." He pressed his lips to the spot just below her earlobe and whispered, "I know you want to come with me."

"Yes, but you can handle this on your own. I really am tired."

Rip gazed into her eyes, his brows puckered. Finally, he opened the door for her and she disappeared inside.

He hadn't liked that she'd given in to him so easily. He'd find out what was eating her later, for now, he had work to do.

NORMALLY TRACIE WOULD have insisted on going with her partner to any planning sessions for the mission they would conduct. But after seeing the camaraderie of the SEAL men, she'd felt like an outsider. With Rip's kiss fresh on her lips and her emotions in a twist over everything that had happened that day, she needed the time alone.

She headed straight for their room and took the opportunity to prepare for bed without Rip making her feel incredibly hot and needy.

Hector's staff had been through the room and removed the dress they'd flung over the camera. Grabbing a lightweight throw blanket, she tossed it over the camera, not in the mood to be on display, now or ever.

Unfortunately, Hank's team had put together the perfect bridal trousseau and the only sleeping garment inside was now spread out across the sheets of the huge bed.

Tracie held up the scraps of material. The incredibly sexy, mostly sheer white teddy sported faux-fur trim around the lower-than-low neckline and where the elastic would stretch along her outer thighs.

How was she supposed to sleep in that? She riffled through drawers of clothing the staff had unpacked from her suitcases and found one dark, long-sleeved T-shirt and a pair of dark jeans, apparently for any night ops they might need to conduct.

Well, it was nighttime and she wasn't sleeping in the faux-fur bit of fluff. Not when Rip would be lying in the bed beside her.

Not only would it tickle her, but every time she moved,

she'd be reminded of how close Rip was and how far he'd pushed away from her since the shower.

The teddy was definitely out. She wadded it into a tight ball and shoved it under the pillow, stripped out of her clothes and pulled the T-shirt over her head. It fit her perfectly. Therein lay the problem. It wasn't long enough to cover her bottom. Her pulse pounding, not knowing when Rip would be back in the room, Tracie slipped beneath the sheets and pulled them up over her. The long-sleeved black T-shirt stood out against the crisp white sheets.

A knock on the door made her jump. "Who is it?" she responded, remembering she hadn't locked the door, leaving the lock open for when Rip returned.

"*Pardon, Señora.* It is Dehlia Perez. I have fresh towels for your bath."

"Just a minute." Knowing how strange she must look in the black T-shirt, Tracie shucked it, grabbed the white teddy and pulled it over her head, tugging it down over her torso. Shoving the black T-shirt beneath the sheet by her feet, she leaned back against the pillow and pulled the sheet up over her breasts. "Okay, you can come in now."

The door opened and the maid entered, wearing the powder-blue uniform and carrying a stack of clean, thick white towels. She closed the door behind her and hurried toward the bathroom. When she came back out, she walked directly over to Tracie.

"*Bueno?*"

"Yes." Tracie smiled at the woman and willed her to leave so that she could change back into the black T-shirt before Rip returned. "*Gracias.*"

Slowly, the woman walked backward, her gaze skimming through the room, looking for anything out of place or needing attention. Her glance shifted to the blanket hanging from the light fixture, but she didn't say anything. She reached the door and opened it. *"Buenos noches, Señora."*

"Good night." Tracie let go of the breath she'd been holding and listened for the sound of footsteps retreating down the hallway before she reached for the snaps between her legs.

No sooner had her hands dived beneath the sheets, the door opened and Rip stepped in.

Tracie froze as Rip's gaze swept across the faux fur barely covering her nipples.

His nostrils flared as his fingers twisted the lock on the door.

Based on his instant response, Tracie knew the man was interested. Though she wished he'd quit giving her mixed signals.

Too late to trade the teddy for the T-shirt, she pulled the sheet up over the faux fur and the rounded swells of her breasts.

"Woman, you don't know what you're doing to me," Rip grumbled, low and barely audible.

Nevertheless, Tracie heard him. Her back straightened and she sat up, letting the sheet fall down around her waist. The teddy was so sheer it didn't hide much beneath the soft white fabric.

"Sweetheart, you had your chance and blew it." Yanking the comforter off the end of the bed, she threw it at him and followed that with a pillow that hit him in the side of his head. "You can sleep on the floor."

She plopped back against the pillow and waited, her breath lodged in her throat. Half of her hoped he'd accept the challenge and crawl into bed with her, while the other half wished he'd just leave her alone. She was tired of the push-me-pull-me game he had been playing.

Rip caught the blanket, his lips thinning. He didn't say a word as he settled on the floor at the foot of the bed.

So that was how he was going to play it?

Tracie turned her back on the man, punched her pillow, wishing it was him, and settled in for a restless night's sleep.

Tomorrow promised to be a long day. With Rip at her side, it would prove more difficult than it had to be.

Chapter Eight

Rip didn't know how long he lay staring up at the ceiling before he fell into a fitful doze. He'd slept on worse than the hard floor beneath him. One time he'd slept in a fox-hole filled with cold water. By the time he'd gotten out of it, he thought for sure he'd sprouted webs between his toes.

Sure the hardwood floors were unforgiving on his back, but the discomfort came solely from the image seared into his mind of Tracie lying against the pillows in that...that... *holy hell.*

That teddy had him tied in knots. He could imagine tasting the rounded swells of her breasts all the way to the edge of the faux fur that would tickle his nose and force him to strip the garment from her body. Then where would they be?

She'd be nude and he'd forget the reason he couldn't allow himself to sleep with her. He slammed a fist into the pillow and turned on his side, the floor biting into his hipbone and shoulder. *Damn it to hell.* The woman was derailing him when he needed to be thinking solely about the mission.

As the gray light of predawn pushed through the blinds on the windows, Rip rose from the hardwood floor, tilt-ing his head from side to side to work the kinks out of his neck. He draped the blanket and pillow on the end of the bed, careful not to disturb Tracie, and he entered the bathroom where he took a long cold shower before donning his disguise of the wealthy young entrepreneur.

The suit he chose was a lightweight gray linen but it was still a suit. He skipped the tie and opted for a black polo shirt. He'd carry the jacket and only wear it when he met with the plantation owner. As hot as it got in Honduras, he didn't want to wear any more clothes than he had to.

When he emerged from the shower, Tracie still lay in the bed her eyes closed.

His gaze lingered on her face. Her dark hair splayed out in a fan across the white pillowcase. If he was not mistaken, her eyelid jerked and lifted halfway before closing tightly.

He strode across the floor and swatted her hip. "You're not fooling me. You might as well get up."

She opened her eyes, rolled onto her back and stretched her arms over her head. The movement edged the sheet down below her chest, making the faux fur of the teddy rise as her back arched.

Rip spun on his heels and marched toward the door. "I'll see you at the breakfast table."

Her warm chuckle halted him as he reached for the door. "Not a morning person, I take it?" she said.

Yes, he was a morning person. But he wanted to do more than just say good morning. She'd made it clear he'd missed his chance, and he wasn't willing to go back on his word, anyway. "We leave in forty-five minutes," he said through clenched teeth and left the room.

Leaving Tracie in that sheer white teddy was harder to do than to storming an enemy position in the middle of a firefight. Every ounce of his being wanted to go right back into the bedroom and show her what lovemaking was all about. Whoever she'd been engaged to before had been a first-class idiot.

After their initial meeting, Rip knew that Tracie was a woman worth fighting for—it was worth taking it slowly and bringing her up to a point where she would be willing to commit to the possibility of a future. She wasn't a one-night stand kind of woman.

"Buenos dias, Señor Gideon." Hector sat at the dining table, buttering a soft tortilla. He pointed to the seat across from him. "Have a seat. My staff will get whatever you'd like to eat for breakfast."

"I'd like coffee. Straight up, black, no cream or sugar."

Hector nodded to a servant who hurried from the room and returned with a mug of steaming brew. The scent of freshly ground coffee cleared the cobwebs from Rip's mind and made a good start to getting him back on track.

Hector set his fork beside his plate and crossed his arms. "Senor Gideon, you strike me as someone who has been a member of the military."

"My father was in the US Marine Corp," he said, avoiding a direct lie.

"Did you follow your father's lead and enter the military?"

Rip was in midsip of his coffee and took the time to phrase his answer, wondering how he could respond without giving anything away.

He was saved by the appearance of one of Hector's male servants who entered the room and spoke in rapid-fire Spanish. Rip could only catch a few of his words.

Hector's eyes narrowed and his brow inched downward as the man spoke.

The lead guard who'd met Rip at the airplane entered, his boots clomping across the smooth tile floor, a deep scowl across his forehead.

Hector glared at the man and pushed to his feet. "Pardon

me, Senor Gideon. It seems we have had a breach in our security that I must deal with."

"By all means. Security of your home takes priority." Rip half stood and dropped back into his seat as Hector moved into the hallway and exchanged harsh words with the guard.

Rip understood Spanish and got by all right speaking it, but he was by no means fluent. Still, he picked up enough of Hector's conversation to get the gist of what had happened.

A truck had crashed into the concrete outer wall. Though it was full of explosive fertilizer, by some gift of fate it had not ignited. However, it had ripped a hole in the concrete that would need to be repaired. Until the repairs were complete, a guard would have to be posted at that point, as well.

Hector wanted to know who was responsible. Who had set the truck in motion to crash into his wall? And when he found that person, he wanted him brought to the compound where he would be made an example of.

Out of the corner of his eye, Rip witnessed his congenial host go from a well-mannered, soft-spoken and civilized man to the steel-edged commander of his little corner of the Honduras countryside.

If Rip was certain he could trust the man, he'd want him on his side not against him. When he finished breakfast, he didn't wait around, preferring to allow Tracie to eat on her own rather than face her after the lousy night's sleep he'd had.

As he left the dining room, Tracie descended the staircase.

Rip stood in the shadows of the dining room until she reached the bottom, enjoying the view. She wore a silky sundress in a soft butter yellow with narrow straps and a hip-hugging skirt. Low, matching heels showed off her trim ankles and well-toned calves. Her hair hung down around her shoulders and she carried a broad-brimmed hat with a sky-blue scarf tied to it.

Rip stepped through the door. "I trust you slept well, Mrs. Gideon?" He greeted her with a quick kiss on her lips.

Tracie's eyes widened at first and then her lips pushed up in a smile. "I did, Mr. Gideon."

He suspected she was lying, playing the part. Makeup barely disguised the dark circles beneath her eyes.

"I'll see to the vehicles for our excursion while you find something to eat."

"I'm ready to go."

"Please, find something to eat. Things don't always go as planned and, for all we know, you might not get another meal today."

Tracie's fists knotted and she stared into his eyes. "You think things will go that bad?"

"A number of scenarios could take place. It's best to go into a fight with fuel in your belly."

"Fine. I'll find something to eat."

"And I'll be outside mustering the troops." He chucked her beneath the chin like a kid sister to keep from yanking her into his arms and crushing her with a kiss. "Now go. If you're not outside in fifteen minutes, I'll leave you here."

"Like hell you will." She spun on her pretty heels and hurried from the foyer, headed toward the dining room.

He liked her spunk but worried about her running in heels. Hopefully, they wouldn't be running today. They'd do their recon and save the running and covert ops for the cover of darkness.

Tracie bypassed the dining room, unwilling to wait for an order to be created and delivered and found her way to the hacienda's spacious, modern kitchen where she used her tenuous grasp on Spanish to ask for a piece of toast and a slice from a ham sitting in a roasting pan on top of the counter. She folded the ham into the toast, wrapped it in napkin, grabbed a cup of freshly squeezed orange juice and hurried outside.

She'd be damned if Rip left her behind now that the two SEALs had arrived. Hank had assigned her to this case. She was Rip's covert bride. They'd established the newly-wed cover story, they had to see it through—SEALs or no SEALs. And she was every bit as qualified to go on this mission as they were.

When she arrived outside in her feminine sundress to find Hector's bodyguards dressed in camouflage uniforms and packing M4A1s, she almost turned around and ran back inside to change into slacks and combat boots.

"There you are." Rip hooked her arm to keep her from changing her clothes. "You look so pretty today, I'm afraid I'll be beating the locals off with a stick."

Falling into his story line, she smiled up at him. "I wanted to wear something nice. If we're going to the fiesta in Colinas Rocosa, I wanted to be dressed for dancing."

"Hopefully our business arrangements won't take all day and we can enjoy the festivities."

The two SEALs joined them dressed in jeans and loose-fitting guayabera shirts. When the wind picked up a little, the shirts pressed against their bellies, outlining suspicious lumps Tracie suspected were the pistols they had strapped beneath their clothing. From all outward appearances, they would blend into a festival crowd with their dark brown hair, bronze skin and fluent Spanish.

On one hand, Tracie was uneasy about Hector's para-military bodyguards following them on the trip. They could be a big fat sign to the guerillas that the people they were guarding might make good kidnapping targets. On the other hand, they looked big, bad and dangerous and might just scare off any unwanted attempts to steal the wealthy play-boy and his bride to hold them for ransom.

Having been kidnapped once, Tracie had no desire to go through that again. She'd been lucky to get out alive. In cat terminology, she'd already used up one of her spare lives. Why tempt fate and use up another?

"Having second thoughts?" Rip whispered as he helped her into her seat in the Jeep. He tucked her skirt around her legs, his big fingers sending electrical shocks up her thighs and to her core as they brushed her skin through the thin fabric of her dress.

Tracie had been around plenty of testosterone-fueled men, having gone through Quantico where women made up less than 20 percent of the trainees. But Rip was some-how more masculine and more dangerous than any man she'd ever known.

She responded with, "No second thoughts about the plan for the day." Definitely second thoughts about the SEAL tucking her into the backseat of the Jeep. She could imag-ine those gentle hands sliding over her naked skin, stirring up so much passion she'd be lost, maybe even forget her vow to never trust a man again.

Julio slid in behind the steering wheel, Carlos rode shot-gun, his hand resting lightly over the weapon beneath his shirt.

As Rip settled into the seat beside her, Tracie's pulse leaped. This was it. Up until this point, they'd been in a fairly safe environment having flown into a private airstrip to be met by armed guards and secluded behind a massive concrete and concertina-wire wall.

She sucked in a deep breath as they drove through heavy gates onto the public road. Rip gathered her hand in his and rested it on his thigh. The gesture made her pulse slow from its frantic beating. It also made her realize how much she'd grown to trust this SEAL in the very short time they'd been together, giving her the confidence to see this mission through. She hadn't realized how affected she'd been by her previous captivity at the hands of Mexican thugs.

Mexico had been much like Honduras. With drug cartels in charge of the country, whoever had the most or the biggest guns were in charge.

In Honduras the guerillas called the shots, undermining and manipulating the government.

Using GPS, Julio sped along the road slowing only for the occasional cattle or goats being herded by small, skinny children or teens. Nothing about the lush green countryside raised red flags. They could have been traveling tourists without a care in the world. Except they were in a guerilla-infested area of Honduras.

As they passed through Colinas Rocosa, Tracie made note of the town. Decorated with crepe-paper streamers, and a sign commemorating the town's patron saint, who they were celebrating, the streets were filled with vendors selling their wares. Most folks smiled and waved, happy to have something to rejoice—grasping at a chance to have fun in a land where danger lurked around every corner.

Tracie found herself peering into every vehicle they passed on the road, wondering if the occupants were part of the guerilla faction.

One particular truck sped toward them moving too fast for the narrow, people-filled streets.

A small child darted out into the middle of the road, directly into the path of the oncoming vehicle.

"Stop!" Tracie shouted.

Julio slammed on the brakes and the Jeep skidded to a halt.

Tracie leaped from the vehicle, snatched the boy from the

middle of the road and stepped back as the truck barreled by, its driver barely glancing her way.

The boy clung to her and burst into tears.

Tracie held him against her breast, rubbing his back and whispering soothing words as she did so. A moment later, a woman's wail broke through the child's sobs and his mother ran out into the street, her eyes wide.

As soon as the boy heard his mother's voice, he struggled to break free Tracie's hold. She set him on the ground and he ran into his mother's arms, crying even louder.

The frightened mother scooped up her errant youngster and hugged him hard to her chest. *"Gracias, Señora. Muchas gracias."* Then bowing and apologizing in Spanish, she hurried away, talking sternly to her little one.

A hand slipped around Tracie's waist and Rip pulled her against him. "That was close."

"Too close." Tracie leaned into Rip's embrace for a moment, willing her pulse to slow to normal. Then she glanced up at him. "That truck driver didn't even slow down."

"No, he didn't. For a moment there, I thought he'd hit you." His hand shook where it rested on her waist. "I admit I've never been more scared."

She stared up at him. "You? Scared?"

"Hey, just because I'm a S— man…doesn't mean I can't get scared." He hugged her hard, then bent to kiss her. A sharp, high-pitched beep made Tracy look around.

A man on a vintage motorcycle passed on the street, grinning.

Her cheeks heating, Tracie realized they were the center of attention with the two SEALs in the front seat of the Jeep, Hector's men in the vehicle behind and the citizens of Colinas Rocosa gathering around them.

A woman walked by and patted Tracie on the back saying something in rapid Spanish she couldn't quite translate.

"What did she say?" Tracie asked.

"Something about young love and having babies of your own."

Her face heating even more, Tracie forced a snort. "Like that's going to happen. Not in my line of work." Her voice was low enough only Rip could hear her.

"It can happen," Rip reassured her.

"Not today." Stepping out of Rip's embrace, Tracie couldn't help the feeling of loss that washed over her. She'd just have to get over it. Their days together were numbered and babies with Rip were completely out of the question.

Then why did a dark-haired, blue-eyed little girl emerge in her mind, holding hands with her and Rip and swinging between them?

Tracie climbed back into the Jeep and tucked her own skirts around her before Rip had the chance. Her thoughts were unsettling. She liked working for Hank and wouldn't want to give up what she did to go all domestic.

Still…that little boy had felt good and somehow right in her arms.

What was she thinking? Her life didn't have room for a husband and children.

But if it did…Rip was the kind of man she'd want to marry. Too bad her job pretty much ensured she would die single.

Chapter Nine

The trip to the plantation went without a hitch. Too easy. Rip's every nerve was on alert.

As they turned onto the gravel road leading to the main house, a man with an automatic weapon stepped out of the shadows of the overhanging trees into the middle of the road aiming the weapon at the driver.

Ah, there it was. The threat.

To Rip, it was almost a relief to finally see the enemy.

The man shouted in Spanish for them to stop.

Julio immediately applied the brakes, jamming his foot on the pedal so hard, Rip and Tracie were thrown forward.

The Jeep behind them slid to a stop mere inches from their bumper and the men aboard leaped to the ground, aiming their guns at the man in the middle of the road.

Rip got out of the Jeep, smiling and holding his hands in the air. "Let's not get crazy here."

Carlos translated to the man in the middle of the road.

He answered back, talking so fast, Rip couldn't understand him.

Five more men emerged from the shadows, all bearing arms.

Rip's chest tightened, but he held his ground. "Tell them that we are here to see the owner of the plantation, that we mean no harm."

Carlos translated.

The guard in charge snarled and jerked his head toward Hector's men.

"He wants your men to put down their weapons."

"Tell him they will when he confirms he works for the plantation owner." Rip gritted his teeth.

Before he could stop her, Tracie stepped out of the vehicle and came around to his side. He wished like hell she'd stayed put in the vehicle.

Instead, she stood beside him in her yellow sundress and curled her arm through his, looking like a ray of sunshine, all soft and feminine, with nerves of steel hidden beneath that pretty dress. "What seems to be the problem, sweetheart?"

Reminding himself that he wasn't armed for combat and others' lives depended on him keeping a cool head, Rip patted her hand. "Nothing but a little misunderstanding."

Carlos spoke in Spanish to the head guard again.

The man pulled a walkie-talkie from a case on his belt and barked into it.

A moment later a voice crackled from the device.

Carlos turned to Rip. "Delgado just gave the go-ahead to let us through as long as we leave Hector's men and all our weapons behind."

"Okay, then." Rip nodded to Carlos.

Carlos and Julio tossed their weapons on the ground and held their hands in the air while the guards patted them down. Then Carlos gave instructions to Hector's men.

They didn't look happy about being left out of the action, but they backed away, still holding their weapons at the ready.

Rip smiled at the plantation gate guards. "Then we're good?"

The guards stepped back, forming a line on either side

of the road with the man in charge climbing aboard a dusty old forty-horsepower motorcycle the likes of which hadn't been built since the end of World War II.

It belched smoke and kicked up dust that streamed through the open doors and windows of the Jeeps, forcing Julio to hang back to let the dust settle before they followed.

The road curved through a hedge of encroaching jungle. On one side of the lane, in the rare gaps between trees, vines and underbrush, Rip could see the coffee orchards spread out over the hills and valleys, lush and green. On the opposite side of the road, the jungle seemed impenetrable and free of the coffee trees that produced the heavenly brew.

The next curve revealed a wide opening in the jungle where a traditional plantation-style house rose up from the surrounding orchard and jungle, the base a dull gray stone with a multitude of arched passages. The stark white of the upper story lay in bright contrast to the surrounding deep green vegetation.

The guard on the motorcycle in front of them parked the vehicle and ducked through one of the arches.

Julio brought the Jeep to a smooth stop. Rip was first out.

The guard emerged again with another man dressed in jeans, a white button-up shirt, black vest and a cowboy hat. On his hips rode a gun holster just like those seen in the Old West. If Rip wasn't mistaken, the gun in the holster was a vintage Colt single-action US Army revolver with a pearl handle, in mint condition. His face was that of the scarred man in the photos Morris Franks had stashed in his car.

"Nice gun you've got there." Rip held out his hand. "Name's Chuck Gideon. This is my wife, Phyllis. We stopped by to talk to the owner of *le Plantación de Ángel*."

The man rested his hand on the pearl grip and in heavily accented English responded. "I, Carmelo Delgado, am the owner of *le Plantación de Ángel*. What do you want?"

Rip curled his arm around Tracie's waist and smiled. "My wife fancies owning a coffee plantation, and she fell in love with the name of this one. Have you considered selling?"

The man's heavy brows V'd toward the bridge of his nose. "No." He turned to go back into the house.

Rip stepped forward. "Surely there is a price we could agree on. Phyllis has her heart set on growing her own coffee."

Delgado shot his riposte over his shoulder. "Then buy another farm. This one is not for sale."

When the man started toward the house, Rip stepped in front of him, blocking his return to the cooler interior.

No sooner had Rip moved, than half a dozen armed men stepped out of the shadows on the other sides of the arches. Each carried a M4A1 rifle, exactly like the ones used by the US Army. Rip used a specially modified version. The ones pointing at him now were pristine and new.

Rip raised his hands. "Hey, hey. No need to get punchy. I'm a businessman not much into playing with guns. I prefer to concentrate my efforts on making money." He addressed Delgado. "Could we talk?" Glancing sideways at the men with the guns, he added, "In private. I might have a deal you'll be interested in."

The man glared down his nose at Rip. "I do not think so."

Rip's smile slipped and his brows descended, all joviality wiped from his expression as he examined the guns the men carried. "I take it you like the weapons your men carry." He nodded toward the closest one. "What would you say if I told you that I could get them for you at a cheaper price?"

Tracie stiffened next to him, but her expression remained the same. The woman could probably play a mean hand of poker.

Delgado's eyes narrowed and he stared from Rip to Tracie and back to Rip. "I'd say for you to get the hell off my land."

Rip shrugged. "Have it your way. If you want to keep buying guns at a higher price, that's your business. We will be on our way." Rip turned toward the Jeep.

Tracie turned with him.

The hired guns blocked their exit.

Rip's muscles bunched, prepared to fight his way out if necessary.

The plantation owner jerked his head and gave an order in Spanish.

The guards stepped back, giving Rip and Tracie an open path to escape.

Delgado sliced the air with his hand. "Now go. You are not welcome here."

"Your loss," Rip said. "You could have sold the plantation and purchased some damned fine weapons at a steal of a price. Come on, sweetheart, at least we can enjoy the festival tonight." Rip shook his head, hooked Tracie's elbow in his hand and guided her to the backseat of the Jeep.

Once they were all in, Julio spun the vehicle around and headed back the way they'd entered.

When they were out of earshot, Tracie leaned close to Rip and demanded, "What in the hell was that all about?"

Rip leaned back in his seat, a grin spreading across his lips. "I think we hit the jackpot."

"Meaning?" she shot back.

"Meaning, I went to the plantation hoping to look around the land for hideouts, thinking maybe the guerilla group is camping out on the grounds. Instead, I think we found some of them."

Tracie nodded. "I get that. They carried the guns from

the DEA agent's photographs. But why did you tell them we had guns to sell?"

"The offer to purchase the plantation wasn't enough. The temptation of cheaper weapons? Now that got his attention. And I was beginning to think he wasn't going to let us leave so easily."

TRACIE INHALED DEEPLY and let it out. "Wow. We've gone from being just a couple on our honeymoon looking for a coffee plantation, to international arms dealers. It's insanely dangerous." She gave a shaky smile. "But what the hell. I'm in."

Rip clapped his hands together. "We have a festival to go to, and I'll bet money that, one, Delgado has something to do with the guerillas since he has access to the weapons we're looking for. And two, he'll have us tailed. All we have to do is identify his men at the festival, plant tracking devices on one or two of them and see where they lead." He grinned. "You ready for a late-night adventure?"

Her heartbeat kicked up when he smiled at her like that, and adrenaline ran through her veins, making her wish they were already following the tracking devices to the guerrilla's hidden location deep in the jungle. "I'm ready."

As they passed the entrance to the plantation, they picked up Hector's vehicle full of mercenaries.

Tracie hadn't liked the mean look in Delgado's eyes. Several times, she'd glanced back over her shoulder, trying to look past Hector's men to the road beyond. A couple of times the road straightened long enough she thought she saw another vehicle kicking up dust.

Within twenty minutes, they were back in Colinas Rocosa, driving slowly through the busy streets.

"Are we stopping here?" Carlos asked.

"No," Rip responded. "We'll come back later this evening. We can go back to Hector's and enjoy the pool during the hottest part of the day."

Tracie touched his arm. "We can't go back to Hector's. Carmelo's men could be following us."

Rip grinned. "We'll take care of that." He leaned forward. "Julio, when we get to the outskirts of Colinas Rocosa pull over."

"Aye, aye!" Julio said and pulled over a moment later.

"Carlos," Rip said. "Could you please explain to Hector's men that they can return to his place? We no longer require their services."

Carlo's brows rose. "If you're sure we can handle it just the four of us."

"Julio assures me he's an expert driver. I'm counting on that to throw Carmelo's men off our trail before we head back to Hector's."

"Muy bueno." When the other Jeep slid to a stop behind them, Carlos met the leader of the group and spoke softly in Spanish. The man nodded and barked an order to the driver. The Jeep left them, headed back to Hector's.

Carlos climbed back into their vehicle. "I told them to take a roundabout route back. But they should get there before us."

"Good, now let's lose our tail." Rip patted Julio's shoulder. "Go."

Tracie glanced back toward the little town and spotted a truck filled with what looked like Delgado's men moving slowly toward them.

Julio slammed his foot on the accelerator. Dust and gravel spewed out behind them as they shot forward.

Tracie held on to the armrest, her hair flying around her face. A rush of excitement filled her as Julio sped away from Delgado's men.

The road twisted and turned through the hills and Tracie

lost sight of the truck for a second. The next turn she spotted it. They were falling behind, but not by enough to lose them.

Ahead the road T-junctioned.

Julio turned to the right, stirring up a lot of dust and then spun around and rolled more slowly back the opposite direction.

Tracie swiveled in her seat to see the road behind her. They'd lost time turning around and going back the other direction.

A curve in the road meant the jungle blocked her view of the intersection.

Abruptly, the Jeep left the road and plowed into the underbrush. Giant trees shaded the spot where they'd entered the jungle, hopefully hiding their entry point.

Julio shut off the engine and jumped out of the Jeep, followed by Carlos and Rip. Together, they pushed and shoved brush and vines over the branches broken by their plunge into the woods. When they were satisfied with their efforts, they stood still.

Dressed in heels, Tracie remained where she was, listening as the sounds of nature resumed, disturbed only by the rumbling of tires on gravel and the heavy roar of a truck's engine.

Rip crossed to Tracie and whispered, "They turned right at the intersection."

She nodded, afraid to speak too loud, even though the men in the truck probably couldn't hear them.

The truck's engine sounds faded the farther away they moved from the team hidden in the vegetation.

"Sounds like they're gone," Tracie said.

Rip held up a hand. "We need to be certain."

Carlos closed the distance between them. "I'm going on recon."

114   *Navy SEAL Newlywed*

Rip nodded.

Slipping into the jungle, Carlos hunched low, moving so quietly Tracie couldn't hear his footsteps. A moment later he disappeared.

Tracie leaned close to Rip and whispered into his ear, "How long should we wait to be certain?"

Rip's lips hovered next to her temple. "Until Carlos returns." His breath stirred the loose tendrils of hair around her ear, sending ripples of awareness across her skin. A thin sheen of sweat built up across her upper lip that had nothing to do with the heat and humidity of the jungle.

Just when Tracie had relaxed and thought they were in the clear, the sound of an engine approaching made her stiffen. "Delgado's men or someone else?" she said, speaking quietly.

The engine noise grew louder and then seemed to hold steady for a moment. Shouts pierced the air. Too far away to make out what was being said, Tracie sent up a silent prayer that Carlos was all right and hadn't been discovered.

The engine's rumble changed and then started to fade again. A few minutes later, Carlos emerged from the darkness of the surrounding jungle.

"They're gone."

"What happened?"

Carlos's lips twisted. "They'd left a couple of soldiers at the intersection. I was only three feet away from one of them before I saw him."

"Damn." Rip grinned. "I take it you saw him, but he didn't see you?"

Carlos gave Rip an answering grin. "Damn right. I lay low, waiting for him to move far enough away I could slip back to you and let you know. But it wasn't until the truck returned that he left his post. Their leader was angry that they'd lost us and mentioned that Delgado wouldn't be happy. They loaded the two guards and headed back to Colinas Rocosa."

"Good." Rip climbed into the Jeep. "We can go back to Hector's now. I hope the others made it back without being followed."

Tracie was glad to see the imposing concrete fence and concertina wire rise up out of the jungle when they arrived at Hector's. She'd be even happier when she got out of the dress and heels. Never had she felt so useless. When they returned to the festival, she planned on wearing a dress, but she'd have serviceable shoes and trousers beneath the skirt.

Having grown up on a ranch, dresses made her itch to be back in her jeans. The FBI had suited her perfectly. She dressed to suit the mission. Usually that was in trousers. This undercover bride stuff was challenging her inner tomboy to the limits.

Though she had to admit, the look in Rip's eye when he'd first seen her in the yellow sundress almost made it worth the discomfort.

This evening the real test would be following the guerillas back to their jungle hideout. If all went as planned, they'd get the information they sought and be on their way back to the States tomorrow.

Chapter Ten

As they pulled in front of the sprawling hacienda, Hector emerged from the house, his brow puckered. "*Mi amigos.* I worried when you did not return with my men."

Rip climbed out of the Jeep and met the man at the base of the steps. "The owner of *le Plantación de Ángel* seemed to want to follow us back to our place of origin. I didn't think you wanted them to know I was staying here, so we led them on what we call a wild goose chase." He grinned. "It was entertaining to say the least."

Hector's gaze shifted to Tracie. "And you, Senora? Were you equally entertained?" he asked, his tone doubtful.

Tracie slipped her hand into the crook of Rip's elbow. "Very much so. I felt like I was on the set of an action-adventure movie. It was exhilarating." She smiled and shook her hair back from her face.

The motion made Rip's pulse quicken. How he'd love to run his hands through her pretty brown hair. She'd been stoic and held it together throughout the entire confrontation with Delgado.

Their host's frown deepened. "Carmelo Delgado is not a man to be toyed with. He will not be happy that he couldn't find you. Were you able to speak to him about buying a coffee plantation?"

Rip pressed his lips together, aiming for a sufficient look of irritation. "He didn't want to sell his place."

Tracie touched his arm. "Oh, honey, he was quite adamant. He even had his people point guns at us." She raised a hand to her breast, although Rip was certain she didn't have to feign her shock at their hostile reception on *le Plantación de Ángel*. She dropped her hand and looked around. "I don't know about you, but all that excitement made me hungry."

Hector hesitated, his eyes narrowing as if he wasn't convinced they were telling him everything. Then his brows rose and he waved toward the door. "Please. I will have my staff prepare a meal."

"And I so look forward to swimming in that lovely pool," Tracie said.

Rip could have kissed her for pulling Hector's attention off their day's adventure and back to his duties as a host. His gut told him that Hector was on the up-and-up and could be trusted with the truth, but Rip wasn't going to risk the lives of Tracie, Carlos and Julio on instinct. They entered the hacienda and settled down to a meal in the airy dining room. Afterward, Tracie excused herself and left the men to talk, claiming a headache.

Hector received a call at the end of the meal and left the room to go to his office to take it.

Rip stood and motioned to Carlos and Julio. "Please, let's go out to the pool to discuss tonight's plan. My wife wishes to attend the festival, but I worry that Delgado's men will be there. I want to make certain we have a way out, should things get sticky."

Carlos's gaze shifted left then right before he nodded. "Let's go."

Once outside, Rip settled in chairs far enough away from the hacienda walls they need not worry about listening devices. Carlos and Julio dragged seats close to him and they put their heads together. The night ahead could prove to be difficult.

"It might be suicide going to the festival tonight," Carlos started.

Rip nodded. He wasn't sure he liked the idea himself. "I'll check in with Hank before we go. If they haven't been able to locate the rebel base, we have to get close enough to Delgado's men to plant GPS devices on them."

"If they attend."

"They will." Rip grinned. "I told them we'd be there."

Carlos's mouth quirked up on the corner. "You did, didn't you?"

"Purposely," Rip said. "And with the suggestion I was a competing weapons supplier, I don't think he will try to kidnap us. Follow, yes. Kidnap or kill, no."

Carlos frowned. "From Hank's briefing, these guerillas prefer to shoot first, question later."

"We'll be prepared."

Julio leaned close. "Hank sent along enough equipment to outfit an entire SEAL team. All we need is for Delgado's team to lead us into their camp."

"Good. Let's be sure to take what we need with us. I have a feeling we'll be headed into the jungle before the night is over."

"What will you tell Hector?" Carlos asked.

"Leave it to me."

Julio's eyes narrowed. "He'll want to send reinforcements with us. I prefer to leave them behind. We can handle this mission without them."

"They might prove a good distraction. Delgado won't know who to target if he has eight people to follow instead of just the four of us. I'll have Hector instruct them to dress casual like they're going to the festival and leave the big guns at the house."

Julio laughed. "Yeah, the camouflage might give them away."

Carlos nodded. "We'll have to lose them, as well, or risk them following us to the rebel camp."

Rip stared at the two men and felt a kinship, even though they'd only met the night before. "What unit were you with?"

"SEAL Team Six," Julio answered.

"And you're working for Hank now?"

Julio nodded. "He recruited us when he'd heard we'd left the Navy."

"Why'd you leave?" Rip asked.

"Our missions were becoming too bogged down in politics," Carlos answered.

"Yeah. Watched one of our own get gunned down because we weren't allowed to fire first."

Rip sucked in a deep breath. "I understand that. We're here because someone in our government ratted out the DEA agent we went in to rescue. Set us up to pull him out far enough for a sniper to take him down and we lost one of our team."

Carlos and Julio nodded.

"That's what Hank told us." Carlos's mouth pressed into a tight line. "Makes you wonder who you're fighting for."

Julio's brows dipped. "When we heard about your situation, we asked to be a part of the team."

Rip's chest tightened. "I'm glad you're on board." A movement out of the corner of his eye caught his attention.

Tracie, emerged from the hacienda wearing a hot-pink bikini and a sheer wrap knotted around her hips. The ends of the wrap billowed out in the breeze and then plastered against her shapely legs.

Carlos gave a low whistle. "None of our buddies looked like that in the Navy."

"Yeah," Julio said. "Glad she's on our team."

Rip's fists clenched. He wanted to tell the guys to back off, but what good would it do? Tracie had been clear about not wanting a relationship with him. On this four-person team, Rip was the outsider. Julio, Carlos and Tracie worked for Hank.

"Hank said she was a Fed," Carlos said.

"Former FBI," Rip confirmed. "I would have thought you three would know each other."

Carlos shook his head. "Julio and I are out of San Diego. We've only been to Hank's ranch once. When he has a job, he either picks up the phone or takes one of his planes and meets with us in California."

"Just how many people does Hank have working for him?"

Julio shrugged. "None of us know. He started with four cowboys from Texas. Since then, he's expanded out. I think he has one in Colorado, the two of us in California and now a woman. All of us were born and raised on ranches."

Which would exclude Rip from Hank's selection criteria. He'd never been on a ranch in his life, having grown up in the suburbs of Atlanta, raised by his father, a member of the Atlanta Police Department. Not that he cared about Hank's methods of choosing his Covert Cowboys. He wasn't interested in giving up on the Navy SEALs yet. He loved his job, despite the corruption within the government.

If he could trace the source of the weapons sales back to the United States, he was almost certain he'd find a corrupt government official at the root of the problem. Clean out the traitor and he could go back to business as usual.

Silence fell over the three men as they sat in the shade, studying Tracie as she strode out into the sunshine, untied the wrap and let it fall onto a lounge chair.

Her body was trim, not an ounce of flab, her muscles

tight and well defined. She'd let her hair hang straight down her back. Her skin was tanned, not too dark, but a perfect contrast to the bright pink of the bikini. For a moment she stood at the edge of the pool, staring across the hilltop to the east, as if she could see all the way to the coast.

Rip's breath caught in his throat. She was as beautiful in the bikini as she'd been naked in the shower and he wanted her even more. What would it take to break through her defenses and convince her they had a chance?

Then she sucked in a deep breath, her lungs expanding before she dove cleanly into the sparkling water.

When she surfaced, Carlos and Julio clapped loudly and whistled.

"Well done, Senora Gideon," Carlos said.

Tracie twisted in the water, pushing the wet hair back from her forehead. "I didn't see y'all there," she said in her soft Texas drawl. "Am I missing anything?"

Rip shook his head. "Not really. We were discussing going to the festival tonight."

"Oh, good. I haven't danced since our wedding." She winked at Rip.

"Ah, the beautiful Senora Gideon is taking advantage of the pool." Hector stepped out of the shadows, wearing swim trunks with a towel slung around his neck. "The pool sees so little use with only me to enjoy its pleasures." He draped the towel over the back of a chair and stood with his arms crossed, facing Rip, Julio and Carlos. "Gentlemen, perhaps you would care to join us?"

"I'm more interested in a siesta," Carlos said.

Julio stood and stretched. "I could use one, as well. If we're to go to the festival tonight, I want to be well-rested and alert in case we encounter trouble."

The two SEALs left the patio. Rip stood. "I suppose I could do with a swim. I'll be right back."

He entered the hacienda, glancing back at the sound of a splash.

Hector surfaced next to Tracie, close enough to touch.

Rip's blood heated. He was tempted to turn around and jump into the pool fully clothed to put a little space between Hector and Tracie.

For a long moment, he clenched his fists and counted, reaching fifty before he finally calmed enough to enter the house. He strode across the living area and ran up the stairs taking the steps two at a time, not slowing until he reached the bedroom he shared with Tracie.

He riffled through the drawers, digging deep, searching for swim trunks. After the first two drawers, he was throwing shirts, shorts and underwear on the floor, grinding his teeth down to the nub. Where the hell were his swim trunks?

Finally, he reached the bottom of the shorts drawer and unearthed what was nothing more than a pair of shiny black men's underwear.

"Really, Hank? Real men don't wear tiny swim briefs unless they're competing in a swim competition." He flung the offending item on the bed and dug through the next drawer. None of the shorts would do. As soon as they got wet, they'd be sheer.

"I'm not wearing that," he grumbled. The image of Tracie laughing into Hector's face flashed in Rip's mind and he grabbed the swimwear, shucked his trousers and yanked the garment up over his thighs. He might as well be swimming naked.

He stood in front of the mirror, his cheeks hot, and almost ditched the entire idea. If not for the thought of Hector flirting with Tracie, he would have. Grabbing a towel from the bathroom, he wrapped it around his waist and ran back down the stairs and out to the pool.

Tracie and Hector glanced up as he skidded to a halt at the edge.

"Join us, sweetheart, the water's wonderful." Tracie stood in water that came up to just beneath her breasts, the reflection of sunlight emphasizing the hot-pink bikini top.

"*Si.* Join us Senor Gideon."

"Oh, Hector, we don't need to be so formal. Call him Chuck."

He smiled at Tracie, his charm turned up full blast and then he faced Rip and dipped his head. "Join us, Chuck." His emphasis on Chuck made it almost sound like an insult.

With both of them watching his every move, Rip didn't want to remove the towel. "I think I'll enjoy the sunshine."

"You have to get in. The water is just the right temperature." Tracie batted her eyes at him, making his stomach do all kinds of flips, even knowing she was putting on a show for Hector's benefit. "Please."

The *please* won. With a sigh, he dropped the towel.

Hector's brows rose.

Tracie's green eyes flared and darkened, but she didn't say a word.

Rip dove into the water, figuring that the sooner he got in, the sooner his swimming apparel wouldn't be as conspicuous. When he surfaced, he came up behind Tracie and pulled her against him. "Did you tell Hector where we're going tonight?"

Tracie shook her head. "I thought I'd let you."

Hector's head canted to the side. "Are you going to the festival as planned tonight?"

"We are."

Hector's brows dipped. "It is dangerous for foreigners to wander around the countryside at night. There have been many kidnappings and murders at the hands of *Los Rebeldes del Diablo*. I wish you to reconsider."

Rip smiled and nuzzled the back of Tracie's neck. "My wife has made up her mind."

"What of Senor Delgado?" Hector asked.

"There will be a lot of people in the town. We'll do our best to blend in."

Hector snorted. "Senora Gideon, your skin is far too pale to blend in and Senor Gideon is much taller and broader than most men of the area. I am afraid you will have difficulty getting lost in the crowd."

"That's where your men could come in. Do you mind loaning us the four men you sent with us this morning?" Rip asked. "I need them to dress in clothes that will help them to blend into the crowd. I will have my men do the same. That way if we run into trouble, no one will know they are there to protect us and they can help us get out."

"Oh, sweetie, I do so want to dance. And the decorations were so cute."

Rip shrugged toward Hector. "You see? I can't disappoint my bride."

Hector's frown deepened. "You are putting yourselves in unnecessary danger when you can stay here, behind the walls where you will remain safe."

"But we'll miss the music and the dancing." Tracie leaned toward Hector, though Rip held her back. "We'll be okay. Chuck will be there to protect me, and the other men will be, as well."

Hector shrugged. "So be it. I will inform my men."

"Good. It's all settled. We'll leave at dark." Rip pulled Tracie closer, nibbling the back of her ear. "Now where was I. Ah, yes. I missed you."

She giggled and responded with, "I missed you, too."

Hector's eyes narrowed and he swam away. Lifting himself out of the water, he rose to stand dripping beside the pool.

"Aren't you going to stay?" Tracie asked, her hands resting on Rip's arms, which he'd wrapped around her waist.

"I have business to conduct and I do not intend to be what you call, the third wheel." He nodded to Rip. "Enjoy for as long as you like."

Once Hector left the patio, Tracie squirmed, pushing Rip's hands away. "Let go."

He didn't release her, instead he turned her in his arms and clamped her to him.

"What are you doing?" she whispered, a smile pasted across her angry lips.

"Hector went inside, but I'd bet my favorite snorkel he's standing in the window watching."

Tracie stopped wiggling and sighed. "I supposed you could be right."

"We really need to act more like a newlywed couple," he said. "For the sake of our cover, of course." Rip tightened his hold on her.

"I thought you didn't want to get closer. You don't want to waste your time on a relationship that isn't going anywhere."

"Maybe I've decided to use my indomitable charm to convince you a relationship with me isn't such a bad idea." He brushed his lips across hers. "Now show Hector that we're crazy in love, and you can't live without me."

"You're impossible," she whispered, her wet hands rising to capture his face between her palms.

"No, I'm indomitable. We SEALs—" Rip was cut off by Tracie's lips pressing against his.

She leaned back for a moment to say, "You SEALs talk way too much."

"Only when we have—"

Her mouth descended on his again and her legs wrapped around his waist beneath the water.

For sure now, he wouldn't be able to leave the pool without displaying just how turned on he was by her. At that moment, he didn't care.

He deepened the kiss, pushing past her teeth to slide along the length of her tongue, stroking, caressing and loving every inch of his possession.

Tracie moaned, her thighs tightening, her center rubbing against the front of his swimsuit, igniting a desire so strong, he wanted to take her, there in the pool and to hell with whoever was watching.

"You want me now, don't you?" Tracie nibbled at his ear.

"I've always wanted you."

"Then let's go to our bedroom."

God, he wanted to. More than he wanted to breathe. If they weren't at Hector's house in his pool, and if he wasn't wearing that damned bathing suit, he might have been beyond temptation and carried her into the house and up the stairs to the massive king-size bed and taken her places she'd never dreamed possible.

But they weren't alone. With the possibility that they were being watched, maybe even recorded, Rip knew he couldn't throw caution to the wind.

Tracie had to want to be with him for longer than just the operation. When they were no longer playing the newlyweds, she had to want him to make love to her as much as he wanted to make love to her.

The physical attraction could not be denied. Rip knew there was so much more to life than that and he wanted Tracie to know that, too. If he could find the bastard who'd betrayed her trust, he'd kill him. On the other hand, he was glad she'd met someone who wasn't trustworthy so that when she met someone who was, she'd eventually know the difference.

The sound of someone clearing his throat broke through

the intense and deeply stirring kiss, and Rip tore his mouth from Tracie's long enough to acknowledge the blue-shirted servant.

"Dinner will be served on the hour."

Rip was surprised to see that the sun had begun its descent to the horizon. Shadows had lengthened and darkness would soon settle over the hacienda. After supper they'd load up in the vehicles and return to the little town of Colinas Rocosa and then the adventure would begin.

Hugging Tracie close one last time, he whispered into her ear. "You don't have to come."

She pushed her hands against his shoulders and stared into his eyes. "What are you talking about?"

"Tonight will be dangerous. You can stay here where it's safe and where I won't have to worry about you."

"Look, mister, don't patronize me." She shoved against him, twin flags of color flying her cheeks. "I might not be a SEAL, but I'm just as much a part of this team as Julio and Carlos. More so. I've been on it longer than they have."

"By a day," he pointed out, loving the fire in her green eyes as her ire spiked.

Tracie pushed at his chest. "A day in an agent's life is like seven years."

Rip laughed out loud. "Now you're talking about dogs."

"I mean it. I'm going." She caught his face in her hands and stared hard into his eyes. "Are you listening? I'm going."

"Okay, okay. You're going. But I'm calling the shots. What I say goes. No questions asked. Agreed?" He kissed the tip of her nose.

Her eyes narrowed. "Don't do that. I'm being serious."

"Yeah, me too. Agreed?" He didn't move, refusing to break eye contact. "On this, he wouldn't waver. "Agree and go, or refuse and stay behind," he challenged.

She breathed in and blew the air out her nose in a soft snort. "Agreed."

He kissed the tip of her nose again. "You could have agreed with a little more enthusiasm."

"Yeah and you could have asked with a little less force." This time, she kissed the tip of his nose.

He liked it. "Why did you do that?"

She pressed her lips together. "To show you how irritating it is."

"Well, I like it when you're playful."

"Don't get used to it. This operation is almost over."

"Maybe so, but we're not."

"You know how I feel."

"Blah, blah, blah. You're all talk." He scooped her legs out from under her and tossed her into the water.

When she came up sputtering, she slapped at the water, sending a wave square into his face. "That was uncalled for."

"Yeah, and you need to get your dancing shoes on. We leave right after supper."

Her lips twisted in a saucy smile. "I'm not getting out until you do."

Rip cringed at the thought of climbing out of the pool in the package-hugging suit. And his package had been far too inspired by his fake bride. "Fine." Forcing a bravado that was hard to feel wearing such a tiny thing, he hiked his body up on the side of the pool and stood.

Tracie's eyelids drooped and her nipples spiked beneath her bikini top. "You should wear that suit more often. It is totally you."

"Shut up." He dipped his foot in the water and sent a splash her way. "Now hurry up, or I'll leave without you."

"Like hell you will." Tracie pulled herself up out of the water and raced ahead of him for the house, slipping a little on the wet concrete. They ran into the house, laughing all the way up the stairs to their bedroom.

Rip let Tracie hit the shower first, slowing down at the dresser, pretending to select his clothing. The way he felt at that moment, he couldn't continue to resist her and he didn't want to go back on his word. He refused to take her until she admitted there could be something between them on a long-term basis.

Standing at the window, he stared out over the jungle-covered hillside and wondered where he'd be next week and where Tracie would be.

"Hey." A wet washcloth hit him in the side of the head and landed with a splat on the floor.

Rip turned to find Tracie standing in the doorway of the bathroom holding a towel up to her front.

"Aren't you going to join me?" she asked, her voice low and sultry. Then she dropped the towel giving him a full-on view of what she had to offer. She turned and gave him the backside of the same and walked away, leaving the door open, inviting him to follow.

Holy hell.

All his good intentions flew out the window and he didn't walk—he ran toward his destiny.

Chapter Eleven

Tracie ducked under the shower spray, sure she'd gotten to him this time. And she wasn't disappointed when Rip's arms slipped around her middle and pulled her back to his front.

"You play dirty, Agent Kosart."

She leaned into him, letting her head fall back on his shoulder. "I do whatever it takes to get the job done."

"Just because I'm here doesn't mean I've given up."

"It doesn't?" She reached behind her to grasp his hips in her hands and press him closer. "I have you right where I want you."

"And I'm telling you, this isn't over when we leave here."

"Whatever."

He spun her around and into his arms. "Look, Tracie. I don't know what's happening between us. All I know is that I don't want it to end. If you're honest with yourself, neither do you."

She walked her fingers up his chest and chin to press her pointer finger to his lips. "You talk a lot for a man. Shut up and make love to me."

"Not without protection."

Tracie reached behind a washcloth hanging on a rail and produced a foil packet like the ones he'd found in the draw the night before. "Is this what you're talking about? While you weren't a Boy Scout, I made a very good Girl Scout. I make it a point to always come prepared."

Rip laughed out loud. "If you were a Girl Scout, I'm the king of England."

"Well, Your Highness, you're not getting any closer to making use of this royal gift." She tore the edge of the packet with her teeth and removed the contents, rolling it down over his stiff shaft.

Rip scooped her legs out from under her and wrapped them around his waist. He turned, pressing her back against the cool stone tiles and positioning himself at her entrance. But he didn't drive home.

Tracie wiggled, trying to lower herself over him, her body on fire, her core aching with the need for him to fill her. "What are you waiting for?" she moaned.

"You're not ready yet."

"Are you kidding me?" Trying again to take him into her, she gave up and glared at him.

He shook his head. "You're not ready." Then he set her on her feet and wrapped a hand around the back of her neck, tipping her head up to accept his kiss.

He took her mouth in a gentle joining, brushing softly over her lips, sliding into her mouth with his tongue.

Tracie rose on her toes, deepening the kiss, pressing her breasts against his naked chest, wanting to get so much closer to him.

Warm water ran down her back and between them, heating with the fire of their rising desire.

"Please," she moaned.

But he didn't press into her, instead, his lips trailed wet kisses down her chin and the length of her neck to the pebbled tips of her breasts.

Tracie arched her back, urging Rip to take more.

He obliged, sucking her nipple into his mouth, rolling it around on his tongue.

Tracie's body undulated to the rhythm of Rip's tongue. When he nibbled at her, she cried out and clasped the back of his head, forcing him to take more of her breast into his mouth.

When he'd finished with one, he moved to the other and paid it equal attention.

Everywhere Rip touched her, her body burned, her skin was so sensitive it rippled as he moved down her body, skimming across her abs.

He dropped to one knee on the shower tiles and parted her folds with his thumbs.

Tracie sucked in a deep breath and flattened her palms against the tile as he slid his tongue along the strip of flesh packed with a fiery bundle of nerve endings, each popping off a fresh round of sensations through her body.

Her belly clenched and her core heated, aching for him to fill her.

"Damn you, sailor," she said through clenched teeth. "Come to me now."

"Almost there," he muttered, blowing a stream of warm air against her heated center, while water dripped over his head and shoulders.

Only she couldn't concentrate past the tongue flicking, licking and sliding over her, drawing her taut like a fully extended bow string.

"I can't…take…any…more." One more touch of his magic tongue launched her over the edge, spinning her out of control. Her body jerked and spasmed as she shot into the stratosphere, tumbling past the moon in a passion-filled flight to the stars.

Still, he wouldn't let up his attack on her senses, bringing her to a frenzied pitch before she fell back to earth.

"Now." Grabbing his ears, she dragged him up her body. "Take me now," she demanded in a desperate, gravelly voice she didn't recognize.

Rip lifted her again, wrapping her legs around him, positioning his member at her entrance. He paused, his breathing ragged, his face tense. "Say you'll see me again stateside."

"Now?" she wailed.

"Say it." He nudged her but refused to enter.

"For the love of Mike!" She pounded her fists on his shoulder. "Take me."

"Not until you say it."

"Fine! I'll see you stateside."

"A date," he insisted.

"A date." She squeezed her legs around his middle and lowered herself as he thrust upward.

They came together in a rush, her channel slick and ready.

Past the point of impatience, Tracie rose and fell, trying to set a fast-paced rhythm.

Rip growled and backed her against the shower wall. With one hand he pinned her wrists above her head. With the other hand, he held her steady while he slammed into her, over and over, picking up speed with every thrust.

Tracie whimpered, feeling herself climbing that slippery slope again, her body tensing with the promise of another shot at ecstasy.

One last thrust and she pitched over the edge.

Rip released her wrists and held her hips in both hands, buried as deeply as he could go, his member throbbing against the walls of her channel.

When Rip finally moved, he pressed his forehead to hers. "You drive a hard bargain," he whispered, his voice unsteady.

"Me?" she laughed, feeling light and satiated. "You were the one doing all the driving."

He breathed in and let go of the breath in a long, shaky sigh. Then he slapped her naked bottom. "We'd better hurry. Dinner will be on the table and Hector will be waiting for us to appear."

Rip lifted her off him and set her on her feet.

Tracie was glad he didn't let go immediately as her legs could barely support her. She laid her cheek on his chest, listening to the rapid beat of his heart. With a smile, she realized he'd been as affected as she was.

When she could stand on her own, he let go, discarded the condom, shampooed her hair and then his, and pulled her under the shower's spray to rinse all the soap off her head and body.

In quick efficient movements he switched off the water and toweled her dry, then himself.

Feeling as limp as a wet noodle, Tracie let him, enjoying the swift vigor with which he ran the towel over her body, between her thighs and across her breasts. Her body responded to his touch her core heating all over again.

"Do we have to go to dinner?" she asked, her fingers skimming over his shoulders.

He took her hands in his, closing his eyes for a moment as if gathering his wits. "Sadly, yes. I came to Honduras to find a traitor. A man who was responsible for the deaths of a DEA agent and one of my SEAL brothers. I'd love to spend the rest of the night making love to you, but duty comes first."

Tracie pushed back her rising desire. "You're right. Duty comes first." She twirled her towel into a tight twist and popped his thigh with it. "Get moving Mr. Gideon, you're taking your bride out on the town to dance."

RIP GLANCED AROUND at the colorful clothing and decorations lit up by twinkle lights in the middle of the town square of Colinas Rocosa. At one end of the square stood an old Spanish-style church that probably dated back to the early 1800s. The buildings on the other three sides of the square were dingy, chipped stucco structures that had seen better days. But tonight with the cheerful lights and the happy crowd spinning and dancing to the music from a local mariachi band, the place was somewhat magical.

Or would have been if they weren't on full alert watching for Carmelo Delgado's men to appear.

Rip spotted Carlos, Julio and the four men Hector had provided dressed to fit in with the crowd. Although the SEALs looked like the locals in most respects, the breadth of their shoulders made them stand out. Hector's men came closer to fitting in. Though they were rugged, they hadn't spent much time lifting weights or even working hard in the local fields to bulk up.

Rip had Carlos instruct them to take up positions at the four corners of the town square where a live band entertained the festival attendees.

"Come on, good-looking, dance with me." Tracie grabbed his hand and dragged him into the middle of the crush of people. The tune was lively like the six other tunes she'd insisted he dance to. He liked to dance all right, and so far, Delgado and his thugs hadn't made a showing.

Their efforts to find the one responsible for the weapons sales had reached an impasse. If they weren't able to tag one of Delgado's men with a tracking device tonight, they'd have to pay another visit to his plantation and hope to get close enough to tag one there.

Or they could sneak in at night and interrogate Delgado himself. He appeared to have some authority over the men who'd carried the illegally purchased weapons.

Tracie danced close, wrapped her arms around his neck and leaned in. "Anything?"

If she meant was he feeling anything, that would be a big fat yes. Mainly her body against his. If she meant had he seen anything of Delgado, which he was sure was what she'd meant, then… "No."

Tracie danced away from him, her bright red, layered skirt swirled out around her legs. She'd told him of the black jeans she'd worn rolled up beneath the skirt, but even as she twirled, they weren't visible to him or others. On her feet, were a pair of black ankle-high boots. Though most people wouldn't think the boots went with the dress, Rip thought they were damned sexy and could imagine them wrapped around his waist.

He grabbed her hand and twirled her around and back into his arms.

When the song came to an end, another song began immediately. Tired and thirsty, Rip tugged Tracie's hand and led her to the edge of the crowd. "Do you want me to find you a bottle of water?"

Her eyes widened, a faint sheen of perspiration made her pretty face glow. She wore very little makeup and her face had that open, earthy look that reminded him of the great outdoors and wide-open spaces. With her hair hanging loose around her shoulders, Tracie looked like a young girl barely out of her teens.

Rip knew better, though. She was a seasoned, former FBI agent bent on going after truth and justice for Hank Derringer's Covert Cowboys, Inc. And she wore the red skirt just as beautifully as the pretty village girls.

She smiled up at him and then her happy glow faded, her

gaze shifting to a point behind him. "Isn't that Delgado?" she asked.

Without appearing too obvious, Rip eased around to stand beside her. As soon as he did, he could pick out the large, gray-haired Honduran. "Yup. That would be Delgado."

He had one of his men on either side of him and several bringing up the rear.

People moved out of his way as he stepped into the square, either because of the heavy scowl on his face or the fact his men carried semiautomatic weapons.

"Looks like he spotted us," Rip confirmed.

Tracie forced a smile of welcome to her lips and spoke through her teeth. "Get ready. He doesn't appear to be very happy."

"Probably still mad that we eluded his thugs." Rip pushed his lips up into a smile and held out his hand in greeting to the older man.

Delgado took it, but didn't shake it. "What are you doing here?"

Rip grinned wider. "We're here for the festival and the dancing. My wife loves to dance."

"You should have left when you still could," Delgado warned.

"I'm not good at taking orders." Rip continued to smile even though his jaw strained under the effort. "You need to understand that if we're going to be doing business together."

Delgado's brows rose and his men pushed closer. "I have not agreed to do business with you."

"Then I'll go around you to the man in charge. I'm only here for a day. Two, max. If you are not the authority I need to speak to, I'll have to ask you to take me to him."

Delgado snorted. "That is not possible."

"Then we have nothing to talk about." Rip snapped his fingers.

Carlos and Julio moved in behind Delgado's men and jammed pistols into their backs. In Spanish, Carlos warned them not to move or they'd blow holes in them.

Delgado reached for his waistband.

Before he could get there, Rip had pulled the small, but deadly HK .40 from the hidden holster around his own waist beneath the loose-fitting shirt he'd worn. "I wouldn't do that."

"I have many men at the festival. You will not get away," Delgado practically growled.

"I bet I will." Rip, still holding his hand, twisted Delgado's arm and spun him, pinning the older man's arm up between his shoulder blades. "Now, tell your men to back off. You and I will be going for a ride.

Tracie leaned close to Rip. Out of the corner of his eye, he could see her drop one of the small tracking devices into the back pocket of Delgado's pants.

A nod from Carlos and Julio indicated they, too, had dropped their devices in the pockets of their targets.

The music had stopped and the festival goers, their eyes wide and frightened, had backed away from the confrontation taking place in the square, whispering to each other. Some herded the women and children down side streets.

Unwilling to put the good citizen's in danger, Rip knew he had to get Delgado out of the square and away from town before he let him loose. "Take their weapons," he ordered.

Julio and Carlos took Delgado's guards' weapons while Tracie grabbed Delgado's nine-millimeter pistol.

"Tell your other men to stay back or I'll shoot you," Rip said.

Delgado hesitated.

Rip shoved his arm up higher and goosed him with the tip of his gun. "Do it."

Delgado shouted in Spanish.

Carlos snarled. "He's telling them to shoot us." He swung his fist, hitting Delgado in the mouth.

Delgado spit blood out and glared at Carlos.

"You plan on dying tonight, don't you?" Rip jacked his arm up higher behind his back.

The old man cursed. "Okay!" He spluttered in Spanish.

Carlos nodded. "That's more like it. He told them to stay back."

"Let's go." Rip led the way, pushing Delgado in front of him to a location just outside of the small town. They'd parked the vehicles behind a rundown building that appeared to have been abandoned.

Hector's men closed in behind Rip, Tracie, Carlos, Julio and their charges. Delgado's other men followed at a distance.

Rip got into the backseat of the Jeep with Delgado. With nowhere else to sit, Tracie sat in Carlos's lap.

If he'd had a free hand, Rip would have knocked the grin off Carlos's face. Since there was no other choice, he kept his mouth shut and retained his grip on Delgado's arm.

The two other men Carlos and Julio had disarmed were released and told to go back to town. They stood still, hesitant to leave their leader.

Delgado shouted for them to leave.

Without a pause, they turned and ran back to the other men carrying weapons.

Rip had Carlos tell Hector's men to go ahead of them, giving them a good lead before Julio pulled out on the road. Once again, they headed out of town, fully expecting to be followed.

Three miles out, Julio pulled to the side of the road.

Carlos handed Rip a roll of duct tape, which he quickly wound around Delgado's wrists behind his back.

"My men will kill you," Delgado warned.

Rip didn't respond, just slapped a length of tape over the rebel leader's mouth and shoved him out of the Jeep onto the road. As the man struggled to break his bonds, Tracie slipped into the backseat and Julio pulled away.

Once on the road again, Julio hit the accelerator, putting as much distance as possible between them and Delgado. The rebel's men would not be far behind them.

When they'd gone a good mile along the twisting turning roads, Julio announced, "Lights out in one minute."

Rip leaned toward Tracie. "Close your eyes, let them adjust to the darkness." Following his own advice, Rip closed his eyes and waited the minute.

"Lights out," Julio announced. A click indicated Julio had switched the lights off.

Rip opened his eyes. Julio would be half-blinded, having closed one eye for the minute prior and could manage to drive while his other eye adjusted to the limited light provided by the stars above.

Before they'd left Hector's place, Rip had Julio pull the wiring on the Jeep's tail and brake lights as well as the lights to the dash. In purely blackout mode, they drove through the night another three miles before pulling off the road into a copse of trees and brush.

Once again, the men climbed out of the Jeep and covered their tracks with vegetation.

Tracie got out of the Jeep and pulled her skirt off. Her legs below her knees glowed white in the night until she unrolled her black jeans.

Rip handed out camouflage sticks and they went to work covering every pale inch of exposed skin.

The roar of an engine alerted them to an approaching vehicle.

Rip pushed his way up to the edge of the bushes where he could peer through as a truck loaded with Delgado's men rumbled past.

One hundred yards down the road, they slowed, their taillights burning bright red, lighting the darkness.

"Are they turning around?" Tracie asked, having moved silently up behind him. She'd pulled her hair back in a ponytail and her face was completely covered in camouflage paint, only her eyes and teeth shone white.

"I don't know. They stopped." He lifted a pair of night-vision goggles to his eyes and focused on the truck. The red taillights glowed bright. After a moment he could see men dropping to the ground, carrying weapons and spreading out. Some of them moved ahead of the vehicle, others ran back the way they'd come. Toward the spot where they'd hidden the Jeep in the brush. Each man carried a flashlight, the beams crisscrossing along the edges of the road.

"They're headed this way." Rip backed away from his vantage point, took Tracie's hand and led her away from the road.

The Jeep had been parked behind a bunch of tree trunks surrounded at the base by a thick weave of vines. As long as Delgado's men didn't walk very far into the woods, they'd be all right.

Rip led Tracie to a thick bush. Together, they crouched behind it, pulling leafy vines over their backsides.

As Rip glanced around, he couldn't see Julio or Carlos. Trained SEALs wouldn't be visible to the naked eye. Only night-vision goggles, more commonly called NVGs, could pick them out of the darkness by reading their heat signature.

Footsteps crunched on gravel too close for Rip's comfort.

Tracie's hand squeezed his and they hunkered low, careful not to make a sound.

A shout rose up from the direction of the truck. An engine revved and headlights flooded the road, moving back toward Rip and his team.

He held his breath until the truck came to a halt near the point they'd left the road.

In the light, he could see a man crouching close to the ground, his hand skimming across the gravel.

A shout in Spanish made the man jerk to his feet. Others ran toward the truck. In a moment, they had all piled into the truck bed and the vehicle took off, headed back toward the small town.

Not until the taillights disappeared in the distance did Rip let go of the breath he'd been holding.

"That was close," Tracie said, laughing shakily.

Still holding her hand, Rip stood and pulled her to her feet and into his embrace. He kissed her black-painted lips and set her at arm's length. "Did I tell you how sexy you look in black lipstick?"

She kissed him again, leaving some of the black paint on his lips. "Same to you, frogman."

He hugged her close, loving the way she felt in his arms. Then, setting her aside, he clapped his hands together, ready to get the show on the road. "Now all we have to do is wait until they go to their hidden camp in the jungle."

"What makes you think they will?" Tracie asked.

"They were attacked and bested. If Delgado is the leader, he'll go for reinforcements. If he's just a pawn, he'll have to report to the leader. Either way, they will go to the camp tonight and we'll find them."

Chapter Twelve

The bright green blips that had been moving for the past half hour had stopped. After Delgado's men had loaded up and passed through the small town hosting the fiesta, Tracie, Rip, Carlos and Julio followed. They skirted Colinas Rocosa's outskirts, careful to avoid any men Delgado might have left behind to watch out for them.

Stopping five miles short of their destination, Rip contacted Hank on the sat phone so that he could pinpoint where they were and tell them if there was a better route into the camp. Fortunately, a river close to where they'd pulled off the road also came within five hundred yards of the camp. They managed to get close enough to the river to unload what they'd need to stage their infiltration op.

Rip had given the handheld tracking device to Tracie to monitor while he, Julio and Carlos pulled the inflatable raft and the mini motor out of the rear storage area of the Jeep.

Tracie slipped her arms into one of the bulletproof vests Hank had included in the care package he'd sent with Carlos and Julio. She wore it over the long-sleeved black T-shirt she'd put on.

While the men spread the rubber boat out, Tracie collected an array of smoke grenades and clips full of nine-millimeter bullets, stuffing them into her pockets or strapping them to the vest. When she'd set out earlier that evening, she'd strapped a nine-millimeter Glock to her thigh beneath her party skirt. It was just like the one she'd used when she'd been part of the FBI, and she'd qualified as an expert with a similar weapon on numerous occasions. When she had to use it, the gun felt like an extension of her hand.

Carlos stared down at the small raft, shaking his head woefully. "It's not a RIB."

"What's a RIB?" Tracie asked.

"Rigid hull inflatable boat, one of the boats we use in the Navy," Rip answered.

Carlos pulled what appeared to be a small engine out of the rear compartment of the Jeep and attached it to the back of the raft. "Nor does it have a 470-horsepower engine. I'd give my right arm for one of those right now."

Julio snorted. "You call that trolling motor an engine? My electric toothbrush has more power than that."

"Hey, that trolling motor will be quiet and get us close to the camp without driving in by roads sure to be lined with sentries." Rip nodded toward the river. "We'll be going up river to get in."

Carlos groaned. "Which will make it even slower."

"Yeah. And faster when we leave," Rip reminded them.

"I don't like it." Julio kicked the boat with his boot. "I feel like a kid going fishing, not a man about to sneak into an enemy camp full of angry men with guns. Can't we call in SBT-22 for a little backup?"

Rip's chest tightened. "No."

Tracie stepped in. "Hank didn't brief you on Rip's status?"

Carlos shook his head. "Just that he had been a member of SBT-22. He didn't say why he wasn't a member anymore."

"Because I'm dead," Rip said, his voice flat. He pushed

past the two SEALs and mounted the trolling motor on the back of the boat.

Carlos's brows came together. "How can you be dead when you're standing right in front of me?"

Tracie waited for Rip to answer for himself. When he didn't, she filled the silence. "His unit thinks he was killed by a sniper who wanted him dead because of the information he received from a DEA agent. The agent had been undercover, embedded in the terrorist training camp we're about to enter."

"Holy crap," Julio said. "And here I thought we were going into a cakewalk. Terrorist training camp? Not just some local boys playing at being rebels?"

Carlos's lips spread in a smile. "You said it would be dangerous."

"It will be." Rip faced Tracie. "Now's the time to change your mind."

"I'm going." Tracie helped Carlos load the boat with every bit of equipment they'd brought with them in the Jeep. Weapons, smoke grenades, explosives and detonators.

Rip faced his SEAL brothers. "The same goes for each of you. If you're not comfortable with the mission, there's no shame in backing out. You didn't know what you were going into."

"Can't let a girl show me up." Carlo's lips quirked upward. "Besides, you know the code. The only easy day was yesterday. Let's get wet."

Rip held out his hand to Julio who gripped his forearm instead. "I could use a little exercise. Dude, let's rock and roll."

Tracie climbed into the boat first, then Julio and Carlos.

"We're going in to collect information, not to engage," Rip reminded them as he pushed the boat off the short and hopped in. "We'll stop short of the camp and go in on foot. We can wait until the camp is asleep before we make our move."

The moon was nothing more than the tip of a fingernail in the sky, leaving the stars to provide all the light they needed.

Keeping close to the narrow river's edge and the inky shadows of the overhanging trees, they traversed upriver in the direction the tracking devices indicated.

The going was slow, but then, they weren't in much of a hurry. Delgado's arrival in the camp would get everyone stirred up. They'd need time to wind down again before Tracie and the team of SEALs could slip in, gather what information they could and get out.

"Anything else you want to tell us now that you have our full attention?" Carlos questioned.

Rip, his hand on the till continued in silence for a moment before answering. "I think whoever is selling the weapons to the terrorists is American and could be connected high up the food chain."

Carlos turned to look at Rip in the light from the stars. "Are you kidding me? You think someone in Washington is dirty?"

"I'd bet my best rifle on it," Rip said. "Whoever it is got to our gunnery sergeant and bribed him to leak information about our mission. That leak got a sniper positioned outside the camp. When we brought out the DEA agent, the sniper took out the agent and got one of our men as collateral damage."

"I'd heard about that. A kid named Gosling," Julio said. "Damned shame." Julio and Carlos hung their heads in deference to their lost comrade.

Tracie sat in silence. The SEALs had a strong bond, even though they hadn't known each other before they'd met at Hector's. From all she'd read, their training was so intense, it reinforced the notion to look out for your own and do whatever it took, no matter what, to get the job done.

Tracie was in good shape, but by no means as ruggedly fit as the men who made it through BUD/S training.

Rip aimed the craft toward an overhanging tree, slowed the boat and cut the engine. The remaining momentum sent them toward shore where the rubber hull bumped soundlessly against mud and roots.

Without waiting to be told, Julio and Carlos jumped out of the boat and dragged it up on the shore beneath the drooping tree.

Tracie scrambled out and gathered whatever weapons she could, handing them to the men, one at a time. They all pulled on helmets rigged with communication devices and NVGs.

Rip turned on his radio and waited while the others did the same. Then he spoke softly, "Check."

Through the crackling of the static that erupted in Tracie's ear, she could make out Rip's word clearly. "Check," she repeated.

Rip nodded.

"Check," Carlos and Julio each said and waited for Rip to indicate he'd heard them.

With the handheld GPS tracker in hand, Rip took the lead, heading east, away from the river.

"Remember where we parked," Carlos whispered.

An answering chuckle helped ease Tracie's tension as they pushed through thick foliage, working their way toward the location where the green lights had stopped.

Rip led the way, moving as swiftly as the jungle would allow. The canopy, high overhead, blocked most of the light from the stars, which meant it also blocked a good portion of the sunlight, needed for vegetation to grow at ground level. Other than the occasional vine with huge leaves, they had it pretty easy. The NVGs helped them navigate through the dark forest floor.

Tracie followed Rip, glad she was in good shape as he moved quickly, barely slowing down to catch his breath. Carlos followed her and Julio brought up the rear.

After fifteen minutes of steady forward movement, Rip held up his fist and came to an abrupt halt.

Tracie had been following so closely, intent on keeping up, she nearly plowed into him.

"Get down," Rip whispered through the headset.

All four of them crouched in the underbrush, inching forward, abreast with Rip.

Through her NVGs, Tracie saw the green blobs of people moving about in a clearing a hundred yards ahead.

"I count ten," Rip said.

"I had eight," Carlos replied. "We'll go with your number."

"Looks like they're unloading a big crate from the back of that truck." Rip touched her arm. "Do you see it?"

Tracie could make out six men heaving a huge crate out of the back of what appeared to be an old army two-ton truck with two men seemingly supervising.

"Watch where they take it. I'll bet that's where we need to go," Rip advised.

Tracie riveted her attention on the men moving the crate. For a moment, they disappeared behind the truck. She could see the green outlines of their legs beneath the truck bed and they appeared on the other side, heading toward what looked like a tent. Then they disappeared inside. Through the canvas, Tracie could see the smudge of light green silhouettes moving about.

"Heads down," Carlos said quietly and flattened himself to the ground.

Out of the corner of her NVGs Tracie saw a big green

blob not ten feet from where they crouched on the ground. She eased down to her belly, making herself as much a part of the jungle floor as she could.

"Damn, he's got NVGs," Rip said quietly.

Tracie held her breath, waiting for all hell to break loose.

The man passed by their location and continued on, making a turn at the far end of camp. He had his NVGs tilted upward. A lucky break for their little party. Tracie released the breath she'd been holding and started to rise to her knees.

"Stay put," Rip said. "There's another one coming."

The next man didn't have NVGs but he carried what looked like an automatic weapon with a long banana clip.

Once again, Tracie sucked in a breath and held it. The man headed their way was closer than the first and he kicked at leaves as he walked, appearing bored and slightly resentful at having to pull guard duty.

"We'll stay here until the camp settles." Rip lay on his belly, probably conserving his strength.

Tracie lay as flat as she could, but her heart pounded so hard, she would be worn out before they moved into the camp. Inhaling, she eased the air out of her lungs, willing her pulse to slow. After a few minutes, she had control of her excitement.

SHE WASN'T SURE how long they waited, an hour, maybe two, before the camp grew quiet, the vehicles' engines had cooled and the camp residents had stopped moving around. All except the men pulling guard duty.

Rip rose to his knees. "I'm going to get closer. Everyone stay here until I give you orders otherwise."

"But—" Tracie started.

"You promised to do as I say," Rip reminded her.

"Yes, but—"

"Then don't argue."

She clamped her lips shut. Carlos and Julio hadn't argued. Feeling like a child who had been reprimanded, Tracie lay back down and watched as Rip low crawled into camp.

She didn't like the idea of him going in alone. What if he ran into trouble? Who would have his six?

No one.

For an excruciatingly long time, she lay counting the seconds. Rip hadn't said a word, hadn't let them know he was okay and most of all, hadn't told them to join him.

The only thing that made her feel better was that camp was still quiet, no one had raised an alarm. So, Tracie waited as instructed, chewing a hole in her lip, praying Rip was all right.

RIP MADE IT all the way to one of the tents without incident. So far so good. He was glad he'd made the others wait in the woods. Infiltrating the inside perimeter with one person was hard enough. Taking four in would be impossible. A guard had been deployed outside the tent he'd identified as the one that could contain the evidence he was looking for. The man had started his sentry duties standing and had eventually squatted and then sat. Now his head was tipped forward and he snored with a light whistling sound.

When he was certain nothing was moving, Rip eased his way around the outskirts to the back of what he had tagged as the supply tent. Slipping his knife from his boot, he slit a one-foot long gash in the canvas and pushed it aside, peering in through his NVGs, while his ears perked for any sounds from behind.

Nothing moved inside the tent and it was filled with crates and boxes stacked three deep in some places. Careful not to make a sound, he crawled beneath the canvas and into the tent. Using the crates for cover, he eased his way to the front of the tent to confirm that the tent was empty of personnel.

Near the entrance, one of the crates was set aside, the lid loose on top.

Rip listened for the whistling sound of the guard snoring. For a long moment, he heard nothing, then the soft whistle came to him through the canvas.

Careful not to make a sound, he eased the lid off the crate, lifting it toward the entrance, propping it up to block any light he might have to shine down into the crate.

As dark as it was outside, it was even darker inside the tent. The NVGs only did so much. He had to see more. Shifting the goggles upward he shone a red penlight into the crate. Clothes and cans of vegetables lay jumbled on top. As he dug deeper, his fingers hit the cold metal and hard plastic of M4A1 carbine rifles.

Easing one out of the crate, he laid it on top of the clothing and held the pen over it, clicking the end to take a photo. Looking closer, he saw that the weapons didn't have serial numbers on them.

On the manufacturing plate where they usually were, the metal was smooth, as if it had been ground down and repainted, the paint color a slightly different shade from the rest of the stock. Even the horse emblem identifying the manufacturer had been removed. It wasn't a clone of the M4A1, it was the real deal, modified to hide that fact.

If this was all they had to go on, they didn't have anything.

Disappointed, Rip laid the weapon back in the box and moved the lid back in place. As he settled the wood over the crate, his fingers slipped and the top landed with a soft whomp.

The guard outside the tent flap door, snorted awake, muttering curse words in Spanish.

Rip ducked behind a large wooden crate just as the tent flap was thrown aside.

Peeking through the gap between two crates he could see the guard enter, weapon first. He shone a flashlight around the interior, pausing on the crates behind which Rip hid.

His breath caught in his throat, Rip froze.

A shout went up outside and the guard spun and ran out of the tent.

As soon as the tent flap fell in place, Rip leaped to his feet and ran to the doorway, edging the flap to the side enough he could see what was going on.

A truck rumbled into the camp, headlights illuminating all the tents. A dozen men emerged, rubbing sleep from their eyes and carrying some of the weapons supplied from the crates.

Delgado hurried by Rip's tent, shouting orders. He had to have come from one of the tents next to the one Rip was in. Only three tents had been erected on this side of the compound. One on the very end and four across from where he hid. He could see the one on the end, but not the ones beside him, narrowing the possibilities.

While the men gathered around the truck, Rip slipped out the hole he'd cut in the back of the supply tent and ran to the one beside it, hoping to find any information regarding the shipment of weapons—a cargo manifest, contact name of the shipper, anything that would help them trace the weapons back to the seller. He tried to listen for any sounds of movement inside the tent, but the commotion outside drowned out anything inside. As he inserted his knife to tear a hole, he prayed the noise from the truck engine was sufficient to mask the sound of ripping canvas.

When he had a gap big enough, he lifted the flap and

peered inside. Half a dozen pallets were spread across the floor along with clothes hanging from a line struck from pole to pole. It appeared to be the equivalent of a portable barracks for the terrorists who trained there.

Delgado held more of position of authority than a lowly grunt.

Rip moved on to the next tent. A loud crash and the sound of splintering wood sounded in the center of the compound, a man cried out and others shouted all at once. Whatever they were unloading from the truck must have crashed onto one of the men.

The confusion would be enough to allow him to check out the next tent. Quickly, he moved into position behind the next tent, slit a tear in the back and peered inside. A makeshift desk had been erected with paper scattered across the top. A cot stood in the corner with mosquito netting hanging from the roof down over the cot. Nothing moved inside the tent.

Rip crawled through the hole and, keeping low, moved toward the desk. Quickly, he snapped pictures of the documents, one after the other until he had all of them. He found a battered briefcase on the floor beside the desk and flicked the clasps open.

A moan behind him made him freeze. He turned to find a woman lying among a pile of blankets on the floor of the tent. She lifted her head and frowned at him in the dim light that shone through the canvas from the truck outside.

"Who are you?" she asked in groggy Spanish.

He replied in Spanish. "No one, go back to sleep."

Her frown deepened. "You are not Carmelo." She straightened, pulling the blankets up over her naked body.

Her scream sliced through the night, piercing Rip's eardrums.

Throwing the briefcase in front of him, he dove for the

slit in the back of the tent, managing to get through before the first man entered the tent behind him. He scooped up the briefcase and ran as fast as he could, the darkness hampering his progress and making him second-guess where he was going. Keeping the light from the truck in his peripheral vision, he circled the camp, watching for the men guarding the perimeter.

The screaming didn't stop until he was halfway around the camp. He heard a shout near the point he'd left Tracie, Carlos and Julio and prayed they hadn't been discovered.

Hunkering low, he moved more slowly toward their position. Before he got within fifty yards, the whole world erupted in a fiery explosion.

Chapter Thirteen

When the truck lumbered into the camp, Tracie could no longer stand by and do nothing. "What if he's trapped somewhere that he can't get out without alerting them to his presence?" she whispered to Carlos.

"He will get out."

"We could set up a diversion just in case." Julio patted the plastic explosives he had tucked into his vest earlier.

"No." Carlos remained firm. "He'll let us know if he needs help."

Julio pointed to a beat-up van parked near the edge of camp, closest to them. "I could be there, set a charge and get back before Rip returns. And no one will see me."

Carlos shook his head, the movement slowing as if he was considering the suggestion. "Remote detonation? I don't want to kill our guy."

A cold chill slithered down the back of Tracie's neck, in direct contrast to the sweat dripping off her brow. "I say let Julio go for it." She positioned her nine-millimeter in front of her. "I've got your back."

Julio stared at her, his brows twisting. "You sure you know how to use that thing?"

"I'll show you just how well if you make another comment like that."

Carlos chuckled softly. "Go."

Julio slipped into the night. Once he left their position, Tracie didn't see him again until he slid beneath the van and then only because she knew he'd be there. The head-lights from the truck provided just enough illumination to see when he finished and rolled out from under the chassis.

Back into the night, he moved, virtually invisible until he slipped up behind Tracie and Carlos.

Tracie started, rolled onto her back and aimed her pis-tol at the man.

On his knees, Julio held up his hands. "It's me. Don't shoot."

"Give me a little warning next time." Her heart ham-mered against her ribs. "I almost shot you."

Julio lay on the ground between them.

"Did you see Rip?" Tracie half hoped he had and then again that he hadn't. If he'd seen him, how many terrorists would be able to see him?

"No."

A scream rose above the noise of the truck's engine.

Tracie watched as the men behind the truck ran for one of the tents on the other side of the camp.

"We've got trouble," Julio said beside her.

"What now?" Tracie asked.

"The sentry with the NVGs is headed this way. And I don't mean sliding by us, he's headed right for us."

"Back up, slowly, stay low," Carlos warned.

"Damn, he's coming faster," Julio said. "Can I shoot him?"

"No!" Tracie said as quietly as she could. "If we fire a weapon, we alert the others to our presence."

They had backed away several yards when the man headed their way shouted.

Julio stopped moving and pulled out the detonator. "Time to blow."

Tracy and Carlos covered their ears a second before Julio hit the switch.

A loud bang shook the ground and the night sky lit up like the Fourth of July. The sentry hit the dirt and covered his ears.

Carlos dropped his hands from his ears and grabbed Tracie's arm. "Let's move."

The initial explosion was followed by a secondary explosion as the van's gas tank erupted in a fiery ball, spewing fuel into the air, catching the nearby tents and some of the men on fire. Gunshots were fired and the whole camp churned in turmoil.

Carlos tugged Tracie's arm. "Come on!"

She dug her heels into the ground. "Not without Rip."

"He'll come when he doesn't find us where he left us." Carlos dragged her away from the burning camp.

Again Tracie dug her heels in the dirt. "I'm not leaving without him."

A shout sounded behind them.

A bullet whizzed past Tracie's head and hit the tree in front of her. She quit fighting Carlos, dropped to her hands and knees and crawled across the ground. When she reached a massive tree trunk, she rolled behind it for cover.

More shouts rose from the fire at the center of the compound. Fortunately, most of them were battling the blaze and unconcerned about one lonely sentry, fighting a battle all on his own.

Tracie aimed her weapon at the man racing toward them and almost pulled the trigger when a rectangular object flew out of the trees and hit the guerilla in the side of the head.

He slammed against a tree trunk and sank into a heap, the rectangular object skidding to a halt on the ground beside him.

A dark silhouette detached itself from a nearby shadow, bent to scoop up what appeared to be a briefcase and ran toward them.

Her heart pounded even harder—Tracie would recognize that form anywhere.

"Rip!" She staggered to her feet and threw her arms around his neck.

He dropped a quick kiss on her lips and said, "We have to get out of here."

"I'm one step ahead of you, buddy." Carlos raced for the river.

Rip, holding the briefcase in one hand and Tracie's hand in the other, ran after him.

Julio brought up the rear, covering their six.

When they reached the overhanging tree where they'd left the boat, everyone tumbled in while Rip pushed off the shore and settled in next to the motor.

Tracie peeked over the sides and spotted the man Rip had knocked over with the briefcase.

He stood on the shore beside a tree and raised his rifle, letting loose a short burst of bullets. The rounds plunked into the water close to the raft.

"Get down!" Rip cranked the motor, grabbed the till and angled it toward the shadows along the far shore, which wasn't far enough for Tracie's tastes. The rubber raft puttered down the river at the pace of a snail's crawl.

Carlos aimed at the man on the shore and fired, but the pistol's range wasn't nearly as far as that of the M4A1. Their attacker was quickly out of their weapons' range.

More bullets pelted the water and one ripped into the little boat's hull.

Air hissed out of the tear and one of the compartments gradually deflated, slowing the boat even more. Tracie pinched the rubber over the hole in an attempt to slow the collapse. Water trickled into the bottom, but they continued downstream moving farther and farther away from the shooter.

Tracie looked ahead at a bend in the river and prayed they'd get there before another bullet sank them completely.

As they rounded the corner, the shooter fired again, missing the boat.

Rip grunted and hunched forward.

"Rip?" Tracie rose up, grabbed Rip's shoulders and leaned him upright. Her right hand came away warm and sticky.

"I'm okay," he said through gritted teeth. "He just nicked me."

"Yeah, right," Carlos reached into his vest and pulled out a pouch. "That's a self-aid kit. As long as it didn't hit an artery—"

"It didn't," Rip said. "I'm fine."

"As I was saying," Carlos eased his way to the back of the boat. "Apply pressure to the wound to stop the bleeding. I'll take the till."

"I've got it," Rip groused.

"He'll live," Julio said. "As grumpy as he is, he'll live."

"I told you I was fine," Rip forced a tight smile.

"Bull." Tracie tugged at his good arm. "Let Carlos steer or you'll run us into the trees."

Rip let Tracie drag him into the center of the raft. She dug her fingers into the hole in his shirt and ripped it away from his shoulder. Tearing open the pouch Carlos had given her, she found a folded wad of gauze and adhesive tape. "Looks like the bullet went clean through."

"Good," Rip said, his voice tight. "At least they won't have to dig it out."

Tracie pressed a wad of gauze to the front wound and taped it tightly in place. She did the same for the exit wound. When she was done, she used her hands to scoop the rising water and blood out of the boat.

Rip leaned close to her. "Thanks."

"You're welcome. And by the way, you make a terrible patient."

"You make a sexy nurse with black lipstick."

"Well, don't get used to it. I prefer you intact."

He chuckled. "I prefer you the same way." With his lips next to her ear, he whispered, "And naked."

Julio coughed and spluttered. "TMI, buddy. I didn't have to hear that."

Tracie's cheeks burned and she was glad the trees hid them from the starlight at that moment. Carlos steered them into the tiny cove they'd departed from what seemed like days ago and could only have been a few hours.

Leaving the half-sunken raft on the shore, they climbed into the Jeep and headed toward Hector's hacienda, lights out, navigating by the light of the stars.

No one spoke, as if each of them was lost in thought. The operation hadn't gone exactly according to plan. Tracie hoped that whatever they found in the briefcase would help them identify the man selling weapons to the terrorists and shut him down.

RIP FADED IN and out of consciousness on the way back to Hector's. The bumps and jolts shot pain through Rip's arm, waking him every time Julio darted off the road to hide in the jungle when he spotted other vehicles on the road.

By the time they reached the hacienda, he could barely stand. Julio and Carlos half dragged, half carried him into the house and up the stairs to the bedroom he and Tracie shared.

Hector sent for a doctor and insisted his staff help Rip out of his dirty clothes and into the shower. None of them had had time to wash the camouflage paint from their faces, but Hector refrained from asking about it. He saved his questions until Rip was clean and the doctor had been there to dress his wounds with sterile bandages and give him a tetanus shot.

To have his guests show up with a gunshot wound and looking like terrorists themselves, was a lot to ask of their host without an explanation. Though he was tired and would rather just sleep it off, Rip figured he owed Hector the truth. The man had been more than helpful and patient with them.

Hector stood beside Rip's bed. "If there's anything else you need, just ask. Either I or one of my servants would be more than happy to get it for you." The man turned and would have walked out of the room, but Rip couldn't let him.

"Wait. I need to tell you what's going on."

Tracie had just walked in. "Do you want me to go or stay?"

"Stay," Rip said.

She turned, closed the door and walked across the room to stand on the other side of the bed, facing Hector.

In a few short minutes, Rip laid it out, telling Hector about what had happened when SBT-22 had attempted to extract the DEA agent, the death of his teammate and his own attempted murder in Mississippi.

He brought Hector up to date on what had occurred in the terrorist training camp that evening and why he had a bullet wound and the four of them wore camouflage paint.

"We have to find out who is selling American military weapons to the terrorists and shut them down," Rip ended.

Hector remained silent throughout.

"We understand if you want us to leave tonight," Tracie added. "It's a lot to ask you to harbor people who have stirred up the hornet's nest. And for all we know, we might have what we came for in that briefcase."

Hector pinched the bridge of his nose. "I wish you had been open and honest with me from the beginning."

Rip nodded. "Hank trusted you enough to send us here, but he asked us not to reveal who we were and why we had come. The fewer people who knew about our mission the more likely our cover story would be accepted."

Hector nodded. "I understand." He turned and paced to the door and back. "Had I known, I could have helped much more than just sending four men out with you. I have a boat you could have used. We could have launched an attack that would have taken every one of those murdering bastards out of existence." He clenched his fist, his face contorted into an angry, tortured mask. "They deserve to die for what they did."

Tracie rounded the bed and laid her hand on his back. "We couldn't go in killing everyone there. If we don't have what we need, we might have to capture their leader and extract that information from him."

"You can't interrogate a dead man." Rip gave a tired smile. "They don't have much to say."

The anger seemed to drain out of Hector. "You are correct. It is just as well I was not involved or I might have ruined the mission."

"As it is, they will have to move their camp again. The fire was big enough to be picked up by the satellites." Rip lay back and closed his eyes. "If you need us to leave tonight, we can."

"No," Hector spoke softly. "You are doing my country a service by attempting to stop the flow of weapons into the hands of the terrorists. I want to help in any way I can."

"A good night's sleep is what I need now. In the morning we'll look over what we got and go from there." His blood loss had affected him more than he'd expected and he fought to stay awake.

"I'll leave you two alone." Hector's brows rose. "Unless Senora Gideon, which I'm certain is not your name—" he laughed softly "—would like another room?"

"No," Tracie spoke firmly. "I'm staying with Senor Gideon." She grinned. "I'm getting used to the name and the man. Plus I want to make sure he doesn't bleed all over your bed."

"Do not worry about the bed." Hector opened the door. "Thank you for all you have done." With that he left Tracie and Rip alone, closing the door behind him.

Rip patted the bed beside him.

"I want to get a shower before I go to bed." She pressed her lips to his forehead.

She must have taken off her shoes because he didn't hear her move across the floor. The bathroom door closed and the shower started.

Rip lay back, tired beyond all measure and his shoulder ached, but they were safe and Tracie hadn't been shot or killed in the process of infiltrating the terrorist camp. He'd call that a good day.

Chapter Fourteen

Tracie hurried through the shower, scrubbing the black camouflage paint from her face, hoping to get back to the bed before Rip fell asleep.

It had been wishful thinking on her part. Still wound up from the explosion, gunfire and hiding in the woods, she knew it would be a while before she was tired enough to sleep. Carlos and Julio had helped get Rip into the house and then gone to their own rooms to rest up for whatever was in store for them the following day.

Tracie slipped into a silk robe and wandered around the room stopping at a small desk set against the wall. The briefcase Rip had used as a weapon lay on the smooth, polished wood. Someone had wiped the exterior clean of the mud it had collected on their race through the jungle.

Sitting at the chair in front of the desk with only the light from the bathroom to see by, she flipped the catches and opened the case.

Before she could peruse the contents, a soft knock sounded on the door. She rose to answer.

Hector stood in the hallway. "I sent twenty of my men to round up as many of the terrorists as they could. We were fortunate and caught Delgado and he is locked up in the cellar of a barn not far from here."

"Good. That will keep him from alerting his supplier that some of his documents are missing."

Although they spoke quietly, Tracie was afraid they'd disturb Rip. "Look, let me bring the case downstairs where we can go through it. Hopefully it will contain something we can use to trace the weapons shipments back to the States."

"I would be honored to help."

Tracie closed the case and carried it from the room and downstairs to Hector's study.

He cleared his massive mahogany desk. Tracie set the briefcase in the middle and flipped it open.

Tracie shuffled through documents and bills of lading, searching for a link between Carmelo and the shipments of weapons, finding only records of food and supplies. She sorted them into stacks. Some were from businesses in Honduras. Others were imports from Costa Rica, Guatemala and the Dominican Republic. Nothing really stood out.

With the briefcase empty, she stared down at it. Something about the case wasn't right. It was much shallower than the exterior would indicate. Not just the difference of the width of the materials used to make the case. There had to be at least an inch and a half's difference.

Tracy felt along the inside lining, dug her fingernail into the fabric and lifted up. The bottom rose, revealing a hidden compartment. "Well, look at this."

Hector leaned over her shoulder. "Delgado is smarter than I expected."

Inside was an array of papers, a passport and an airline ticket for Dulles International Airport for a man named Enrique Perez. The name wasn't familiar to Tracie, but the photograph was of the man Tracie knew as Carmelo Delgado.

"Check this out." She handed the passport and the ticket to Hector.

Beneath the papers lay a thin mobile phone.

Tracie lifted it and pressed the button to switch it on. The screen blinked to life, but it was password protected. "Hector, do you have access to the internet?"

He nodded. "I have satellite connection."

"I need to connect my laptop."

"Anything you need."

Tracie hurried back to the bedroom, checked on Rip and returned with the thin laptop she'd stashed in her suitcase. While she'd been upstairs, she had also claimed the satellite phone Hank had given her. Now that they had some information, she could turn it over to her boss and his computer genius to figure out.

Tracie placed the call. "Hank, it's Kosart."

"Hi, Tracie. How are things going?" Though his voice started out groggy, it cleared quickly. "Did you make it into the terrorist camp?"

"We did. If the spy satellites were over it an hour ago, they should have picked up an image of it. The whole camp was lit up like the Fourth of July."

Hank chuckled. "I take it you made a splash."

"Yes, sir." Her lips quirked. "Julio is amazing with pyrotechnics."

"The Navy does a helluva job training SEALs on demolition. We're lucky to have him on the CCI team," Hank agreed. "Were you able to retrieve any data?"

"We're not sure. My partner managed to snag a briefcase belonging to the leader of the *Diablos*. Unfortunately, during our escape, he took a bullet to the shoulder."

"Is he okay?"

Tracie's gut knotted. "He lost a lot of blood, but Hector brought a doctor in to treat him. He's holding his own."

"Good. He's a good man. We could use more men like him on our team."

Tracie smiled. "I think he already has a job."

"See what you can do to recruit him."

Her heart skittered at the thought of working with Rip in the Covert Cowboys, Inc. The man was a dedicated SEAL. What were the chances of him giving up a life he loved to go to work for a billionaire? The SEALs were a tight-knit community.

But then there was Carlos and Julio, both SEALs who'd decided they'd had enough. Tracie wondered if Rip would do the same. Dragging her thoughts back to the present, she continued, "We found a cell phone in a hidden compartment of the case, but it's password protected."

"Connect the phone to the computer. I'll get Brandon on it right away."

"Already set up and ready for him." No sooner were the words out of her mouth then the cursor moved on the screen even though her hand was nowhere near the touchpad.

"Leave it to Brandon," Hank said. "He'll have it hacked and the numbers downloaded in no time. Anything else?"

"Not much. I'll scan the documents and send them your way to see if you can find a connection to the weapons shipments. Also, Delgado had a ticket to Virginia and a fake US passport under the name of Enrique Perez."

"Scan and send the documents. Brandon's already working on the phone. We'll get back to you as soon as we have anything."

"Roger." Tracie ended the call and looked at Hector. "I don't suppose you have a scanner I could use? I have a portable one, but it will take forever."

"I do." He opened a cabinet next to his desk revealing a state-of-the-art, combination printer and scanner.

For the next hour, Tracie scanned documents and sent

them to Hank. She also downloaded and sent the photos Rip had taken with his penlight camera. When she was done, she stretched and yawned. "I think that's all we can do for now."

Hector nodded. "You might as well get some rest."

"You, too."

"I'd planned to after I check with the men holding Delgado."

Tracie climbed the stairs so tired she could barely lift her feet. The adrenaline high she'd been on was long gone and all she wanted was to lie down and sleep.

Other than a light she'd left on in the bathroom, the massive bedroom was dark. She could make out Rip's form lying so still, she touched his chest to see if he was breathing.

He grabbed her wrist and pulled her down to him. "You smell good," he said, his voice like warm syrup over gravel.

"Better than river water and camo paint?" she whispered, pressing her lips to his forehead.

"I kinda like that scent on you, too. You're pretty hot when you're dressed for battle."

"You weren't so bad yourself." She smoothed a lock of his hair back from his forehead.

"Are you going to stand there all night, or get in bed?"

"I'm afraid I'll hurt you."

"My shoulder's sore, but I'll hurt a lot more if I have to get up and put you in the bed."

"Okay, okay. I'm getting in."

He let go of her wrist, his gaze slipping over her body in the silk robe. "I like that robe on you."

"You'll like what's under it better." Tracie untied the sash and let the garment slip from her shoulders to pool around her ankles to reveal the white teddy.

Rip moaned. "You sure know how to hurt a guy."

"Oh, if this is going to be too much for you…"

"Don't you dare walk away now." When he reached for her, she danced out of range.

"I really don't want to cause you any more pain."

"Come here."

She straddled his hips and lowered herself over him, careful not to touch his injured shoulder as she nuzzled his neck on the opposite side. "I thought maybe I could do all the work this time."

He lifted the hand of his good arm and cupped her cheek. "I'm all for equal opportunity." Then he covered her lips with his, capturing the back of her head to deepen the kiss.

"You scared me tonight." Tracie lay down pressing her ear to his chest, listening to the beat of his heart.

"When I got back to where I left you, I about had a heart attack when you and the team weren't there." His tongue slipped between her teeth, probing her mouth, caressing her in urgent strokes.

"I wouldn't have left without you." She kissed her way down his chest and tongued a dark brown nipple, nibbling on it before she moved to the other.

"You know, I could get used to this," he said.

"Get used to what? Me doing all the work?" She sank her teeth into his skin, biting gently. "Don't. I like it when you're on top."

"No, I could get used to having you around."

She stopped midlick, her heart heavy, her stomach knotting. Then she slid off him to his uninjured side, resting her hand on his chest, her thigh draped over his. Resting her head in the crook of his shoulder, she sighed.

Why was she fighting this so hard? She liked him. He liked her. Their chemistry was off the charts. So why not go with it?

Because it would lead to heartache and Tracie wasn't

sure she was strong enough to have her heart broken again. Especially by this man. Where Bruce had been handsome and exciting, he'd also been a liar and a traitor.

Cord Schafer was a good man, dedicated to his country and the men in his unit. He was a man she could respect and maybe even fall in love with. But the time and distance that would be between them would make anything they might want to have impossible. She didn't want to risk her heart again, but damn. She suspected it was too late.

RIP LAY STILL for a long moment, wishing he'd kept his big mouth shut. Everything had been going so well. She'd worried about him in the thick of things and had been right there, tending his wounds when he'd been shot. Then to come to him in that teddy…

And he had to go and ruin it all by talking about the future.

"Look, I understand how you feel about long-term relationships. I've already told you how I feel about them and that I think we'd be good together."

He pulled in a deep breath and let it out, twinges of pain shooting through his shoulder with every movement. "I promise not to bug you about it again. After nearly dying several times in the past couple months, I've come to the conclusion that maybe I need to loosen up and live in the moment. No expectations, no commitments. What I'm trying to say, and doing a terrible job of it, is that I just want to hold you. When you want me to let go, I will." His arm tightened around her. "I'll take what I can get for as long as I can get it."

Tracie sighed, pressing her lips to his skin. "Thank you." Nestling closer she slipped an arm over his chest. "Much as I'd like to make love to you, it's probably better if you rest. Who knows what Hank will have for us when Brandon decodes the phone."

"Phone?" Rip lifted his head to stare down at Tracie's face. "What phone?"

With her eyes already closed, she yawned and said. "The one Hector and I found in the secret compartment in the briefcase."

"I feel like Rip van Winkle instead of Rip Schafer. Did I miss anything else?"

"Just that Hector collected Delgado and some of his men and is holding them in the basement of a building nearby."

"He did what?" Rip half sat up, pain stabbing through his shoulder. He eased back down, wincing. "Catch me up on that, will you?"

"He sent a large contingent of his men to where the camp had been. Hector's men surprised those of Delgado's men who were still there trying to salvage what they could. Hector's men captured some of them who willingly disclosed Delgado's location. When they got to Delgado, the terrorist leader's men scattered and they were able to capture Delgado."

"Did Delgado talk? Did he tell Hector who sold him the guns?"

"Not a chance." Tracie yawned again and buried her cheek against his side. "Hank will let us know what he finds on the phone."

"Anything else interesting in the briefcase or on my penlight camera?"

"Delgado had a plane ticket and US passport under another name. Hank and his team back in Texas are going over the data."

When Rip opened his mouth to ask another question, Tracie pressed her finger to his lips. "Hank will call when he knows anything. I've told you everything. Now get some rest and regenerate all that blood you lost. We're not done yet, and I'm tired."

He lay still for a while, his good arm curled around Tracie, holding her close. Before long her deep, even breaths blew warm air against his skin. She'd fallen to sleep, wearing that damned teddy and pressing her breasts to his ribs. He was in pain from more than just his shoulder, but he wouldn't wake her. She'd been through as much as he had that day. She needed to sleep.

If Hank's techie was half as good as Tracie said, he'd get something off that cell phone or glean something from the data found in the briefcase.

In the meantime, he would enjoy the moment, holding Tracie as if there would be no tomorrow, only today. And with Tracie, that could be true.

He was out of ideas or ways to convince her that their relationship was worth making the effort for. But he wasn't giving up yet. They had until they resolved this case. He'd take all he could get.

Exhaustion claimed him and he slept, dreaming about explosions, firefights and losing sight of Tracie in the confusion. No matter which way he turned, he couldn't find her. The fire burned high, creeping closer until he saw her standing with her back to the flames, nothing but a faceless silhouette. She reached out to him, but he couldn't quite touch her hand. Just as the fire swept over her, he felt as though his heart would explode, his pulse pounding so hard he heard ringing in his ears.

The ringing continued, growing lower until he surfaced from the dream.

Beside him, Tracie leaned over to the nightstand and made a grab for the satellite phone, knocking it to the floor. She rolled over.

Before he could catch her, she tumbled off the bed, landing on her knees on the carpeted floor, fumbling with the phone until it stopped ringing.

"Yeah." Her voice cracked as she sat cross-legged. She listened for a moment, pushing her hair back from her face. "Sounds like an excellent place to start...Good...We'll be on it." She ended the call and glanced up at Rip. "The plane will be here in less than an hour. Are you up to flying?"

Rip sat up and shoved the sheet aside. He was light-headed and his arm was sore, but he could move. "Where are we headed?"

"Virginia."

Chapter Fifteen

Tracie stared out over the wing of the Citation as it took off from Hector's grass landing strip.

Carlos and Julio stayed with Hector's team of guards, providing ground support and protection as the airplane rolled down the runway and launched into the sky over the Honduran jungle. Once in the air at a decent cruising altitude, Tracie tapped into the satellite Wi-Fi and connected a live video feed into the Raging Bull Ranch.

Hank Derringer's face filled the screen.

"No problems getting out of the country?" he asked.

"None," Tracie responded. "Hector and his men were invaluable in their support."

"I knew he would be. He's a good man. It's a shame about his family."

An image flashed in her mind of the portrait hanging in the hallway in Hector's hacienda. She was glad the *Diablos* had been crippled by their intel-gathering operation. Anyone who would gun down a six-year-old or condone their men firing on a child was worse than an animal. The leader of the *Diablos* deserved no mercy. But as much as Tracie would have loved to let Hector deal with Delgado, the US government would need to interrogate him.

"As I said earlier, Brandon was able to trace the phone numbers on the cell phone. Most of them were to a disposable phone that was purchased in Virginia. The purchaser used a fake ID and listed a bogus address."

"Then it's a good thing we're headed to Virginia." Tracie said.

Hank grinned. "Fortunately, one of the phone numbers was from a cell phone registered to a Belinda Tate who lives in Alexandria, Virginia. The call didn't last long, only five seconds."

"So why is this Tate woman important?" Rip stood behind Tracie, leaning over so that Hank could see his face on the screen.

She could feel the heat from his body and smell the clean, fresh scent of his aftershave. A thrill rippled the length of her spine and out across her skin in goose bumps.

Hank's eyes narrowed. "She might not be important, but her husband, Vance, is. He works at the Blackburn Gun Manufacturing plant outside of Alexandria."

Tracie sat forward, all thoughts of how good it felt to have Rip leaning over her pushed to the back of her mind. "But the weapons at that terrorist training camp looked exactly like M4A1s they issue to soldiers in the US Army. If I'm not mistaken, Blackburn isn't the manufacturer that makes them."

"And there are plenty of knockoffs," Hank said. "I need you two to infiltrate Blackburn, find out if they are making knockoffs and supplying the weapons. If they are, find out who authorized it."

"From what I saw in that camp, those weapons were the real McCoy, not knockoffs. But their manufacturing plates had been ground off and the stock had been repainted."

"Perhaps that's what Blackburn has been doing. It's up to you two to find out. And, if that's what's happening, we also need to find out how they're getting the guns. Brandon hasn't found any records in their system indicating shipments from the usual government supplier."

"Which means they aren't getting them legally," Tracie concluded.

"Exactly. Let me know what you find and if you need backup." Hank signed off, leaving Rip and Tracie staring at the screen.

"How do you propose we get into Blackburn?" Tracie asked. "Think we could try to sneak in at night?"

Rip shook his head. "They will have that place covered in surveillance cameras."

Tracie tapped a finger to her lip. "We could disable the cameras…"

Rip's gaze locked on the point where her finger touched her lip, his eyes flaring. He swallowed before he answered, "We'd have to find them first."

Tracie's pulse quickened at the way Rip was staring at her lip, and she dropped her hand to her lap. Having him so close and not touching him was hard enough as it was. They had a job to do and the four- or five-hour flight gave them ample time to plan their attack. "How do we get in to check them out?"

Rip's lips spread into a wide grin. "Mrs. Gideon, it's time to arm the security staff around your six-million-dollar home in Costa Rica."

Tracie's brows arrowed into a tight V. "What six-million-dollar home?"

Crossing his arms over his chest, Rip answered, "The one we need to buy arms to protect." He nodded toward the computer. "For a start, we need a home. Do you mind?"

Tracie scooted over one seat and let Rip have the helm of the computer.

His fingers tapped the keyboard, bringing up a search

engine to find real estate in Costa Rica. "What kind of home would you like?"

"I don't care."

After another call to Hank, giving him the bare-bones of their plan, they spent the next hour, combing through high-end homes. Tracie was amazed at how similar their tastes were in the home they finally settled on. It almost made her feel as though they were actually selecting a home they could live in.

She sighed. "It's a beautiful home and who wouldn't love to own it?"

"It's okay, if you have that kind of money. And it's great for our pretend home." He downloaded pictures to the computer and sent them to his cell phone. "It's a good start to consult with a firm about setting up security cameras and arming it with the kinds of weapons we'd need to deter thieves."

"You know, even if I had the money to own something like that, it's still too big." Tracie shrugged. "I'd much rather have a small cabin in the mountains with a stone fireplace."

"I've always loved the Colorado Rockies. I can picture that cabin perched on a hillside with large picture windows, overlooking a mountain valley."

"Flowers in the spring and summer, and snow-covered in the winter." Tracie smiled. "I grew up in West Texas. It's arid and hot there."

"I grew up in Illinois farmland," Rip said. "Not many hills there. Lots of snow, but no mountains. I've always wanted to live where there were mountains."

"But you're a SEAL." Tracie shook her head. "I thought SEALs loved being around the water."

"No doubt about it. I do. But I love the mountains, too." He frowned. "It doesn't matter. I belong to the Navy until I retire or get out."

Tracie sighed. Playing make-believe with Rip was a self-defeating effort. "We do what we have to do and go where we're needed."

"I live where I have to live, because I'm in the military. With you, the sky's the limit. You have choices."

"I work for Hank. I go where he wants me to go."

"But if you wanted, you could live where you wanted to live and deploy from there to where Hank needs you to go."

She narrowed her eyes. "I suppose. But that doesn't mean I'm going to follow a man around the world. My work is just as important to me. I don't ever want to be dependent on a man for my income or identity."

"No one gets that more than I do." Rip cupped her cheek. "I never said I'd expect any woman I was involved with to give up her life to follow me."

"No? But that's what would happen if you wanted any time together when you're not deployed."

Rip's brows drew together. "The personal life of a SEAL is not an easy one. The woman who chooses to get involved with one *needs* to be independent and ready to handle anything. When we deploy, we don't know if we're coming back, much less on our own two feet or in a body bag."

Tracie's chest clenched and her eyes stung. "All the more reason not to get involved with a frogman, if you ask me." Tracie swallowed hard. "What woman would want to sit around twiddling her thumbs waiting for someone to show up on her doorstep announcing her man was dead?"

Rip smoothed the hair back from her forehead. "What about you? You work in a dangerous job. You could be killed by whatever bad guy you're trying to nail for Hank."

"Yeah, but I don't expect a man to stay at home twiddling his thumbs waiting for me to throw a few crumbs of attention and affection his way when I'm home. He'd get bored and go looking for a woman willing to satisfy his needs. I don't want that for either of us."

"Because you had one bad experience with a jerk who took advantage of your affection, doesn't mean you should give up on all of us." He kissed her again. "On me. You don't know what you're going to get out of love until you give it a chance."

"And you're asking me to give you a chance? A man who could come back from a mission in a body bag?" Her words caught on a sob that she choked back.

"No, I'm asking you to give me a chance to see if what we're feeling is more than just lust, which I highly suspect it is. To grab for whatever happiness you can, while you can."

"And when I'm not around, will you grab another woman to find happiness?"

"I told you before, life is too short to waste on one-night stands. I'm in it for the full package." He bent to take her lips in a gentle, coaxing connection that made her heart swell with so much emotion she could barely breathe past it.

Tracie wrapped her hand around the back of his neck and pulled him closer, deepening the kiss, wanting it to go on forever.

The sound of the flight attendant clearing her throat brought Tracie back to reality. Her cheeks heated and she moved back from Rip.

"Sorry to interrupt, but you two need to buckle up. We'll be landing shortly."

Fumbling with her seat belt, Tracie refused to look into Rip's face, afraid of what she'd see. He wanted an answer, but she wasn't ready to give him one. She was afraid that if she put him off too long, he'd quit asking, yet she was more afraid to accept his offer, commit her heart and have it crushed again.

The plane banked to the left and circled a small airport in the Virginia countryside. When the craft came to a complete stop, Tracie unbuckled her seat belt and stood, stretching.

Rip did the same, wincing when he moved his injured arm. His gaze connected with hers. "Ready?"

"Ready." She led the way down the gangway to the ground where a limousine stood. With a deep breath and she stepped into the limo and slid over for Rip to climb in next to her.

"Where to first?" Tracie asked Rip.

The chauffeur, his hand pausing in the process of closing the door, answered, "Mr. Derringer suggested I take you shopping for appropriate attire at, as he put it, a high-end establishment. He has made arrangements for you two to meet with Vance Tate at Blackburn Manufacturing at four o'clock this afternoon."

Tracie nodded. If they were going in as an insanely affluent couple, they need to look the part. Nothing like a little shopping therapy to calm the nerves.

RIP HELPED TRACIE out of the limousine at the entrance to the Blackburn Gun Manufacturing building in Alexandria, Virginia. The large building stood in an industrial park surrounded by similar buildings.

Tracie stretched one silky, sexy leg out of the limo, followed by the other and stood, smoothing the slim-fitting, simple, black designer dress she'd purchased for the occasion. It hugged every inch of her body and the neckline dipped low, displaying an ample amount of her breasts. Accessorized with a simple diamond drop necklace and earrings, a large designer handbag and Jimmy Choo black stilettos, Tracie was stunning.

When she'd walked out of the dress shop wearing the complete ensemble, Rip had to swallow several times before he could comment. Now, all he wanted to do was take her somewhere private and strip the damned dress off and make love to her.

He'd chosen a gray suit and black button-down shirt beneath the jacket, leaving it opened several buttons and wearing no tie. Hank had insisted on a Rolex watch and designer shoes to complete the disguise.

"Mrs. Gideon, shall we?" He settled a hand in the small of her back and guided her toward the front entrance.

Vance Tate met them at the door, wearing a charcoal-gray suit, white shirt and red power tie. He held the door open as Rip and Tracie strode through. "Welcome, Mr. and Mrs. Gideon. So glad you could make it to tour the factory."

"It was nice of you to make time for us on such short notice. Mr. Tate, was it?" Tracie said.

Tate held out his hand. "Vance Tate."

She ignored his outstretched hand and continued. "Chuck and I are only in town for a few hours and we have dinner plans with friends in DC."

Rip took the man's hand and shook it. "Nice to meet you, Mr. Tate."

"Please, call me Vance." The man gestured toward a door on the other side of the lobby entrance. "If you'll come into our conference room, I can show you what we manufacture here at Blackburn."

Rip held up a hand. "We've done our homework and we know *what* you make. We'd like to see your facilities to ensure that you don't skimp on the materials used to manufacture the weapons we're interested in purchasing."

"We use only the best materials," Vance assured him. "I can show you around the factory, then we can sit and discuss your needs."

"Very well." Rip crossed his arms, hoping to convey to the man that he was waiting to be impressed.

Vance led the way past a reception desk, slid his identification badge through a card reader and held the door for Tracie and Rip. "Your secretary gave us an idea of what you were looking for, but perhaps you could elaborate?"

"As my secretary was to inform you, the weapons we require are to provide security to our villa in Costa Rica. I do not intend to take my wife there until the security personnel and their weapons are in place." Rip slipped his arm around Tracie's waist and pulled her against him. "I will spare no expense to keep my wife safe. She is my most important possession."

Anticipating her elbow jab to his gut, his muscles were tight, ready to take the blow, knowing she'd take offense to being called a possession. Rip could barely contain his smile.

Vance handed them safety glasses and ear protection headsets. He led them through the different buildings of the manufacturing facility. They started in an area where materials and spare parts were received, their certification documents scanned and filed. From there, they entered a large room filled with machines that cut away the metal to shape the outside of the barrels and rifled the insides. In a clean room, several workers along a line assembled the parts by hand.

Tate entered a long hallway with doors along the length, walking past several without stopping.

"What's behind these doors?" Tracie asked.

"Offices and storerooms." Vance passed the restrooms and took them to the end of the hallway. "I think you will find this interesting." He pushed through a door into another building. "We have an indoor range where each weapon is tested with live rounds. If you'd like, you could fire one of the weapons you're interest in purchasing." He reached for a rifle hanging on a rack along the wall. When he turned to face the two of them, Tracie stepped forward and held out her hands. "I'd like that."

Vance's brows rose as he handed the weapon over. "A gun enthusiast?"

Rip smiled over Tracie's head. "My wife is a woman of many talents. I assure you, she's an expert shot. All those skeet-shooting lessons paid off. Right, sweetheart?" He kissed her temple. "This rifle is similar to the M4A1, is it not?"

Vance nodded, his brow furrowed. "Yes, sir."

Rip looked down at Tracie, "While you get set up, I'd like to retrieve my hearing protection headset I left in the car." He grimaced and pointed to his ears. "The doctor warned me that I could lose what's left of my hearing if I don't take care."

"I'll need to go with you." Vance glanced from Rip to Tracie and back to Rip, his frown deepening. "Visitors aren't allowed to be in the factory without an escort."

"I'll be all right. I know the way back. It's not as though I'd be wandering through the manufacturing areas."

Tracie lifted the weapon to her shoulder and stared down the site. "Do you have a clip and bullets, Mr. Tate?" she asked.

Vance hesitated for a moment. "I guess it will be okay if you go straight there and return directly. And yes, I can get those bullets for you." The salesman turned to help Tracie.

Rip took the opportunity to slip out of the range building and back into the hallway. He opened several doors belonging to offices. One was empty with Vance's name plate on the desk inside. Another had a woman seated at a desk piled high with paperwork. "May I help you?" she asked, barely looking up.

"Just looking for the restroom," Rip said with his most charming smile.

The woman's eyes and her harried expression softened. "Down the hall on the left."

"Thank you." Rip ducked out and moved to the next door. It was locked. Using a slim metal file, he slipped it into the keyhole and turned it, triggering the locking mechanism. When he twisted the door handle the door opened.

The room was too dark to see very far inside. Pulling a small flashlight from his pocket, he switched it on to reveal a much larger work area, with an overhead door at the far side. Crates lined up along the floors and were stacked against the walls. Inside the crates were more parts to be used in the assembly of the weapons. In the ceiling corners of the large room were cameras, the green blinking lights indicating they were active. Someone at the other end of the cable was monitoring this room.

Rip checked the hallway behind him—*clear*—and stepped inside, closing and locking the door behind him. Without the overhead lights shining down on him, the video cameras wouldn't be able to make out his face.

Making a quick turn around the room, using a red filter on his flashlight and creating a barrier between the light and the security cameras with his body, he checked the contents of several boxes. Nowhere did he find anything resembling M4A1s.

When he'd run out of time, he stopped at the door and listened before opening it a crack and peering out into the hallway. The click, click, click of a lady's high heels alerted him to someone coming down the hallway.

Closing the door, he twisted the lock just as the heels stopped clicking directly in front of the door.

Rip held his breath and inched to the side of the door, resting his hand lightly on the knob. If someone opened it, he'd be hidden temporarily behind the door. But not for long. If the woman turned on the lights, entered and shut the door behind her, he'd be exposed.

The cool metal knob beneath his fingers shifted slightly. The lock held and the knob stopped moving. The knob turned slightly again. A moment later the heels tapped against the tile floor of the hallway and the sound diminished, leaving silence in its wake.

Knowing Vance would come looking for him soon, Rip edged the door open. The hallway was clear. Leaving the room, he locked the door behind him and returned the way he'd come, pausing at the door to Vance's office.

He opened it, peered inside and almost left before he spotted a door nearly hidden by a file cabinet. After glancing over his shoulder, he slipped into the office, noting a distinct lack of cameras here.

The possibility of finding a key was slim—if there were something worth hiding in the room beyond, the key would not be in the man's desk, it would be on him. Rip stuck the metal file he'd used on the other door into the keyhole and jiggled the lock. It wasn't budging.

He tried the file in the keyhole again and this time, the lock released.

Rip pushed through the door. As he suspected, the door led into a large storage room and workspace. He checked the upper corners of the room for cameras. Finding none, he flipped the light switch and illuminated the dark room. Near the end of the row, he located four large crates marked Spare Parts. The lids were nailed shut.

Quickly locating a crowbar from a long workbench on the wall, Rip levered the nails loose and pushed the lid aside. Brown paper covered the top. Below were brand-new M4A1 military-issue rifles complete with serial numbers and the manufacturers logo engraved on the manufacturing identification plate.

A bill of lading indicated this shipment had been meant to go to a US Army warehouse at Fort Lee, Virginia. Nothing on the outside of the box indicated the destination. In fact, there was no writing on the outside of the box. Whatever shipping documents had been originally attached to the box had been removed.

Rip snapped photos of the weapons with his cell phone.

His chest squeezed. He'd found the source of the modified M4A1 rifles and Vance Tate was knee deep in the operation.

The big question was who had diverted the shipment of military weapons to Blackburn Gun Manufacturing? Whoever it was had some connection to military procurement somewhere along the supply chain. Vance was his only link to the misappropriated weapons, and he was with Tracie. How desperate would he be if he knew his illegal arms trade had been discovered?

His gut clenching, Rip set the box lids in place, left the room and turned out the light. The sooner he got back to Tracie the better.

Once he made it to Vance's office, his cell phone vibrated in his back pocket. He whipped out the phone and read the text message from Hector on the screen, his heartbeat skidding to a stop.

Delgado escaped. My sources say he boarded a plane for the US.

Even if Delgado hadn't boarded a plane for the States, he would still notify his supplier that he'd been captured and the weapons' supply chain had been compromised. Any minute now, Vance Tate would get the word.

Rip and Tracie had to get out. *Now.*

Chapter Sixteen

Tracie knew she had to keep Vance Tate distracted long enough for Rip to search the immediate premises for any sign of illegal arms trade.

"I suppose you're an expert shot, are you not, Mr. Tate?"

"I am. I have the weapons and the range to practice as much as I want. I wouldn't be a good salesman if didn't familiarize myself with the weapons I'm selling in order to provide the best information to my customers."

"You're a very good salesman, Mr. Tate." Tracie lined up her sites and pulled the trigger, hitting the target dead center of the silhouette's heart.

"Nice shot, Mrs. Gideon." Vance stood beside her, one earpiece of his headset pulled off his ear. "Do you mind if I call you Phyllis?"

She shrugged and lined up her sights again. "I don't mind. But my husband is a very jealous man." If she were in a relationship with Rip, would he be jealous of other men if they found her attractive? Pulling the trigger, she hit the target just barely off the original bullet hole.

"How many semiautomatic rifles are you interested in ordering for you security guards?" Vance asked.

Without hesitating, she answered, "At least fifty."

A beep sounded from Vance's breast pocket and he

dug out a cell phone, as he stated, "That's a lot of guns for a villa."

"I intend to hire fifty guards. I want each of my guards to have his own weapon in case of an emergency or uprising."

Vance's lips twisted. "I thought Costa Rica was pretty stable at this time."

Tracie raised her brows and gave Vance what she hoped was a questioning, yet sexy look, not that she was used to playing the sex-kitten wife of a billionaire. "You of all people know that no Central American country is completely stable. Where there are desperately poor people, there are thieves and opportunists."

Vance held the cell phone without looking down at the screen, a slight frown making lines across his forehead. "If you're not comfortable with the location, why buy a villa there?"

Tracie finished off the rounds in the clip, nailing the target with one after the other. When the clip was empty, she released it and handed it to Vance, her hand lingering in his. "Where else can I go where I can make the rules?" She faced him, a smile curling her lips. "If I feel like it, I can sunbathe in the nude and make love to my husband in broad daylight without being thrown in jail for indecent exposure."

Vance's eyes flared and his attention drifted to the V-neckline of her little black dress. He swallowed, Adam's apple bobbing as he handed her another clip. "I suppose of all the countries in Central America, Cost Rica is the least dangerous. And if you have the money to hire your own army, you can live anywhere you want."

"Precisely." Tracie shoved the clip into the rifle, lifted the rifle to her shoulder again and aimed. "I like things a certain way, and I get what I want." She fired the weapon and turned to glance at Vance.

His gaze had shifted to the cell phone in his hand.

From the corner of her eye, Tracie saw the man stiffen, his jaw tightening, his fingers curling around the device. "Mrs. Gideon, did you say you and your husband were only in town for a couple of days?"

Her pulse kicking up a notch, Tracie feigned a calm she didn't feel as she answered. "That's right. We have dinner with friends in DC later tonight."

"Where did you fly in from?"

Still holding the rifle, she faced Vance, unwaveringly. "Dallas, why?"

Vance held a nine-millimeter Glock in his hand, pointed at her gut. "I don't think so." In his other hand, he held up his cell phone and showed her a picture of her and Rip, standing outside Delgado's house on *le Plantación de Ángel*.

Her heart plummeted to the pit of her belly.

"How interesting that you have a picture of my husband and me on our vacation to Honduras." Tracie leaned toward Vance and frowned. "I'm appalled at the arrogance of the paparazzi." She waved her hand at the weapon in his hand. "Am I firing that one next?" she asked, reaching out to take the handgun from him.

Vance jerked his hand back. "Hell no. What you're going to do is tell me why you were in Honduras in the first place."

"My dear, Mr. Tate. We take vacations in a variety of locations. Honduras just happens to be one of them."

Vance shook his head. "Save your lies for some dumb schmuck who'll believe them. I suspect you and Mr. Gideon, if those are even your real names, are casing my factory."

"Should we be? Only men with something to hide would be concerned about being played for a fool."

"Doesn't matter. My boss knows what went down in

Honduras and he's mad as hell. Guess you and I will be paying him a visit." Vance snatched at her arm.

Tracie slammed the rifle she'd been carrying into Vance's chest, knocking his handgun from his grip. She dodged him and made a run for the door, her slim-fitting skirt hampering her stride.

He caught her before she reached it, wrapped his arms around her middle, clamping her arms to her sides. Vance held on as she kicked, bucked and fought to throw him off.

Tracie had to warn Rip that they'd been discovered. If she didn't, he could be walking right into a trap. Gathering all her strength, she planted her feet on the ground, hunched over and nearly tossed Vance over her back.

He lost his balance for a moment, then dug his heels into the ground and lifted her off her feet, carrying her toward a door on the far side of the range, opposite the one Rip had disappeared through what seemed like such a long time before.

The door he carried her through led to another short hallway with an exit. As they neared, he fought to free one of his hands.

Now would be the time to make her break for it.

Tracie braced her feet against the door and shoved backward, knocking Vance onto his backside.

He hit with such force, his arms loosened momentarily. Just long enough for Tracie to roll to the side and spring to her feet.

Two steps brought her to the door. She twisted the knob, threw it open and ran outside and straight into the arms of one of Vance's oversize henchmen.

He crushed her to his chest and squeezed until she thought every one of her bones would snap beneath the pressure. She couldn't breathe and she couldn't move.

A cloth was shoved over her nose.

Desperate to breathe, Tracie inhaled, a biting scent stinging her nostrils. Her world went black.

RIP BURST THROUGH the doorway leading to the indoor range. The absolute silence struck him first. No voices, no pop or bang of rounds being fired.

His heart plummeted as he ran to the spot where he'd left Tracie. On the floor lay the rifle she'd held when he'd excused himself to go to the restroom.

He hadn't passed anyone in the hallway, nor had he heard a scuffle. Vance and Tracie had to have taken an alternate exit from the range. After a quick scan of the range facility, he spotted a doorway on the opposite end of the firing stations. Rip grabbed the rifle Tracie had been firing from the floor and ran for the door and flung it open. A short, empty hallway led to yet another doorway. By the time he reached it, he already knew what he'd find.

He opened it and stared out onto an empty parking lot. Tracie was gone. Rip knew in his gut, Vance had taken her. How had he walked away without planting a tracking device on her?

Her cell phone. If she'd managed to keep it, they had a way of tracking her.

Rip pulled his mobile phone from his pocket and dialed Hank's number.

He answered on the first ring. "Rip, what did you find out at the Blackburn factory?"

"I found the room where they grind the serial numbers and logos off the M4A1s. But that's not why I'm calling."

"What's wrong?" Hank asked.

"Vance Tate has Tracie."

"Where?"

"I don't know. I need you to locate her cell phone. If she still has it on her, we have a chance of finding her."

Hank's voice faded out as he gave orders to someone in the same room with him. Then he was back on the line. "I have men on the ground in DC. They've been on alert since you and Tracie landed."

"They won't do me any good if we don't find Tracie."

"Brandon is bringing up the tracking device on her cell phone. It's moving."

Rip let go of the breath he'd been holding. "Which way?" Rather than waste his time searching the factory, he ran back to the room with the guns, took one of the originals and one of the modified weapons, stuffed them into a gym bag he found in Vance's office and ran back to the entrance where he'd met Vance.

A security guard stepped in front of him. "I'm sorry, but I have to search all bags leaving the premises."

"Like hell you do." Rip jerked the bag up, clipping the guard in the chin. The man staggered backward and fell to the floor. The woman behind the reception counter screamed and ducked below her desk, probably dialing 911 as Rip raced for the door.

He didn't give a damn. Vance had Tracie. If he was scared enough, he might try to kill her.

The limousine that had dropped them off pulled up to the curb. The passenger window already down, the driver yelled, "Get in!"

Rip dove into the passenger seat and slammed the door.

The driver hit the accelerator so hard, the rear of the long limousine skidded on the pavement, burning rubber.

Rip was thrown against the door he'd just closed. When the vehicle straightened, Rip did, too, and buckled his seat belt.

"Here, hold this." The driver shoved his cell phone into Rip's hands. "Tell me which way to turn while I drive."

"Rip?" Hank's voice shouted into the headset.

"Yeah, Hank. It's me. Which way?"

Hank guided them through the streets and onto an expressway.

"It appears as though they're exiting into a rest area. If you hurry, you might catch up with them."

Rip peered through the windshield, willing the limo to go faster. The flash of a blue information sign caught his attention and his heart beat faster. The sign indicated a rest area in one mile. "Take the exit for the rest area."

Leaning forward, Rip couldn't get closer to the windshield without bumping his forehead. "Are they moving?"

"No," Hank said.

Hope swelled in Rip's chest as they barreled down the exit ramp into the rest area.

"We're here," Rip said, staring into every car parked along the curbs. One held a heavyset man, his equally heavyset wife and children. A man in jeans and a T-shirt climbed into a pickup and backed out of a space.

The limo driver pulled along the curb taking up several spaces while Rip hopped out and ran along the line of cars, clutching the phone to his ear. He didn't find Tate or Tracie. "Are you sure they're still here?"

"Yes, the tracker says the phone is there."

His hope fading, Rip came to a stop in front of the brick bathroom buildings. "Hank, call Tracie."

"Calling," he responded.

A moment later, Rip heard a cell phone ring. He followed the sound to a trash receptacle, dug down inside and found the new handbag Tracie had bought for the tour through Blackburn. Inside was the cell phone Tracie had carried with her since she'd found him in Biloxi.

Lifting Tracie's phone to his ear, he pressed the talk button, his gut clenched. "She's gone. Her cell phone was dumped."

"Damn." Hank said something to whoever was in the room with him. "Sorry, Rip. I have Brandon backtracking through Belinda's phone numbers to find Vince Tate's personal cell phone. As soon as we have anything, I'll call."

Rip stood on the sidewalk in the rest area and stared around. He had nothing to go on, nowhere to look and had never felt more helpless in his life. Instead of shouting his frustration, he climbed into the limousine.

"Where to?" the driver said.

The only answer he could think of was, "DC."

As the driver shifted into gear, the cell phone in Rip's hand beeped and a message flashed onto the screen.

If you want to see her alive, meet me at the Lion Shipyard in Norfolk, pier 10 at midnight. Bring 5 million dollars. Come alone.

"Change of plan." Rip turned to the driver. "We're headed for Norfolk."

Rip contacted Hank and relayed the demands.

"I'll have the money brought to you by ten o'clock tonight, along with my best men."

"I have to go in alone."

"I understand. But that doesn't mean you won't have backup. Get to Norfolk. The money will be there by ten."

Rip settled back in the passenger seat of the limousine and watched as they passed rural farmland, cities and traffic congestion.

"My name's Ben Harding." The driver stuck out his hand.

Rip looked over at the man and took his hand. Ben's grip was firm and he nodded.

"So are you one of Hank's men?"

"Yeah, I was one of the original Covert Cowboys."

"You know Tracie?"

"Not really. I've been away on assignment. We've met in passing, but I haven't gotten to know her, although Kosart's reputation as an FBI special agent was solid. It got her on as the first female Covert Cowboy. I think she was ready to leave the FBI after her fiancé and the regional director double-crossed her. She almost died in the hands of the Mexican mafia."

"She's tough." *And beautiful, and has a heart of gold.* Rip would give anything to have her back and safe.

"It's hard enough when you're the one being shot at. At least you feel like you have some control. But when it's your partner…" Ben sighed. "I'd tell you not to worry, she can handle herself, but that won't do any good if she's outnumbered."

Rip's fingers clenched into a fist. If they hurt her…

Ben continued, "I will tell you, though, Hank is a good man. If there's a way out of this, he'll throw everything he owns at it to see that Kosart comes home safely. He's done it before. He's the one who sent the Covert Cowboys in to rescue her from the mafia. He didn't give up on her then, he sure as hell won't give up on her now that she works for him."

"That's nice to know." As they neared the outskirts of Norfolk, Rip had Ben take him to the airport where he rented a nondescript two-door sedan that looked like anything else on the streets.

On Hank's orders, Ben rented an SUV. In the separate vehicles, they drove farther out to a smaller, local airport and waited. The sun set around eight, which gave them two full hours to kill until Hank's plane would arrive with the money.

Rip leaned back in his vehicle and closed his eyes. Before each mission he'd performed with the Navy SEALs he'd force himself to relax, to let his body gather the strength he'd need to face the enemy. Each time he had known his skills and awareness were what stood between the enemy and his team. If he wasn't at his best, he was letting his team down.

With Tracie's life on the line, he had a harder time relaxing. Every sound made him jump and his body twitched with the need to take action. There was no way he'd relax until he had her back in his arms. His gunshot wound didn't help with the tension, but he ignored the pain, pushing it aside for now.

A few minutes before ten, the blinking lights of an incoming aircraft brought Rip out of the car and onto his feet.

The Citation X landed on the tarmac and pulled to a stop. When the stairs were lowered, a man in peak condition but with a shock of white hair stepped out of the plane and settled a cowboy hat on his head. Rip knew that face from the video feeds on board the Citation.

Ben joined Rip as they strode through the hangar and out onto the tarmac. "You haven't met Hank, have you?"

"Not in person." Rip stepped forward. "Mr. Derringer, I'm Cord Schafer. Folks call me Rip."

Hank's grip was firm. "Would rather have met you under better circumstances, but that's not important. What is important is getting Ms. Kosart back alive."

"I like the way you think."

Hank turned to the plane gangway and nodded at the man standing at the top with a suitcase in his hand. The man was big like a linebacker, making the door to the plane seem too small for his broad shoulders. He turned sideways and descended the steps.

Two more men followed him out of the plane.

"Rip, meet Chuck Bolton." Hank indicated the man with the suitcase.

Chuck held out a hand and shook Rip's, practically crushing his fingers.

"Zachary Adams and Thorn Drennan will also be joining the team," Hank said.

Zachary and Thorn both shook hands with Rip and then smiled and shook hands with Ben.

"Good to see you, Harding," Adams said.

Ben turned to Chuck. "I hear you're expecting another kid. Congrats."

Chuck nodded, a grin spreading across his face. "Didn't know being a dad was going to be so much work and so rewarding."

Rip didn't have time for pleasantries.

Adams turned to Rip, his jaw tight, his brows furrowed. "Just so you know, I have a stake in this rescue operation. Tracie Kosart is my fiancée's twin. If I don't come back with good news, I've been told not to come back."

Adam's words hit Rip in the chest. He hadn't known Tracie had a twin. Hell, he didn't know much about her at all. But damn it, *he would*. Once this thing was over, he would make Tracie see reason and go out with him. Then he'd ask all those questions they hadn't had time for since they'd met.

"We will get Ms. Kosart back," Hank said. "There's no *if* about it." He motioned Chuck forward and had him set the case on the ground. Then he bent to flick the catches open and stood back for the men to see inside.

Adams, Bolton, Harding and Drennan whistled, as impressed by the amount of cash packed into the case as Rip was.

"That's a lot of money to be carrying around," Thorn said, his tone deep, resonant.

"A man could get killed carrying around such a stash." Ben's voice filled the darkness.

"That's why I brought along a security detail." Hank crossed his arms. "Though you'll be going in alone, my men will infiltrate the shipyard ahead of you and be there for you."

Rip shook his head. "I don't know. If they get wind of any of you, it could jeopardize Tracie's safety."

"My men are highly skilled, each coming to me with excellent records in their prior lives and positions."

Rip's lips thinned. "Are you willing to bet Tracie's life on them?"

"I'm counting on them to help you get Tracie back alive." Hank's eyes narrowed. "I value each and every member of my team and the people we swear to defend and protect. I won't let the men who've taken her hurt her. I give you my word."

For a long moment Rip stared into Hank's eyes. The man appeared sincere and committed to getting Tracie back. "If that's the case, we need to be going. I'm due to meet with them at midnight."

Bolton, Harding, Adams and Drennan helped offload an astonishing array of weapons from the plane into the SUV and then climbed in.

Hank stood beside Rip. "You need to arm yourself."

"I have a .40 caliber strapped around my calf and a nine-millimeter Glock under my shirt. Anything more than that and they'll see it. I'm risking enough as it is. The idea is to give them the money and get Tracie out of there. If you and your men want to go after them, that's fine. I'll help as long as we get Tracie clear first."

"I agree." Hank touched a hand to Rip's arm. "We'll get her back." The older man extended his hand and Rip shook it. When Hank withdrew his hand, he left what appeared to be a coin in Rip's palm. "I want you to have this."

"What is it?" Rip turned the coin over. It looked like

one of the gold-colored dollar coins he occasionally got for change from a soda machine.

"My good-luck charm. Although, for the most part, I believe in making my own luck. But it doesn't hurt to carry some with you."

Rip shrugged and stuffed the coin in his pocket. "Thanks. I'm not supposed to be there until midnight. You and your men have until then to get into place."

Hank climbed into the SUV with the other four operatives and they set off.

A glance at his watch made his stomach clench. One hour until he was to meet the men who held Tracie captive. For the first time in a long time he prayed. In the few days he'd known her, she'd come to mean more to him than any other woman he'd ever met. Never one to believe in love at first sight, he could be well on his way there with Hank's only female Covert Cowboy.

As he climbed into the little sedan, he thought back over all he and Tracie had been through together. No other woman he knew would have handled it as well. She was tough, but sensitive, passionate and gentle.

When he got her back, he'd insist they go out on a real date before he had to go back to Mississippi, and she headed back to Texas or wherever Hank chose to send her. Somehow he'd convince her that they should continue seeing each other.

The drive to Lion Shipyard took thirty minutes. For the next twenty, he parked in an empty parking lot outside the fenced-in compound, waited and prayed.

Chapter Seventeen

Tracie woke in a very dark, cramped place that smelled of old tires and gasoline. An engine rumbled, making her tomb vibrate. Based on the noise, darkness and movement beneath her, she was locked in the trunk of a car. The metal hood and walls of the vehicle seemed to close in around her. Her heart raced and her breaths came in short, spiky gasps. She had to calm herself or she'd pass out again.

Taking deep breaths of the smelly air, she forced herself to think of a way out of the vehicle. The backseats of many sedans were equipped with a fold-down seat to carry a long load from the trunk into the cab of the car.

Running her hands along the seam of the trunk lid, she searched for the emergency release lever. Her fingers encountered a ragged piece of metal she guessed was the broken lever. She redirected her search to the back of the seat, hoping to find a lever to release the locks holding the seat in place. If she could get through the backseat without being detected, she could somehow take out the driver and the passenger and make her escape. She found nothing but the hard back of the seat. What she needed was a weapon. The dress she'd worn had been so tight, hiding a gun or knife beneath it hadn't been an option, and they'd ditched her purse somewhere along the way. Tracie felt around the trunk, finding nothing but the shoes she'd been wearing and a hard metal tab.

Her heart thumped in her chest. Most new cars stored the spare tire beneath a panel in the trunk. The tab had to be there to allow access to the tools needed to change a tire, like a jack, the crank and a heavy wrench to loosen the lug nuts.

Tracie tried to roll to one side and out of the way so that she could get to the tools before the vehicle came to a stop. If she didn't have some way to defend herself, she could be dragged out on the ground and dispatched with a bullet in the back of her head.

She'd sworn she'd never allow herself to be kidnapped ever again. Not after Mexico. Yet here she was, captive in the trunk of a car heading who knew where. Her only hope was that Rip would be tearing up heaven and earth to find her.

She laughed, the sound choked by a sob. If only she could get the cover off the storage compartment, she might find a lug wrench or something heavy to hit her captors with and distract them long enough to get away. If Rip found her, she didn't want him to walk into a trap.

The SEAL had grown on her and she wanted to see him again. Preferably under better circumstances. She'd been toying with the idea and now knew, if she didn't die that night, she wanted to go out on that date with her "husband."

Her lips curled at the irony of the situation. They were married before they'd had a first date. Okay, so the marriage had never taken place, but they'd done a helluva job pretending to be a married couple, and they had more in common than most married couples she knew.

They both loved a good firearm. They were both in dangerous lines of business, and they both wanted to live in a cabin in the mountains. Those few things she knew about him only made her want to know so much more. Like which was his favorite football team, could he ride a horse and did he have any living family members?

Thinking of family, Tracie wished she could get word to her sister. And tell her what? *I'm alive for the moment, but all bets are off when the car stops.*

The car made a turn, rolling her to the side. With her hand on the tab, the cover came up with her and she shoved it aside.

Patting the well beneath her she felt around for the familiar hard steel of a lug wrench. A small temporary doughnut tire lay in the middle of the well. Beside it was what felt like a jack stand. She couldn't find a tire iron or lug wrench.

Damn. What idiot drove a vehicle without the proper emergency equipment? She almost laughed hysterically at her thought, then sobered as the car slowed to a stop.

Fumbling to remove the jack stand from where it was screwed into the bottom of the well, she found a wing nut and twisted it loose as fast as she could. When she had it out, she set it aside.

The engine cut off and doors opened and closed.

Moving as quietly as she could, she slid the lid over the well and rolled over it. She pushed the jack stand behind her, hiding it and her hand from view.

When her captors opened the trunk, they'd be in for a big surprise.

The lock on the trunk popped and the lid rose, letting in only a small amount of light.

Tracie kept her eyes closed most of the way, peeking through the slits. When a man bent over and grabbed her arm, she launched herself at him, swinging her other hand with the jack stand in it at her attacker's head. It hit with a dull thump.

The man's grip loosened and he crumpled to the ground with a groan.

Tracie scrambled out of the trunk, falling to the ground beside the man she'd hit. Before she could scramble to her feet, the big man who'd captured her outside Blackburn grabbed her around the middle and held on.

She fought, kicking and biting until he slammed a fist into her face, hitting her cheek so hard, her head jerked back and everything faded to gray. She tried to hang on, willing her eyes to stay focused.

In the meantime, Vance Tate rose to his feet and backhanded her. "Bitch! I oughta kill you for that." Blood oozed from a gash on Tate's temple and he wiped it away with the back of his sleeve.

Dizzy, her knees threatening to buckle, Tracie's head swayed in the dark searching for another escape plan. From what she could tell, they were in a dark alley between brick warehouses that were completely dark. Even if she screamed, she doubted anyone would hear her.

Headlights illuminated the darkness. A vehicle sped toward them. For a moment Tracie thought it wasn't going to stop, would run them over.

At the last minute, the vehicle, a black SUV, screeched to a halt, kicking up gravel and dust in their faces.

A man wearing a suit and a dark fedora stepped out of the vehicle, the hat pulled down over his forehead, hiding his eyes from them. "What's the meaning of this?" the man growled. "Why is she here?"

Vance jerked a thumb toward her. "This woman and her husband came to Blackburn today asking about purchasing guns."

The man crossed his arms over his chest. "So?"

"They are the ones Delgado told us about. He's mad as

hell and is on his way here. He thinks this woman and her husband are responsible for destroying his entire camp."

"What does that have to do with me? You know I don't get involved in the details."

"If this woman and her husband are responsible, as Delgado says they are, we could be in big trouble. I want out. I don't even know if she was involved, but it was too much of a coincidence."

"Where's the husband?" Fedora demanded.

"I don't know. When I heard Delgado was on his way here, I left with the woman and called you immediately."

"Look," Tracie said, struggling against the arms locked around her middle. "I have no idea what you're talking about. This is just a big mistake. If you let me go, I'll walk away, no harm, no foul."

"Shut up!" Vance popped the side of her head with a forceful slap.

Tracie tried to break free of the big man's hold, but he was stronger and refused to release her.

"It's too late," Fedora said. "She already knows more than she should."

"What do I know?" Tracie argued. "I came to buy guns for my vacation home in Costa Rica. I don't know what you two are talking about or who this Delgado guy is. Just let me go. My husband will be worried sick."

As if she hadn't said a word, Fedora focused on Vance. "You know my policy."

Vance's entire body shook. "Yes, sir, but—"

The mystery man held up his hand. "You've compromised my cover."

"I had to. They know."

"Know what? Really." Tracie shook her head. "I have no idea what you're talking about. I just want to go home, kick up my feet and drink a very dry martini. Maybe two."

Fedora man didn't move a muscle. In a voice that sent chills up and down Tracie's spine, he said, "Kill her."

"Whoa, wait a minute," Tracie said. "This is one big ugly mistake. If it's all the same to you, I'll buy my guns somewhere else."

Vance backed up a step. "I'm not doing your dirty work for you. This is Delgado's mess. Other than a grainy photo and Delgado's text, I'm not even certain they did anything wrong."

"We can settle that right now." Fedora raised his hand and motioned for someone to join them. The passenger door of the SUV opened and a man dropped to the ground.

At first all Tracie could see was his silhouette. When he passed beside the headlights, she caught a glimpse of his face.

Carmelo Delgado.

Tracie's blood ran cold and she leaned her head forward, letting her hair fall partially over her face, praying the man didn't recognize her for the woman who had come to ask about his coffee plantation.

"Is this the woman?" Fedora asked.

Delgado walked straight up to her, grabbed a handful of hair and yanked it back, exposing her face to the headlights.

"Si." He cursed in Spanish and then backhanded her so hard, she almost fell. If not for the big guy's arm around her middle, she would have been knocked to the ground.

Her jaw and cheek ached and the tissue around her right eye began to swell.

"Kill her," Fedora demanded.

Delgado's eyes narrowed and he pulled his fist back to hit her again.

"Wait." Vance held up a hand. "You can't kill her. Her husband is still running around out there. I've arranged for him to meet me at Lion's Shipyard at midnight. He'll want proof she's alive before he reveals himself to us."

Delgado looked to Fedora.

For a long moment, Fedora paused. "How did you get him to agree to come?"

"I told him to bring five million dollars in cash in exchange for his wife."

"Where exactly are you meeting him?" Fedora straightened the sleeve of his suit jacket, appearing to be in no hurry.

Warning bells went off in Tracie's head. The man was like a snake, quietly tensing to strike.

"At Lion's Shipyard, pier ten." Vance added, "At midnight."

"How did you arrange this?"

Vance pulled a cell phone out of his pocket. "I used this disposable phone. I signed up for it using a fake name."

"Clever," Fedora said. "Let me see that." He held out his hand.

Vance placed the phone in the man's hand.

In the next second, the world exploded around Tracie, and Vance fell. Knocking into the man holding her and taking them both down.

Another gunshot made the big guy jerk and then his arm loosened.

Slightly dazed, Tracie fought to free herself from the tangle of bodies.

Delgado yanked her up by the hair, jerked her hands behind her back and secured them with a zip tie. He tossed her over his shoulder and carried her to the back of the SUV and dumped her inside.

Her night wasn't going very well at all, but Vance and his bouncer friend's had ended even worse.

Tracie vowed to live long enough to return Delgado's

favor and slug him in the face. Then she'd figure a way out of the mess she was in and expose the man in the Fedora. He seemed to have the power, and she planned to bring him down.

AT TEN MINUTES to midnight, Rip found a gap beneath the fence and slid the suitcase full of money under the chain link, then he dropped to the ground and rolled beneath the wire. Once inside he patted the gun in the holster under his shirt. It was little reassurance against an enemy he didn't know much about. All he knew was that Vance had taken Tracie. How many more men would show up to protect his investment was a mystery.

He walked between tall stacks of huge metal containers, aiming for the end of the dock where pier ten was located. Right at midnight he arrived and waited in the shadows of the containers, craning his neck to see beyond, hoping to catch a glimpse of Tracie. Nothing moved. He didn't know whether or not Hank's team was in place.

At three minutes past twelve, his cell phone rang.

He fumbled in his pocket for the device and answered.

"There is a forklift three rows from where you are standing. Get in it and drive it down to pier number six. Leave your cell phone where you're standing. If anyone follows you, the girl is dead. You have exactly two minutes to get there. If you aren't there by then, the girl dies. Now go!"

"I want to hear her voice. Prove to me she's alive," he demanded. His demand was greeted with the silence of the call having ended. With less than a minute to spare, he dropped his phone, ran two aisles of containers over and found the forklift with the key still in it. Rip pushed the lever toward the front of the device and the forklift shot forward. Manipulating the many levers, he finally got the forklift heading in the right direction, having wasted too much time already.

He raced past several piers, counting backward from Pier ten to the sixth one. He would have to handle the exchange alone. If the others moved closer to pier six, they would be seen and risk tipping off Tracie's kidnappers. The money didn't mean anything to him. Tracie did.

Hopefully, with the amount of money they'd demanded, her captors wouldn't feel the need to kill her. Then again, they'd killed the DEA agent to keep their secret. Rip figured there was little chance they'd take the money and leave the girl. Alive.

As he pulled to a halt in front of pier six, he remained in the forklift, hunkered low, using the heavy-duty frame of the machine to shield himself as best he could. He didn't care if he lived or died, but he had to make sure Tracie was safe. He couldn't do that if he was picked off by a sniper.

Shutting off the forklift's engine, he sat for a moment, waiting for Vance to emerge with Tracie. Poised to throw himself off the forklift, he twitched, ready for action, ready to get this over with.

When no one emerged, Rip couldn't wait any longer. "I have the money. Give me the girl."

Again silence.

"One more minute and I leave, taking the money with me. Fifty-nine, fifty-eight, fifty-seven…"

His countdown made it to fifty before a figure detached itself from the shadow of a container stack. "Are you alone?" A man in a Fedora stood in the open, his face still hidden by the brim of his hat.

"Yes. Where's my wife?"

"Come down from the forklift so that I can see you're not armed."

"Show me my wife."

"She's in a safe place." The man waited with his legs slightly apart, his arms crossed. "Show me the money."

"It's in a safe place."

"Touché." Fedora touched a finger to his hat. "Tell me, why would a man and his wife go all the way to Honduras to buy a coffee plantation and then leave without negotiating?"

"We didn't find one for sale."

"Perhaps you didn't ask nicely enough," Fedora said.

Another man emerged from the shadows, and in his arms, he held Tracie, his hand clamped over her mouth. A shaft of light spilled over the man's face, revealing who it was.

Carmelo Delgado.

Rip's heart lurched. He wanted to drop down off the forklift and run to her. But he couldn't tell whether Fedora had a gun in his hand or not. He couldn't take the chance with Tracie's life hanging in the balance.

Tracie struggled to free herself, but Delgado had a powerful hold on the trained agent and it appeared he had her hands tied behind her back.

Thinking fast, Rip called out, "Tell you what. You send the girl halfway and I'll send the money halfway. She can show you that the case is in fact full of the five million dollars you asked for. When I have my wife safely over here, I'll leave and you can take the case. I won't try to stop you. All I ask is that no harm comes to my wife."

"Bring her." Fedora waved Delgado forward with Tracie.

Using the forklift's bulky frame as cover, Rip slipped out of his seat and dropped to the ground. He took the suitcase full of money from behind the seat of the forklift and held it against his chest.

"You need to untie my wife's hands so that she can open the case."

Fedora and Delgado whispered to each other.

Delgado pulled a switchblade out of his pocket and hit the button, popping it open. Then he cut the tie binding Tracie's wrist, immediately pressing the knife to her throat.

Rip's heart stopped and then raced on.

Fedora shouted, "If you do something stupid, I'll have him kill you and then kill your wife."

"Okay, I'll leave the stupid out. On the count of three, send her over, and I'll send the case." Still using the fork-lift for cover, Rip bent and laid the case on the pavement, slipped the strap holding the small .40 caliber pistol from around his calf and buckled it to the handle of the case. If the strap held, the gun would arrive at the midpoint be-tween him and Tracie's captors. "If you want the money, you have to give me the girl."

"Okay. But if you make one wrong move, I'll kill your wife," Fedora warned. Using Delgado and Tracie as a human shield, he backed toward the SUV and ducked be-hind the door.

Rip held his breath. They could be walking her back to the SUV to take off and find another place to hide her or leave her body.

When they didn't shove her into the vehicle, Rip remem-bered to breathe. He'd feel better when she was with him and away from Fedora and Delgado.

"Ready?" Fedora called out.

"Ready," Rip responded. "On the count of three. One… two…three."

Delgado gave Tracie a shove, sending her flying to-ward the case. He ducked behind the door with Fedora and waited.

Rip shoved the case, gun and all toward Tracie, praying she'd see the gun before the others did.

Surreptitiously pulling his Glock from beneath his shirt,

he waited for the fun to begin. As soon as Tracie started out across the pavement, Rip wanted to run out and throw his body over hers to protect her from being shot.

"I have a gun aimed at Mrs. Gideon," Fedora noted. "One false move and she is dead."

Tracie walked toward the case and bent down beside it. She fumbled with the clasps until they popped open, taking more time than Rip liked.

When he was sure she'd found the gun and had sufficient time to pull it from the holster, he held his breath.

Tracie swiveled on her heels, squatting beside the case, turning it so that they could see inside. "The money is all here."

Rip almost laughed.

Tracie held the gun behind her back, her legs tense, appearing spring-loaded, ready for action. "Coming your way," she said and shoved the case hard enough it went flying at Fedora. Rip had been ready and fired at the same time as Fedora, hitting him square in the chest.

Delgado threw his knife at Tracie.

She dropped to the ground, clutching at the knife in her belly. With a quick jerk, she pulled it out and blood spurted from her body.

Rip fired back at Delgado and lurched toward her, his heart in his throat.

"Look out, Rip!" she yelled.

Fedora sat up and aimed at Rip, but didn't get the chance to pull the trigger.

A shot rang out from somewhere to Rip's right, clipping Fedora in the temple, knocking the hat off his head.

Chapter Eighteen

Rip reached Tracie and gathered her in his arms, pressing his hand against her wound to slow the blood loss.

"Hey, Mrs. Gideon, you doing all right?" he asked, brushing the hair out of her eyes so that he could see them.

She smiled up at him. "Never better, Mr. Gideon," she answered, her voice weak, her face turning a chalky white.

"Hang in there, we're going to get you fixed up."

"Good. I have a date with my husband I wouldn't want to miss…" Her voice faded and her eyes closed.

Rip's chest squeezed so hard he could barely breathe. "We need an ambulance here!" he yelled.

"Could you keep it down, sweetheart?" Tracie whispered. "A girl needs her beauty sleep."

Keeping his hand pressed to her wound, Rip hugged her close. "That's my girl. You're going to be just fine."

Covert Cowboys surrounded them. Hank brought up the rear, already on the phone calling for assistance. Within minutes, the fire department's emergency vehicle arrived and they loaded Tracie into the ambulance.

Rip couldn't remember a longer trip in his entire life.

Two hours later, he stood in the waiting room, waiting for the surgeon to appear. Hank, Adams, Bolton, Harding and Drennan had gathered around him, awaiting news of Tracie's prognosis.

The entire time they were in the waiting room, Hank had been on and off his cell phone with the authorities, with Rip's commander and with Brandon back at the Raging Bull Ranch.

Hank finally hung up and faced the men. "Brandon verified the identity of the man with Delgado. His name was Mark Kuntz. He's a former soldier from the US Army Special Forces. He was in the same unit as the sniper who tried to kill you several weeks ago, Rip."

Rip's chest felt hollow. "Fenton Rollins?"

"Yes. Brandon found several photographs of the two together in Iraq. And, get this—Kuntz was Senator Thomas Craine's executive assistant."

"Wasn't Craine the one who was working on trade negotiations with several Central American countries?" Rip ran a hand through his hair, sick at the thought of his own countrymen selling them out.

Hank nodded. "I had Brandon search the photographs of Senator Craine's visit to Central America, including the one in which we saw him with Delgado. Mark Kuntz was in that photo, as well. Not prominently featured, but there in the background."

Rip's fists clenched. "Is Senator Craine involved in the illegal arms deals with the terrorists?"

Hank shook his head. "So far, we haven't found a definitive connection other than Kuntz working for Craine. I have Brandon searching every link he can find, digging into their emails, their phone records and their bank accounts. Senator Craine has several corporations he's associated with, some of which have offshore accounts. So far we have nothing and Senator Craine has refused to be interviewed. It's in the Feds' hands now."

Rip drew in a deep breath to calm the rage he felt toward these men who'd become traitors to their own country. "You're not stopping the investigation, are you?"

Hank smiled, though his eyes narrowed. "Not on your life…or Tracie's."

"Good."

"With Mark Kuntz and Fenton Rollins out of the picture now, are you planning to go back to your unit?" Hank asked.

Rip hadn't even gotten past leaving the hospital. He wouldn't leave until he knew for sure Tracie was going to be all right. "I haven't gotten that far."

"When Tracie is released, I'd like you two to take some time off. I'll clear it with your unit commander if you don't mind me arranging things. You need it, and I'm sure Tracie would feel better if you were with her during her recuperation."

Rip glanced at the doorway to the surgical waiting room. "I'm okay with whatever." He didn't care about anything at that moment but getting news from the doctor.

Then a man in scrubs, a hair cap and surgical booties entered the waiting room. "Are you the folks with Tracie Kosart?"

All six of the men answered as one. "Yes."

"Good news. She's going to be just fine. No major damage to internal organs. After a night of observation, she could be ready to go home."

All the air rushed out of Rip's lungs and, for a moment, he felt light-headed. "Can I see her?"

"She's in recovery now and asking for her husband." The doctor's brows rose. "Is that you?"

Rip nearly laughed out loud before he nodded, "That's me." He ran for the door, happier than he'd been since graduating BUD/S.

A WEEK LATER, Tracy lounged in a deck chair, staring out over a mountain valley with a cup of hot cocoa cradled in her hands. "It's just like I imagined it."

"It's better than I had imagined it because you're here." Rip held out his hand, taking one of hers.

"You're a smooth talker, for a frogman." Tracie squeezed his fingers. She couldn't remember a time she was more content.

Rip shot a twisted smile at her. "How would you rank this as a first date?"

"Right up there." She sipped her cocoa. "Although I don't think most first dates last an entire week."

"No?" Rip stood and took the mug from her hands. "Well, we have your boss to thank for that. It was nice of him to offer his mountain cabin for your recuperation and the plane to get us here in comfort." Rip eased her out of her chair and into his arms, so careful not to disturb her stitches.

Tracie leaned into him, wrapping her arms around his rock-hard waist and resting her cheek against his chiseled chest. Feeling very lucky to have him, she lifted her face and stood on her toes to press a kiss to Rip's lips. He tasted of marshmallows and cocoa and she loved it. "Mmm. Remind me to thank Hank."

Despite the tug at her stitches, she didn't want the kiss to end and pushed up on her toes again, deepening it until their tongues writhed together and her body heated.

The cell phone on the table beside the lounge chair buzzed and vibrated, shattering the silence of the mountainside.

Rip looked up, brushing a strand of her hair behind her ear. "Should we answer it?"

Tracie shook her head. "No."

Rip glanced at the cell phone. "It's yours and, if I'm not mistaken, it's Hank."

Tracie sighed and bent to grab the phone. "Kosart here."

"Tracie, are you with Rip?"

She smiled, tipping her head so that the man in question could nibble her neck. "Yes, sir, I am."

"Turn on the television."

Tracie couldn't think straight with Rip's lips angling lower, his hands parting her silk robe. "What?"

"Put me on speaker," Hank demanded.

She hit the button for speakerphone and Hank's voice came over loud and clear, "Turn on the television. Senator Craine is about to make a statement on live TV."

Rip sighed. "Come on." He slipped an arm around her waist, guided her back into the cabin and hit the on button for the state-of-the-art video system. It had taken him half an hour to figure out all the controls, but he had them down now.

Following Hank's instructions, they found the channel and waited.

Senator Craine appeared in front of a podium with several microphones. He started by stating that he didn't have any idea that his executive assistant Mark Kuntz was running arms to rebel fighters in Honduras and that he was sorry for the deaths of the DEA agent and the SEAL who'd been sent in to retrieve him. While he made his statement, a disturbance occurred as uniformed FBI agents pushed through the crowd, walked up onto the stage and cuffed the senator.

The reporter covering the story described what was happening in an excited tone. "They're charging him with treason and misappropriation of government equipment!"

The press went wild, cameras flashed and the senator was led away.

Shocked, Tracie stood with her mouth open, struggling to comprehend what had just occurred.

"Tracie? Rip?" Hank's voice sounded nearby and Tracie realized she hadn't hung up.

"What the hell just happened?" she asked.

Hank laughed. "Brandon kept digging and found the bank accounts that connected Craine to Kuntz's dirty dealings with Delgado and the terrorist training camp. It just took longer than we expected. Although, I can't argue with the timing. Perhaps the public arrest of Senator Craine will serve as a reminder to our other elected officials to keep it clean."

"We can always hope." Tracie shook her head. "You don't know who to trust anymore."

"You can trust me," Hank said.

"And me." Rip kissed her cheek and leaned over the phone she still held. "Hank, just in case I didn't tell you before, thanks for this week, and for sending Tracie to help me. You couldn't have picked a better cowboy from Covert Cowboys, Inc."

"Glad to be of service," Hank said. "And thank you for your service. The Citation will be there tomorrow to take you back to Mississippi where your unit is anxious to receive you with a hero's welcome."

"I don't know about hero." Rip's hand slid around Tracie's waist and he dropped a kiss on her forehead. "Gosling was the hero."

"Speaking of Gosling," Hank said. "I've set up a trust fund for his wife and baby. They won't want for anything for the rest of their lives."

A lump formed in Tracie's throat. She knew money couldn't replace a husband and father.

She glanced up at Rip, noting the sheen of moisture in his eyes. He'd been thinking the same thing.

"Thanks, Hank," Rip said.

Tracie hung up and leaned into Rip's embrace. "I feel so bad for Gosling's widow and child."

"I know Jeanette." Rip smoothed Tracie's hair back and tipped her head up so that he could stare into her eyes. "I even asked her if she'd have done anything different if she had known he'd die. She said no. She loved him with all her heart and knew the risks that came with loving a SEAL."

"She would have wanted every moment of happiness she could grab," Tracie finished, finally understanding that concept.

"So CCI Agent Kosart," Rip pressed a featherlight kiss to the tip of her nose. "What's it to be? Are you ready to end what we just started?"

She leaned up on her toes and pressed a kiss to his lips. "No way in hell." She wrapped her arms around him and held on tight. "I'm going for all the happiness I can squeeze into the time we have together."

"Are you going to come visit me in Mississippi or anywhere else I might be stationed?"

"Wild horses couldn't keep me away." She stared up at him. "Would you mind terribly if I stayed with you between my CCI assignments?"

Rip's lips spread into a wide grin and he laughed out loud. "Honey, I wouldn't have it any other way."

* * * * *

MILLS & BOON®

Why not subscribe?

Never miss a title and save money too!

Here's what's available to you if you join the exclusive **Mills & Boon Book Club** today:

✦ *Titles up to a month ahead of the shops*
✦ *Amazing discounts*
✦ *Free P&P*
✦ *Earn Bonus Book points that can be redeemed against other titles and gifts*
✦ *Choose from monthly or pre-paid plans*

Still want more?

Well, if you join today we'll even give you
50% OFF your first parcel!

So visit **www.millsandboon.co.uk/subs**
or call Customer Relations on **020 8288 2888**
to be a part of this exclusive Book Club!